"WORDS FOR THE HOUR"

"WORDS FOR THE HOUR"

A New Anthology of American Civil War Poetry

EDITED BY
FAITH BARRETT AND
CRISTANNE MILLER

University of Massachusetts Press
AMHERST AND BOSTON

Printed in the United States of America

LC 2005018477
ISBN 1-55849-510-X (library cloth ed.); 509-6 (paper)

Designed by Dennis Anderson
Set in Adobe Caslon and Veljovic Medium by Graphic Composition, Inc.
Printed and bound by The Maple-Vail Book Manufacturing Group

Library of Congress Cataloging-in-Publication Data

Words for the hour : a new anthology of American Civil War poetry / edited by Faith Barrett and Cristanne Miller.
p. cm.
Includes bibliographical references and index.
ISBN 1-55849-509-6 (pbk. : alk. paper)—ISBN 1-55849-510-X (lib. bdg. : alk. paper)
1. United States—History—Civil War, 1861–1865.—Poetry. 2. American poetry—19th century.
3. War poetry, American. I. Barrett, Faith, 1965– II. Miller, Cristanne.

PS595.C55W67 2005
811.008'0358—dc22
2005018477

British Library Cataloguing in Publication data are available.

CONTENTS

List of Illustrations xiii

Preface by Cristanne Miller xv

A Civil War Time Line xxiii

Abbreviations: Source Collections of Civil War Poetry for Part I xxix

Introduction: "Words for the Hour": Reading the American Civil War through Poetry by Faith Barrett 1

PART I: POEMS PUBLISHED IN NEWSPAPERS AND PERIODICALS

Antebellum Poetry 25

SARAH LOUISA FORTEN
My Country 27

ELLA (SARAH MAPPS DOUGLASS?)
The Mother and Her Captive Boy 28

JAMES RUSSELL LOWELL
The Present Crisis 29

SAMUEL HENRY DICKSON
I Sigh for the Land of the Cypress and Pine 30

WILLIAM GILMORE SIMMS
Southern Ode 33
Song of the South 35

JOSHUA MCCARTER SIMPSON
Song of the "Aliened American" 37

HENRY DAVID THOREAU
The Vessel of Love, the Vessel of State 38

ALFRED GIBBS CAMPBELL
Lines 38

DAN EMMETT
I Wish I Was in Dixie's Land 40

CHARLOTTE FORTEN GRIMKÉ
The Two Voices 41

1861 45

RICHARD HENRY STODDARD
To the Men of the North and West 47

LUCY LARCOM
The Nineteenth of April 48

JAMES R. RANDALL
My Maryland 49

JANE T. H. CROSS
Over the River 51

FRANCIS ORRAY TICKNOR
The Old Rifleman 52
OLIVER WENDELL HOLMES
Brother Jonathan's Lament for Sister Caroline 54
MRS. JAMES NEALL
The Harvest-Field of 1861 55
ELLEN KEY BLUNT
The Southern Cross 56
AUGUSTUS JULIAN REQUIER
Our Faith in '61 58
CATHERINE A. W. WARFIELD
Manassas 60
WILLIAM CULLEN BRYANT
Not Yet 61
ANONYMOUS
Cotton-Doodle 62
M. JEFF THOMPSON
Price's Appeal to Missouri 64
ETHELINDA BEERS
The Picket-Guard 65
ELIZABETH STODDARD
A Thought 66
ANONYMOUS
Soldiers' Aid Societies 67
ANONYMOUS
Let My People Go: A Song of the "Contrabands" 69

1862 73

JULIA WARD HOWE
Battle Hymn of the Republic 75
CAROLINE MASON
Anomalies 76
GEORGE HENRY BOKER
A Battle Hymn 77
The Sword-Bearer 78
HENRY WADSWORTH LONGFELLOW
The Cumberland 80
R. M. ANDERSON
The Song of the South 82
R. R.
The Stars and Bars 83
JOHN WILLIAMSON PALMER
Stonewall Jackson's Way 85
LUCY LARCOM
Weaving 86
JOHN JAMES PIATT
To Abraham Lincoln 89
EDMUND CLARENCE STEDMAN
Wanted—A Man 89
AUGUSTUS JULIAN REQUIER
Clouds in the West 91
JAMES SLOAN GIBBONS
Three Hundred Thousand More 92
WILLIAM E. PABOR
Emancipation 93
ELLEN MURRAY
Half Way 94
MARY H. C. BOOTH
"While God He Leaves Me Reason, God He Will Leave Me Jim" 96
ANONYMOUS
A Southern Scene 97
F. T. ROCKETT
Melt the Bells 99
NATHANIEL GRAHAM SHEPHERD
Roll Call 100

1863 103

Ralph Waldo Emerson
Boston Hymn 105
Bret Harte
The Reveille 108
Anonymous
Conservative Chorus 109
S. A. Jonas
Only a Soldier's Grave 109
Elizabeth Akers Allen
Spring at the Capital 110
George Henry Boker
The Black Regiment 112
Alexander Beaufort Meek
Wouldst Thou Have Me Love Thee 114
Della Jerman Weeks
The Wood of Gettysburg 115
Anonymous
Chickamauga, "The Stream of Death!" 117
J. Augustine Signaigo
On the Heights of Mission Ridge 120
Anonymous
Negro Song of Mission Ridge 121
Anonymous
My Army Cross Over 122
Anonymous
Ride In, Kind Saviour 123
Phoebe Cary
Ready 123
Caroline A. Ball
The Jacket of Gray 124
Ellen Flagg
Death the Peacemaker 125
Bret Harte
The Copperhead 127
Severn Teackle Wallis
A Prayer for Peace 128
Frederick A. Bartleson
In Libby Prison—New-Year's Eve 1863–4 130

1864 133

James Madison Bell
From The Day and the War 135
Charles Graham Halpine
Sambo's Right To Be Kilt 138
Emily M. Washington
Confederate Song of Freedom 139
James R. Randall
At Fort Pillow 140
George Henry Boker
In the Wilderness 142
Sonnet 144
William H. Hayward
The Patriot Ishmael Day 144
Frank H. Gassaway
The Pride of Battery B 146
Thomas Buchanan Read
Sheridan's Ride 149
Thomas Manahan
Brother, Tell Me of the Battle 151
J. R. Bagby
The Empty Sleeve 152

Anonymous
Reading the List 154
Julia L. Keyes
Only One Killed 155
Thomas Bailey Aldrich
Fredericksburg 156
Jane T. H. Cross
The Confederacy 157

1865 159

William Cullen Bryant
My Autumn Walk 161
Mary H. C. Booth
I'm Dying, Comrade 163
Anonymous
The Voices of the Guns 164
Kate Putnam Osgood
Driving Home the Cows 167
Joseph Blythe Allston
"Stack Arms" 168
Robert Falligant
Doffing the Gray 169
Augustus Julian Requier
Ashes of Glory 170
William Cullen Bryant
The Death of Lincoln 171
Christopher Pearse Cranch
The Death-Blow 172
The Martyr 173
Bret Harte
A Second Review of the Grand Army 173
Sidney Lanier
The Dying Words of Jackson 175
Sarah E. Shuften
Ethiopia's Dead 176

The Aftermath of the War 179

Anonymous
"Is There, Then, No Hope for the Nations?" 181
Henry Wadsworth Longfellow
Killed at the Ford 182
Abram Joseph Ryan
The Sword of Robert Lee 183
Joshua McCarter Simpson
Let the Banner Proudly Wave 185
Mary Eliza Tucker
Christmas, South, 1866 187
William Gilmore Simms
"Ay De Mi, Alhama!" 188
Sidney Lanier
To Our Hills 189
Francis Miles Finch
The Blue and the Gray 191
Francis Orray Ticknor
Little Giffen 193
Bayard Taylor
Gettysburg Ode 194
Henrietta Cordelia Ray
Lincoln 195

PART II: COLLECTIONS AND VOLUMES OF CIVIL WAR POETRY

George Moses Horton 201

Slavery 202
Lines 203
The Poet's Feeble Petition 205
General Grant—The Hero of the War 205
The Southern Refugee 207
Lincoln Is Dead 208
Like Brothers We Meet 208
The Dying Soldier's Message 209
The Spectator of the Battle of Belmont 210
The Terrors of War 211
Jefferson in a Tight Place 212
The Soldier on His Way Home 213
Weep 214

John Greenleaf Whittier 216

The Hunters of Men 217
A Word for the Hour 218
Ein feste Burg ist unser Gott 219
At Port Royal 222
The Battle Autumn of 1862 225
What the Birds Said 226
Barbara Frietchie 228

Walt Whitman 230

Eighteen Sixty-One 231
Beat! Beat! Drums! 232
Virginia—The West 233
Cavalry Crossing a Ford 233
Bivouac on a Mountain Side 233
An Army Corps on the March 234
By the Bivouac's Fitful Flame 234
Come Up from the Fields Father 234
Vigil Strange I Kept on the Field One Night 236
A March in the Ranks Hard-Prest, and the Road Unknown 237
A Sight in Camp in the Daybreak Gray and Dim 238
Not the Pilot 238
Year That Trembled and Reel'd Beneath Me 239
The Wound-Dresser 239
Dirge for Two Veterans 241
Over the Carnage Rose Prophetic a Voice 242
The Artilleryman's Vision 243
Ethiopia Saluting the Colors 244
Not Youth Pertains to Me 244

Look Down Fair Moon 245
Reconciliation 245
How Solemn as One by One 245
As I Lay with My Head in Your Lap Camerado 246
To a Certain Civilian 246
Adieu to a Soldier 247
Turn O Libertad 247
To the Leaven'd Soil They Trod 248
Pensive on Her Dead Gazing 248
When Lilacs Last in the Dooryard Bloom'd 249

Herman Melville 257

The Portent 258
Apathy and Enthusiasm 259
The March into Virginia 260
Ball's Bluff 261
Dupont's Round Fight 262
Donelson 263
A Utilitarian View of the *Monitor*'s Fight 275
Shiloh 276
Malvern Hill 277
The House-top 278
Sheridan at Cedar Creek 279
In the Prison Pen 280
The College Colonel 281
The Martyr 282
Rebel Color-bearers at Shiloh 283
"Formerly a Slave" 284
Magnanimity Baffled 285
On the Slain Collegians 285
On the Slain at Chickamauga 287
An uninscribed Monument 288

Frances Ellen Watkins Harper 289

The Slave Mother 290
Bible Defence of Slavery 291
Eliza Harris 292
The Slave Auction 294
Bury Me in a Free Land 295
To the Cleveland Union-Savers 296
Lines to Miles O'Reiley 298
Words for the Hour 299
An Appeal to My Countrywomen 300
The Deliverance 302
Learning to Read 309

Henry Timrod 311

Ethnogenesis 312
The Cotton Boll 315
I Know Not Why 320
A Cry to Arms 320
Charleston 322
The Two Armies 323

Carmen Triumphale 324
The Unknown Dead 326
We May Not Falter 327
Ode 328
1866 329

Sarah Morgan Bryan Piatt 331

Hearing the Battle.—July 21, 1861 332
Army of Occupation 333
Giving Back the Flower 334
Shoulder-Rank 335
Another War 336
Mock Diamonds 337
Over in Kentucky 339
The Black Princess 340
The Old Slave-Music 342
Counsel—In the South 343
A Child's Party 344

PART III: UNPUBLISHED OR POSTHUMOUSLY PUBLISHED POEMS

Emily Dickinson 351

To fight aloud, is very brave - 352
Unto like Story - Trouble has enticed me - 353
I like a look of Agony 353
After great pain, a formal feeling comes - 354
The name - of it - is "Autumn" - 354
He fought like those Who've nought to lose - 354
When I was small, a Woman died - 355
It feels a shame to be Alive - 356
One Anguish - in a Crowd - 356
They dropped like Flakes - 357
If any sink, assure that this, now standing - 357
The Battle fought between the Soul 357
No Rack can torture me - 358
My Portion is Defeat - today - 358
My Life had stood - a Loaded Gun - 359
Color - Caste - Denomination - 360
Dying! To be afraid of thee 360
My Triumph lasted till the Drums 360
I never hear that one is dead 361

Obadiah Ethelbert Baker 362

After the Battle: The Dirge 363
Nov. 30th To an absent Wife 365
Do You 365
My Army Birth 365

The Charge at Monterey 366
The Charge at Farmington 367
August 3rd, 1886 368
The Unknown Grave 369

Civil War Poetry Glossary 371
Biographies of Poets 375
Index of Authors and Titles 397

ILLUSTRATIONS

"The Brave Wife" xiv

Men of the 1st Virginia Militia, also known as "The Richmond Grays" xxii

African American soldiers posing with their teachers 26

Militiamen guarding the Chain Bridge over the Potomac River 46

Fair Oaks, Virginia. Lt. James B. Washington, a Confederate prisoner, with Captain George A. Custer of the 5th Cavalry, U.S.A. 74

Company E, 4th U.S. Colored Infantry, at Fort Lincoln 104

"Compromise with the South" 134

"The Halt"—A Scene in the Georgia Campaign 160

"Home from Andersonville" 180

"The Brave Wife." Lithograph published by Currier & Ives, New York, ca. 1861.
Harry T. Peters Collection, Museum of the City of New York.

PREFACE

During the American Civil War, people from all walks of life—famous, unknown, scholarly, and uneducated—and from all segments of the population in the United States responded to the war by writing poetry. Thousands of these poems, representing a variety of perspectives and commemorating various events, were published in newspapers and magazines; others were written in letters, diaries, and scrapbooks. Beginning only shortly after the end of the war and continuing through the present, editors gathered hundreds of these poems and songs—sometimes collecting only texts written during and explicitly about the conflict and sometimes ranging more broadly. William Gilmore Simms must have begun collecting poems for his *War Poetry of the South* immediately following the war to achieve publication in 1866; Emily V. Mason published *The Southern Poems of the War* in 1867; and in his 1865 volume *The Civil War in Song and Story, 1860–1865,* Frank Moore reprinted much of the short fiction and poetry he had published so far in *The Rebellion Record,* a twelve-volume "diary" of Civil War documents, newspaper accounts, and literature put out by Moore between 1861 and 1868. The 1886 *Bugle-Echoes: A Collection of the Poems of the Civil War Northern and Southern,* edited by Francis F. Browne, aims to present "a record of the feelings and experiences of that heroic epoch" through poetry, as Browne puts it; in the 1943 compilation *The Blue and the Gray: The Best Poems of the Civil War,* Claudius Meade Capps, its editor, similarly selects what he regards as the best of the poetry published in earlier collections; and the 1994 *Columbia Book of Civil War Poetry: From Whitman to Walcott,* edited by Richard Marius and Keith W. Frome, includes over a century of poetic responses to the war. Especially these, and other, early volumes have been useful to us in making our own compilation of Civil War poetry, which focuses on the period from 1861 to 1865—including a handful of both antebellum poems on issues leading up to the war and postbellum responses to the war's conclusion.

While we, too, aim in part to present "a record" of responses to the Civil War and to collect the best of the poetry written during the war years, our volume has both a larger and a more complex intent. In our experience, volumes of Civil War poetry tend to focus on poems of heroism or battle, with a few very famous and popular exceptions. In ours, by contrast, we attempt to include poetry written by women as well as men, noncombatants as well as soldiers or veterans, and pacifists as well as supporters of both the North and the South. Similarly, whereas some editors lean toward popular representations of the war and others toward the work of more canonical poets, we have tried to balance presentation of what a contemporary reader would have found in popular periodicals and newspapers with a generous selection of the work of major poets writing extensively in response to the war, sometimes in dedicated volumes—not just Walt Whitman, with his *Drum-Taps,* and Herman Melville, with his *Battle-Pieces and Aspects of the War,* but also Southern poets such as George Moses Horton and Henry Timrod. Additionally, we include generous selections of poems by writers rarely regarded as Civil War poets, either because they did not publish volumes of poems explicitly dedicated to the war—for example, Sarah Piatt—or because they did not publish during the period—such as Emily Dickinson, who published only ten poems during her lifetime, and Obadiah Baker, whose work is first published here.

Hundreds of poems were set to music and sung in public gatherings or sung by troops, in camp and while marching to and from battle, during the war. Many songs were also later published as poems. While we have not attempted a representative sample of Civil War songs as such, we do include here a few of the best known, and many of the poems we reprint were put to music and became popular as songs during the war. Dan Emmett's song "I Wish I Was in Dixie's Land" became so highly identified with the Confederate cause that it served as a popular national anthem, especially after it was performed at Jefferson Davis's inauguration as president of the Confederacy. Julia Ward Howe's "Battle Hymn of the Republic" was almost equally popular in the North, although it was first published as a poem in a prestigious literary journal. The African American sorrow songs "Let My People Go" (better known as "Go Down, Moses"), "My Army Cross Over," and "Ride In, Kind Saviour" similarly represent a popular genre of music both for African Americans and for sympathetic Northern whites. Many sorrow songs were printed as sheet music in the North during the war years, and Northerners spending their first prolonged periods in the South during the war published essays describing and transcribing these songs. This was the period in which such music began to become known outside black communities. As one of the first published sorrow songs, "Let My People Go" has particular status in representing this genre of tremendous significance to a large population of African Americans in the South and North and of great influence on the development of American music after the war.

Our volume is also distinctive in its inclusion of framing information about the war—information that we hope will orient readers without extensive historical knowledge of the period. This historical apparatus provides multiple levels of specificity. First, we provide a brief historical time line listing major battles and events immediately preceding, during, and following the war. Second, a glossary of important names and terminology relevant to understanding the poems gives basic factual information. Third, we include a brief biographical sketch for every poet whose work appears in the volume, as well as a longer biographical sketch for the most significant poets writing in response to the war during the period. Because so many of the poems published in contemporary newspapers were written by ordinary women and men who did not publish volumes of verse or in other ways leave a lasting public record of their lives, little or no information is available for some authors. Many of the poems we include were first published under pseudonyms or anonymously, and the authors of some of these poems have not yet been identified. Finally, Faith Barrett's introductory essay provides a scholarly overview of the function of poetry during the Civil War period, with attention both to poetry's popularity and to some elements of the differing responses of the individual poets we include. To facilitate use of our volume's informational apparatus, we mark names and terms included in the glossary with an asterisk (*) and names of other poets and poems included in the volume with boldface type (**"My Maryland"**); we also provide an index of authors and titles.

Our goal has been to present an eminently readable as well as a representative and illuminating collection, telling many of the nation's stories of the Civil War through poetry. Part I shows the range of poems written immediately preceding and during the war and published in popular periodicals, providing a kind of poetic newspaper account of the war as one might have read it then—from the early days of optimistically heralded victory on both sides, through the brutal deaths of the long middle years of the war, up to the war's conclusion and President Lincoln's assassination. Reading through the war from the perspective of many different poets with distinctive experiences of its progress and various stakes in its outcome gives the reader a complex and direct access to how people from various backgrounds understood the trajectory of the war. Civilians and soldiers, free blacks and adamant proponents of slavery, women and men from Massachusetts and Virginia and from barely developed states or territories, writers with their eyes on the national political stage and those focused on personal domestic consequences of the conflict: only by hearing these multiple voices and perspectives in conflict and concert with each other can one begin to get a sense of how thoroughly engaged all communities of this nation were in seeking to articulate their relation to the national catastrophe. Our representation of African American poets is stronger in the antebellum period than thereafter because it has proved difficult to find poems published during or immediately following the war by black poets—a result, perhaps, of their different preoccupations during the war or of these poems having appeared in journals that were not preserved. Whatever the reason, few poems by African Americans were reprinted in the collections published soon after the war.

Part II of our volume presents selections of poets who published extensively in response to the war, providing more concentrated perceptions of the conflict from the individual angles of a variety of poets—some of whom were famous during this period and others of whom have since become canonical. Part III presents the work of two poets who did not publish during their lifetimes, giving a sense of the richness of private as well as public responses to the war. That one of these two poets is now renowned (Emily Dickinson) while the other (Obadiah Ethelbert Baker) is first published in this volume also gives some sense of the significance of the genre for meditative people of all levels of talent.

Editing this volume has involved challenges, primarily that of negotiating the appropriate boundaries between scholarly accuracy and pleasurable reading. It has been a priority of our selection that the poems in Part I present a narrative with all the turns and twists of the primary stories of the period—from high drama to low humor, sentimentality, pathos, ghastly realism, and emotional response in many registers. The poems tell of heroic efforts, mighty victories, tragic deaths (sometimes of hundreds of comrades), a mother's or sweetheart's loss, the sorrowful reflections of the prisoner or contemplative observer, and the keen yearning of various speakers for freedom, democracy, reunion, and peace—differently defined. At the same time, we have attempted to ascertain the original date and place of publication for as many of the poems we include in the dated sections of the volume as possible, a task monumental in scope because few collections of Civil War poems contain bibliographic information about either poem or poet.

For example, Frank Moore's *Rebellion Record*—one of the richest resources for any scholar interested in publications of the war years—prints James Russell Lowell's "The Present Crisis" in volume 1, 1860–61, not mentioning that it first appeared in the *Boston Courier* in 1845: *The Rebellion Record* recirculates poems, often without reference to original dates of composition or publication. Likewise, many of the other best resources for poems or bibliographic information (*Bugle-Echoes*; *The Blue and the Gray*; *Southern War Songs*, edited by W. L. Fagan in 1890; the bibliographic guide *The Southern War Poetry of the Civil War*, edited by Esther Parker Ellington in 1918; *The Poetry of the American Civil War*, edited by Lee Steinmetz in 1960) give only a state identification for the author, date a poem according to the battle it describes, or refer at most to other collections (Simms's 1866 *War Poetry of the South*, Mason's 1867 *The Southern Poems of the War*, or Edmund Clarence Stedman's 1900 *An American Anthology, 1787–1900*). Such information is at times misprinted (F. T. Rockett in Simms's *War Poetry* is listed as F. V. Rocket in Ellington's *Southern War Poetry*). Since we can find no bibliographic or biographical information for either spelling of the author's name, it is impossible to determine with certainty which is correct. In such cases, we have gone with the earlier (or what we judge to be the more reliable) record.

At other times, information is contradictory or incomplete. Sheila Weems Johnston's *The Blue and the Gray from Hawkins County, Tennessee, 1861–65* (1995) lists a poem called "Two Soldiers Lay Dying" as found in a November 9, 1863, letter written by Joseph A. Bare (a name she also spells Bear). According to Johnston, the poem refers to the death of two soldiers near Lickor Creek Bridge in Greene Country, Tennessee, on February 3, 1863. She speculates that the poem was written shortly after the incident. The same poem, however, is published in Capps's *The Blue and the Gray* as "Death the Peacemaker" by "Ellen Flagg (New Hampshire)"—almost certainly a pseudonym, given the overt patriotism of the name "Flagg" and the fact that we could find no historical reference to a person of this name. New Yorker Ethelinda Beers's "The Picket-Guard" was also attributed to a Confederate soldier, with the claim that the poem was found on his dead body—a claim made about many Civil War poems—which raises questions about Johnston's attribution. Furthermore, Bare might have copied "Flagg's" poem into a letter without attribution (a common practice), leading to the assumption that he wrote the poem. Agnes Leonard of Kentucky used "Death the Peacemaker" as a major segment of her much longer "After the Battle," without attributing the lines borrowed to any other author, and recently on a Civil War Web site a user seeks information about this poem, written by "a family member," calling it "Blue and Grey." We have listed the poem as by "Ellen Flagg" and given it Flagg's title, "Death the Peacemaker." Such confusion about authorship occurs with great frequency for poems of this period. "Brother, Tell Me of the Battle," attributed by several sources to George F. Root, was in fact written by Thomas Manahan; Root (a composer of classical music and popular songs) set this poem, and many others, to music—as well as writing some lyrics for songs, most famously "The Battle Cry of Freedom" (1864). The lack of careful distinction between composers and poets as the "author" of popular war songs contributes to the confusion in accurate attribution.

Some false attribution has been caught by previous editors of Civil War poems. A famous example is "The Picket-Guard" (also known as "All Quiet Along the Potomac"), which was attributed to Northern and Southern, male and female authors but was written and published by Ethelinda Beers, who went to some lengths to prove that she had indeed composed the poem. We see ourselves as continuing in the process of bibliographic clarification that has preceded our volume and will no doubt follow it. Given the nature of this kind of detective work and of our volume—intended primarily as a reader, not as a scholarly bibliographic resource—we have not always returned to original periodical and newspaper publications to find appropriate documentation for all poems and have no doubt inadvertently passed along some false information in the form of scholarly best guesses. Nonetheless, our work moves the field of Civil War poetry closer to accuracy in representing the authorship and dating of poems. Where we have not been able to find a year of publication or approximate date of composition, we have placed the poem according to topical references within the poem or principles of arrangement in our source text.

In this collection, we have relied on the excellent available twentieth-century editions of such poets as Emily Dickinson, Ralph Waldo Emerson, Frances Watkins Harper, George Moses Horton, Sidney Lanier, Herman Melville, Sarah Piatt, William Gilmore Simms, and Walt Whitman. Poems by George H. Boker and Bret Harte are taken from early collections of their work, published in 1864 and 1882, respectively. Obadiah Ethelbert Baker's poetry was discovered and selected by Faith Barrett from the archives of the Huntington Library. The poems of Part I come primarily from *The Rebellion Record, Civil War in Song and Story, War Poetry of the South, Bugle Echoes,* and *The Blue and the Gray,* as well as from two more-recent anthologies, Joan R. Sherman's *African-American Poetry of the Nineteenth Century: An Anthology* (1992) and Paula Bernat Bennett's *Nineteenth-Century American Women Poets: An Anthology* (1998). Full bibliographic information for these and other frequently cited texts, with the short titles or abbreviations used throughout our volume, is given in "Source Collections of Civil War Poetry for Part I."

We have in as far as possible maintained chronological order and used the text of either a definitive recent edition or of the first printing for our presentation of poems. For Whitman, where both a first edition and later editions are available, we have used the 1881–82 version of *Drum-Taps,* as edited by Sculley Bradley, Harold W. Blodgett, Arthur Golden, and William White in *Leaves of Grass: A Textual Variorum of the Printed Poems* (1980). This version includes some poems written later than 1865, the first printing of *Drum-Taps,* but not some of the earlier poems; "Pensive on Her Dead Gazing" is the sole omitted poem that we include here. Because Whitman followed his 1865 first printing of *Drum-Taps* with *Sequel to Drum-Taps* in 1865–66 and then continued to rearrange, add to, and subtract from these two volumes until 1881, we have chosen to follow the order of his final edition of this volume. By this logic, we include significant poems added after 1866—"Adieu to a Soldier" and "Ethiopia Saluting the Colors" (added in 1871) and "Virginia—The West" (added in 1872)—and use the titles with which most readers will be familiar ("The Wound-Dresser" rather than the 1865 title "The Dresser," and "The Artilleryman's Vision" rather than "The Veteran's Vision").

We are indebted to several institutions and individuals for support in completing the work on this book. Foremost, we thank the Huntington Library, San Marino, California, for a fellowship that allowed Faith Barrett to study their Civil War–era holdings and for permission to quote and reproduce the poems of Obadiah Ethelbert Baker; particular thanks go to Mona Shulman for her assistance with these materials. We also thank the American Antiquarian Society for the research assistance they provided in the later stages of this project. Pomona College has generously funded copying, postage, and research assistance—the latter in the very able persons of undergraduate students Susanne Liaw and David Newman, who assisted with the organization of our hundreds of pages of material, bibliographic research, and proofreading, and Barbara Clonts, English Department administrative assistant. California State Polytechnic University at Pomona provided research funding and invaluable release time to Faith Barrett. Lawrence University provided a faculty research grant for Faith Barrett's work at the American Antiquarian Society and funded two student research assistants, Kendall Surfus and Elizabeth Breese, who provided skillful help with biographical research and the proofing of the manuscript. Reference librarians Gretchen Revie at Lawrence and Carrie Marsh at Pomona helped us track down information about elusive writers and publication sources. Civil War historian Stuart McConnell of Pitzer College provided a detailed historical time line that served as the skeleton for our more sharply focused document. Our thanks also to Bruce Wilcox, director of the University of Massachusetts Press, for his frank enthusiasm from the moment we broached the project to him and his support throughout, and to our two outside readers. Paula Bernat Bennett was particularly helpful in providing suggestions for alternative or additional poems we might include and for giving hard-to-find bibliographic and historical information. Finally, I thank Faith Barrett, whose extensive scholarly work on the poetry of this period gave intellectual impetus to our decision to publish this collection and whose knowledge has provided the backbone of our collective efforts throughout the enterprise. While we have worked jointly in the selection and organization of the materials printed here, Faith's greater familiarity with the materials inevitably facilitated our procedure.

We hope you will take as much pleasure and find as profound an interest in the juxtapositions and concurrences of these poems as we have.

Cristanne Miller

Men of the 1st Virginia Militia, also known as "The Richmond Grays," at the time of John Brown's Trial. Valentine Richmond History Center, Richmond, Virginia.

A CIVIL WAR TIME LINE

1820 Missouri Compromise: Congress admits Maine as a free state and Missouri as a slave state, preserving the balance in the Senate between free and slave state votes; the compromise bars slavery from the remainder of the Louisiana Purchase—the current states of Kansas, Nebraska, and the Dakotas and parts of Montana, Wyoming, and Colorado.

1848 End of Mexican War: Mexico cedes five hundred thousand square miles of land to the United States—the current states of California, Nevada, and Utah, most of Arizona and New Mexico, and parts of Colorado and Wyoming—and cedes claim to the Republic of Texas.

1850 The Compromise of 1850 admits California as a free state, bars the slave trade—but not slavery itself—in Washington, D.C., and provides for a much tougher Fugitive Slave Law*.

1854 The Kansas-Nebraska Act creates two new territories from land in the Louisiana Purchase—Kansas Territory and Nebraska Territory—and specifies that a decision on slavery will be the result of "popular sovereignty." That both territories are north of 36° 30' means the de facto repeal of the Missouri Compromise. Northerners denounce the act, and a new antislavery party forms as a result: the Republican Party. Five years of violence between pro- and antislavery forces in Kansas ensue ("Bloody Kansas"*).

1857 *Dred Scott v. Sanford:* The Supreme Court rules the Missouri Compromise unconstitutional, in determining that a slave (Scott) taken from Missouri to Illinois and then back was not free when living in a free state. According to the decision, Congress has no right to deprive white citizens of their property—including slaves—anywhere in the United States.

October 1859 John Brown's raid at Harpers Ferry: A white radical abolitionist, Brown leads a raid on the federal arsenal at Harpers Ferry, Virginia (now West Virginia), hoping to seize arms and inspire a slave revolt; he is caught and hanged, but his actions panic the white South, and he becomes a martyr for Northern abolitionists.

1860 Abraham Lincoln (Republican Party candidate) is elected president in November; as a result, South Carolina secedes from the Union in December.

January 1861 Mississippi, Florida, Alabama, Georgia, and Louisiana secede.

February 1861 Texas secedes. The first meeting of the Confederate Congress takes place at Montgomery, Alabama, and Jefferson Davis is inaugurated as president of the Confederacy.

April–June 1861 The Confederacy takes Fort Sumter, in the harbor of Charleston, South Carolina, April 12–14. Virginia secedes on April 17, followed within a few months by Arkansas, North Carolina, and Tennessee. Lincoln calls for troops to quell the rebellion. Though deeply divided, Kentucky, Maryland, and Missouri do not secede.

July 21, 1861 Battle of Bull Run, Virginia (Confederate name: First Manassas)—Confederate victory. Union troops flee, and Confederate troops are too weary and confused to pursue. Expecting an easy victory, many Northern civilians come out to see the battle and have to flee with the Union retreat.

Winter 1861–62 The Union navy blockades thirty-five hundred miles of Confederate coastline.

February 6 and 16, 1862 In Tennessee, Forts Henry and Donelson are captured by Union forces under Ulysses S. Grant, which brings his skills into the public eye and gains a key strategic position on the western front for the Union.

April 6–7, 1862 Battle of Shiloh, Tennessee (Union name: Pittsburg Landing)—Union victory. A total of more than twenty thousand Union and Confederate soldiers are killed and wounded. Confederate commander Albert Sidney Johnston is killed; Union general William T. Sherman, serving under Grant, is wounded twice.

April 24, 1862 Union victories at Baton Rouge and Natchez leave Vicksburg, Mississippi, the last Confederate stronghold on the Mississippi River.

April–July 1862 Robert E. Lee assumes command of the Army of Northern Virginia. In the Shenandoah Valley, Confederate cavalry commander Thomas J. "Stonewall" Jackson defeats a Union force twice his size five times in five days, then joins Lee. During the Seven Days' battles (June 25–July 1), Lee drives McClellan back to Washington. Total losses are ten thousand Union and twenty thousand Confederate soldiers killed and wounded. Lincoln becomes increasingly concerned about McClellan's reluctance to attack. These battles persuade both sides that the war will be longer than anticipated and establish Lee's reputation as an invincible leader and brilliant tactician.

August 25, 1862 Orders from Secretary of War Edwin Stanton provide for the enlistment of up to five thousand black troops, to be trained as guards for captured plantations and settlements.

August 28–29, 1862 Second battle of Bull Run, Virginia (Confederate name: Second Manassas)—Confederate victory. Union commander John Pope is soundly thrashed by Lee and Jackson, suffering sixteen thousand casualties to the Confederates' ten thousand and retreating to Washington. Lee decides to invade the North, to secure European recognition of the Confederacy and to entice Maryland to leave the Union.

September 16, 1862 Battle of Antietam (Confederate name: Sharpsburg)—draw, favoring Union. McClellan heads off Lee's invasion in western Maryland, but Lee's army escapes back across the Potomac after one day of fighting that produces twenty-three thousand casualties. The battle persuades England not to recognize the Confederacy and gives Lincoln something close enough to a Northern victory that on September 22 he can make public a preliminary emancipation proclamation, to become effective January 1, 1863.

December 13, 1862 Battle of Fredericksburg, Virginia—Confederate victory. Appointed by Lincoln to replace McClellan as commander of the Army of the Potomac, Ambrose E. Burnside renews Union efforts to capture the Confederate capital of Richmond. He attempts a frontal assault on Confederates entrenched with artillery on heights above half a mile of open field. The Union suffers thirteen thousand casualties to five thousand for the Confederates; it is one of the worst Union defeats of the war.

January 1, 1863 Lincoln signs the Emancipation Proclamation, declaring all slaves held within Confederate states or parts of states controlled by the Confederacy to be free. This document goes beyond the preliminary proclamation by sanctioning the enlistment of black soldiers for combat positions. By the war's end, approximately two hundred thousand African Americans would serve in the Union army and navy.

April 2, 1863 Bread riots occur in Richmond; the Confederacy has severe food shortages.

May 2–6, 1863 Chancellorsville campaign, Virginia—Confederate victory. Now under the command of Joseph Hooker, the Union Army of the Potomac is routed by Lee, in spite of the Union's much greater numbers. Total losses are thirteen thousand Confederates, seventeen thousand Union. Stonewall Jackson is mistakenly and fatally shot in the dark by one of his own men. Lee proposes a second invasion of the North.

May–July 1863 Siege of Vicksburg, Mississippi—Union victory. Grant and Sherman win five small engagements against the army protecting Vicksburg and set siege to the city; the garrison at Vicksburg surrenders to Grant on July 4, followed by the surrender of the garrison at Fort Hudson on July 9. This crucial victory gives the Union control of the Mississippi River and cuts the Confederacy in half.

May 28, 1863 The first regiment of black troops trained for combat, the 54th Massachusetts, leaves Boston for fighting in the Sea Islands of South Carolina.

July 1–3, 1863 Battle of Gettysburg—Union victory. As Lee moves into the North, a small skirmish between advance units of both armies near Gettysburg, Pennsylvania, becomes a general battle. On July 3, Lee gambles on breaking the center of the Union line with a direct attack—Pickett's Charge. The assault is a disaster: fifteen thousand men march across an open field to attack dug-in infantry supported by cannon. In the three days of fighting, Lee suffers twenty-three thousand casualties—more than one-quarter of his army—while the Federals lose twenty-eight thousand, more than one-third of their army. Because this was Lee's first major defeat, it was a psychological turning point for both the Union and the Confederacy.

July 13–17, 1863 Draft riots in New York City in response to the Conscription Act leave more than one thousand people dead and wounded. Racism incites these riots. Democratic slogans proclaim that white working men will be forced to fight to free blacks who will then move North and take their jobs, and in June, African Americans had in fact been hired to replace striking Irish dockworkers. Following the announcement of the draft, a violent mob (made up largely of Irish workers) murders blacks, burns a black orphanage, and destroys the property of blacks and abolitionists. Federal troops are needed to quell the rioting. Many white Northerners react with horror to the racist violence of the rampage; combined with the bravery of black troops in battle in July, these riots help persuade many Northerners to support emancipation.

September–November 1863 Chickamauga/Chattanooga campaign—eventual Union victory. Union troops are attacked and nearly destroyed by Confederates, holding the line only after a last-ditch stand at the Battle of Chickamauga, Georgia, on September 19. Confederates lose twenty thousand men in the assault and settle in for the Union siege of Chattanooga, Tennessee. Grant directs a breakout attack at the battle of Lookout Mountain on November 24, and Chattanooga falls.

March 1864 Frustrated with the failures of numerous Union generals on the eastern front and impressed by Grant's successes in the West, Lincoln appoints Grant the head of all Union forces.

April 12, 1864 Battle of Fort Pillow*, Tennessee—Confederate victory. Confederate cavalry commander Nathan Bedford Forrest attacks Union forces. The number of black soldiers killed in and after this battle raises vehement protest in the North.

May–July 1864 Overland Campaign: Moving toward Richmond, Virginia, Grant for the first time commands troops fighting against Lee, resulting in seven weeks of almost continuous combat and huge Union losses. Major battles include the Wilderness (May 5–6) and eighteen hours of hand-to-hand fighting at the Bloody Angle at Spotsylvania (May 12). The carnage is so intense that Confederate officers salvage 120,000 pounds of lead from the battlefields for recasting. On June 3, Grant attacks Confederates at Cold Harbor. By the time

Grant's army reaches Petersburg, it has suffered sixty-five thousand casualties—60 percent of the total losses suffered by the Army of the Potomac in the previous three years. Nonetheless, Lincoln recognizes that Grant may well be the kind of leader who can defeat Lee.

May–September 1864 Starting from Chattanooga, Tennessee, Union general Sherman begins a campaign to capture Atlanta, Georgia, that will last for four months.

June 8, 1864 Lincoln is renominated for president; Andrew Johnson, a Tennessee War Democrat, is his running mate. Throughout the summer, it seems unlikely that they will win.

June 15, 1864 Congress grants equal pay to black soldiers serving in the Union army.

June 18, 1864 Beginning of the ten-month-long siege of Petersburg, Virginia—eventual Union victory.

July 30, 1864 Battle of the Crater—Confederate victory. Union miners explode 320 kegs of dynamite beneath the Confederate line at Petersburg, but errors by Union leaders and troops result in a failed attack. The long stalemates in the Union campaigns for Petersburg and Atlanta increase Northern opposition to the war.

September 2, 1864 Sherman's army cuts last railroad line into Atlanta, and five days later, Sherman orders the remaining civilians to evacuate the city. His success at Atlanta is greeted with jubilation in the North and helps rebuild waning support for Lincoln's presidency.

November 8, 1864 Lincoln takes 55 percent of the vote overall and 78 percent of the soldier vote in reelection victory.

November 15, 1864 Determined to destroy any property, supplies, or railroad lines that could possibly support the Confederate army, Sherman burns the city of Atlanta and then leads his forces in the now infamous March to the Sea. By the time his army captures Savannah in December, it has left a fifty-mile-wide swath of destruction.

January 31, 1865 Congress passes the Thirteenth Amendment to the Constitution, outlawing slavery.

February 1865 With the goal of joining Grant's forces against Lee, Sherman's army heads north through the Carolinas. On February 17, Sherman burns the South Carolina capital of Columbia; the next day, Federal forces recapture Charleston and the symbolic Fort Sumter.

March 4, 1865 Lincoln delivers his second inaugural address.

April 1, 1865 Lee flees Petersburg to the west with thirty-five thousand troops. Richmond becomes indefensible, and the Confederate government flees.

April 3, 1865 Lincoln makes a triumphal entry into Richmond, walking the streets, where he is greeted by throngs of freed slaves.

April 9, 1865 Lee surrenders to Grant at Appomattox, Virginia.

April 14, 1865 On Good Friday, John Wilkes Booth shoots Lincoln in Ford's Theatre, Washington, D.C. Lincoln dies the next morning, and Andrew Johnson is sworn in as president.

ABBREVIATIONS

Source Collections of Civil War Poetry for Part I, listed chronologically

Poems of the War	Boker, George H. *Poems of the War.* Boston and New York: Ticknor and Fields, 1864.
CWSS	Moore, Frank, ed. *The Civil War in Song and Story, 1860–1865.* New York: Peter Fenelon Collier, 1865.
Rebellion Record	*The Rebellion Record,* 12 vols. Volumes 1–6, New York: Putnam, 1861–63. Volumes 7–12, New York: Van Nostrand, 1864–68.
War Poetry	Simms, William Gilmore, ed. *War Poetry of the South.* New York: George C. Rand and Avery, 1866.
Southern Poems	Mason, Emily Virginia, ed. *The Southern Poems of the War.* Baltimore: J. Murphy & Co., 1867.
Poems	Harte, Bret. *Poems and Two Men of Sandy Bar: A Drama.* Boston and New York: Houghton Mifflin Company, 1882.
Bugle-Echoes	Browne, Francis Fisher, ed. *Bugle-Echoes: A Collection of Poems of the Civil War Northern and Southern.* New York: White, Stokes, and Allen, 1886. Second edition, Chicago: McClurg, 1916.
Southern Poets	Parks, Edd Winfield. *Southern Poets: Representative Selections.* New York: American Book Company, 1936.
Blue and Gray	Capps, Claudius Meade, ed. *The Blue and the Gray: The Best Poems of the Civil War.* Boston: B. Humphries, Inc., 1943. Reprint, Freeport, N.Y.: Books for Librairies Press, 1969.
Selected Poems	Kibler, James Everett, ed. *Selected Poems of William Gilmore Simms.* Athens: University of Georgia Press, 1990.

African-American Poetry	Sherman, Joan, ed. *African-American Poetry of the Nineteenth Century: An Anthology.* Mineola, N.Y.: Dover Publications, 1997.
NAWP	Bennett, Paula Bernat, ed. *Nineteenth-Century American Women Poets: An Anthology.* Oxford, Eng., and Malden, Mass.: Blackwell, 1998.

“WORDS FOR THE HOUR”

INTRODUCTION

"Words for the Hour"

Reading the American Civil War through Poetry

FAITH BARRETT

In September of 1861, twenty-three-year-old Obadiah Ethelbert Baker left his wife and home and enlisted in the Second Iowa Cavalry Volunteers. Baker fought in the Union army for the next three and half years, taking part in battles in Mississippi, Missouri, Louisiana, and Tennessee, before being honorably discharged in April of 1865. During the war years, Baker kept detailed accounts of daily events in the form of journal entries, which he addressed and regularly sent to his wife; by the war's end, he had filled thirteen volumes of pocket diaries with his responses to the war, responses that include journal entries and long poems, as well as the lines of verse he sometimes used to close out journal entries.[1] Over the next forty years, Baker would continue drafting and revising his poetry; between 1861 and the 1890s, he wrote about two hundred poems, many of which respond either directly or indirectly to his experiences on Civil War battlefields and in military hospitals.

Baker's example is instructive insofar as it underlines the crucial role that poetry played in American culture by the middle of the nineteenth century. The American Revolution had prompted an outpouring both of patriot ballads and of poems in praise of Washington and other military heroes. With the rise of public education in the 1830s and 1840s, the centrality of poetry to American cultural life was effectively codified as part of schoolroom practice. Children across the United States memorized and recited patriotic poems both for the classroom and for

---

I thank Cristanne Miller, first for proposing the idea of this anthology and then for offering to coedit the volume with me. Her expertise and advice have been essential and inspiring at every stage of the project. I am particularly grateful for her generous and helpful responses to this essay. I also thank the students in my Civil War literature courses at California State University at Pomona and at Lawrence University for their suggestive responses to many of the poems I discuss here.

1. The papers of Obadiah Ethelbert Baker are housed at the Huntington Library in San Marino, California.

public performances. Poetry—recited by both adults and children—was also regularly included as part of the lectures and meetings organized by church leaders, abolitionists, temperance and women's rights activists, and other reformers of the nineteenth century. Poets like Ralph Waldo Emerson wrote civic-minded occasional poems for events such as the unveiling of the Revolutionary War monument at the Concord Bridge in Massachusetts. Emerson's "Concord Hymn" was distributed as a broadside and sung at the dedication of the monument on July 4, 1837; it then went on to circulate in newspapers and achieved widespread popular acclaim because of the numerous occasions on which it was recited by schoolchildren.

The example of Emerson's "Concord Hymn" underlines how ubiquitous poetry was in American life at this time, both in oral performance and in print. Americans not only heard poems at many civic events, but they also read poetry in broadsides, pamphlets, daily newspapers, and magazines, as well as in books and anthologies. The second half of the nineteenth century witnessed explosive growth in the number of newspapers and magazines available to American readers, and publishers delighted in the equally rapid growth in their subscriber base. Poems that appeared in newspapers and magazines were read aloud after dinner around the fireplace, copied into album books of favorite poems, and sent through the mail to family and friends. Not surprisingly, many Americans also wrote poetry as a pastime or a hobby. These poems celebrated births and birthdays, addressed sweethearts, mourned losses, and reflected on American history and heroes; some writers sent their poems to newspapers and magazines. Far more, however, contented themselves with circulating their work through letters to friends and relatives and reading it aloud at social gatherings. If we consider Obadiah Ethelbert Baker's output of two hundred poems in its historical context, his achievement becomes not something exceptional but rather a representative example of a wider cultural practice.

The national crisis of the Civil War did nothing to lessen Americans' interest in poetry; because poetry was seen as an integral part of American political culture, the war only heightened Americans' commitment to the discursive strategies of poetry. Yet the onset of war wrought changes—some subtle, some pronounced—in the landscape of that poetry. Boundaries between once-distinct poetic stances became remarkably fluid. Earlier in the century an occasional civic poem such as Emerson's "Concord Hymn" would have seemed diametrically opposed to a woman poet's meditation on the death of a child—for example, Lydia Sigourney's "Death of an Infant" (1824). In the Civil War era, however, when a poem represents the death of a son in battle, grieving becomes a process that is at once collective and individual, and the staged or dramatic quality of poetic expression enables a mingling of publicly expressed and privately felt emotions. Because of the rhetorical and imaginative possibilities poetry offered for speaking not only for oneself but also for one's family, state, region, or nation, an astonishing variety of people—men and women from all walks of life—turned to poetry in order to respond to the events of the war.

Writing in 1962, Edmund Wilson dismisses the poetry of the Civil War as "versified journalism," suggesting that the writers' emphasis on politics undermines the artistic merits of their work.[2] Writing a decade later, Daniel Aaron agrees with Wilson, suggesting that few writers of the Civil War era were able to say anything revealing about the "meaning . . . of the War."[3] And this critical assessment of the poor performance of American poets of the Civil War era begins in the immediate aftermath of the war itself. Writing a hundred years earlier in 1867, William Dean Howells observes: "Our war has not only left us a burden of a tremendous national debt, but has laid upon our literature a charge under which it has hitherto staggered very lamely."[4] In dismissing Civil War poetry as "versified journalism," Edmund Wilson overlooks the cultural function of poetry in nineteenth-century America. In reading nineteenth-century poetry from a twenty-first-century standpoint, we must bear in mind that in this era, poetry was seen as serving a vital political function. A nineteenth-century reader of poetry would not have considered a politically engaged stance to be an artistic liability; indeed, both during and after the Civil War, poetry was seen as playing a central role in defining new versions of American identity. When William Dean Howells laments that few writers have been adequate to the task of representing the war, he is suggesting that only a few writers have—in his view—risen to the challenge of writing work that is both aesthetically pleasing and politically accountable.

With this collection, we hope to encourage a reassessment of the claims of Howells, Wilson, and Aaron by emphasizing the quantity, variety, and quality of the poetry written in response to the war.[5] Whereas scholars of American literature have traditionally focused on just a few canonical poets who explicitly address the war in their work (Walt Whitman in *Drum-Taps,* for example, or Herman Melville in *Battle-Pieces*), in this collection we seek to emphasize both the tremendous outpouring of poetry produced in response to the war and the

2. Edmund Wilson, *Patriotic Gore: Studies in the Literature of the American Civil War* (New York: Oxford University Press, 1962), 479.

3. Daniel Aaron, *The Unwritten War: American Writers and the Civil War* (1973; reprint, Madison: University of Wisconsin Press, 1987), xxii.

4. Cited from ibid., xix.

5. In her wide-ranging study of the popular literature of the Civil War, Alice Fahs discusses numerous examples of the poetry of this era, arguing for the richness and thematic complexity of these texts. See *The Imagined Civil War: Popular Literature of the North and South, 1861–1865* (Chapel Hill: University of North Carolina Press, 2001).

extraordinary range of tones and stances within that production. In choosing poems for inclusion in this collection, we began with the premise that nineteenth-century American poets are responding not only to momentous historical changes but also to one another: the conversation that results between and among these communities of writers sheds light both on nineteenth-century visions of national identity and on the development of the American poetic tradition.[6] The sense of urgency that propels this conversation becomes still more apparent if we read across the spectrum of nineteenth-century American poetry, rather than focusing on only a few canonical poets. As we read and selected pieces for the anthology, we were able to confirm our sense that the poetry of this era has much to recommend it: a surprising formal variety and thematic range, complex and compelling aesthetic ambitions, and an equally complex and ambitious engagement with the political discourses of the day. These are poems which merit closer study and which offer many and varied pleasures to the reader.

As Alice Fahs points out in her study of the popular literature of the Civil War, the distinctions that we as contemporary readers draw between "high" literary texts and "low," or popular, writing are not distinctions that a nineteenth-century reader would have recognized.[7] During the war years, poems appeared regularly in the columns of the daily and weekly newspapers, between military officers' detailed accounts of battles, lists of the dead and wounded, and advertisements for fabric or farm equipment. Some of these poems were written by local writers; others were written by the likes of Emerson or John Greenleaf Whittier. Fahs notes that *Harper's Weekly* had an audience of more than a hundred thousand readers during the war years; if we consider both its content and its audience, a publication such as *Harper's* clearly resists easy classification as either "high" or "low" in its commitments.[8] In the chronological structure of Part I of this anthology, then, we have aimed to re-create something like the experience of the nineteenth-century reader encountering poetry in contemporary newspapers and magazines as the events of the war unfolded.

If we read across the selections from the four years of the war, certain patterns become evident: as the number of deaths mounts, poems which argue that it is right for young men to sacrifice themselves for the greater good of their country are increasingly answered by poems that focus on individual losses. The many poems, both Northern and Southern, which hint that the war may soon be over give way to poems in which speakers are resigned to the fate of a long and bloody

6. I develop these ideas more broadly in a book-length manuscript titled "'To fight aloud is very brave': American Poetry and the Civil War."

7. Fahs, 3.

8. Ibid.

conflict; poems from the war's later years sometimes call for peace or protest the conflict's high death toll. Given the heightened religious rhetoric of the era, it is not surprising that many writers engage with the theological discourses that surrounded the moral dilemmas of war; given the popularity of sentimental literature in the mid-nineteenth century, it is also no surprise that an abundance of poems rely on the conventions of sentimentality or the imagery of Victorian domesticity in responding to war's violence. Some poems celebrate the heroism of the war's great generals and leaders; still others celebrate the contributions of foot soldiers. White Northerners and Southerners mourning the deaths of loved ones write poems that are often almost indistinguishable if references to uniforms, flags, and geography are removed; as Cristanne Miller points out in her preface, many of the same poems were published in both the North and the South during the war—often with incorrect accounts of the regional allegiances of their writers. Not surprisingly, questions of race marked a deep divide between Northern and Southern poets. Poets who had already been responding positively to the war's impact on the African American slave community gained a renewed sense of purpose and commitment with Lincoln's Emancipation Proclamation. When blacks were officially authorized to fight as soldiers for the Union army, poets began to meditate on their position in the military, their valor in battle, and racial-ethnic tensions in the ranks. Meanwhile, Southern writers compared the South's treatment at the hands of the Union to a form of slavery; Southern writers also figured African American slaves as Southern loyalists who were content with their lot.

Reading across the spectrum of the poetry of this era, we gain a sense not only of the powerful impact that the war had on women but also of the powerful impact that women had on the war. As writers, as editors of poetry collections and memorial volumes, as workers for the soldiers' aid societies, as hospital nurses, as encouraging or grieving or angry mothers, wives, and sisters, women played key roles both in endorsing and in questioning the war's ideologies. Poets sometimes figure women's work in support of the troops as a form of combat, and as Fahs observes, poems describing a soldier's decision to enlist are far more likely to represent the mother's perspective on his enlistment than that of the father.[9] Both Northern and Southern writers figure the nation-state in feminine terms, thereby heightening the stakes in representing women's commitment to the war effort. Moving away from the front lines of battle, then, writers consider the wartime roles of women in the family and in their relief work; they also address children's relationship to the war, the culture of the military hospital, and life in a prison camp. As the wounded return from the battlefields, writers begin to reflect on the

9. Ibid., 108.

challenges faced by disabled veterans coming home. Not surprisingly, Southern declarations of regional pride remain strong throughout the war years, culminating in the outrage and anguish of poems lamenting the Southern defeat. Northern hymns of praise for Lincoln begin early on in the war years and reach their apex in the outpouring of elegies written after his assassination. When Whitman declares that the war "was you and me," he is emphasizing all the ways in which the war was intricately woven into the everyday lives of most Americans at this time, even and especially those who lived far from battlefields and got all their news of the war by way of the telegraph, letters, and newspapers.[10] The poetry of this era suggests that the war touched issues of identity and culture which were fundamental to most Americans; the majority of the poetry written in response to the war was written by men and women who had no direct experience of combat.

Both because of their enormous popularity with nineteenth-century audiences and because of their critical dismissal in the twentieth century, sentimental poems merit special attention in any discussion of Civil War poetry. As Part I of this anthology makes clear, sentimental poems were not the exclusive province of women writers; rather, they were written by men as well. Indeed, the poetry of this era often unsettles a reader's expectations about the kinds of poetic stances men and women might assume; while men often write sentimental poems, women are equally capable of writing angry battle cries.[11] As a rejoinder to early poems that emphasized masculine strength and courage in articulating a call to arms, later sentimental poems representing dying soldiers often figure those soldiers as feminized boy-children.[12] These images of soldiers as gentle, waning youths were particularly successful and influential, appealing to male and female readers from across the political spectrum and often becoming best-selling items for publishers of broadsides or sheet music. The success of such poems results in part from their continuance of the antebellum cultural focus on the rituals of death and mourning. More important still, the sentimental poems of death also served two seemingly contradictory, yet actually complementary, purposes. On the one hand, as Fahs suggests, the sentimental poem reasserts the presence and worth of the individual in the face of the massive numbers of the war dead;[13] on the other hand,

---

10. Walt Whitman, "By Blue Ontario's Shore," line 278, in *Leaves of Grass: A Textual Variorum of the Printed Poems,* ed. Sculley Bradley et al. (New York: New York University Press, 1980), 1:207.

11. See Frank Gassaway's "The Pride of Battery B," Thomas Manahan's "Brother, Tell Me of the Battle," and Longfellow's "Killed at the Ford," for just a few of the many examples of male-authored sentimental poems. For a representative sample of the angry battle cries written by women authors, see Catherine Warfield's "Manassas," Ellen Blunt's "The Southern Cross," or, for that matter, Julia Ward Howe's "Battle Hymn of the Republic."

12. Here again I draw on the analysis of Alice Fahs. For a fuller discussion of this issue, see chap. 3, "The Sentimental Soldier," 93–119.

13. Ibid., 93–94.

the sentimental poem frequently represents the dying soldier not as a unique individual but rather as a type of martyred youth and innocence. Such poems enable readers to mourn the loss of the individual soldier without losing sight of the larger national cause for which he died. The sentimental poem thus becomes a kind of release valve for the pressures of an otherwise unbearable loss: the weeping and grieving that the poem permits and indeed encourages are often contained by the poem's conclusion, which offers reassurance that the soldier's death supports the ideologies of his nation. Sentimental poems both threaten to undermine military ideologies and also frequently endorse them, thereby allowing a wide range of readers to assume multiple and contradictory emotional stances in relation to the war's violence.

As this brief overview indicates, given the range and complexity of work from this era, we had to make some difficult decisions about categories of poems that we could not fully represent within the scope of this project. Whereas previous anthologies of Civil War poetry have often included reflective poems written in the 1880s and 1890s, we have included only poems written within a handful of years after the war's end; as the volume's title, *Words for the Hour,* suggests, we have aimed to focus on contemporary writers' more immediate and urgent responses to the conflict. The relatively brief antebellum section is intended to provide a partial context for understanding the themes and ideological stances of the Northern and Southern poems published during the war years. We have included only a limited selection from the rich and varied tradition of the abolitionist poem; we have likewise limited ourselves to a few representative antebellum paeans to the Southern landscape and culture. Because Civil War poetry anthologies have in the past included few poems discussing the relationship of African Americans to the war, we have included several; more broadly, we have also tried to include a range of poems that foreground issues of race.

Three of the best-known Civil War–era songs we have included speak directly to the racial issues that worked to propel the nation toward war. In the nineteenth century, the relationship between poetry and popular song was much closer than it is at the present time. Broadsides and sheet music lyrics were two of the most affordable and popular ways of circulating poetry during the war years, and many publishers also offered pamphlet-sized songsters of war poems for soldiers on the march.[14] In a brief discussion of Dan Emmett's "I Wish I Was in Dixie's Land," Julia Ward Howe's "Battle Hymn of the Republic," and the slave song "Let My People Go: A Song of the 'Contrabands'" (popularly known as "Go

14. See, for example, the collection by Francis Child, *War Songs for Freemen* (Boston: Tick-nor and Fields, 1862), or William H. Hayward, *Camp Songs for Soldiers and Poems of Leisure Moments* (Baltimore: H. Robinson, 1864). Hayward's "The Patriot Ishmael Day" is drawn from this volume.

Down, Moses"), I want to suggest that what links all three songs is not only the strength of their commitment to unifying their respective communities but also the strength of their investment in the American landscape.

Dan Emmett's "Dixie" resists easy categorization in several ways.[15] A white minstrel who performed in blackface, Emmett was born in Ohio. He composed the piece for Dan Bryant's Minstrels, who were based in New York, and the song received its first performance there in 1859. The central conceit of the song's chorus is the black slave speaker's nostalgic longing for his lost homeland, "de land ob cotton"; the song ironically offers no explanation for the circumstances that have compelled the speaker to leave home. Mimicking the call and response of African American singing in the chorus's repeated cries of "Look away" and "Hooray," the song was an instant hit with white audiences and was soon a popular choice for performances in both the North and the South. It was a particular favorite of Lincoln, who first heard it performed at a minstrel show in Chicago in 1860 and who asked to hear it played immediately after the war's end.[16] Minstrel performances of the piece—like all blackface performance—involved portraying crude stereotypes of black characters; Emmett imitates Southern black dialect in the lyrics.[17]

Clearly, both Northern and Southern whites were engaged and amused by the cartoon image of a poor black speaker who looks with longing back toward the South. Yet even as Northern and Southern whites sat in minstrel halls listening and laughing, the song points toward the violence to come, the violence that will effectively divide the American landscape: "In Dixie Land, I'll took my stand / To lib an die in Dixie." In the lyrics Emmett published for the song, his imitation of black dialect tones down the threat of collective black violence by focusing on a solitary speaker and by mingling past and present tenses in "I'll took my stand."[18]

---

15. Judith and Howard Sacks suggest that Emmett's songwriting—and the writing of "Dixie" in particular—may have been influenced by the Snowdens, a family of African American musicians who lived in the town next to Emmett's hometown of Mount Vernon, Ohio, and gave frequent performances in that part of the state. See Howard L. Sacks and Judith Rose Sacks, *Way Up North in Dixie: A Black Family's Claim to the Confederate Anthem* (Washington, D.C.: Smithsonian Institution Press, 1993).

16. Henry Clay Whitney, *Life on the Circuit with Lincoln* (Caldwell, Idaho: Caxton Printers, 1940), 102–103, 161.

17. For analysis of blackface performance in nineteenth-century American culture, see Eric Lott, *Love and Theft: Blackface Minstrelsy and the American Working Class* (New York: Oxford University Press, 1993); William J. Mahar, *Behind the Burnt Cork Mask: Early Blackface Minstrelsy and Antebellum American Popular Culture* (Urbana: University of Illinois Press, 1999); and Dale Cockrell, *Demons of Disorder: Early Blackface Minstrels and Their World* (New York: Cambridge University Press, 1997).

18. The singular pronoun "I" is perhaps particularly surprising here given that "I Wish I Was in Dixie's Land" was written as a "walk-around," the finale of the program in which all the performers came back onstage to dance, play, and sing. Performances undoubtedly introduced variations on Emmett's published lyrics.

As whites enjoyed the idea of black nostalgia for slavery and for Southern landscapes, they were indeed "look[ing] away" from the violence of slavery and the violence of the impending national conflict. And though on the eve of war the song was popular with whites in both the North and the South, in the months leading up to secession, "Dixie" was played in Washington, D.C., to express Southern loyalists' discontent with Lincoln's election. Jefferson Davis had "Dixie" played at his inauguration in February of 1861, and by the time the war had entered its second year, the song had become a Southern anthem. When Confederate soldiers sang "Dixie," they used a plural pronoun and the future tense in the crucial line of the chorus to underline their determination to build a Southern nation: "In Dixie Land, we'll take our stand / To lib an die in Dixie."

First published in the North in 1861 both in the *New York Tribune* and in the form of sheet music, the slave song "Let My People Go: A Song of the 'Contrabands'" displays an equally strong commitment to the idea of a homeland for African Americans. Echoing the Puritan reading of the Old Testament, with its emphasis on God's covenant with his chosen people, the song captured the imagination of many Northern white listeners who supported the idea of linking the war to the emancipation of blacks; with its invocation of a God of wrath who will guide his people to a promised land, it also articulated the rage and longing of blacks who were willing to fight for their freedom and for the Union but who were initially relegated to menial labor and service duties behind the front lines. The song's popularity with abolitionists no doubt resulted from the force of its argument that African Americans had a God-given right to freedom. The image of God dividing the waters of the Red Sea in verse nine ("At the command of God it did divide") points toward the ways in which the nation was divided by the question of slavery.

Like "Let My People Go," Julia Ward Howe's "Battle Hymn of the Republic" imagines a God of wrath who descends to earth to right the wrong of slavery; Howe's God wreaks his vengeance on the landscape itself, in a process that yields a harvest of redemptive blood. Howe's poem is just one of many from this era that conjures up the image of a blood-drenched field. On a trip to Washington in the fall of 1861, Howe wrote her "Battle Hymn" when one of her companions suggested that she might write more-elegant words for "John Brown's Body," a popular hit often sung by Union soldiers at that time. Although both songs argue that the war is being fought to free the slaves, Howe's version rewrites the soldier's bravery in a loftier and more literary vein. Howe's song achieved rapid success, and Northern troops quickly began to sing it, though they continued to sing "John Brown's Body" as well; it is, of course, unlikely that all the soldiers who sang these songs wholly endorsed the ideal of black emancipation these lyrics articulated. The tremendous success of both versions nonetheless attests to the permeability of the boundary between the "literary" and the popular and the boundary between song and poem in this era.

While in Part I of the anthology we arrange a variety of popular and literary poems in chronological order, Part II presents the work of a group of poets who published their Civil War poems either in collections of poems on various themes or in volumes dedicated solely to the war. In what follows, I will offer a brief introduction to each poet's work and a few suggestions for approaching the poems. This section begins with the work of the remarkable North Carolina poet George Moses Horton.[19] Born into slavery, Horton published two volumes of poetry in the South while still a slave. As a young man, Horton made a name for himself by composing love poems made to order for University of North Carolina students; his work as a poet-for-hire clearly helped him hone his skills at writing poems that would be successful with white Southern audiences. When the Union army passed through Chapel Hill in April of 1865, the sixty-eight-year-old Horton traveled for three months with the Ninth Michigan Cavalry Volunteers, publishing his third volume of poems that summer. Probably a year or so later, he moved north to Philadelphia.

Though less carefully polished than some of his earlier work, the war poems which Horton wrote while on the march with the Ninth Michigan and which he then included in *Naked Genius* reveal all the nuance and complexity of his relationship to the war; indeed, they seem particularly revealing because of their rough edges, presenting a remarkable range of literary stances and political commitments. From songs of praise for Union war heroes to a poem about brotherly reunion between Confederate and Federal soldiers, to the sentimental "Dying Soldier's Message," Horton demonstrates his skill at working in the many different poetic conventions of the Civil War era. Still other poems rely on those conventions to call into question the war's ideologies. In "The Spectator of the Battle of Belmont," Horton examines the ethical dilemmas of being a spectator of a war ("Spectators the pain of the conflict explore"). In "The Terrors of War," he offers a nightmarish vision of battle as apocalypse; in the extraordinary poem "Weep," he laments the devastation that war has wrought both North and South and anticipates the pain and struggles that the still deeply divided nation will face ("And of the gloom which still the future waits").

Some of what Horton may have felt on leaving his home of sixty-eight years after the war's end can be gleaned from "The Southern Refugee"—a poem which

19. Joan Sherman's edition of Horton's poems, *The Black Bard of North Carolina: George Moses Horton and His Poetry* (Chapel Hill: University of North Carolina Press, 1997), also includes an insightful essay on Horton's life and work.

suggests that Horton had already decided to leave the South when the war ended. This piece offers an eloquent and moving reply to Dan Emmett's "Dixie," puncturing the racist caricature of Emmett's blackface speaker by giving voice to the complex mix of emotions that Horton's speaker feels as he considers what he will lose by leaving the South. The poem begins with the speaker's declaration that he "deplore[s] the bitter fate" which impels him "to straggle" from his "native home." Here Horton seems to allude to the plight of both whites and blacks in the South, many of whom were displaced, homeless, and destitute in the war's aftermath. The stanza employs conventional poetic imagery in evoking a natural world that expresses all the sorrow the speaker feels:

> The verdant willow droops her head,
> And seems to bid a fare thee well;
> The flowers with tears their fragrance shed,
> Alas! their parting tale to tell.

The speaker declares that his decision to leave the South will mean "the loss of Paradise." Yet he also goes on to state that this paradise has been marred. When he describes the South with the phrase "Eden's garden left in gloom," he seems to imply that, whether or not he departs, the beauty of the landscape has been irrevocably lost, that it can never recover from the ravages of war and of slavery. And there will be, he argues, no relief from this burden of loss, for "grief affords us no device." Gesturing implicitly toward the complex ties of power, fear, hate, and love that bound blacks and whites together in the South, he likens his departure to the end of a marriage, when the "lone deserted bride" bids her "bridegroom fare thee well." Yet unlike Emmett's song, in which the speaker reiterates his homesickness for Dixie in every chorus, Horton's poem offers its speaker emotional closure on this longing in the final stanza:

> I trust I soon shall dry the tear
> And leave forever hence to roam,
> Far from a residence so dear,
> The place of beauty—my native home.

While the poem's last two lines again evoke the memory of a beloved Southern home, the first two lines clearly argue for the finality of the speaker's departure and the end of his period of grieving. In "The Southern Refugee," Horton dismisses the fantasy of "old times" in "Dixie" as fantasy, implicitly suggesting that this is a white fantasy which blacks can never share.

One of the foremost white abolitionist poets of the nineteenth century, the second writer in Part II of the volume is John Greenleaf Whittier, who used his pen in support of the Union cause, ultimately winning widespread public acclaim from Northern audiences. With satirical antebellum poems such as "The Hunters of Men," Whittier pressed his Northern readers to acknowledge the injustice and cruelty of slavery. Because he was already writing a popular and politically engaged poetry before the war, the outbreak of violence only confirmed Whittier's sense of mission as a civic-minded poet. In "At Port Royal," Whittier reveals his fascination with the tradition of "sorrow songs," the name W. E. B. DuBois gives slave songs; Whittier seeks to make that tradition come alive for white Northern audiences. The abolitionist poems of his later years are now considered by many scholars to be some of his finest work. With its patriotic depiction of an older woman's bravery, "Barbara Frietchie" was arguably his most successful poem of the war years. Whittier's towering stature in nineteenth-century America is a testament to the centrality of poetry in American culture at this time.

Like Whittier, both Walt Whitman and Herman Melville found in the war a powerful sense of artistic purpose; both published individual volumes of poems that focus specifically on the war. Though Whitman would later observe that "the real war will never get in the books," he nonetheless took up the task of representing war's violence and binding the nation together again at the war's end; Whitman now enjoys a reputation as the leading poet of the Civil War.[20] *Drum-Taps* first appeared in 1865, though the dates of composition for the poems ranged throughout the war; it was followed the next year by the *Sequel to Drum-Taps,* which included the now well-known Lincoln elegies as well additional war poems. With his Civil War poems, as with all his work, Whitman continued to arrange, rearrange, and revise long after he wrote his first versions of these pieces. Some of the more conciliatory poems in *Drum-Taps* were first published after the war ended; "Reconciliation," for example, first appeared in the 1865–66 *Sequel.* Still others, however, were written before the outbreak of war: "Over the Carnage Rose Prophetic a Voice" was first published as one of the *Calamus* poems in 1860.

---

20. The quotation is from Walt Whitman, *Specimen Days,* in *Prose Works, 1892,* ed. Floyd Stovall (New York: New York University Press, 1963), 1:115. In view of Whitman's reputation as the poet of the war, it is not surprising that there has been so much scholarship on this part of Whitman's work. Among many others, recent studies that discuss Whitman's Civil War poetry include Timothy Sweet's insightful *Traces of War: Poetry, Photography, and the Crisis of the Union* (Baltimore: Johns Hopkins University Press, 1990); Michael Moon's *Disseminating Whitman: Revision and Corporeality in* Leaves of Grass (Cambridge: Harvard University Press, 1991); Mark Maslan's "Whitman's 'Strange Hand': Body as Text in *Drum-Taps,*" *ELH* 58 (1991): 935–955; George Hutchinson, "Race and the Family Romance: Whitman's Civil War," *Walt Whitman Quarterly Review* 20, nos. 3–4 (2003): 134–150; and M. Wynn Thomas, "Weathering the Storm: Whitman and the Civil War," *Walt Whitman Quarterly Review* 15, nos. 2–3 (1997–98): 87–109.

In the 1881–82 version of *Drum-Taps*, then, Whitman carefully arranges the poems to create a narrative that balances the speaker's moments of doubt with moments of moral certainty, always with the overarching goal of reunifying the nation and binding together its disparate elements.

The antebellum fascination with panoramic views of landscape both in paintings and photography not surprisingly leads to photographic and painterly depictions of battlefields, and Whitman, like many poets of this era, was influenced by these images.[21] In some of the landscape poems in particular, Whitman inaugurates a brevity and simplicity of style which are new to his work and which foreshadow developments to come in modernist poetry. In "Cavalry Crossing a Ford," the speaker provides a description of a military unit on the move. The language is almost journalistic in its detachment and compression: "A line in long array where they wind betwixt green islands, / They take a serpentine course, their arms flash in the sun—hark to the musical clank." Yet the poem also echoes the conventions of pastoral poetry in the way that it seamlessly mingles the landscape and the human figures. "Look Down Fair Moon" is still briefer, and here too Whitman mingles traditional literary devices with an innovative graphic realism. In "Look Down Fair Moon," the combination of the high literary address to the moon and the poem's brevity suggests that the speaker is stunned into silence by what he sees: the horror of the dead on the battlefield. One of Whitman's masterpieces, the poem offers no closing reassurance, no easy resolution after such a terrifying vision.[22]

While Whitman met with a certain degree of success in styling himself as the nation's bard in the aftermath of the war, Melville's 1866 collection *Battle-Pieces and Aspects of the War* was panned by the critics when it appeared and has, until recently, received only limited attention from scholars and readers.[23] Melville was clearly disappointed by the lack of positive response. One of the most fascinating aspects of *Battle-Pieces* is the hybridity of the text, and that hybridity likely

21. A primary purpose of Timothy Sweet's *Traces of War* is to read Whitman's *Drum-Taps* and Melville's *Battle-Pieces* in relation to visual images of battlefield landscapes.

22. For a fuller discussion of landscape imagery and poetic devices in "Cavalry Crossing a Ford" and "Look Down Fair Moon," see my essay "Addresses to a Divided Nation: Images of War in Emily Dickinson and Walt Whitman," *Arizona Quarterly* 61, no. 4 (Winter 2005).

23. Timothy Sweet's incisive study of Whitman, Melville, and Civil War photography has clearly helped launch a revival of interest in Melville's poetry in general and in *Battle-Pieces* in particular. See Sweet's *Traces of War*. Stanton Garner's *The Civil War World of Herman Melville* (Lawrence: University Press of Kansas, 1993) presents thorough historical research on Melville's relationship to the events of the war. Other more-recent studies of *Battle-Pieces* include Rosanna Warren, "Dark Knowledge: Melville's Poems of the Civil War," *Raritan* 19, no. 1 (Summer 1999): 100–121, and Robert Milder, "The Rhetoric of Melville's *Battle-Pieces*," *Nineteenth-Century Literature* 44, no. 4 (September 1989): 173–200.

accounts for the lukewarm reviews the work received. In addition to the prose "Supplement" that Melville appended to the text, he also included a series of footnotes, and these notes make plain the fact that Melville relied on newspaper accounts of battles as he wrote the poems of *Battle-Pieces*.[24] Then as now, it is unconventional for a poet to include a prose supplement or a series of footnotes in a volume of poems. Some reviewers seemed to have trouble deciding whether Melville was writing poetry or prose.[25]

In "Donelson," a poem that both intrigued and puzzled the critics, the mingling of poetry and prose foregrounds three of Melville's central aims in *Battle-Pieces*: first, Melville is trying to invent a new kind of poetry, one that can represent the indescribable horrors of war without sentimentality or excessive ornament; second, Melville is interested in examining the ways in which war is represented in all kinds of texts, including newspapers, telegrams, and poetry; and third, Melville wants to record the experience of those who observed the war not on its battlefields but through the newspapers, letters, and bulletins they read. The scene of "Donelson" alternates between a newspaper office where people gather to read the latest posted news and seemingly firsthand descriptions of battlefields provided by reporters at the front. Over the course of the poem, however, the reliability of those reporters and of the newspaper's system for providing information is called into question, as erroneous information is published and then retracted, as smeared ink runs down the posted bulletins, and as the telegraph service on which the journalists depend breaks down. By emphasizing these aspects of war reporting, Melville points out that journalistic representations of war are inherently limited, flawed, and subjective. By presenting these descriptions in metrical verse, Melville probes the boundary between poetry and prose, suggesting that poetry—a new kind of poetry—might have a role to play in representing the war's horrors. He does not claim that poetic representations of war might be any less flawed than journalistic ones. He does, however, argue that we must read both kinds of texts with caution and with a skeptical eye. Ultimately, "Donelson" suggests that language is inadequate to the task of representing the violence of war—even as it also suggests that language is one of the only means at our disposal in seeking to understand that violence.

While Melville's volume of densely written and philosophical war poems was a critical failure in its own time, Frances Ellen Watkins Harper's stirring and accessible narrative poems were highly acclaimed and enormously popular with

24. In the interest of conserving space, we have opted to present the Melville poems in this edition without their accompanying footnotes and without the "Supplement."

25. For an overview and analysis of those reviews, see Hershel Parker's *Herman Melville: A Biography*, vol. 2 (Baltimore: Johns Hopkins University Press, 2002), chap. 27, 606–625.

both readers and listeners. Famous in the nineteenth century as a tireless speaker and activist on the abolitionist, temperance, and women's rights lecture circuits, Harper frequently gave dramatic oral performances of her poems when she spoke. The poems are clearly shaped both by her activist commitments—they are politically explicit and emotionally powerful, often including fast-paced narration of events—and by her interest in oral performance: Harper's poems were written to be read, spoken, and chanted aloud. Like Whittier, Harper chose to use her poetry in the service of her political convictions. She saw poetry as the means by which she might reach skeptics left otherwise unmoved, and she recognized that vigorous meter and rhymes worked to fix her arguments in a listener's mind. As an orator, she also understood how to use her femininity as a means to further her message: listeners at Harper's lectures invariably commented on her "slender and graceful form" and her "soft musical voice."[26] The moral authority of Harper's presence on the lecture platform echoes in the authoritative voices of her poem's speakers. It is that moral authority which allows her speaker to address the "men of the North" in "Words for the Hour," urging them to keep on fighting for racial justice and against racist violence in the war's aftermath.

Like many of the poets in Part II, the South Carolina poet Henry Timrod found in the crisis of the war an intensity of artistic purpose that made his Civil War–era poems some of his strongest.[27] Like Whitman, Melville, and Emily Dickinson among many others, Timrod often evokes scenes of battle through landscape description. Already an accomplished poet of nature before the onset of war, Timrod presents the beauty of Southern landscapes with a renewed sense of political and artistic urgency after the conflict begins. His early war poems are marked by a fiery patriotism; in these he often imagines the landscape itself as the source of a Southern nation's sustenance and grandeur, as he does in "The Cotton Boll." Not surprisingly, the later poems are much darker, mourning Southern losses and expressing a profound sense of foreboding about the future of the South. In "The Unknown Dead," Timrod's speaker mourns the fact that nature will not always reflect the sorrow felt by those who have suffered losses in the war. Imagining on a rainy day the "nameless graves on battle-plains," Timrod argues: "Just such a sky as this should weep / Above them, always, where they sleep." He acknowledges, however, that nature may prove "oblivious of the crimson debt" paid by fallen soldiers; these lines suggest a sense of betrayal as the beauty of the landscape belies the presence of the "unknown dead."

---

26. Frances Smith Foster, introduction to *A Brighter Coming Day: A Frances Ellen Watkins Harper Reader* (New York: Feminist Press of the City University of New York, 1990), 15.

27. For a discussion of Timrod's Civil War poetry, see John Budd's "Henry Timrod: Poetic Voice of Southern Nationalism," *Southern Studies* 20, no. 4 (1981): 437–446.

Like her fellow Southerner Henry Timrod, the Kentucky-born Sarah Morgan Bryan Piatt represents the devastation of the South by means of the contrast with the beauty of its natural landscapes. And like her Northern contemporary Herman Melville, Piatt found that her attempts at rewriting poetic conventions were often misunderstood by her contemporaries. Both the dialogic structures she often relies on and her mingling of Victorian imagery with biting irony pose significant challenges for the reader. Piatt moved to the North with her husband, John James Piatt (see his "To Abraham Lincoln" in "1862"), at the outbreak of war; yet she continued for the rest of her poetic career to meditate on the lost glories of the South of her childhood, the complex power relations between master and slave, and the relationship between the war's violence and the ideologies of Southern culture.[28] Steeped in a Victorian domestic femininity, Piatt's poetry meditates on the consequences of the war through the lens of women's fascination with violence and the lens of romantic attachments between men and women.

"Hearing the Battle.—July 21, 1861" is an interesting case in point. At first glance the poem might seem to present a sentimental scene in which a young woman urges her beloved to go and join the fight, thereby demonstrating his valor, defending his country, and also proving his love for her. A closer examination of the poem, however, reveals that it includes no direct references to bravery, love, or loyalty to the nation. Rather, the poem presents the shocking juxtaposition of a scene of domestic tranquillity with a scene of wartime carnage. While "a delicate wind" rustles the "dewy odors" of the "jessamine-flowers" on this "beautiful night," corpses from a recent battle lie on a field nearby: "things with blinded eyes / That stared at the golden stillness / Of the moon in those lighted skies." Like Whitman in "Look Down Fair Moon," Piatt here offers a Romantic landscape gone awry, with the moon casting its light on the gory aftermath of a battle. When the speaker urges her beloved to go to war, this plea seems to result from the disparity between the "beautiful night" she sees around her and the "ghastly" violence she knows is taking place at the same time. Moreover, the speaker also suggests that she can never understand the experience of other women unless her lover joins the fight:

> . . . I shall never know
> How the hearts in the land are breaking,
> My dearest, unless you go.

28. Paula Bennett's groundbreaking edition of Piatt's poems includes an introductory essay in which Bennett discusses the scope of Piatt's aesthetic and political interests and the history of critical responses to her work; Bennett also offers a brief discussion of Piatt's Civil War poems, arguing that, unlike many other poets, Piatt is particularly interested in analyzing the war's aftermath. My analysis of Piatt's poetry is indebted to Bennett. See *Palace-Burner: The Selected Poetry of Sarah Morgan Bryan Piatt* (Carbondale: University of Illinois Press, 2001).

In view of Piatt's divided loyalties—she was born in the South yet moved North in 1861— it is not surprising that when she evokes this community of suffering women, she does so without separating North from South; indeed, these lines unify the two groups of women into one. Indirectly, these lines also suggest that the knowledge of love can only result from the loss of it. Significantly, the poem does not reveal whether the man in question chooses to enlist or remains at home, an omission that means the emotional dilemma of the poem's speaker remains unresolved at the poem's end.[29] Will she share the collective experience of other women by experiencing the heartbreak of wartime loss? Or will she remain trapped in a domestic world of "delicate" winds and "dewy" flowers? Offering no answer to these questions, the poem leaves its speaker caught in that genteel world of isolation, living at a painful remove from both the "fierce words of war" and the "worlds unknown" of the battlefield.

The two poets in Part III of the anthology published little or no work during their lifetimes. Both, however, chose poetry as their means to meditate on the costs and consequences of war. Emily Dickinson's reputation as one of the leading American poets of the nineteenth century has long been firmly established. Until recently, however, few scholars and readers have seen connections between her dense and hermetic body of work and the political crisis that engulfed the nation throughout her adult life. In her study *Emily Dickinson: A Voice of War,* Shira Wolosky notes that the Civil War years correspond to Dickinson's most productive period as a poet, arguing that this productivity is too striking to be mere coincidence.[30] R. W. Franklin's dating of Dickinson's manuscripts would suggest that she wrote an astonishing 937 poems between 1861 and 1865.[31] This outpouring of creative work indicates that Dickinson was profoundly affected by the Civil War—that she was both inspired and deeply troubled by the war's events.

---

29. Biographical readings of Piatt poems are particularly risky in view of her heavy reliance on personae and dialogic voices. Some biographical context may nonetheless be helpful as background for this poem: Piatt was twenty-five and her husband twenty-six at the outbreak of war. He held a political appointment in the Treasury Department from 1861 until 1867 and did not serve in the military, though he did encourage others to do so.

30. Shira Wolosky, *Emily Dickinson: A Voice of War* (New Haven: Yale University Press, 1984), 32–63. For other analyses of Dickinson's engagement with the Civil War, see Cristanne Miller's "Pondering 'Liberty': Emily Dickinson and the Civil War," in *American Vistas and Beyond: A Festschrift for Roland Hagenbüchle,* ed. Marietta Messmer and Josef Raab (Trier: Wissenschaftlicher Verlag Trier, 2002), 45–64; Christopher Benfey, "Emily Dickinson and the American South," in *The Cambridge Companion to Emily Dickinson,* ed. Wendy Martin (New York: Cambridge University Press, 2002), 30–50; and Leigh-Anne Urbanowicz Marcellin, "'Singing Off the Charnel Steps': Soldiers and Mourners in Emily Dickinson's War Poetry," *Emily Dickinson Journal* 9, no. 2 (2000): 64–74.

31. R. W. Franklin, *The Poems of Emily Dickinson* (Cambridge: Harvard University Press, Belknap Press, 1998).

While Dickinson's seclusion in her father's house might suggest that she was isolated from war news, this interpretation cannot be sustained when one considers the circumstances of her life more closely. Both Dickinson's father and brother were intellectual and political leaders in Amherst, thus the two households around which Dickinson's world revolved were centers for political debate in the war years. Although Dickinson became more and more reluctant to leave the grounds of her father's house in the early 1860s, she continued to carry on an avid correspondence with relatives and friends, many of whom were writers, editors, and intellectuals. Dickinson read voraciously, and her house was filled with the leading newspapers, magazines, and books of the day. In both her letters and her poems, she offers vivid responses to battlefield scenes, individual deaths in battle, the deaths of Amherst students, and the violence of the war. While some of the poems are marked by Dickinson's characteristically oblique and indirect stances, still others read like conventional elegies or sentimental depictions of soldiers' Christian martyrdom on the battlefield. If we read Dickinson's poems in the context of American poetry of the Civil War, we can begin to see not only the commitments which *separate* her work from that of her contemporaries but also the many interests and themes which *connect* her work to theirs.

In many of Dickinson's war poems, her oblique stance in relation to the conflict seems to underline the idea that women writers face particular difficulties in maintaining their credibility as they try to represent the male-dominated world of combat. Dickinson often addresses this credibility problem by writing poems that permit multiple interpretive possibilities and even resist a single dominant reading, a strategy which allows her to evade the accusation that she's writing outside her own sphere. Her interest in panoramic vistas and landscape painting also furthers her attempts to represent battlefields by means of indirection. For example, if Dickinson describes a beautiful landscape by means of pastoral imagery, then she appears to be writing the kind of poem that would be considered acceptable and appropriate for a genteel female writer. Yet in several of her more remarkable poems from the war years, images that present descriptions of nature simultaneously evoke the horror of war. "The name - of it - is 'Autumn'" (F 465) offers a striking example of this technique. The poem was probably written in the fall of 1862 and may well be a response to the September battle at Antietam, a battle that produced twenty-three thousand casualties in a single day. In the poem, Dickinson offers an autumnal scene saturated with the vivid color of the season; at the same time, she presents a blood-soaked landscape. Images that ostensibly describe the colors and patterns of leaves—"An Artery - opon the Hill - / A Vein - along the road -"—simultaneously evoke rivers of blood. Particularly in the second stanza, these metaphors become increasingly strained, as the poem turns to language that sounds more and more like medical terminology and less and less like the language of poetry: the speaker describes "Great Globules - in the Alleys -" and a "Scarlet Rain" spilling from a "Basin." The scene of battle has moved from a field in the country to a more urban setting and perhaps to a hospital with its basins of blood. The change of scene suggests an ever-widening arena of conflict, as if no corner of the nation will be left untouched by war. The third and final stanza points to the impact of war on women, describing the "Bonnets - far below -" which have been "sprinkle[d]" with blood. Whereas the blood which soaks the landscape in Howe's "Battle Hymn of the Republic" is redemptive, Dickinson's poem offers no such reassurance; rather, Dickinson's poem implies that the language of poetry is inadequate to describe this kind of bloodshed.[32]

If we read this poem in relation to Sarah Piatt's "Hearing the Battle—July 21, 1861," key parallels and contrasts become apparent in the two poets' methods. Although both poems rely on the juxtaposition of a pastoral scene with a battlefield scene, Piatt creates a shock effect by alternating between the two, whereas Dickinson creates her shock effect by collapsing the two scenes into one. Piatt takes a risk in writing about battle, but she controls that risk by positioning her feminine speaker away from the front and by emphasizing her separation from it: for Piatt's speaker, the worlds of battle are "worlds unknown." Dickinson, on the other hand, plunges her speaker into the midst of the war's carnage, yet she does so in such an oblique manner that the kind of reader who might be unsettled by her representation of violence can read the poem as presenting nothing more than an autumnal scene. To name just one example of this kind of reading, "The name - of it - is 'Autumn'" first appeared in print in September of 1892 in *Youth's Companion,* one of the leading children's magazines of the nineteenth century. One can only assume that its editors imagined they were printing a poem about fall in New England, not a poem about the battle of Antietam. Seemingly conventional poetic gestures like those of Dickinson and Piatt can conceal strategies of political engagement.

Unlike Dickinson, who often approaches the representation of battlefields from an oblique position, the final poet in our collection had direct experience of combat, and he represents that experience with a characteristic directness both in his prose and poems. While Obadiah Ethelbert Baker is clearly not a professional poet, the very ungainliness of his poetry breathes life into his writing voice. Like Dickinson, Baker circulated his poems in letters sent to friends and family, and at

32. For a fuller discussion of landscape imagery and poetic devices in "The name - of it - is 'Autumn'" (F 465), see my essay "Addresses to a Divided Nation.

the time of his death he also left a wealth of notes, drafts, and finished poems. As I mentioned at the start of this introduction, Baker wrote many of his war poems during the war years themselves: some are drafted or recopied in the pocket journals that he sent to his wife from the front or from the military hospitals where he later stayed. What Baker's poems lack in originality of form or sentiment, they make up for in the ways that they convey his lived experience of the war. Rhymes that are forced or mechanical bring alive for us the soldier-poet who was struggling to encompass the sights and sounds he had heard in battle in the kind of stirring and rhythmic ballads that he liked best. In "My Army Birth," which Baker wrote in 1863, he evokes the mix of emotions that ultimately led him to enlist:

I tried to be content at home,
  But no, I could not stay,
While rebel feet were tramping o'er,
  The flag that sheltered me.[33]

The poems often lack the gestures of closure and balance that we recognize and admire in the work of accomplished poets, but their very lack of closure signals the extent to which the memory of the war is still immediate and present to Baker—even when the war is over. His recollection of "the charge at Monterey" thus ends with a metaphorically awkward but nonetheless moving paean to the horse he rode and lost that day:

The king of all our mounts was he,
  A daisy on the road.
In drill he knew all the commands,
  And did not need a goad.

The poem slides abruptly from the scene of battle to an earlier scene of mounted drill; one senses in that shift Baker's glowing pride—pride that he had the chance to fight and drill with such a skilled mount, a mount that was also admired by other soldiers. In "The Charge at Farmington," as in many of his other poems, he carefully registers in poetic form the exact details of military formations—the batteries "in a half moon shape," for example—details that he draws from his journals.

The poem "After the Battle: The Dirge" is particularly noteworthy because of its date of composition; a draft of the poem appears in Baker's journal just a few pages after an October 5, 1862, entry describing his experience in the battle of Corinth. If Baker did in fact write the poem in October of 1862, then it is re-

33. All citations from Baker's poetry are reproduced by permission of the Huntington Library, San Marino, California.

markable that he writes of recent events as if they occurred in a more distant, elegiac past; it is also remarkable that his speaker strikes such a conciliatory tone toward the Southern soldiers against whom he had so recently fought. While most of the poems we have chosen to include were left as discrete manuscripts in Baker's papers, we have also included two selections from the verses that Baker used to close out his journal entries. As I mentioned earlier, Baker's journal takes the form of a series of letters addressed to his wife; particularly during the first two years of the war, he often ends entries with a few lines of poetry that directly address her. The lines titled "Nov. 30th To an absent Wife" were written in 1862 when Baker was in a camp in Mississippi. The quatrains and stanzas Baker uses to close entries often evoke his loneliness and homesickness, and these lines follow that pattern:

Wish I was sitting by thy side
  My dear beloved wife;
Far from the cannon's awful roar,
  Far from this awful strife.

My thoughts are of thee through the day,
  I dream of thee at night;
I long to kiss thy lips once more
  And see thy face so bright.

O God! When will this strife be o'er?
  When will we learn to war no more?

The first two stanzas of this poem are in Baker's usual style and tone: the telegraphic compression of "Wish I was sitting by thy side" contrasts with the self-consciously literary stance of "My thoughts are of thee through the day." The final couplet, however, breaks the pattern of control in the first two quatrains, and it also breaks out of Baker's usual formal habits: he rarely uses couplets. It gives us a taste of the weariness, boredom, loneliness, and fear that were part of his everyday experience during the war years. For Baker, the fighting would last for another two and a half years. Though his poems rarely dwell on his own heroism in battle, it is clear from his careful revision and copying of his Civil War papers that Baker makes sense of his life by defining himself as a soldier long after the war is over; "August 3rd, 1886" confirms the profound impact of Baker's military experience on his sense of self. A teacher and a struggling farmer in his civilian life, Baker writes poetry not only to remind himself of the way in which he participated in the making of the nation's history but also to participate—as a writer—in the great outpouring of poetry produced during the war years.

For all the poets we have gathered here, writing poetry offered a means of defining one's own position in relation to the war, its causes, and the ideals of nationhood it contested. By means both explicit and implicit, these writers argue that poetry offers a crucial form of engagement; they contend that the war was fought not only with weapons but also with what Piatt calls the "fierce words of war." Contemporary reports of the Civil War abound with references to poems and songs read and sung in camps, on battlefields, and on the home front. Poems were used as recruitment tools for soldiers and for military hospital nurses; poems set to music were sung by soldiers as they marched into—and in some cases away from—battle. Countless newspaper articles refer to poems found in the pockets of slain soldiers on the field. The poetry of the Civil War era suggests how profoundly people's lives and identities were changed by the war; these poems also indicate that poetry had a profound impact on the events that took place both on and off the battlefields.

Part I

POEMS PUBLISHED IN NEWSPAPERS AND PERIODICALS

Antebellum Poetry

African American soldiers posing with their teachers. Library of Congress, Civil War Photograph Collection, LC-B8184-10061.

My Country[1]

Sarah Louisa Forten

Oh! speak not of heathenish darkness again,
Nor tell me of lands held in error's dread chain!
Where—where is the nation so erring as we,
Who claim the proud name of the "HOME OF THE FREE"?
What a throb do the lov'd ties of country awake
In the heart of the exile!—for time cannot break
The sweet vision of home, and all he loved well,
Which has thrown o'er his pathway a magical spell.
Can the name of "MY COUNTRY"—the deeds which we sing—
Be honored—revered—'midst pollution and sin?
Can the names of our fathers who perished in fight,
Be hallowed in story, midst slavery's blight?
When America's standard is floating so fair,
I blush that the impress of falsehood is there;
That oppression and mockery dim the high fame,
That seeks from all nations a patriot's name.
Speak not of "my country," unless she shall be,
In truth, the bright home of the "brave and the free!"
Till the dark stain of slavery is washed from her hand,
A tribute of homage she cannot command.

1. *Liberator* 1834, published under the pseudonym "Ada"; cited from NAWP.

The Mother and Her Captive Boy[2]

ELLA (SARAH MAPPS DOUGLASS?)

Wilt thou, when long years roll o'er thee,
Years of toil, and woe, and scorn,
Still remember her who bore thee?
Still when thou art most forlorn?

"The Negro Mother: To Her Child, the Night Before their Separation"

No, he will not! —they who can rend apart
The strongest chords that bind the human heart,
They, in whose breasts no mercy e'er is found,
Will crush his feelings, —pois'ning as they wound.
Each tender, generous impulse of his soul,
Must bow beneath a tyrant's harsh control;
Oppress'd, degraded, beaten and reviled,
Witness of darkest crimes while yet a child,—
If in his infant bosom there are sown
The germs of actions men are proud to own,
They'll bear most bitter fruit. —Deeds, that would be
Applauded, honored, in the *white* and *free,*
By *him* attempted, will but gain the brand
Of crime and treason. —In this "*happy land,*"
Which owes its boasted freedom to a hand
That fought against oppression, there are found
Thousands of men—of *souls* in fetters bound.
Souls that too soon forget the pure, the mild,
Unsullied feelings of a "sinless child,"
And turn to bitterness; for "woe and scorn,"
Are all they meet,—and how may these be borne?
How, by their hapless victim, who ne'er knows
What a kind mother's priceless love bestows?
Or mildness, that a father's precepts lend?

2. Published in the *National Enquirer* October 8, 1836, under the pseudonym "Ella," and attributed to Sarah Mapps Douglass. "Ella" quotes stanza 5 of "The Negro Mother: To Her Child," which was published anonymously in the *National Enquirer* August 17, 1836.

Who knows not *one,* or loses *every* friend?
What marvel that the "still small voice" should be
Unheeded, where not even thought is free?
Death, only death can purchase peace and joy,
For her that's parted from her captive boy.

The Present Crisis[3]

JAMES RUSSELL LOWELL

When a deed is done for Freedom, through the broad earth's aching breast
Runs a thrill of joy prophetic, trembling on from east to west,
And the slave, where'er he cowers, feels the soul within him climb
To the awful verge of manhood, as the energy sublime
Of a century bursts full-blossomed on the thorny stem of Time.

Through the walls of hut and palace shoots the instantaneous throe,
When the travail of the Ages wrings earth's systems to and fro;
At the birth of each new Era, with a recognizing start,
Nation wildly looks at nation, standing with mute lips apart,
And glad Truth's yet mightier man-child leaps beneath the Future's heart.

So the Evil's triumph sendeth, with a terror and a chill,
Under continent to continent, the sense of coming ill,
And the slave, where'er he cowers, feels his sympathies with God
In hot tear-drops ebbing earthward, to be drunk up by the sod,
Till a corpse crawls round unburied, delving in the nobler clod.

For mankind are one in spirit, and an instinct bears along,
Round the earth's electric circle, the swift flash of right or wrong;
Whether conscious or unconscious, yet humanity's vast frame,
Through its ocean-sundered fibres, feels the gush of joy or shame;—
In the gain or loss of one race all the rest have equal claim.

3. Lowell prints this poem as "dated December, 1844"; it was published in the *Boston Courier* December 11, 1845. This was Lowell's first significant publication, and the poem was reprinted widely, often in abridged form, for the next twenty years. The poem's representative significance was also marked by the National Association for the Advancement of Colored People, whose journal *The Crisis* was named in homage to this poem. Some stanzas were set to music and are still sung as a hymn in Protestant churches. Cited from *The Poetical Works of James Russell Lowell* (1896).

Once, to every man and nation, comes the moment to decide,
In the strife of Truth with Falsehood, for the good or evil side;
Some great cause, God's *new* Messiah, offering each the bloom or blight,
Parts the goats upon the left hand, and the sheep upon the right,
And the choice goes by forever 'twixt that darkness and that light.

Hast thou chosen, O my people, on whose party thou shalt stand,
Ere the Doom from its worn sandals shakes the dust against our land?
Though the cause of Evil prosper, yet 'tis Truth alone is strong,
And albeit she wander outcast now, I see around her throng
Troops of beautiful, tall angels, to enshield her from all wrong.

Backward look across the ages and the beacon-moments see,
That, like peaks of some sunk continent, jut through Oblivion's sea;
Not an ear in court or market for the low foreboding cry
Of those Crises, God's stern winnowers, from whose feet earth's chaff must fly;
Never shows the choice momentous till the judgment hath passed by.

Careless seems the great Avenger; history's pages but record
One death-grapple in the darkness 'twixt old systems and the Word;
Truth forever on the scaffold, Wrong forever on the throne,—
Yet that scaffold sways the future, and, behind the dim unknown,
Standeth God within the shadow, keeping watch above his own.

We see dimly, in the Present, what is small and what is great;
Slow of faith, how weak an arm may turn the iron helm of fate;
But the soul is still oracular—amid the market's din,
List the ominous stern whisper from the Delphic cave within;—
"They enslave their children's children who make compromise with sin!"

Slavery, the earth-born Cyclops, fellest of the giant brood,
Sons of brutish Force and Darkness, who have drenched the earth with blood,
Famished in his self-made desert, blinded by our purer day,
Gropes in yet unblasted regions for his miserable prey;—
Shall we guide his gory fingers where our helpless children play?

Then to side with Truth is noble when we share her wretched crust,
Ere her cause bring fame and profit, and 't is prosperous to be just;
Then it is the brave man chooses, while the coward stands aside,
Doubting in his abject spirit, till his Lord is crucified,
And the multitude make virtue of the faith they had denied.

Count me o'er earth's chosen heroes, —they were souls that stood alone,
While the men they agonized for hurled the contumelious stone,
Stood serene, and down the future saw the golden beam incline
To the side of perfect justice, mastered by their faith divine,
By one man's plain truth to manhood and to God's supreme design.

By the light of burning heretics Christ's bleeding feet I track,
Toiling up new Calvaries ever with the cross that turns not back,
And these mounts of anguish number how each generation learned
One new word of that grand *Credo* which in prophet-hearts hath burned
Since the first man stood God-conquered with his face to heaven upturned.

For Humanity sweeps onward: where to-day the martyr stands,
On the morrow couches Judas with the silver in his hands;
Far in front the cross stands ready and the crackling fagots burn,
While the hooting mob of yesterday in silent awe return
To glean up the scattered ashes into History's golden urn.

'Tis as easy to be heroes, as to sit the idle slaves
Of a legendary virtue carved upon our father's graves,
Worshippers of light ancestral make the present light a crime;—
Was the Mayflower launched by cowards, steered by men behind their time?
Turn those tracks toward Past or Future, that make Plymouth Rock sublime?

They were men of present valor, stalwart old iconoclasts,
Unconvinced by axe or gibbet that all virtue was the Past's;
But we make their truth our falsehood, thinking that hath made us free,
Hoarding it in mouldy parchments, while our tender spirits flee
The rude grasp of that great Impulse which drove them across the sea.

They have rights who dare maintain them; we are traitors to our sires,
Smothering in their holy ashes Freedom's new-lit altar-fires;
Shall we make their creed our jailer? Shall we, in our haste to slay,
From the tombs of the old prophets steal the funeral lamps away
To light up the martyr-fagots round the prophets of to-day?

New occasions teach new duties; Time makes ancient good uncouth;
They must upward still, and onward, who would keep abreast of Truth;
Lo, before us gleam her campfires! we ourselves must Pilgrims be,
Launch our Mayflower, and steer boldly through the desperate winter sea,
Nor attempt the Future's portal with the Past's blood-rusted key.

I Sigh for the Land of the Cypress and Pine[4]

SAMUEL HENRY DICKSON

I sigh for the land of the cypress and pine,
Where the jessamine blooms, and the gay woodbine;
Where the moss droops low from the green oak tree,—
Oh, that sun-bright land is the land for me!

The snowy flower of the orange there
Sheds its sweet fragrance through the air;
And the Indian rose delights to twine
Its branches with the laughing vine.

There the deer leaps light through the open glade,
Or hides him far in the forest shade,
When the woods resound in the dewy morn
With the clang of the merry hunter's horn.

There the hummingbird, of rainbow plume,
Hangs over the scarlet creeper's bloom;
While 'midst the leaves his varying dyes
Sparkle like half-seen fairy eyes.

There the echoes ring through the livelong day
With the mock-bird's changeful roundelay;
And at night, when the scene is calm and still,
With the moan of the plaintive whip-poor-will.

Oh! I sigh for the land of the cypress and pine,
Of the laurel, the rose, and the gay woodbine,
Where the long, gray moss decks the rugged oak tree,—
That sun-bright land is the land for me.

4. First published under the title "Song—Written at the North" in Simms's *The Charleston Book* (1845). Reference to cypress and the "sun-bright land" marks this clearly as a poem of the South. Cited from *Southern Poets.*

Southern Ode[5]

William Gilmore Simms

Once more the cry of Freedom peals,
From broad Potomac's wave to ours,
The invader's cunning footstep steals,
Usurping fast our rights and powers.
He proffers love, he prates of ties
That still should bind our fates in one,
Yet weaves his subtle web of lies,
To share and leave us all undone.
What bond of faith, however strong,
Thus taught by lust of pelf and sway,
He would not, in his march of wrong,
Hurl scornful from his treacherous way?
The bond that's sacred in our sight,
Made pliant by his arts of shame,
Is but the means to rob of right,
The race he cannot rob of fame!
But we have seen the serpent's trail,
Have heard the wolf's base howl, and now,
Taught by the past, we cannot fail,
To brand his blackness on his brow.
To crush the viper in his path,
Beat down the were-wolf in our wrath,
And severing bonds so idly known,
Strike, though we stand and strike alone!

Oh! they are brethren these, who seek
To weave their snares about our feet;—
Their prayers how bland, their pleas how meek,
Most philanthropic all, and sweet!
We see their guile, and when we cry,
In scorn and anger, at each wrong,

5. *Charleston Mercury* February 7, 1850, under the pseudonym "Tyrtaeus" (Spartan war poet); republished as four separate "Lyrics of the South" in the *Charleston Mercury* 1859–60. Cited from *Selected Poems.*

How Christianly they answer—"Fie!"—
    "Brethren!" the burden of their song!
We show our bonds of union broke,
    Each shatter'd tie, each sunder'd string,
And toiling still our necks to yoke,
    How well of "Union" do they sing!
This marriage bond they plead, while still
    In most adulterous arts they strive;
On us bestow its fruits of ill,
    While they on all its profits thrive.
Their bondmen we, who wage the fight,
    Achieve the spoil and win the day;
They, the keen knaves, with trick of sleight,
    The danger o'er, to steal the prey!
Thus, upon Sinbad's back astride,
The Old Man of the Sea would ride,
While preaching, ever and anon,
"Still let us ride together, son!"

Throw by the Harp! 'tis mockery now—
    Decree that dance and revel cease;
The shame spot darkens on your brow,
    And death is in the snares of peace!
It mocks the past our fathers knew;
    To sing the oppressions we must bear;
To swords, not songs, they bravely flew,
    And broke the very chains we wear.
They only felt the wrong, to spring,
    With fury to the desperate fray;
And did not, like their children, cling
    To bonds that crushed their souls to clay.
They too, had ties, long sacred known,
    With loyal hearts they loved the true;
But, when a tyrant filled the throne,
    They trampled throne and tyrant too.
What union firmer knit than theirs,
    With Britain from their earliest hours;
And yet, when Britain moved their fears,
    For freedom, they o'erthrew her powers.

The tie that cunning makes its plea,
To rob the birthright from the free,
Though by our sires with blessings given,
Is fit for Hell, though forged in Heaven!

'Tis peace no more! for peace is rest,
In mutual faith, so well bestow'd,
That doubt and danger fill no breast,
And lust and envy never goad.
What hope have we of state like this?
Who that has seen the fraudful past,
But feels that still the serpent's hiss,
Our hour of dreaming peace must blast.
Our Union still hath been the plea,
To strip us of our natural strength,
Our peace—its future ye should see
In utter deep despair at length.
A dull, dread wearisome repose,
Low crouching still in trembling hush,
In moment fear of bonds and blows,
When power feels bold enough to crush!
With, day by day, some birthright lost,
Some pride depress'd, some purpose cross'd,
Cursed with each thought that brings the past,
And utter slaves to knaves at last!

Song of the South[6]

William Gilmore Simms

i

Oh, the South! the sunny, sunny South!
Land of true feeling, land forever mine;
I drink the kisses of her rosy mouth,
And my heart swells as with a draught of wine!
She brings me blessings of maternal love—

6. A shorter version was first published in *Southern and Western* 1845. The longer version presented here was published in the *Southern Literary Messenger* 1857. Cited from *Selected Poems.*

I have her praise which sweetens all my toil:
Her voice persuades, her loving smiles approve—
She sings me from the sky and from the soil!
Oh! by her lonely pines that wave and sigh—
Oh! by her myriad flowers that bloom and fade;
By all the thousand beauties of her sky,
And the sweet solemn of her forest shade—
She's mine, forever mine!
Nor will I aught resign
Of what she gives me, mortal or divine;
Will sooner part
With life—hope—heart—
Will die—before I fly!

ii

Oh! Love is hers, such love as ever glows
In souls where leaps affection's living tide;
She is all fondness to her friends;—to foes
She glows a thing of passion, strength and pride!
She feels no tremors when the Danger's nigh;
But the fight over, and the victory won,
How, with strange fondness, turns her loving eye,
In tearful welcome, on each gallant son!
Oh! by her virtues of the cherished past—
By all her hopes of what the future brings—
I glory that my lot with her is cast,
And my soul flushes, and exultant sings
She's mine, forever mine!
For her will I resign
All precious things—all placed upon her shrine;
Will freely part
With life—hope—heart—
Will die!—do aught but fly!

Song of the "Aliened American"[7]

Joshua McCarter Simpson

My country, 'tis of thee,
Dark land of Slavery,
In thee we groan.
Long have our chains been worn—
Long has our grief been borne—
Our flesh has long been torn,
E'en from our bones.

The white man rules the day—
He bears despotic sway,
O'er all the land.
He wields the Tyrant's rod,
Fearless of man or God,
And at his impious nod,
We "fall or stand."

O! shall we longer bleed?
Is there no one to plead
The black man's cause?
Does justice thus demand
That we shall wear the brand,
And raise not voice nor hand
Against such laws?

No! no! the time has come,
When we must not be dumb,
We must awake.
We now "Eight Millions Strong,"
Must strike sweet freedom's song
And plead ourselves, our wrong—
Our chains must break.

7. Probably included in Simpson's 1852 *Original Anti-slavery Songs*; reprinted in *Emancipation Car*, 1874, our source. It is written to the tune of "America."

The Vessel of Love, the Vessel of State[8]

HENRY DAVID THOREAU

The vessel of love, the vessel of state,
Each is ballasted with hate.
Every Congress that we hold
Means the union is dissolved.
But though the south is still enslaved,
By that oath the Union's saved,
For 'tis our love and not our hate
Interests us in their fate.

Lines[9]

ALFRED GIBBS CAMPBELL

Wake not again the cannon's thundrous voice,
Nor to the breeze throw out the stars and stripes;
'Tis not the time to revel and rejoice
Beneath the shadow of our nation's types—
Types of her ancient glory, present shame.
The stars have faded of her old renown,
For Liberty is but an empty name,
While Slavery wields the scepter, wears the crown.

Why should we to the lie, persistent, cling,
And falsely boast our freedom on this day?
What though we are not governed by a king?
A sterner tyrant o'er our land holds sway,
And tramples on the dearest rights of man;—
Transforms God's image into merchandise;
Places free speech beneath his impious ban,
And all our God-given liberties denies.

8. Composed September 1852; first published July 4, 1855. Cited from *Collected Poems of Henry Thoreau*, 1864.

9. First published July 4, 1855, and reprinted in Campbell's 1883 *Poems*. Cited from *African-American Poetry*.

Each foot of land within our wide domain
He claims as hunting-ground, whereon to chase
The hero-fugitive who breaks his chain,
And earns his freedom by advent'rous race.
On *our* limbs, too, the shackles he would bind;
Pluck out our hearts, or change them into stone;
Crush all our sympathies for human kind,
And bid us God and manhood to disown.

Give but a crust of bread to one of these
God's weary wanderers in search of rest,
Point out to him the North-star as he flees,
Or make him but an hour your welcome guest; —
And on your head the Robber Despot lays
With violence his unrelenting hand,
And with imprisonment and fine repays
Simple obedience to God's clear command.

We are not free! In every Southern State
Speech and the Press are fettered; —and for him
Who dares speak out, the martyr-fires await,
Or hangman's rope from tallest pine-tree's limb.
We are not free! One man in every seven,
Throughout our false Republic, groans beneath
The vilest despotism under heaven,
Which leaves no hope of freedom but in death.

Nearly four millions in our land in chains!
One-half our country slave-land! and the whole
Man-hunting ground! And Kansas' virgin plains*,
(Once pledged to Freedom,) under the control
Of the Slave Power! Say, Boaster, are we free?
See if the huge lie blister not your lips:
Where Slavery reigns, there Freedom cannot be!
Light vanishes beneath the sun's eclipse.

I Wish I Was in Dixie's Land[10]

Dan Emmett

I wish I was in de land ob cotton,
Old times dar am not forgotten;
    Look away! Look away! Look away! Dixie Land.
In Dixie Land whar I was born in,
Early on one frosty mornin,
    Look away! Look away! Look away! Dixie Land.

Chorus:
Den I wish I was in Dixie, Hooray! Hooray!
In Dixie Land, I'll took my stand,
To lib an die in Dixie,
  Away, Away, Away down south in Dixie,
  Away, Away, Away down south in Dixie.

Old Missus marry "Will-de-weaber,"
Willium was a gay deceaber;
    Look away! Look away! Look away! Dixie Land.
But when he put his arm around 'er,
He smiled as fierce as a 'forty-pound'er.
    Look away! Look away! Look away! Dixie Land.

His face was sharp as a butcher's cleaber;
But dat did not seem to greab 'er;
    Look away! Look away! Look away! Dixie Land.
Old Missus acted de foolish part,
And died for a man dat broke her heart.
    Look away! Look away! Look away! Dixie Land.

Now here's a health to the next old Missus,
An all de galls dat want to kiss us;
    Look away! Look away! Look away! Dixie Land.

---

10. Composed and first performed in New York City in 1859 and reprinted here from the 1860 sheet music version, reproduced in facsimile in *The Civil War Songbook,* 1977. The song was written by a white blackface (minstrel) performer from Ohio. It was first performed in the South in New Orleans in 1860 and quickly became a popular favorite with whites in both the South and the North. After it was performed at Jefferson Davis's inauguration in February 1861, however, it was identified as a Southern anthem.

But if you want to drive 'way sorrow,
Come an hear dis song tomorrow.
    Look away! Look away! Look away! Dixie Land.

Dar's buckwheat cakes an 'Ingen' batter,
Makes you fat or a little fatter;
    Look away! Look away! Look away! Dixie Land.
Den hoe it down an scratch your grabble,
To Dixie land I'm bound to trabble.
    Look away! Look away! Look away! Dixie Land.

The Two Voices[11]

Charlotte Forten Grimké

In the dim December twilight,
  By the fire I mused alone;
And a voice within me murmured
  In a deep, impassioned tone—

Murmured first, and then grew stronger,
  Wilder in its thrilling strain—
"Break, sad heart, for, oh, no longer
  Canst thou bear this ceaseless pain.

"Canst thou bear the bitter anguish,
  All the wrong, and woe, and shame
That the world hath heaped upon thee,
  Though it hath no cause for blame?

"True it is that thou dost give it
  Hate for hate, and scorn for scorn;
True it is that thou would'st gladly
  Make it bear what thou hast borne.

"But does such a vengeful spirit
  Soothe thee, make thee calm and strong?

11. Published under the initials C. L. F. in the *National Anti-Slavery Standard* 1859, dated "Philadelphia, December 1858."

No; thy inmost life it poisons,
  Makes the strife more fierce and long.

"Wouldst thou live, oh, foolish dreamer?
  What to thee are life and joy?
Know'st thou not the cruel future
  All thy visions shall destroy?

"Would'st thou live, oh, homeless outcast,
  Tossed upon life's restless wave?
Thou canst find a haven only
  In the quiet of the grave.

"There a sweet and soothing stillness
  From thee never shall depart;
There the angel Peace shall fold thee
  Closely to her loving heart."

To the earnest voice I hearkened,
  And within my troubled breast
Deeper, stronger grew the longing
  For the blessed boon of rest.

"Grant," I prayed, "O gracious Father!
  Grant the simple boon I crave.
Let me leave this weary conflict,
  Let me rest within the grave!"

Deep the silence that succeeded;
  Gleamed the firelight warm and bright,
But, for me, its warmth and brightness
  Gladdened not the cold, dark night.

But, without, the dreary night-wind,
  With its wild and mournful moan,
From the sad soul of the pine trees,
  Found an echo in my own.

Then another voice spake to me,
  Spake in accents strong and clear;
Like the proud notes of a trumpet
  Fell its tones upon my ear.

"Shame," it cried, "oh, weak repiner!
Hast thou yielded to despair?
Canst thou win the crown immortal
If the cross thou wilt not bear?

"Hast thou nothing left to live for?
Would'st thou leave the glorious strife?
Know, the life that's passed in struggling
Is the true, the only life.

"Canst thou see the souls around thee
Bravely battling with the wrong,
And not feel thy soul within thee
In the cause of Truth grow strong?

"Art thou, then, the only wronged one?
With thy sorrows will all cease?
Thou forgettest other sufferers,
In thy selfish prayer for peace.

"Live for others; work for others;
Sharing, strive to soothe their woe,
Till thy heart, no longer fainting,
With an ardent zeal will glow.

"Of thyself thou art unworthy,
False to all thy early vows,
If thy once unbending spirit
Now beneath its burden bows.

"Prayest thou for death? pray, rather,
For the strength to live, and bear
All thy wrongs with brave endurance.
Scorn to yield thee to despair;

"Knowing that to strive and suffer,
With a purpose pure and high,
In a holy cause, is nobler
Than ingloriously to die.

"Sweet the grave's unbroken quiet
To thy aching heart would be;

But, believe, to live for others
  Is a higher destiny."

Ceased the voice; again, in silence,
  By the fire I mused alone;
Darkly closed the night around me;
  But my soul had stronger grown.

And I said—"I thank Thee, Father,
  For the answer thou hast given.
Bravely will I bear earth's burdens,
  Ere I pray to rest in heaven."

1861

Militiamen guarding the Chain Bridge over the Potomac River at Washington, D.C., in 1861. Rinhart Galleries.

To the Men of the North and West[1]

Richard Henry Stoddard

Men of the North and West,
  Wake in your might,
Prepare, as the Rebels have done,
    For the fight;
You cannot shrink from the test,
Rise! Men of the North and West!

They have torn down your banner of stars;
  They have trampled the laws;
They have stifled the freedom they hate,
    For no cause!
Do you love it, or slavery best?
Speak! Men of the North and West!

They strike at the life of the State—
  Shall the murder be done?
They cry, "We are two!" And you?
    "*We are one!*"
You must meet them, then, breast to breast,
On! Men of the North and West!

Not with words; they laugh them to scorn,
  And tears they despise;
But with swords in your hands, and death
    In your eyes!
Strike home! leave to God all the rest,
Strike! Men of the North and West!

1. According to the *Rebellion Record* Vol. 1, 1860–61, this poem was composed on April 17 and published on April 18, 1861, in the *Evening Post* (New York).

The Nineteenth of April[2]

Lucy Larcom

This year, till late in April, the snow fell thick and light:
Thy truce-flag, friendly Nature, in clinging drifts of white,
Hung over field and city: now everywhere is seen,
In place of that white quietness, a sudden glow of green.

The verdure climbs the Common, beneath the leafless trees,
To where the glorious Stars and Stripes are floating on the breeze.
There, suddenly as Spring awoke from Winter's snow-draped gloom,
The Passion-Flower of Seventy-six is bursting into bloom.

Dear is the time of roses, when earth to joy is wed,
And garden-plot and meadow wear one generous flush of red;
But now in dearer beauty, to her ancient colors true,
Blooms the old town of Boston in red and white and blue.

Along the whole awakening North are those bright emblems spread;
A summer noon of patriotism is burning overhead:
No party badges flaunting now, no word of clique or clan;
But "Up for God and Union!" is the shout of every man.

Oh, peace is dear to Northern hearts; our hard-earned homes more dear;
But freedom is beyond the price of any earthly cheer;
And freedom's flag is sacred; he who would work it harm,
Let him, although a brother, beware our strong right arm!

A brother! ah, the sorrow, the anguish of that word!
The fratricidal strife begun, when will its end be heard?
Not this the boon that patriot hearts have prayed and waited for;—
We loved them, and we longed for peace: but they would have it war.

Yes; war! on this memorial day, the day of Lexington,
A lightning-thrill along the wires from heart to heart has run.

2. *Boston Transcript* April 25, 1861; reprinted in *The Poetical Works of Lucy Larcom* 1884, the source for this text. The attack on Fort Sumter* occurred on April 12, 1861. On April 19, the Sixth Massachusetts Regiment, the first Northern unit to be mustered after Lincoln's call for troops, was attacked by a mob as it traveled through Baltimore en route to Washington; four Union soldiers and twelve civilians were killed in the violence. These were the first deaths of the Civil War. Larcom also refers to the Battle of Lexington, which occurred on April 19, 1775, and was the first battle in the American Revolutionary War against the British.

Brave men we gazed on yesterday, to-day for us have bled:
Again is Massachusetts blood the first for Freedom shed.

To war,—and with our brethren, then,—if only this can be!
Life hangs as nothing in the scale against dear Liberty!
Though hearts be torn asunder, for Freedom we will fight:
Our blood may seal the victory, but God will shield the Right!

My Maryland[3]

James R. Randall

The despot's heel is on thy shore,
　　Maryland!
His torch is at thy temple door,
　　Maryland!
Avenge the patriotic gore
That flecked the streets of Baltimore,
And be the battle queen of yore,
　　Maryland, my Maryland!

Hark to an exiled son's appeal,
　　Maryland!
My Mother State, to thee I kneel,
　　Maryland!
For life or death, for woe or weal,
Thy peerless chivalry reveal,
And gird thy beauteous limbs with steel,
　　Maryland, my Maryland!

Thou wilt not cower in the dust,
　　Maryland!
Thy beaming sword shall never rust,
　　Maryland!
Remember Carroll's sacred trust,

3. *New Orleans Delta* April 6, 1861. The text reprinted here is that corrected and sent to Browne for *Bugle-Echoes*. When Randall read in a newspaper of the April 1861 attack on Fort Sumter,* he felt compelled to express his desire that Maryland secede from the Union in verse, composing "My Maryland" during one sleepless night. This poem was set to music and was extremely popular in the South.

Remember Howard's warlike thrust,
And all thy slumberers with the just,
          Maryland, my Maryland!

Come! 'tis the red dawn of the day,
          Maryland!
Come with thy panoplied array,
          Maryland!
With Ringgold's spirit for the fray,
With Watson's blood at Monterey,
With fearless Lowe and dashing May,
          Maryland, my Maryland!

Dear Mother, burst the tyrant's chain,
          Maryland!
Virginia should not call in vain,
          Maryland!
She meets her sisters on the plain,
"*Sic semper!*" 'tis the proud refrain
That baffles minions back amain,
          Maryland!
Arise in majesty again,
          Maryland, my Maryland!

Come! for thy shield is bright and strong,
          Maryland!
Come! for thy dalliance does thee wrong,
          Maryland!
Come to thine own heroic throng
Stalking with Liberty along,
And chant thy dauntless slogan-song,
          Maryland, my Maryland!

I see the blush upon thy cheek,
          Maryland!
But thou wast ever bravely meek,
          Maryland!
But lo! there surges forth a shriek,
From hill to hill, from creek to creek,
Potomac* calls to Chesapeake,
          Maryland, my Maryland!

Thou wilt not yield the Vandal toll,
    Maryland!
Thou wilt not crook to his control,
    Maryland!
Better the fire upon thee roll,
Better the shot, the blade, the bowl,
Than crucifixion of the soul,
    Maryland, my Maryland!

I hear the distant thunder-hum,
    Maryland!
The "Old Line's" bugle, fife, and drum,
    Maryland!
She is not dead, nor deaf, nor dumb;
Huzza! she spurns the Northern scum—
She breathes! She burns! She'll come! She'll come!
    Maryland, my Maryland!

Over the River[4]

Jane T. H. Cross

We hail your "Stripes" and lessened "Stars,"
    As one may hail a neighbor;
Now forward move! no fear of jars,
    With nothing but free labor;
And we will mind our slaves and farm,
And never wish you any harm,
    But greet you—over the river.

The self-same language do we speak,
    The same dear words we utter;
Then let's not make each other weak,
    Nor 'gainst each other mutter;
But let each go his separate way,
And each will doff his hat, and say:
    "I greet you—over the river!"

4. *Nashville Christian Advocate* 1861; cited from *Blue and Gray*.

Our flags, almost the same, unfurl,
And nod across the border;
Ohio's waves between them curl—
Our stripe's a little broader;
May yours float out on every breeze,
And, in our wake, traverse all seas—
We greet you—over the river!

We part as friends of years should part,
With pleasant words and wishes,
And no desire is in our heart
For Lincoln's loaves and fishes:
"Farewell," we wave you from afar,
We like you best—just where you are—
And greet you—over the river!

The Old Rifleman[5]

Francis Orray Ticknor

Now, bring me out my buckskin suit,
My pouch and powder too;
We'll see if seventy-six can shoot
As sixteen used to do.

Old Bess, we've kept our barrels bright,
Our triggers quick and true—
As far, if not as *fine* a sight,
As long ago we drew.

And pick me out a trusty flint—
A real white and blue;
Perhaps 'twill win the *other* tint
Before the hunt is through.

Give boys your brass percussion caps;
Old "shut-pan" suits as well:
There's something in the *sparks,*—perhaps
There's something in the smell.

5. *Richmond Dispatch* May 23, 1861; cited from CWSS.

We've seen the red-coat Briton bleed;
The red-skin Indian too;
We never thought to draw a bead
On Yankee-doodle-doo.

But, Bessie, bless your dear old heart,
Those days are mostly done;
And now we must revive the art
Of shooting on the run.

If Doodle must be meddling, why,
There's only this to do—
Select the black spot in his eye,
And let the daylight through.

And if he doesn't like the way
That Bess presents the view,
He'll, may be, change his mind, and stay
Where the good Doodles do,—

Where Lincoln lives—the man, you know,
Who kissed the Testament;
To keep the constitution? No,
To keep the Government!

We'll hunt for Lincoln, Bess, old tool,
And take him half and half;
We'll aim to *hit* him, if a fool,
And *miss* him, if a calf.

We'll teach these shot-gun boys the tricks
By which a war is won;
Especially, how Seventy-six
Took Tories on the run.

Brother Jonathan's Lament for Sister Caroline[6]

Oliver Wendell Holmes

She has gone—she has left us in passion and pride—
Our stormy-browed sister, so long at our side!
She has torn her own star from our firmament's glow,
And turned on her brother the face of a foe!

O Caroline, Caroline, child of the sun,
We can never forget that our hearts have been one,—
Our foreheads both sprinkled in Liberty's name,
From the fountain of blood with the finger of flame!

You were always too ready to fire at a touch;
But we said, "She is hasty,—she does not mean much."
We have scowled, when you uttered some turbulent threat;
But Friendship still whispered, "Forgive and forget!"

Has our love all died out? Have its altars grown cold?
Has the curse come at last which the fathers foretold?
Then Nature must teach us the strength of the chain
That her petulant children would sever in vain.

They may fight till the buzzards are gorged with their spoil,
Till the harvest grows black as it rots in the soil,
Till the wolves and the catamounts troop from their caves,
And the shark tracks the pirate, the lord of the waves:

In vain is the strife! When its fury is past,
Their fortunes must flow in one channel at last,
As the torrents that rush from the mountains of snow
Roll mingled in peace through the valleys below.

Our Union is river, lake, ocean, and sky:
Man breaks not the medal, when God cuts the die!
Though darkened with sulphur, though cloven with steel,
The blue arch will brighten, the waters will heal!

O Caroline, Caroline, child of the sun,
There are battles with Fate that can never be won!

---

6. *Atlantic Monthly* May 1861. Jonathan is the stereotypical name of a New Englander, and Caroline refers to South Carolina.

The star-flowering banner must never be furled,
For its blossoms of light are the hope of the world!

Go, then, our rash sister! afar and aloof,—
Run wild in the sunshine away from our roof;
But when your heart aches and your feet have grown sore,
Remember the pathway that leads to our door!

The Harvest-Field of 1861[7]

Mrs. James Neall

Lo! the fields of Harvest whiten with the heavy bending grain:
Hither bring the patient oxen, yoke them to the empty wain;
Call the Reapers; for the Summer has put on her crown again.

And her minister of Plenty stands with overflowing horn,
While the serried ranks in waiting, of the fully ripened corn,
Gaily wave their golden tassels in the soft midsummer morn.

Fair Pomona bendeth lowly 'neath the chrism of her hope,
Summer has fulfilled the promise of the Spring-times' horoscope,
For her fruit is ripe and mellow over many a sunny slope.

Rounded are the rich grape clusters, for the vintage time is near,
Let them fall in purple glory, when the vintagers appear;
Press the juices warm and glowing from each perfect pulpy sphere.

Lo! the fields of Harvest whiten—and the plains are dry and hot,
And the golden fruit is mildewed, and the grain is garnered not,
And the maidens sit in silence while the grapes are left to rot.

Listening to the tread of armies, and the clanging noise of War,
Ploughshares into swords are beaten, and the scythe is wet with gore,
For the Harvesters are gathered, where the smoking cannons roar.

And the reapers reap together, spear on spear-top falling low,
And the serried ranks are parted, be it friend or be it foe,
While the Summer days are waning and the Harvest-moon is low.

7. First published in the *California Farmer* and reprinted in the *National Anti-Slavery Standard* 1861. Cited from NAWP.

And the dust lies on the vintage. Ah! the tendrils torn away,
For the crimson wine is flowing, which no human hand may stay,
And the stain is darkly resting on the sad hearts far away.

Lo! the empty field of Harvest! tread the rank grain in the soil,
Cover all with "dust and ashes," let the gleaners take the spoil,
Call the Mowers and the Reapers, thus to rest them from their toil,

Listening to the glad evangel, "Freedom for the coming years!"
While the Nation shouts in triumph. And the broad world rings with cheers
That the Spring-time brings in gladness, what the Autumn sowed in tears.

The Southern Cross[8]

ELLEN KEY BLUNT

In the name of God! Amen!
  Stand for our Southern rights;
On your side, Southern men,
  The God of battles fights!
Fling the invader far—
  Hurl back their work of woe—
The voice is the voice of a brother,
  But the hands are the hands of a foe.
They come with a trampling army,
  Invading our native sod—
Stand, Southrons, fight and conquer!
  In the name of the mighty God!

They are singing our song of triumph,[9]
  Which *was* made to make us free,
While they are breaking away the heart-strings
  Of our nation's harmony.
Sadly it floateth from us,
  Sighing o'er land and wave,

8. Probably composed in 1861 and published as a broadside under this title (our source for the text) and also as "God and Liberty"; reprinted in the *Southern Literary Messenger* September 1862. The "Southern Cross" is another name for the Confederate flag.

9. "Our song" is "The Star Spangled Banner," written during the War of 1812 by Francis Scott Key of Baltimore, who was Blunt's grandfather and whose descendants were Confederates.

'Till mute on the lips of the poet,
  It sleeps in his Southern grave.
Spirit and song! departed!
  Minstrel and minstrelsy!
We mourn thee heavy hearted!
  But we will, we shall be free!

They are waving our flag above us,
  With the despot's tyrant will;
With our blood they have stained its colors,
  And call it holy still.
With tearful eyes, but steady hand,
  We'll tear its stripes apart,
And fling them like broken fetters,
  That may not bind the heart—
But we'll save our stars of glory,
  In the might of the sacred sign
Of Him! who has fixed forever
  Our "Southern Cross" to shine.

Stand, Southrons, fight and conquer!
  Solemn and strong and sure!
The fight shall not be longer
  Than God shall bid endure.
By the life that only yesterday
  Waked with the infant's breath!
By the feet which ere the morn may
  Tread to the soldier's death!
By the blood which cries to heaven!
  Crimson upon our sod!
Stand, Southrons, fight and conquer
  In the name of the mighty God!

Our Faith in '61[10]

AUGUSTUS JULIAN REQUIER

That governments are instituted among men, deriving their just powers from the consent of the governed: that whenever any form of government becomes destructive of these ends, it is the right of the people to alter or abolish it, and to institute a new government, laying its foundation on such principles, and organizing its powers in such form, as TO THEM SHALL SEEM *most likely to effect their safety and happiness.*

Declaration of Independence, July 4, 1776

Not yet one hundred years have flown
Since on this very spot,
The subjects of a sovereign throne—
Liege-master of their lot—
This high degree sped o'er the sea,
From council-board and tent,
"No earthly power can rule the free
But by their own consent!"

For this, they fought as Saxons fight,
On bloody fields and long—
Themselves the champions of the right,
And judges of the wrong;
For this their stainless knighthood wore
The branded rebel's name,
Until the starry cross they bore
Set all the skies aflame!

And States co-equal and distinct
Outshone the western sun,
By one great charter interlinked—
Not blended into one;
Whose graven key that high decree
The grand inscription lent,
"No earthly power can rule the free
But by their own consent!"

10. *Southern Monthly* 1861; cited from *War Poetry*.

Oh! sordid age! Oh! ruthless rage!
  Oh! sacrilegious wrong!
A deed to blast the record page,
  And snap the strings of song;
In that great charter's name, a band
  By grovelling greed enticed,
Whose warrant is the grasping hand
  Of creeds without a Christ—

States that have trampled every pledge
  Its crystal code contains,
Now give their swords a keener edge
  To harness it with chains—
To make a bond of brotherhood
  The sanction and the seal,
By which to arm a rabble brood
  With fratricidal steel.

Who, conscious that their cause is black,
  In puling prose and rhyme,
Talk hatefully of love, and tack
  Hypocrisy to crime;
Who smile and smite, engross the gorge
  Or impotently frown;
And call us "rebels" with King George,
  As if they wore his crown!

Most venal of a venal race,
  Who think you cheat the sky
With every pharisaic face
  And simulated lie;
Round Freedom's lair, with weapons bare,
  We greet the light divine
Of those who throned the goddess there,
  And yet inspire the shrine!

Our loved ones' graves are at our feet,
  Their homesteads at our back—
No belted Southron can retreat
  With women on his track;
Peal, bannered host, the proud decree
  Which from your fathers went,

"No earthly power can rule the free
But by their own consent!"

Manassas[11]

CATHERINE A. W. WARFIELD

They have met at last—as storm-clouds
Meet in heaven;
And the Northmen back and bleeding
Have been driven:
And their thunders have been stilled,
And their leaders crushed or killed,
And their ranks, with terror thrilled,
Rent and riven!

Like the leaves of Vallambrosa[12]
They are lying;
In the moonlight, in the midnight,
Dead and dying:
Like those leaves before the gale,
Swept their legions, wild and pale;
While the host that made them quail
Stood, defying.

When aloft in morning sunlight
Flags were flaunted,
And "swift vengeance on the Rebel"
Proudly vaunted:
Little did they think that night
Should close upon their shameful flight,
And rebels, victors in the fight,
Stand undaunted.

---

11. The first battle at Manassas, called the Battle of Bull Run in the North, took place July 21, 1861. The poem is dated July 1861 and collected in *Southern Poems*.

12. In John Milton's *Paradise Lost*, book 1, Satan's angels lay "Thick as the autumnal leaves that strow the brooks. / In Vallambrosa." Vallambrosa is a famously shady valley near Florence, hence a place where leaves fall thick; Milton's subsequent reference in this passage to "Etrurian shades" represents the valley as one of death (a valley of shades). There were frequent references in nineteenth-century verse, and especially in Civil War poetry, to the dead as falling or lying "like the leaves of Vallambrosa."

But peace to those who perished
In our passes!
Light be the earth above them;
Green the grasses!
Long shall Northmen rue the day
When they met our stern array,
And shrunk from battle's wild affray
At Manassas!

Not Yet[13]

WILLIAM CULLEN BRYANT

Oh country, marvel of the earth!
O realm to sudden greatness grown!
The age that gloried in thy birth,
Shall it behold thee overthrown?
Shall traitors lay that greatness low?
No! Land of Hope and Blessing, No!

And we who wear thy glorious name,
Shall we, like cravens, stand apart,
When those whom thou hast trusted aim
The death-blow at thy generous heart?
Forth goes the battle-cry, and lo!
Hosts rise in harness, shouting, No!

And they who founded in our land
The power that rules from sea to sea,
Bled they in vain, or vainly planned
To leave their country great and free?
Their sleeping ashes from below
Send up the thrilling murmur, No!

Knit they the gentle ties which long
These sister States were proud to wear,
And forged the kindly links so strong,
For idle hands in sport to tear—

13. *New York Ledger* August 17, 1861; cited from CWSS.

For scornful hands aside to throw?
No, by our fathers' memory, No!

Our humming marts, our iron ways,
  Our wind-tossed woods on mountain crest,
The hoarse Atlantic, with his bays,
  The calm, broad Ocean of the West,
And Mississippi's torrent-flow,
And loud Niagara, answer, No!

Not yet the hour is nigh when they
  Who deep in Eld's dim twilight sit,
Earth's ancient kings, shall rise and say,
  "Proud country, welcome to the pit!
So soon art thou, like us, brought low!"
No, sullen group of shadows, No!

For now, behold, the arm that gave
  The victory in our fathers' day,
Strong as of old to guard and save—
  That mighty arm which none can stay—
On clouds above, and fields below,
Writes, in men's sight, the answer, No!

Cotton-Doodle[14]

Anonymous

Hurrah for brave King Cotton!
  The Southerners are singing;
From Carolina to the Gulf

14. According to Moore's *Civil War in Song and Story*, this poem was written "by a lady on hearing that Yankee Doodle had been hissed in New Orleans." In stanza 2, the author refers to poet **James Russell Lowell**, a strong abolitionist; the phrase "sacred compromises" may be taken from a December 7, 1859, speech to Congress by Representative Lucius Lamar (Mississippi), in which Lamar states: "We [of the South] are determined to maintain [the Constitution's] sacred compromises. You being a majority, and looking upon it as an instrument of restraint upon your power, have taken issue with the Constitution and are attempting to throw off its restrictions." Lamar refers to the compromise in which "your fathers and my fathers" put "the negro" into the Constitution "not as property, but as 'persons not free.'"

The echo's loudly ringing;
In every heart a feeling stirs
'Gainst Northern abolition!
Something is heard of compromise,
But nothing of submission.

Cotton-doodle, boys, hurrah!
We've sent old Yankee hissing;
And when we get our Southern rights,
I guess he'll turn up missing!

His poet, Lowell, is singing
'Gainst "sacred compromises";
Prays, "God confound the dastard word,"
At which his "gall arises."
No wonder that he hates it,
He surely has good reason;
He broke the faith of Seventy-six,
And it proclaims his treason.
Cotton-doodle, boys, hurrah!

He does not love the negro;
That's but a pretext hollow
To hide his greedy longing
For the "almighty dollar."
Where was his tender conscience,
When for "blood-stained gold"
His Narraganset captives
Were into slavery sold?
Cotton-doodle, boys, hurrah!

'Gainst nullifying tariffs
He raised a mighty din,
And loudly talked in Thirty-two
Of Carolina's sin;
But now appeals from Congress
To the "higher law" of Heaven!
'Twas horrible in one, you know,
But God-like in eleven!
Cotton-doodle, boys, hurrah!

Thank God, his day is passing!
He can no longer vex us;
For, State by State, we'll firmly stand,
From Maryland to Texas.
King Cotton is a monarch
Who'll conquer abolition,
And set his foot upon the neck
Of treason and sedition.

Cotton-doodle, boys, hurrah!
We've sent old Yankee hissing;
And when we get our Southern rights,
I guess he'll turn up missing!

Price's Appeal to Missouri[15]

M. Jeff Thompson

Missouri! Missouri! Awake from thy slumbers:
Canst thou not hear the hammer that rivets thy chains?
Can't the death-shriek of fathers, the wail of thy mothers,
The tears of thy daughters, arouse thee again?
Come! rise in thy might, shake the dewdrops of morning
From thy limbs, and walk forth as a lion to war,
For fanatics are forging bonds stronger than iron,
To bind thee forever to a conqueror's car.

Can thy slumbering senses be so callous and dead
That even in dreams thou canst hear not nor see
That the chains they are striking from Afric's black sons
Are being welded again to be placed upon thee?
Canst thou not see through the world the finger of scorn
Is pointed at those who submissively stand
Beneath the foul yoke, while their brothers are striking
For the freedom and glory of our dearly loved land?

15. Sterling Price was a Missouri politician who, although initially a Unionist, became a secessionist during the first summer of the war. In August of 1861, he led the Missouri state militia into combat against Federal soldiers at Wilson's Creek, joining forces with Confederate soldiers from Arkansas. This key Confederate victory left a large portion of the deeply divided state of Missouri under Southern control. Cited from CWSS.

O, rise in thy might; drive the "Huns" from thy borders,[16]
And stand by thy Southern sons in the fight;
Pour forth all thy men to help them to battle
For Freedom, for Glory, for Justice, for Right!
Let thy watch-fires glow, and thy bugles blast high
O'er thy mountains and valleys, o'er woodland and lea.
Then the glad shout shall ring o'er thy prairies and streams,
"Hail! brothers, hail! Missouri is free!"

The Picket-Guard[17]

ETHELINDA BEERS

"All quiet along the Potomac*," they say,
"Except, now and then, a stray picket
Is shot as he walks on his beat to and fro,
By a rifleman hid in the thicket.
'Tis nothing—a private or two, now and then,
Will not count in the news of the battle;
Not an officer lost—only one of the men
Moaning out, all alone, his death-rattle."

* * * * * *

All quiet along the Potomac to-night,
Where the soldiers lie peacefully dreaming;
Their tents, in the rays of the clear autumn moon
Or the light of the watch-fire, are gleaming.
A tremulous sigh, as the gentle night-wind
Through the forest-leaves softly is creeping;
While stars up above, with their glittering eyes,
Keep guard—for the army is sleeping.

16. Huns were an Asiatic people who ravaged Europe in the fourth and fifth centuries; Confederates called Northerners "Huns" to indicate that they were uncivilized and destructive.

17. *Harper's Weekly* November 30, 1861, under the initials E. B. Widely known under the title "All Quiet Along the Potomac," this poem was claimed by both the North and the South and has been attributed to various authors. It was published in the *Southern Literary Messenger* in February 1863 as "written by Lamar Fontaine, private of Company I, Second Regiment Virginia Cavalry, while on picket, on the bank of the Potomac, in 1861."

There's only the sound of the lone sentry's tread,
As he tramps from the rock to the fountain,
And thinks of the two in the low trundle-bed
Far away in the cot on the mountain.
His musket falls slack—his face, dark and grim,
Grows gentle with memories tender,
As he mutters a prayer for the children asleep—
For their mother—may Heaven defend her!

The moon seems to shine just as brightly as then,
That night, when the love yet unspoken
Leaped up to his lips—when low-murmured vows
Were pledged to be ever unbroken.
Then drawing his sleeve roughly over his eyes,
He dashes off tears that are welling,
And gathers his gun closer up to its place,
As if to keep down the heart-swelling.

He passes the fountain, the blasted pine-tree,
The footstep is lagging and weary;
Yet onward he goes, through the broad belt of light,
Toward the shade of the forest so dreary.
Hark! was it the night-wind that rustled the leaves?
Was it moonlight so suddenly flashing?
It looked like a rifle— "Ha! Mary, good-by!"
And the life-blood is ebbing and plashing.

All quiet along the Potomac to-night,
No sound save the rush of the river;
While soft falls the dew on the face of the dead—
The picket's off duty forever!

A Thought[18]

Elizabeth Stoddard

Falling leaves and falling men!
When the snows of winter fall,

18. Published anonymously in CWSS.

And the winds of winter blow,
  Will be woven Nature's pall.

Let us, then, forsake our dead;
  For the dead will surely wait
While we rush upon the foe,
  Eager for the hero's fate.

Leaves will come upon the trees;
  Spring will show the happy race;
Mothers will give birth to sons—
  Loyal souls to fill our place.

Wherefore should we rest and rush?
  Soldiers, we must fight and save
Freedom now, and give our foes
  All their country should—a grave!

Soldiers' Aid Societies[19]

ANONYMOUS

To the quiet nooks of home,
  To the public halls so wide,
The women, all loyal, hurrying come,
  And sit down side by side,
To fight for their native land,
  With womanly weapons girt,
For dagger a needle, scissors for brand,
  While they sing the song of the shirt.

O women with sons so dear,
  O tender, loving wives,
It is not money you work for now,
  But the saving of precious lives.
'Tis roused for the battle we feel—
  O for a thousand experts,

19. This poem plays on Thomas Hood's "The Song of the Shirt" (*Punch* December 1843), a popular poem about the plight of British seamstresses, working long hours in dismal conditions, "In poverty, hunger, and dirt." Cited from CWSS.

Armed with tiny darts of steel,
   To conquer thousands of shirts!

Stitch—stitch—stitch
   Under the sheltering roof,
Come to the rescue, poor and rich,
   Nor stay from the work aloof;
To the men who are shedding their blood,
   To the brave, devoted band,
Whose action is honor, whose cause is good,
   We pledge our strong right hand.

Work—work—work
   With earnest heart and soul—
Work—work—work
   To keep the Union whole.
And 'tis O for the land of the brave,
   Where treason and cowardice lurk,
Where there's all to lose or all to save,
   That we're doing this Christian work.

Brothers are fighting abroad,
   Sisters will help them here,
Husbands and wives with one accord
   Serving the cause so dear.
Stand by our colors to-day—
   Keep to the Union true—
Under our flag while yet we may
   Hurrah for the Red, White, and Blue.

Let My People Go: A Song of the "Contrabands"[20]

ANONYMOUS

When Israel was in Egypt's land,
O let my people go!
Oppressed so hard they could not stand,
O let my people go!

Chorus: O go down, Moses
Away down to Egypt's land,
And tell King Pharaoh
To let my people go!

Thus saith the Lord bold Moses said,
O let my people go!
If not, I'll smite your first born dead,
O let my people go!

No more shall they in bondage toil,
O let my people go!
Let them come out with Egypt's spoil,
O let my people go!

Then Israel out of Egypt came
O let my people go!
And left the proud oppressive land,
O let my people go!

O 'twas a dark and dismal night,
O let my people go!
When Moses led the Israelites,
O let my people go!

20. Reverend Lewis Lockwood first heard escaped slaves (the "contrabands"*) sing the song now well known as "Go Down, Moses" at Fortress Monroe, Virginia, in early September 1861. Harwood Vernon sent Lockwood's transcription of the song to the *New York Tribune* where it appeared on December 2, 1861, as "Let My People Go: A Song of the 'Contrabands'"; it subsequently appeared in the *National Anti-Slavery Standard* December 1861. Our source for this text is Dena Epstein's transcription of the 1861 *Tribune* text in *Sinful Tunes and Spirituals* 1977. A sheet music edition of the song appeared on December 14, 1861. "Let My People Go" was one of the first of the sorrow songs to appear in print.

'Twas good old Moses, and Aaron, too,
O let my people go!
'Twas they that led the armies through,
O let my people go!

The Lord told Moses what to do,
O let my people go!
To lead the children of Israel through,
O let my people go!

O come along, Moses, you'll not get lost,
O let my people go!
Stretch out your rod and come across,
O let my people go!

As Israel stood by the water side,
O let my people go!
At the command of God it did divide,
O let my people go!

When they had reached the other shore,
O let my people go!
They sang a song of triumph o'er,
O let my people go!

Pharaoh said he would go across,
O let my people go!
But Pharaoh and his host were lost,
O let my people go!

O Moses, the cloud shall cleave the way,
O let my people go!
A fire by night, a shade by day,
O let my people go!

You'll not get lost in the wilderness,
O let my people go!
With a lighted candle in your breast,
O let my people go!

Jordan shall stand up like a wall,
O let my people go!

And the walls of Jericho shall fall,
O let my people go!

Your foe shall not before you stand,
O let my people go!
And you'll possess fair Canaan's land,
O let my people go!

'Twas just about in harvest time,
O let my people go!
When Joshua led his host Divine,
O let my people go!

O let us all from bondage flee,
O let my people go!
And let us all in Christ be free,
O let my people go!

We need not always weep and mourn,
O let my people go!
And wear these Slavery chains forlorn,
O let my people go!

This world's a wilderness of woe,
O let my people go!
O let us on to Canaan go,
O let my people go!

What a beautiful morning that will be!
O let my people go!
When time breaks up in eternity,
O let my people go!

1862

Fair Oaks, Virginia. Lt. James B. Washington, a Confederate prisoner, with Captain George A. Custer of the 5th Cavalry, U.S.A., taken after the Seven Days' battles. Photograph by James F. Gibson. Library of Congress, Brady Civil War Photograph Collection, LC-B815-428.

Battle Hymn of the Republic[1]

Julia Ward Howe

Mine eyes have seen the glory of the coming of the Lord:
He is trampling out the vintage where the grapes of wrath are stored;
He hath loosed the fateful lightning of His terrible swift sword:
His truth is marching on.

I have seen Him in the watch-fires of a hundred circling camps;
They have builded Him an altar in the evening dews and damps;
I can read His righteous sentence by the dim and flaring lamps:
His day is marching on.

I have read a fiery Gospel writ in burnished rows of steel:
"As ye deal with my contemners, so with you my grace shall deal;
Let the Hero, born of woman, crush the serpent with his heel,
Since God is marching on."

He has sounded forth the trumpet that shall never call retreat;
He is sifting out the hearts of men before His judgment-seat:
Oh, be swift, my soul, to answer Him! be jubilant, my feet!
Our God is marching on.

In the beauty of the lilies Christ was born across the sea,
With a glory in his bosom that transfigures you and me:
As he died to make men holy, let us die to make men free,
While God is marching on.

---

1. *Atlantic Monthly* February 1862. Urged by a friend in 1862 to write new lyrics for the popular song "John Brown's Body," Howe woke in the middle of the night to write out the verses that had just occurred to her and then sold the poem for five dollars to the editor of the *Atlantic Monthly*. This poem was reprinted widely and became one of the most popular songs of the North and, after the war, of American popular culture. The poem was first published without the "glory hallelujah" chorus, although Howe knew the chorus from "John Brown's Body"; for Howe's poem, the chorus repeats the final line of each stanza as its final phrase—for example, "Glory! Glory! Hallelujah! Glory! Glory! Hallelujah! / Glory! Glory! Hallelujah! His truth is marching on."

Anomalies[2]

Caroline Mason

The North is armed, but it is an armed neutrality, rather than an armed crusade; it is marshaled in the array of battle, but not for the extermination of its foe. The South is in arms that slavery may be perpetuated; the North is in arms, determined that slavery shall not be injured; two great armies diligently guarding the one stupendous wrong of the earth; two great armies of countrymen carefully guarding the dragon that has stung them both into fratricidal madness, and will sting them both to death.

Rev. O. B. Frothingham's Sermon, "The Year's Record of Sadness and Gladness."

Two armies drawn up in battle array,
Both fighting for slavery—each in its way!

Two Governments—hostile, but both agreed
Of all the trouble to save the seed!

A War that has festered nine months or more,
And nobody daring to touch the sore!

A thousand remedies all applied,
And the only true one left untried!

Merciful Heaven! Is the Nation mad?
Or—truth more terrible yet, and sad—

Has God departed and left us still
To follow the bent of our own wild will?

To work out, under His wrathful eyes,
Our fearful measure of wrong and lies?

Oh, for some Prophet, with burning word,
Straight from the presence of the Lord,

To thunder the truth in our guilty ears,
That God has been whispering us for years: —

"Hear, oh People; the Lord has spoke!
Loose each shackle and break each yoke.

---

2. *National Anti-Slavery Standard* February 8, 1862.

"Let my opprest and my poor go free;
The voice of their sighing has come to me.

"Not oblations and altar fires,
Mercy and Justice my Hand requires.

"Mercy and Justice; as I am true,
As ye give others, I give to you."

A Battle Hymn[3]

George Henry Boker

God, to Thee we humbly bow,
With hand unarmed and naked brow;
Musket, lance, and sheathéd sword
At Thy feet we lay, O Lord!
Gone is all the soldier's boast
In the valor of the host;
Kneeling here, we do our most.

Of ourselves we nothing know:
Thou, and Thou alone, canst show,
By the favor of Thy hand,
Who has drawn the guilty brand.
If our foemen have the right,
Show Thy judgment in our sight
Through the fortunes of the fight!

If our cause be pure and just,
Nerve our courage with Thy trust:
Scatter, in Thy bitter wrath,
All who cross the nation's path:
May the baffled traitors fly,
As the vapors from the sky
When Thy raging winds are high!

God of mercy, some must fall
In Thy holy cause. Not all

3. *Rebellion Record* Vol. 4, 1862; collected in *Poems of the War*, our source for this text.

Hope to sing the victor's lay,
When the sword is laid away.
Brief will be the prayers then said;
Falling at Thy altar dead,
Take the sacrifice instead!

Now, O God, once more we rise,
Marching on beneath Thy eyes;
And we draw the sacred sword
In Thy name and at Thy word.
May our spirits clearly see
Thee, through all that is to be,
In defeat or victory.

The Sword-Bearer[4]

George Henry Boker

Brave Morris* saw the day was lost;
  For nothing now remained,
On the wrecked and sinking Cumberland*,
  But to save the flag unstained.

So he swore an oath in the sight of Heaven,—
  If he kept it the world can tell:—
"Before I strike to a rebel flag,
  I'll sink to the gates of hell!

"Here, take my sword; 'tis in my way;
  I shall trip o'er the useless steel;
For I'll meet the lot that falls to all
  With my shoulder at the wheel."

So the little Negro took the sword;
  And O with what reverent care,
Following his master step by step,
  He bore it here and there!

4. *Rebellion Record* Vol. 4, 1862; collected in *Poems of the War*, our source for this text.

A thought had crept through his sluggish brain,
And shone in his dusky face,
That somehow—he could not tell just how—
'T was the sword of his trampled race.

And as Morris, great with his lion heart,
Rushed onward, from gun to gun,
The little Negro slid after him,
Like a shadow in the sun.

But something of pomp and of curious pride
The sable creature wore,
Which at any time but a time like that
Would have made the ship's crew roar.

Over the wounded, dying, and dead,
Like an usher of the rod,
The black page, full of his mighty trust,
With dainty caution trod.

No heed he gave to the flying ball,
No heed to the bursting shell;
His duty was something more than life,
And he strove to do it well.

Down, with our starry flag apeak,
In the whirling sea we sank,
And captain and crew and the sword-bearer
Were washed from the bloody plank.

They picked us up from the hungry waves;—
Alas! not all!—"And where,
Where is the faithful negro lad?"—
"Back oars! avast! look there!"

We looked; and, as Heaven may save my soul,
I pledge you a sailor's word,
There, fathoms deep in the sea, he lay,
Still grasping his master's sword!

We drew him out; and many an hour
We wrought with his rigid form,

Ere the almost smothered spark of life
By slow degrees grew warm.

The first dull glance that his eyeballs rolled
Was down towards his shrunken hand;
And he smiled, and closed his eyes again
As they fell on the rescued brand.

And no one touched the sacred sword,
Till at length, when Morris came,
The little negro stretched it out,
With his eager eyes aflame.

And if Morris wrung the poor boy's hand,
And his words seemed hard to speak,
And tears ran down his manly cheeks,
What tongue shall call him weak?

The Cumberland*[5]

HENRY WADSWORTH LONGFELLOW

At anchor in Hampton Roads we lay,
On board of the Cumberland sloop-of-war;
And at times from the fortress across the bay
The alarm of drums swept past,
Or a bugle blast
From the camp on shore.

Then far away to the south uprose
A little feather of snow-white smoke,
And we knew that the iron ship of our foes
Was steadily steering its course,
To try the force
Of our ribs of oak.

Down upon us heavily runs
Silent and sullen, the floating fort;

5. Composed early in 1862 and published in 1863 in Longfellow's *Songs of War* and *Tales of a Wayside Inn*; cited from CWSS.

Then comes a puff of smoke from her guns,
And leaps the terrible death,
With fiery breath,
From each open port.

We are not idle, but send her straight
Defiance back in a full broadside!
As hail rebounds from a roof of slate,
Rebounds our heavier hail
From each iron scale
Of the monster's hide.

"Strike your flag!" the rebel cries,
In his arrogant old plantation strain.
"Never!" our gallant Morris* replies;
"It is better to sink than to yield!"
And the whole air pealed
With the cheers of our men.

Then, like a kraken huge and black,
She crushed our ribs in her iron grasp!
Down went the Cumberland all a wrack,
With a sudden shudder of death,
And the cannon's breath
For her dying gasp.

Next morn, as the sun rose over the bay,
Still floated our flag at the mainmast-head.
Lord, how beautiful was Thy day!
Every waft of the air
Was a whisper of prayer,
Or a dirge for the dead.

Ho! brave hearts that went down in the seas,
Ye are at peace in the troubled stream,
Ho! brave land! with hearts like these,
Thy flag that is rent in twain,
Shall be one again,
And without a seam.

The Song of the South[6]

R. M. Anderson

Another star arisen, another flag unfurled;
Another name inscribed among the nations of the world;
Another mighty struggle 'gainst a tyrant's fell decree.
And again a burdened people have uprisen, and are free.

The spirit of the fathers in the children liveth yet,—
Liveth still the olden blood that hath dimmed the bayonet;
And the fathers fought for freedom, and the sons for freedom fight;
Their God was with their fathers, and is still the God of right.

Behold, the skies are darkened! a gloomy cloud hath lowered!
Shall it break in happy peacefulness, or spread its rage abroad?
Shall we have the smiles of friendship, or feel the fierce, foul blow,
And bare the red right hand of war to meet an insulting foe?

In peacefulness we wish to live, but not in slavish fear;
In peacefulness we dare not die, dishonored on our bier;
To our allies of the Northern land we offer heart and hand;
But if they scorn our friendship, then the banner and the brand.

Honor to the new-born nation! honor to the brave!
A country freed from thralldom, or a soldier's honored grave!
Every rock shall be a tombstone, every rivulet run red,
And the invader, should he conquer, find the conquered in the dead.

But victory shall follow where the sons of freedom go,
And the signal for the onset be the death-knell of the foe;
And hallowed be the sacred spot where they have bravely met,
And the star that rises yonder shall never, never set.

6. First published in the *Southern Literary Messenger*; cited from CWSS.

The Stars and Bars[7]

R. R.

'Tis sixty-two!—and sixty-one,
With the old Union, now is gone,
Reeking with bloody wars—
Gone with that ensign, once so prized,
The Stars and Stripes, now so despised—
Struck for the stars and bars.

The burden once of patriot's song,
Now badge of tyranny and wrong,
For us no more it waves;
We claim the stars—the stripes we yield,
We give *them* up on every field,
Where fight the Southern braves.

Our motto this, "God and our right,"
For sacred liberty we fight—
Not for the lust of power;
Compelled by wrongs and sword t'unsheath,
We'll fight, be free, or cease to breathe—
We'll die before we cower.

By all the blood our fathers shed,
We will from tyranny be freed—
We will not conquered be;
Like them, no higher power we own
But God's—we bow to him alone—
We will, we will be free!

For homes and altars we contend,
Assured that God will us defend—
He makes our cause his own;
Not of our gallant patriot host,
Not of brave leaders do we boast—
We trust in God alone.

7. A nickname for the Confederate flag, which kept the two major icons of the United States flag (stars and stripes or "bars") but widened the stripe and arranged both icons differently on its field; the name alludes in contrast to the U.S. "stars and stripes." Cited from CWSS.

Sumter*, and Bethel, and Bull Run
Witnessed fierce battles fought and won,
By aid of Power Divine;
We met the foe, who us defied,
In all his pomp, in all his pride,
Shouting, "Manasseh's mine!"

It was not thine, thou boasting foe!
We laid thy vandal legions low—
We made them bite the sod;
At Lexington the braggart yields,
Leesburgh, Belmont,* and other fields;—
Still help us, mighty God!

Thou smiledst on the patriot seven—
Thou smilest on the brave eleven[8]
Free, independent States;
Their number thou wilt soon increase,
And bless them with a lasting peace,
Within their happy gates.

No more shall violence be heard,
Wasting, destruction no more feared
In all this Southern land;
"Praise," she her gates devoutly calls,
"Salvation," her Heaven-guarded walls—
What shall her power withstand?

"The little one," by heavenly aid,
"A thousand is—the strong one made,
"A nation—oh! how strong!"
Jehovah, who the right befriends,
Jehovah, who our flag defends,
Is hastening it along!

8. The first seven states to secede were South Carolina, Mississippi, Florida, Alabama, Georgia, Louisiana, and Texas. They were followed by Virginia, Arkansas, North Carolina, and Tennessee, bringing the total to eleven. Despite Southern anticipation of further secessions, these were the only states to secede.

Stonewall Jackson's* Way[9]

John Williamson Palmer

Come, stack arms, men! Pile on the rails,
Stir up the camp-fire bright;
No matter if the canteen fails,
We'll make a roaring night.
Here Shenandoah brawls along,
There burly Blue Ridge echoes strong,
To swell the brigade's rousing song
Of "Stonewall Jackson's way."

We see him now—the old slouched hat
Cocked o'er his eye askew,
The shrewd, dry smile, the speech so pat.
So calm, so blunt, so true.
The "Blue-Light Elder"* knows 'em well;
Says he, "That's Banks—he's fond of shell;
Lord save his soul! we'll give him"—well,
That's "Stonewall Jackson's way."

Silence! ground arms! kneel, all! caps off!
Old Blue-Light's going to pray.
Strangle the fool that dares to scoff!
Attention! it's his way.
Appealing from his native sod,
In *forma pauperis* to God—
"Lay bare thine arm, stretch forth thy rod!
Amen!" That's "Stonewall's way."

He's in the saddle now. Fall in!
Steady, the whole brigade!
Hill's at the ford, cut off—we'll win
His way out, ball and blade!
What matter if our shoes are worn?
What matter if our feet are torn?

9. *Southern Literary Messenger* September 17, 1862; collected in CWSS (our source for this text) and Palmer's *For Charlie's Sake, and Other Lyrics and Ballads* of 1901. In stanza 2, Nathaniel Prentiss Banks served as a Union general in Maryland and Virginia.

"Quick-step! we're with him before dawn!"
  That's "Stonewall Jackson's way."

The sun's bright lances rout the mists
  Of morning, and, by George!
Here's Longstreet* struggling in the lists,
  Hemmed in an ugly gorge.
Pope and his Yankees, whipped before,
"Bay'nets and grape!" hear Stonewall roar;
"Charge, Stuart*! Pay off Ashby's score!"
  Is "Stonewall Jackson's way."

Ah, maiden, wait, and watch, and yearn
  For news of Stonewall's band!
Ah, widow, read, with eyes that burn,
  That ring upon thy hand!
Ah, wife, sew on, pray on, hope on!
Thy life shall not be all forlorn.
The foe had better ne'er been born
  That gets in "Stonewall's way."

Weaving[10]

LUCY LARCOM

All day she stands before her loom;
  The flying shuttles come and go:
By grassy fields, and trees in bloom,
  She sees the winding river flow:
And fancy's shuttle flieth wide,
And faster than the waters glide.

Is she entangled in her dreams,
  Like that fair weaver of Shalott,

10. This poem was composed and may have been published during the Civil War. It was (re)published in Larcom's *Poems* (1869), our source for this text. Larcom alludes to the title character in Alfred, Lord Tennyson's 1833 "The Lady of Shalott" as a personification of female passivity and romanticism. In contrast, the speaker's reference to the Merrimack River places her in Lowell, Massachusetts, the site of huge cotton mills worked by women. As she notes, the cotton they spin is provided by slave labor in the South.

Who left her mystic mirror's gleams,
  To gaze on light Sir Lancelot?
Her heart, a mirror sadly true,
Brings gloomier visions into view.

"I weave, and weave, the livelong day:
  The woof is strong, the warp is good:
I weave, to be my mother's stay;
  I weave, to win my daily food:
But ever as I weave," saith she,
"The world of women haunteth me.

"The river glides along, one thread
  In nature's mesh, so beautiful!
The stars are woven in; the red
  Of sunrise; and the rain-cloud dull.
Each seems a separate wonder wrought;
Each blends with some more wondrous thought.

"So, at the loom of life, we weave
  Our separate shreds, that varying fall,
Some stained, some fair; and, passing, leave
  To God the gathering up of all,
In that full pattern wherein man
Works blindly out the eternal plan.

"In his vast work, for good or ill,
  The undone and the done he blends:
With whatsoever woof we fill,
  To our weak hands His might He lends,
And gives the threads beneath His eye
The texture of eternity.

"Wind on, by willow and by pine,
  Thou blue, untroubled Merrimack!
Afar, by sunnier streams than thine,
  My sisters toil, with foreheads black;
And water with their blood this root,
Whereof we gather bounteous fruit.

"There be sad women, sick and poor;
  And those who walk in garments soiled:

Their shame, their sorrow, I endure;
  By their defect my hope is foiled:
The blot they bear is on my name;
Who sins, and I am not to blame?

"And how much of your wrong is mine,
  Dark women slaving at the South?
Of your stolen grapes I quaff the wine;
  The bread you starve for fills my mouth:
The beam unwinds, but every thread
With blood of strangled souls is red.

"If this be so, we win and wear
  A Nessus-robe of poisoned cloth;
Or weave them shrouds they may not wear,—
  Fathers and brothers falling both
On ghastly, death-sown fields, that lie
Beneath the tearless Southern sky.

"Alas! the weft has lost its white.
  It grows a hideous tapestry,
That pictures war's abhorrent sight:—
  Unroll not, web of destiny!
Be the dark volume left unread,—
The tale untold,—the curse unsaid!"

So up and down before her loom
  She paces on, and to and fro,
Till sunset fills the dusty room,
  And makes the water redly glow,
As if the Merrimack's calm flood
Were changed into a stream of blood.

Too soon fulfilled, and all too true
  The words she murmured as she wrought:
But, weary weaver, not to you
  Alone was war's stern message brought:
"Woman!" it knelled from heart to heart,
"Thy sister's keeper know thou art!"

To Abraham Lincoln*[11]

John James Piatt

Stern be the pilot in the dreadful hour
When a great nation, like a ship at sea
With the wroth breakers whitening at her lee,
Feels her last shudder if her helmsman cower;
A Godlike manhood be his mighty dower,
Such and so gifted, Lincoln, mayest thou be,
With thy high wisdom's low simplicity
And awful tenderness of voted power.
From our hot records then thy name shall stand
On Time's calm ledger out of passionate days—
With the pure debt of gratitude begun,
And only paid in never-ending praise—
One of the many of a mighty Land,
Made by God's providence the Anointed One.

Wanted—A Man[12]

Edmund Clarence Stedman

Back from the trebly crimsoned field
  Terrible words are thunder-tost;
Full of the wrath that will not yield,
  Full of revenge for battles lost!
  Hark to their echo, as it crost
The Capital, making faces wan;
  "End this murderous holocaust;
Abraham Lincoln, give us a MAN!

"Give us a man of God's own mould,
  Born to marshal his fellow-men;
One whose fame is not bought and sold

11. Collected in *Blue and Gray*.

12. According to Browne in *Bugle-Echoes*, Abraham Lincoln was so impressed by this poem that he read it to his cabinet in 1862. Stedman here articulates popular dissatisfaction with the lack of success of Northern generals.

At the stroke of a politician's pen;
 Give us the man of thousands ten,
Fit to do as well as to plan;
 Give us a rallying-cry, and then,
Abraham Lincoln, give us a MAN!

"No leader to shirk the boasting foe,
 And to march and countermarch our brave,
Till they fall like ghosts in the marshes low,
 And swamp-grass covers each nameless grave;
 Nor another, whose fatal banners wave
Aye in Disaster's shameful van;
 Nor another, to bluster, and lie, and rave,—
Abraham Lincoln, give us a MAN!

"Hearts are mourning in the North,
 While the sister rivers seek the main,
Red with our life-blood flowing forth—
 Who shall gather it up again?
 Though we march to the battle-plain
Firmly as when the strife began,
 Shall all our offering be in vain?—
Abraham Lincoln, give us a MAN!

"Is there never one in all the land,
 One on whose might the Cause may lean?
Are all the common ones so grand,
 And all the titled ones so mean?
 What if your failure may have been
In trying to make good bread from bran,
 From worthless metal a weapon keen?—
Abraham Lincoln, find us a MAN!

"O, we will follow him to the death,
 Where the foeman's fiercest columns are!
O, we will use our latest breath,
 Cheering for every sacred star!
 His to marshal us high and far;
Ours to battle, as patriots can
 When a Hero leads the Holy War!—
Abraham Lincoln, give us a MAN!"

Clouds in the West[13]

AUGUSTUS JULIAN REQUIER

Hark! on the wind that whistles from the West
A manly shout for instant succor comes,
From men who fight, outnumbered, breast to breast,
With rage-indented drums!

Who dare for child, wife, country—stream and strand,
Though but a fraction to the swarming foe,
There—at the flooded gateways of the land,
To stem a torrent's flow.

To arms! brave sons of each embattled State,
Whose queenly standard is a Southern star:
Who would be free must ride the lists of Fate
On Freedom's victor-car!

Forsake the field, the shop, the mart, the hum
Of craven traffic for the mustering clan:
The dead themselves are pledged that you shall come
And prove yourself—a man.

That sacred turf where first a thrilling grief
Was felt which taught you Heaven alone disposes—
God! can you live to see a foreign thief
Contaminate its roses?

Blow, summoning trumpets, a compulsive stave,
Through all the bounds, from Beersheba to Dan;
Come out! come out! who scorns to be a slave,
Or claims to be a man!

Hark! on the breezes whistling from the West
A manly shout for instant succor comes,
From men who fight, outnumbered, breast to breast,
With rage-indented drums!

Who charge and cheer amid the murderous din,
Where still your battle-flags unbended wave,

13. Cited from *War Poetry*.

Dying for what your fathers died to win
  And you must fight to save.

Ho! shrilly fifes that stir the vales from sleep,
  Ho! brazen thunders from the mountains hoar;
The very waves are marshalling on the deep,
  While tempests tread the shore.

Arise and swear, your palm-engirdled land
  Shall burial only yield a bandit foe;
Then spring upon the caitiffs, steel in hand,
  And strike the fated blow.

Three Hundred Thousand More[14]

James Sloan Gibbons

We are coming, Father Abraham, three hundred thousand more,
From Mississippi's winding stream and from New England's shore;
We leave our ploughs and workshops, our wives and children dear,
With hearts too full for utterance, with but a silent tear;
We dare not look behind us, but steadfastly before:
We are coming, Father Abraham, three hundred thousand more!

If you look across the hill-tops that meet the northern sky,
Long moving lines of rising dust your vision may descry;
And now the wind, an instant, tears the cloudy veil aside,
And floats aloft our angled flag in glory and in pride,
And bayonets in the sunlight gleam, and bands brave music pour:
We are coming, Father Abraham, three hundred thousand more!

---

14. First published anonymously in the *Evening Post* on July 16, 1862, as "We Are Coming, Father Abraham"; cited from *Bugle-Echoes*, where it was also published anonymously. This poem was frequently republished under various titles and authors' names. An 1864 Lincoln Campaign Songster uses the title "We Are Coming, Father Abraham, 600,000 More" and lists J. Cullen Bryant as author. L. O. Emerson, Stephen Foster, and D. A. Warden provided popular musical settings for the poem. On the first Emerson sheet music edition, **William Cullen Bryant** was listed as author (probably the source of the later confused attribution to J. Cullen Bryant), but Bryant quickly made it known that the lyrics were by Gibbons. Gibbons wrote the poem in response to President Lincoln's July 2 call for three hundred thousand men to enlist in the Union army, and he sang it to Lincoln after the December battle of Fredericksburg. After the 1863 Conscription Act, stipulating that one could escape the draft by paying a three-hundred-dollar commutation fee, the song was parodied as "We Are Coming, Father Abraham, Three Hundred Dollars More."

If you look all up our valleys where the growing harvests shine,
You may see our sturdy farmer boys fast forming into line;
And children from their mother's knees are pulling at the weeds,
And learning how to reap and sow against their country's needs;
And a farewell group stands weeping at every cottage door:
We are coming, Father Abraham, three hundred thousand more!

You have called us, and we're coming, by Richmond's bloody tide
To lay us down, for Freedom's sake, our brothers' bones beside,
Or from foul treason's savage grasp to wrench the murderous blade,
And in the face of foreign foes its fragments to parade.
Six hundred thousand loyal men and true have gone before:
We are coming, Father Abraham, three hundred thousand more!

Emancipation[15]

William E. Pabor

Print the glad tidings in letters of gold;
  And scatter it broadcast over the nation!
Ring, merry bells, while the story is told
In palace, in hovel, by fireside and fold
And over the prairie in gladness is rolled,
  All in the dawn of the country's salvation.

Wind of the mountain and wind of the plain,
  Bear on your bosom the Grand Proclamation!
Into the cane-brake drop it like rain!
Into the cotton-field, in the rice swamp.
Into the heart of the Enemy's Camp
  Scatter the boon of Emancipation!

Waited for patiently, waited for long
  All through the evil days, sorely and sadly;
Called for through trial and hoped for through wrong,
See! how the heart of the nation grows strong!
See! how the lips break in Thanksgiving song!
  Never could tidings be welcomed more gladly.

15. *National Anti-Slavery Standard* October 11, 1862, dated "Oct. 2d, 1862."

These the glad tidings: the shackles shall fall,
The gyves from the wrists of slaves shall be broken!
In th' name of th' Nation, there's Freedom for all!
All through the length and the breadth of our land
Each in his Liberty equal shall stand
Blessing our Chief for the words he has spoken.

Half Way[16]

ELLEN MURRAY

The purple of the storm
Came mantling on the sun,
Came darkly on the summer earth,
Before the day was done.

The slumberous shade of storm,
The purple of the cloud,
Closed round the cabin of the slave,
A night, a pall, a shroud.

Withered and bent and old,
A woman by the door
Lifted her white head from her hands,
To hear the thunder roar.

A smile of holy trust
Upon her wrinkled face
Smoothed out awhile the heavy lines,
The grief-mark of her race.

The yellow lightning spears
Fell broken to the ground,
The lightning's crimson arrow-heads
Were flashing all around.

The fig tree o'er her hut
Stirred, as to summer air;

16. *National Anti-Slavery Standard* October 4, 1862. Murray indicates that the long quoted section of her poem consists of "the exact words of an old freed-woman of St. Helena, South Carolina."

Then stood, a blackened skeleton,
A dead, dry ruin there.

But as the thunder-crash
Rolled heavily and dread,
There was no tone of fear or doubt
In the calm words she said:

"If the next lightning-flash
Should miss my shattered tree,
And glancing through my empty hut,
Should do its work on me;

"Should fold my weary hands,
Should end my failing sight,
At once should send me on my way
Across the land of night;

"Though sudden it might be,
I would not shrink or care,
For ere I had gone half the way,
My Lord would meet me there.

"He knows my eyes are dim,
He knows my limbs are weak,
He will not miss me in the dark,
He'll not forget to speak.

"Lest I should lose the path
Along the lonesome vale,
He'll meet me half-way to my home
Lest I should faint or fail.

"Beneath the tree of life
My dwelling he will make,
Where thunders only speak His word,
Or into hymnings break."

The thunder rolled again—
It only seemed to her
The words of angels, welcoming
A fellow-worshipper.

"While God He Leaves Me Reason, God He Will Leave Me Jim"[17]

MARY H. C. BOOTH

"Soldier, say, did you meet my Jimmy in the fight?
You'd know him by his manliness, and by his eyes' sweet light."
"I fought beside your gallant son—a brave, good fellow he;
Alas! he fell beneath the shot that should have taken me."

"And think you that my Jimmy cared about a little fall?
Why make a great ado of what he would not mind at all?
When Jimmy was a little boy, and played with Bobby Brown,
He always played the enemy, and Bob he shot him down.

"I've seen him fall a hundred times, the cunning little sprite;
He can't forget his boyish tricks though in an earnest fight.
But never mind about the fall; I want to hear of him;
Perhaps you've heard the Captain speak of what he thinks of Jim."

"I've often heard the Captain say Jim was a splendid lad,
The bravest and the handsomest of all the boys he had.
And here's a lock of Jimmy's hair, and here's a golden ring;
I found it tied around his neck upon a silken string."

The mother took the matted tress, she took the ring of gold,
But shook her head, and laughed aloud at what the soldier told.
"Soldier," said she, "where is my boy? where is my brave boy, Jim?
I gave the others all to God, but God he left me him.

"Hush, there is Uncle Abraham a-knocking at the door;
He calls for other mothers' sons, '*Three hundred thousand more!*'
Be still, Old Uncle Abraham; 'twill do no good to call;
You think my house is full of boys; ah, Jimmy was my all."

17. Moore's *Civil War in Song and Story* includes the following note with this poem: "Words of a soldier's mother, who, on hearing that her only son had fallen in battle, became hopelessly insane, though continually declaring that his having 'fallen' was of no consequence."

A Southern Scene[18]

ANONYMOUS

"O mammy! have you heard the news?"
  Thus spake a Southern child,
As in her nurse's aged face
  She upward glanced and smiled.

"What news you mean, my little one?
  It must be mighty fine,
To make my darling's face so red,
  Her sunny blue eyes shine."

"Why, Abram Lincoln, don't you know,
  The Yankee President,
Whose ugly picture once we saw,
  When up to town we went.

"Well, he is going to free you all,
  And make you rich and grand,
And you'll be dressed in silk and gold,
  Like the proudest in the land.

"A gilded coach shall carry you
  Where'er you wish to ride;
And, mammy, all your work shall be
  Forever laid aside."

The eager speaker paused for breath,
  And then the old nurse said,
While closer to her swarthy cheek
  She pressed the golden head:

"My little missus, stop and res'—
  You' talking mighty fas';
Jes' look up dere, and tell me what
  You see in yonder glass?

18. *Rebellion Record* Vol. 4, 1862. Most dialect pieces of this era were white authored, as this one almost certainly was.

"You sees old mammy's wrinkly face,
As black as any coal;
And underneath her handkerchief
Whole heaps of knotty wool.

"My darlin's face is red and white,
Her skin is soff and fine,
And on her pretty little head
De yallar ringlets shine.

"My chile, who made dis difference
'Twixt mammy and 'twixt you?
You reads de dear Lord's blessed book,
And you can tell me true.

"De dear Lord said it must be so;
And, honey, I, for one,
Wid tankful heart will always say,
His holy will be done.

"I tanks mas' Linkum all de same,
But when I wants for free,
I'll ask de Lord of glory,
Not poor buckra man like he.

"And as for gilded carriages,
Dey's notin' 'tall to see;
My massa's coach what carries him,
Is good enough for me.

"And, honey, when your mammy wants
To change her homespun dress,
She'll pray like dear old missus,
To be clothed with righteousness.

"My work's been done dis many a day,
And now I takes my ease,
A waitin' for de Master's call,
Jes' when de Master please.

"And when at las' de time's done come,
And poor ole mammy dies,

Your own dear mother's soff white hand
  Shall close dese tired old eyes.

"De dear Lord Jesus soon will call
  Old mammy home to him,
And he can wash my guilty soul
  From ebery spot of sin.

"And at his feet I shall lie down,
  Who died and rose for me;
And den, and not till den, my chile,
  Your mammy will be free.

"Come, little missus, say your prayers;
  Let ole mas Linkum 'lone,
The debil knows who b'longs to him,
  And he'll take care of his own."

Melt the Bells[19]

F. T. Rockett

Melt the bells, melt the bells,
  Still the tinkling on the plains,
And transmute the evening chimes
Into war's resounding rhymes,
  That the invaders may be slain
    By the bells.

Melt the bells, melt the bells,
  That for years have called to prayer,
And, instead, the cannon's roar
Shall resound the valleys o'er,
  That the foe may catch despair
    From the bells.

Melt the bells, melt the bells,
  Though it cost a tear to part

19. In 1862, General Beauregard appealed to the people of Memphis to give their church bells to the Confederacy so that they might be melted into cannons. Cited from *Blue and Gray*.

With the music they have made,
Where the friends we love are laid,
  With pale cheek and silent heart,
    'Neath the bells.

Melt the bells, melt the bells,
  Into cannon, vast and grim,
And the foe shall feel the ire
From each heaving lung of fire,
  And we'll put our trust in Him
    And the bells.

Melt the bells, melt the bells,
  And when foes no more attack,
And the lightning cloud of war
Shall roll thunderless and far,
  We will melt the cannon back
    Into bells.

Melt the bells, melt the bells,
  And they'll peal a sweeter chime,
And remind of all the brave
Who have sunk to glory's grave,
  And will sleep thro' coming time
    'Neath the bells.

Roll Call[20]

Nathaniel Graham Shepherd

"Corporal Green!" the Orderly cried;
  "Here!" was the answer, loud and clear,
  From the lips of a soldier who stood near;
And "Here!" was the word the next replied.

"Cyrus Drew!"—then a silence fell—
  This time no answer followed the call;
  Only his rear man had seen him fall,
Killed or wounded, he could not tell.

20. *Harper's New Monthly Magazine* December 1862; cited from CWSS.

There they stood, in the falling light,
  These men of battle, with grave, dark looks,
  As plain to be read as open books,
While slowly gathered the shades of night.

The fern on the hill-sides was splashed with blood,
  And down in the corn, where the poppies grew,
  Were redder stains than the poppies knew,
And crimson-dyed as the river's flood.

For the foe had crossed from the other side,
  That day, in the face of a murderous fire,
  That swept them down in its terrible ire;
And their life-blood went to color the tide.

"Herbert Cline!" At the call there came
  Two stalwart soldiers into the line,
  Bearing between them this Herbert Cline,
Wounded and bleeding, to answer his name.

"Ezra Kerr!"—and a voice answered, "Here!"
  "Hiram Kerr!" but no man replied:
  They were brothers, these two: the sad wind sighed,
And a shudder crept through the cornfield near.

"Ephraim Deane!"—then a soldier spoke;
  "Deane carried our regiment's colors," he said,
  "When our ensign was shot; I left him dead,
Just after the enemy wavered and broke.

"Close to the road-side his body lies;
  I paused a moment, and gave him to drink;
  He murmured his mother's name, I think.
And Death came with it and closed his eyes."

'Twas a victory—yes; but it cost us dear;
  For that company's roll, when called at night,
  Of a hundred men who went into the fight,
Numbered but twenty that answered, "*Here!*"

1863

Company E, 4th U.S. Colored Infantry, at Fort Lincoln. Library of Congress, Selected Civil War photographs compiled by Milhollen and Mugridge, LC B817-7890.

Boston Hymn[1]

Ralph Waldo Emerson

The word of the Lord by night
To the watching Pilgrims came,
As they sat by the seaside,
And filled their hearts with flame.

God said, I am tired of kings,
I suffer them no more;
Up to my ear the morning brings
The outrage of the poor.

Think ye I made this ball
A field of havoc and war,
Where tyrants great and tyrants small
Might harry the weak and poor?

My angel,—his name is Freedom,—
Choose him to be your king;
He shall cut pathways east and west,
And fend you with his wing.

Lo! I uncover the land
Which I hid of old time in the West,
As the sculptor uncovers his statue
When he has wrought his best;

I show Columbia, of the rocks
Which dip their foot in the seas
And soar to the air-borne flocks
Of clouds, and the boreal fleece.

I will divide my goods;
Call in the wretch and slave:

1. Read in Music Hall in Boston, January 1, 1863, to hail Lincoln's Emancipation Proclamation and collected in the *Rebellion Record* Vol. 7, 1863. Cited from *Ralph Waldo Emerson: Collected Poem and Translations*, 1994.

None shall rule but the humble,
And none but Toil shall have.

I will have never a noble,
No lineage counted great;
Fishers and choppers and ploughmen
Shall constitute a state.

Go, cut down trees in the forest,
And trim the straightest boughs;
Cut down trees in the forest,
And build me a wooden house.

Call the people together,
The young men and the sires,
The digger in the harvest field,
Hireling and him that hires;

And here in a pine state-house
They shall choose men to rule
In every needful faculty,
In church, and state, and school.

Lo, now! if these poor men
Can govern the land and sea,
And make just laws below the sun,
As planets faithful be.

And ye shall succor men;
'Tis nobleness to serve;
Help them who cannot help again:
Beware from right to swerve.

I break your bonds and masterships,
And I unchain the slave:
Free be his heart and hand henceforth,
As wind and wandering wave.

I cause from every creature
His proper good to flow:
As much as he is and doeth,
So much he shall bestow.

But, laying his hands on another
To coin his labor and sweat,
He goes in pawn to his victim
For eternal years in debt.

To-day unbind the captive,
So only are ye unbound;
Lift up a people from the dust,
Trump of their rescue, sound!

Pay ransom to the owner,
And fill the bag to the brim.
Who is the owner? The slave is owner,
And ever was. Pay him.

O North! give him beauty for rags,
And honor, O South! for his shame;
Nevada! coin thy golden crags
With Freedom's image and name.

Up! and the dusky race
That sat in darkness long,—
Be swift their feet as antelopes,
And as behemoth strong.

Come, East and West and North,
By races, as snow-flakes,
And carry my purpose forth,
Which neither halts nor shakes.

My will fulfilled shall be,
For, in daylight or in dark,
My thunderbolt has eyes to see
His way home to the mark.

The Reveille[2]

Bret Harte

Hark! I hear the tramp of thousands,
And of armed men the hum;
Lo! a nation's hosts have gathered
Round the quick-alarming drum,—
Saying: "Come,
Freemen, come!
Ere your heritage be wasted," said the quick-alarming drum.

"Let me of my heart take counsel;
War is not of life the sum;
Who shall stay and reap the harvest
When the autumn days shall come?
But the drum
Echoed: "Come!
Death shall reap the braver harvest," said the solemn-sounding drum.

"But when won the coming battle,
What of profit springs therefrom?
What if conquest, subjugation,
Even greater ills become?"
But the drum
Answered: "Come!
You must do the sum to prove it," said the Yankee-answering drum.

"What if, mid the cannons' thunder,
Whistling shot and bursting bomb
When my brothers fall around me,
Should my heart grow cold and numb?"
But the drum
Answered: "Come!
Better there in death united than in life a recreant,—Come!"

Thus they answered—hoping, fearing,
Some in faith and doubting some,

2. Harte published several poems during the Civil War in California newspapers and magazines; the first known publication of this poem is in an 1882 collection of Harte's *Poems*—the source of this text.

Till a trumpet-voice proclaiming,
Said: "My chosen people, come!"
Then the drum,
Lo! was dumb;
For the great heart of the nation, throbbing, answered: "Lord, we come!"

Conservative Chorus[3]

Anonymous

Abraham, spare the South,
Touch not a single slave;
Nor e'en by word of mouth
Disturb the thing, we crave.
'Twas our forefathers' hand
That Slavery begot;
There, Abraham, let it stand;
Thine acts shall harm it not.

Only a Soldier's Grave[4]

S. A. Jonas

Only a soldier's grave! Pass by,
For soldiers, like other mortals, die.
Parents he had—they are far away;
No sister weeps o'er the soldier's clay;
No brother comes, with a tearful eye:
It's only a soldier's grave—pass by.

True, he was loving, and young, and brave,
Though no glowing epitaph honors his grave;
No proud recital of virtues known,
Of griefs endured, or of triumphs won;
No tablet of marble, or obelisk high;—
Only a soldier's grave—pass by.

3. Cited from CWSS.
4. Collected in *War Poetry*.

Yet bravely he wielded his sword in fight,
And he gave his life in the cause of right!
When his hope was high, and his youthful dream
As warm as the sunlight on yonder stream;
His heart unvexed by sorrow or sigh;—
Yet, 'tis only a soldier's grave:—pass by.

Yet, should we mark it—the soldier's grave,
Some one may seek him in hope to save!
Some of the dear ones, far away,
Would bear him home to his native clay:
'Twere sad, indeed, should they wander nigh,
Find not the hillock, and pass him by.

Spring at the Capital[5]

Elizabeth Akers Allen

The poplar drops beside the way
Its tasseled plumes of silver gray;
The chestnut points its great brown buds, impatient for the laggard May.

The honeysuckles lace the wall;
The hyacinths grow fair and tall;
And mellow sun and pleasant wind and odorous bees are over all.

Down-looking in this snow-white bud,
How distant seems the war's red flood!
How far remote the streaming wounds, the sickening scent of human blood!

For Nature does not recognize
This strife that rends the earth and skies;
No war-dreams vex the winter sleep of clover-heads and daisy-eyes.

She holds her even way the same,
Though navies sink or cities flame;
A snow-drop is a snow-drop still, despite the Nation's joy or shame.

5. Although its composition and first publication dates are unknown, this poem was written between 1863 and 1865, when Allen lived in Washington, D.C.; cited from *Bugle-Echoes*.

When blood her grassy altar wets,
She sends the pitying violets
To heal the outrage with their bloom, and cover it with soft regrets.

O crocuses with rain-wet eyes,
O tender-lipped anemones,
What do you know of agony, and death, and blood-won victories?

No shudder breaks your sunshine trance,
Though near you rolls, with slow advance,
Clouding your shining leaves with dust, the anguish-laden ambulance.

Yonder a white encampment hums;
The clash of martial music comes;
And now your startled stems are all a-tremble with the jar of drums.

Whether it lessen or increase,
Or whether trumpets shout or cease,
Still deep within your tranquil hearts the happy bees are humming "Peace!"

O flowers! the soul that faints or grieves
New comfort from your lips receives;
Sweet confidence and patient faith are hidden in your healing leaves.

Help us to trust, still on and on,
That this dark night will soon be gone,
And that these battle-stains are but the blood-red trouble of the dawn—

Dawn of a broader, whiter day
Than ever blessed us with its ray—
A dawn beneath whose purer light all guilt and wrong shall fade away.

Then shall our nation break its bands,
And, silencing the envious lands,
Stand in the searching light unshamed, with spotless robe and clean white hands.

The Black Regiment[6]

George Henry Boker

Dark as the clouds of even,
Ranked in the western heaven,
Waiting the breath that lifts
All the dread mass, and drifts
Tempest and falling brand
Over a ruined land;—
So still and orderly,
Arm to arm, knee to knee,
Waiting the great event,
Stands the Black Regiment.

Down the long dusky line
Teeth gleam and eyeballs shine;
And the bright bayonet,
Bristling and firmly set,
Flashed with a purpose grand,
Long ere the sharp command
Of the fierce rolling drum
Told them their time had come,
Told them what work was sent
For the Black Regiment.

"Now," the flag-sergeant cried,
"Though death and hell betide,
Let the whole nation see
If we are fit to be
Free in this land; or bound
Down, like the whining hound,—
Bound with red stripes of pain
In our old chains again!"
Oh, what a shout there went
From the Black Regiment!

---

6. Published by the Supervisory Committee for Recruiting Colored Regiments, Port Hudson, Louisiana, May 27, 1863; cited from *Bugle-Echoes*.

"*Charge!*" Trump and drum awoke,
Onward the bondmen broke;
Bayonet and sabre-stroke
Vainly opposed their rush.
Through the wild battle's crush,
With but one thought aflush,
Driving their lords like chaff,
In the guns' mouths they laugh;
Or at the slippery brands
Leaping with open hands,
Down they tear man and horse,
Down in their awful course;
Trampling with bloody heel
Over the crashing steel,
All their eyes forward bent,
Rushed the Black Regiment.

"Freedom!" their battle-cry—
"Freedom! or leave to die!"
Ah! And they meant the word,
Not as with us 'tis heard,
Not a mere party shout:
They gave their spirits out;
Trusted the end to God,
And on the gory sod
Rolled in triumphant blood.

Glad to strike one free blow,
Whether for weal or woe;
Glad to breathe one free breath,
Though on the lips of death.
Praying—alas! in vain!—
That they might fall again,
So they could once more see
That burst to liberty!
This was what "freedom" lent
To this Black Regiment.

Hundreds on hundreds fell;
But they are resting well;

Scourges and shackles strong
Never shall do them wrong.

Oh, to the living few,
Soldiers, be just and true!
Hail them as comrades tried;
Fight with them side by side;
Never, in field or tent,
Scorn the Black Regiment.

Wouldst Thou Have Me Love Thee[7]

Alexander Beaufort Meek

Wouldst thou have me love thee, dearest!
  With a woman's proudest heart,
Which shall ever hold thee nearest,
  Shrined in its inmost heart?
Listen, then! My country's calling
  On her sons to meet the foe!
Leave these groves of rose and myrtle;
  Drop thy dreamy harp of love!
Like young Korner—scorn the turtle,
  When the eagle screams above!

Dost thou pause?—Let dastards dally—
  Do thou for thy country fight!
'Neath her noble emblem rally—
  "God, our country, and our right!"
Listen! now her trumpet's calling
  On her sons to meet the foe!
Woman's heart is soft and tender,
  But 'tis proud and faithful too:
Shall she be her land's defender?
  Lover! Soldier! up and do!

Seize thy father's falcion,
  Which once flashed as freedom's star!

7. *Richmond Dispatch*, reprinted under the title "War Song" and collected in *War Poetry*.

Till sweet peace—the bow and halcyon,
Stilled the stormy strife of war.
Listen! now thy country's calling
On her sons to meet her foe!
Sweet is love in moonlight bowers!
Sweet the altar and the flame!
Sweet the spring-time with her flowers!
Sweeter far the patriot's name!

Should the God who smiles above thee,
Doom thee to a soldier's grave,
Hearts will break, but fame will love thee,
Canonized among the brave!
Listen, then! thy country's calling
On her sons to meet the foe!
Rather would I view thee lying
On the last red field of strife,
'Mid thy country's heroes dying,
Than become a dastard's wife!

The Wood of Gettysburg[8]

Della Jerman Weeks

The ripe red berries of the wintergreen
Lure me to pause awhile
In this deep, tangled wood. I stop and lean
Down where these wild-flowers smile,
And rest me in this shade; for many a mile,
Through lane and dusty street,
I've walked with weary, weary feet;
And now I tarry mid this woodland scene,
'Mong ferns and mosses sweet.

Here all around me blows
The pale primrose.

8. *Legends of the War*, 1863, our source for this text; also published as "The Wood at Chancellorsville"—an earlier battle in 1863—in CWSS.

I wonder if the gentle blossom knows
The feeling at my heart—the solemn grief
So whelming and so deep
That it disdains relief,
And will not let me weep.
I wonder that the woodbine thrives and grows,
And is indifferent to the nation's woes.
For while these mornings shine, these blossoms bloom,
Impious rebellion wraps the land in gloom.

Nature, thou art unkind,
Unsympathizing, blind!
Yon lichen, clinging to th' o'erhanging rock,
Is happy, and each blade of grass,
O'er which unconsciously I pass,
Smiles in my face, and seems to mock
Me with its joy. Alas! I cannot find
One charm in bounteous nature, while the wind
That blows upon my cheek bears on each gust
The groans of my poor country, bleeding in the dust.

The air is musical with notes
That gush from wingéd warblers' throats,
And in the leafy trees
I hear the drowsy hum of bees.
Prone from the blinding sky
Dance rainbow-tinted sunbeams, thick with motes.
Daisies are shining, and the butterfly
Wavers from flower to flower—yet in this wood
The ruthless foeman stood,
And every turf is drench'd with human blood.

O heartless flowers!
O trees, clad in your robes of glistering sheen,
Put off this canopy of gorgeous green!
These are the hours
For mourning, not for gladness. While this smart
Of treason dire gashes the Nation's heart,
Let birds refuse to sing,
Or flowers to bloom upon the lap of spring.

Let Nature's face itself with tears o'erflow,
In deepest anguish for a People's woe.

While rank Rebellion stands
With blood of martyrs on his impious hands;
While Slavery, and chains,
And Cruelty, and direst Hate,
Uplift their heads within th'afflicted state,
And freeze the blood in every patriot's veins—
Let these old woodlands fair
Grow black with gloom, and from its thunder-lair
Let lightning leap, and scorch th'accursed air,
Until the suffering earth,
Of Treason sick, shall spew the monster forth—
And each regenerate sod
Be consecrate anew, to Freedom and to God!

Chickamauga, "The Stream of Death!"[9]

Anonymous

Chickamauga! Chickamauga!
  O'er thy dark and turbid wave
Rolls the death-cry of the daring,
  Rings the war-shout of the brave;
Round thy shore the red fires flashing,
  Startling shot and screaming shell—
Chickamauga, stream of battle,
  Who thy fearful tale shall tell?

Olden memories of horror,
  Sown by scourge of deadly plague,
Long had clothed thy circling forests
  With a terror vast and vague;
Now to gather fiercer vigor
  From the phantoms grim with gore,
Hurried by war's wilder carnage
  To their graves on thy lone shore.

9. *Richmond Sentinel*; cited from CWSS.

Long, with hearts subdued and saddened,
  As th'oppressor's hosts moved on,
Fell the arms of Freedom backward,
  Till our hopes had almost flown;
Till outspoke stern Valor's fiat—
  "Here th' invading wave shall stay;
Here shall cease the foe's proud progress;
  Here be crushed his grand array!"

Then, their eager hearts all throbbing
  Backward flashed each battle-flag
Of the veteran corps of Longstreet*,
  And the sturdy troops of Bragg*;
Fierce upon the foeman turning,
  All their pent-up wrath breaks out
In the furious battle-clangor,
  And the frenzied battle-shout.

Roll thy dark waves, Chickamauga;
  Trembles all thy ghastly shore,
With the rude shock of the onset,
  And the tumult's horrid roar:
As the Southern battle-giants
  Hurl their bolts of death along,
Breckinridge, the iron-hearted,
  Cheatham, chivalric and strong;—

Polk and Preston, gallant Buckner,
  Hill and Hindman, strong in might;
Cleburne, flower of manly valor;
  Hood, the Ajax of the fight;
Benning, bold and hardy warrior;
  Fearless, resolute Kershaw,
Mingle battle-yell and death-bolt,
  Volley fierce and wild hurrah!

At the volleys bleed their bodies,
  At the fierce shout shrink their souls,
While their fiery wave of vengeance
  On their quailing column rolls;

And the parched throats of the stricken
  Breathe for air the roaring flame;
Horrors of that hell foretasted,
  Who shall ever dare to name?

Borne by those who, stiff and mangled,
  Paid, upon that bloody field,
Direful, cringing, awe-struck homage
  To the sword our heroes wield;
And who felt, by fiery trial,
  That the men who will be free,
Though in conflict baffled often,
  Ever will unconquered be!

Learned, though long unchecked they spoil us,
  Dealing desolation round,
Marking with the tracks of ruin
  Many a rod of Southern ground.
Yet, whatever course they follow,
  Somewhere in their pathway flows,
Dark and deep, a Chickamauga,
  Stream of death to vandal foes!

They have found it darkly flowing
  By Manassas' famous plain,
And by rushing Shenandoah
  Met the tide of woe again:
Chickahominy! immortal,
  By the long, ensanguined flight,
Rappahannock, glorious river,
  Twice renowned for matchless fight.

Heed the story, dastard spoilers,
  Mark the tale these waters tell,
Ponder well your fearful lesson,
  And the doom that there befell:
Learn to shun the Southern vengeance,
  Sworn upon the votive sword,
"Every stream a Chickamauga
  To the vile, invading horde!"

On the Heights of Mission Ridge[10]

J. Augustine Signaigo

When the foes, in conflict heated,
  Battled over road and bridge,
While Bragg* sullenly retreated
  From the heights of Mission Ridge—
There, amid the pines and wildwood,
  Two opposing colonels fell,
Who had schoolmates been in childhood,
  And had loved each other well.

There, amid the roar and rattle,
  Facing Havoc's fiery breath,
Met the wounded two in battle,
  In the agonies of death.
But they saw each other reeling
  On the dead and dying men,
And the old time, full of feeling,
  Came upon them once again.

When that night the moon came creeping,
  With its gold streaks, o'er the slain,
She beheld two soldiers, sleeping,
  Free from every earthly pain.
Close beside the mountain heather,
  Where the rocks obscure the sand,
They had died, it seems, together,
  As they clasped each other's hand.

10. Collected in *War Poetry*. This and the next poem refer to the final battle of a series of encounters from September through November 1863 over control of Chattanooga, Tennessee, and a passage through the mountains to Alabama and Georgia. Confederates succeeded in holding back the Union army in the Battle of Chickamauga on September 18–20, 1863, but the Union army finally overpowered Confederate forces on November 25 at Missionary Ridge—often referred to as Mission Ridge.

Negro Song of Mission Ridge[11]

ANONYMOUS

Ole massa he come dancin' out,
And call de black uns roun',
Oh—O! Oh—O!
He feel so good he couldn't stan'
Wid boff feet on de groun'.
Oh—O—ee!

Say! don't you hear dem 'tillery guns
You niggers? don't you hear?
Oh—O! Oh—O!
Ole Gen'ral Bragg's* a mowin' down
De Yankees ober dar!
Oh—O—ee!

You Pomp, and Pete, and Dinah too,
You'll catch it now, I swear,
Oh—O! Oh—O!
I'll whip you good for mixin' wid
Dem Yanks when dey was here.
Oh—O—ee!

Here comes our troops! in crowds on crowds!
I knows dat red and gray.
Oh—O! Oh—O!
But, Lord! what makes dem hurry so,
And frow dere guns away?
Oh—O—ee!

Ole massa den keep boff feet still,
And stared wid boff he eyes,
Oh—O! Oh—O!
Till he seed de blue-coats jes behin',
Which cotch him wid surprise!
Oh—O—ee!

11. Collected in CWSS. Many dialect poems were written by white poets at this time; this is probably one of them.

Ole massa's busy duckin' 'bout
In de swamps up to he knees.
                    Oh—O! Oh—O!
While Dinah, Pomp, and Pete, de look
As if dey's mighty pleas'.
                    Oh—O—ee!

My Army Cross Over[12]

Anonymous

My army cross over,
My army cross over,
O, Pharaoh's army drownded!
My army cross over.

We'll cross de mighty river,
    My army cross over;
We'll cross de river Jordan,
    My army cross over;
We'll cross de danger water,
    My army cross over;
We'll cross de mighty Myo,
    My army cross over.

My army cross over,
My army cross over,
O, Pharaoh's army drownded!
My army cross over.

---

12. Thomas W. Higginson, the white abolitionist who served as the colonel of the first regiment of emancipated slaves, heard black soldiers sing this song in training camp on the Sea Islands off the South Carolina coast and printed it in his *Army Life in a Black Regiment*, 1870, the source of this text.

Ride In, Kind Saviour[13]

ANONYMOUS

Ride in, kind Saviour!
No man can hinder me.
O, Jesus is a mighty man!
No man can hinder me.
We're marching through Virginny fields.
No man can hinder me.
O, Satan is a busy man,
No man can hinder me.
And he has his sword and shield,
No man can hinder me.
O, old Secesh* done come and gone!
No man can hinder me.

Ready[14]

PHOEBE CARY

Loaded with gallant soldiers,
A boat shot into the land,
And lay at the right of Rodman's Point,
With her keel upon the sand.

Lightly, gayly, they came to shore,
And never a man afraid;
When sudden the enemy opened fire
From his deadly ambuscade.

Each man fell flat on the bottom
Of the boat; and the captain said:
"If we lie here, we all are captured,
And the first who moves is dead!"

13. Visiting the schools for emancipated slaves in the Sea Islands, Charles Northam described hearing this song in an article he wrote for the *New York Evening Post* of March 25, 1863. Cited from Higginson's *Army Life in a Black Regiment*.

14. Collected in *Bugle-Echoes*; cited from *The Poetical Works of Alice and Phoebe Cary*, 1882.

Then out spoke a negro sailor,
No slavish soul had he:
"Somebody's got to die, boys,
And it might as well be me!"

Firmly he rose, and fearlessly
Stepped out into the tide;
He pushed the vessel safely off,
Then fell across her side:

Fell, pierced by a dozen bullets,
As the boat swung clear and free;—
But there wasn't a man of them that day
Who was fitter to die than he!

The Jacket of Gray[15]

Caroline A. Ball

Fold it up carefully, lay it aside;
Tenderly touch it, look on it with pride;
For dear to our hearts must it be evermore,
The jacket of gray our loved soldier-boy wore.

Can we ever forget when he joined the brave band
That rose in defense of our dear Southern land,
And in his bright youth hurried on to the fray,
How proudly he donned it—the jacket of gray?

His fond mother blessed him, and looked up above,
Commending to heaven the child of her love;
What anguish was hers mortal tongue can not say,
When he passed from her sight in the jacket of gray.

But her country had called and she would not repine,
Though costly the sacrifice placed on its shrine;
Her heart's dearest hopes on its altar she lay,
When she sent out her boy in the jacket of gray.

15. An extremely popular poem, set to music by Stratford Benjamin Woodbury, and one of the many focused on women's sacrifices, grief, and pride in encouraging husbands and sons to fight. Collected in *Southern Poems*.

Months passed, and war's thunder rolled over the land,
Unsheathed was the sword, and lighted the brand;
We heard in the distance the sound of the fray,
And prayed for our boy in the jacket of gray.

Ah vain, all in vain, were our prayers and our tears,
The glad shout of victory rang in our ears;
But our treasured one on the red battle-field lay,
While the life-blood oozed out on the jacket of gray.

His young comrades found him, and tenderly bore
The cold lifeless form to his home by the shore;
Oh, dark were our hearts on that terrible day,
When we saw our dead boy in the jacket of gray.

Ah, spotted and tattered, and stained now with gore,
Was the garment which once he so proudly wore;
We bitterly wept as we took it away,
And replaced with death's white robe the jacket of gray.

We laid him to rest in his cold narrow bed,
And graved on the marble we placed o'er his head
As the proudest tribute our sad hearts could pay—
"He never disgraced it, the jacket of gray."

Then fold it up carefully, lay it aside,
Tenderly touch it, look on it with pride;
For dear must it be to our hearts evermore,
The jacket of gray our loved soldier-boy wore!

Death the Peacemaker[16]

Ellen Flagg

A waste of land, a sodden plain,
  A lurid sunset sky,
With clouds that fled and faded fast
  In ghastly phantasy;

16. The authorship and title of this poem are disputed, as detailed in the preface to this volume; cited from *Blue and Gray*.

A field upturned by trampling feet,
    A field up-piled with slain,
With horse and rider blent in death
    Upon the battle-plain.

Two soldiers, lying as they fell
    Upon the reddened clay,
In daytime, foes; at night, in peace,
    Breathing their lives away.
Brave hearts had stirred each manly breast;
    Fate only made them foes;
And lying, dying, side by side,
    A softened feeling rose.

"Our time is short," one faint voice said.
    "Today we've done our best
On different sides. What matters now?
    Tomorrow we're at rest.
Life lies behind. I might not care
    For only my own sake;
But far away are other hearts
    That this day's work will break.

"Among New Hampshire's snowy hills
    There pray for me, tonight,
A woman and a little girl,
    With hair like golden light."
And at the thought broke forth, at last,
    The cry of anguish wild
That would no longer be repressed—
    "O God! my wife and child!"

"And," said the other dying man,
    "Across the Georgia plain
There watch and wait for me loved ones
    I'll never see again.
A little girl with dark bright eyes
    Each day waits at the door;
The father's step, the father's kiss,
    Will never meet her more.

"Today we sought each other's lives;
Death levels all that now
For soon before God's mercy-seat
Together we shall bow.
Forgive each other while we may;
Life's but a weary game;
And right or wrong, the morning sun
Will find us dead the same."

The dying lips the pardon breathe,
The dying hands entwine;
The last ray dies, and over all
The stars from heaven shine:
And the little girl with golden hair,
And one with dark eyes bright,
On Hampshire's hills and Georgia Plain,
Were fatherless that night.

The Copperhead*[17]

BRET HARTE

There is peace in the swamp where the Copperhead sleeps,
Where the waters are stagnant, the white vapor creeps,
Where the musk of Magnolia hangs thick in the air,
And the lilies' phylacteries broaden in prayer.
There is peace in the swamp, though the quiet is death,
Though the mist is miasma, the upas-tree's breath,
Though no echo awakes to the cooing of doves,—
There is peace: yes, the peace that the Copperhead loves.

Go seek him: he coils in the ooze and the drip,
Like a thong idly flung from the slave-driver's whip;

17. *The Golden Era* March 29, 1863; collected in *Poems*. Also known as Peace Democrats, Copperheads often promoted peace that would either give the South independence or readmit Southern states into the Union on the old terms, as slave states. Such peace was seen as especially treasonous to the Union because it masqueraded as merely opposing the violence of the war. Especially during times when the Union was not faring well on the military field, Peace Democrats gained in relative political strength.

But beware the false footstep,—the stumble that brings
A deadlier lash than the overseer swings.
Never arrow so true, never bullet so dread,
As the straight steady stroke of that hammer-shaped head;
Whether slave or proud planter, who braves that dull crest
Woe to him who shall trouble the Copperhead's rest!

Then why waste your labors, brave hearts and strong men.
In tracking a trail to the Copperhead's den?
Lay your axe to the cypress, hew open the shade
To the free sky and sunshine Jehovah has made;
Let the breeze of the North sweep the vapors away,
Till the stagnant lake ripples, the freed waters play;
And then to your heel can you righteously doom
The Copperhead born of its shadow and gloom!

A Prayer for Peace[18]

Severn Teackle Wallis

Peace! Peace! God of our fathers, grant us Peace!
Unto our cry of anguish and despair
Give ear and pity! From the lonely homes,
Where widowed beggary and orphaned woe
Fill their poor urns with tears; from trampled plains,
Where the bright harvest Thou hast sent us rots—
The blood of them who should have garnered it
Calling to Thee—from fields of carnage, where
The foul-beaked vultures, sated, flap their wings
O'er crowded corpses, that but yesterday
Bore hearts of brother, beating high with love
And common hopes and pride, all blasted now—
Father of Mercies! not alone from these
Our prayer and wail are lifted. Not alone
Upon the battle's seared and desolate track!
Nor with the sword and flame, is it, O God,
That thou hast smitten us. Around our hearths,

18. Cited from *Blue and Gray.*

And in the crowded streets and busy marts,
Where echo whispers not the far-off strife
That slays our loved ones; in the solemn halls
Of safe and quiet counsel—nay, beneath
The temple roofs that we have reared to Thee,
And 'mid their rising incense—God of Peace!

The curse of war is on us. Greed and hate
Hungering for gold and blood; Ambition, bred
Of passionate vanity and sordid lusts,
Mad with the base desire of tyrannous sway
Over men's souls and thoughts, have set their price
Of human hecatombs, and sell and buy
Their sons and brothers for the shambles. Priests,
With white, anointed, supplicating hands,
From Sabbath unto Sabbath clasped to Thee,
Burn in their tingling pulses, to fling down
Thy censers and Thy cross, to clutch the throats
Of kinsmen, by whose cradles they were born,
Or grasp the hand of Herod, and go forth
Till Rachel hath no children left to slay.
The very name of Jesus, writ upon
Thy shrines beneath the spotless, outstretched wings
Of Thine Almighty Dove, is wrapt and hid
With bloody battle-flags, and from the spires
That rise above them angry banners flout
The skies to which they point, amid the clang
Of rolling war-songs tuned to mock Thy praise.

All things once prized and honored are forgot;
The freedom that we worshipped next to Thee;
The manhood that was freedom's spear and shield;
The proud, true heart; the brave, outspoken word,
Which might be stifled, but could never wear
The guise, whate'er the profit, of a lie;
All these are gone, and in their stead have come
The vices of the miser and the slave—
Scorning no shame that bringeth gold or power,
Knowing no love, or faith, or reverence,
Or sympathy, or tie, or aim, or hope,

Save as begun in self, and ending there.
With vipers like to these, oh! blessed God!
Scourge us no longer! Send us down, once more,
Some shining seraph in Thy glory clad
To wake the midnight of our sorrowing
With tidings of good-will and peace to men;
And if that star, that through the darkness led
Earth's wisdom the guide, not our folly no,
Oh, be the lightning Thine Evangelist,
With all its fiery, forked tongues, to speak
The unanswerable message of Thy will.

Peace! Peace! God of our fathers, grant us peace!
Peace to our hearts, and at Thine altars; peace
On the red waters and their blighted shores;
Peace for the 'leaguered cities, and the hosts
That watch and bleed around them and within,
Peace for the homeless and the fatherless;
Peace for the captive on his weary way,
And the mad crowds who jeer his helplessness;
For them that suffer, them that do the wrong
Sinning and sinned against. O God! for all;
For a distracted, torn, and bleeding land—
Speed the glad tidings! Give us, give us Peace!

In Libby Prison*—New-Year's Eve 1863–4[19]

Frederick A. Bartleson

'Tis twelve o'clock! Within my prison dreary—
My head upon my hand—sitting so weary,
Scanning the future, musing upon the past,
Pondering the fate that here my lot has cast,
The hoarse cry of the sentry, pacing on his beat
Wakens the echoes of the silent street:
"All is well!"

19. *Rebellion Record* Vol. 8, 1865.

Ah! is it so? My fellow-captive sleeping
Where the barred window strictest watch is keeping,
Dreaming of home and wife and prattling child—
Of the sequestered vale, the mountain wild—
Tell me, when cruel morn shall break again,
Wilt thou repeat the sentinel's refrain,
"All is well!"

And thou, my country! wounded, pale, and bleeding,
Thy children deaf to a fond mother's pleading—
Stabbing with cruel hate the nurturing breast,
To which their infancy in love was prest—
Recount thy wrongs, thy many sorrows name;
Then to the nations—if thou canst—proclaim:
"All is well!"

But through the clouds the sun is slowly breaking—
Hope from her long, deep sleep is awaking:
Speed the time, Father! when the bow of peace,
Spanning the gulf, shall bid the tempest cease—
When to men, clasping each other by the hand,
Shall shout once more, in a united land:
"All is well!"

1864

"Compromise with the South." Lithograph by Thomas Nast, reproduced in *Harper's Weekly*, September 3, 1864. General Research Division, The New York Public Library, Astor, Lenox and Tilden Foundations.

From The Day and the War[1]

JAMES MADISON BELL

Though Tennyson, the poet king,
  Has sung of Balaklava's charge,
Until his thund'ring cannons ring
  From England's center to her marge,
The pleasing duty still remains
To sing a people from their chains—
To sing what none have yet assay'd,
The wonders of the Black Brigade.
The war had raged some twenty moons,
Ere they in columns or platoons
To win them censure or applause,
Were marshal'd in the Union cause—
Prejudged of slavish cowardice,
While many a taunt and foul device
Came weekly forth with Harper's sheet,
To feed that base, infernal cheat.

  But how they would themselves demean,
Has since most gloriously been seen.
'Twas seen at Millikin's dread bend!
Where e'en the Furies seemed to lend
To dark Secession all their aid,
To crush the Union Black Brigade.

The war waxed hot, and bullets flew
  Like San Francisco's summer sand,

1. Composed and recited for the first anniversary celebration of the Emancipation Proclamation; cited from *African-American Poetry*. The complete poem is 750 lines long and reviews the history of African American life from slavery through emancipation; these lines describe the June 1863 battle of Millikin's Bend, in which black troops fought valiantly. Tennyson's 1854 "The Charge of the Light Brigade" memorializes the Crimean War's allied victory at the Battle of Balaclava. The upas tree, which has poisonous sap, was understood as a metaphor for discrimination against blacks—here, apparently a reference to the Kansas-Nebraska Act (see Time Line, 1854).

But they were there to dare and do,
    E'en to the last, to save the land.
And when the leaders of their corps
    Grew wild with fear, and quit the field,
The dark remembrance of their scars
    Before them rose, they could not yield:
And, sounding o'er the battle din,
    They heard their standard-bearer cry—
"Rally! and prove that ye are men!
    Rally! and let us do or die!
For war, nor death, shall boast a shade
    To daunt the Union Black Brigade!"

And thus he played the hero's part,
    Till on the ramparts of the foe
A score of bullets pierced his heart,
    He sank within the trench below.
His comrades saw, and fired with rage,
Each sought his man, him to engage
In single combat. Ah! 'twas then
The Black Brigade proved they were men!
For ne'er did Swiss! or Russ! or knight!
    Against such fearful odds arrayed,
With more persistent valor fight,
    Than did the Union Black Brigade!

As five to one, so stood their foes,
When that defiant shout arose,
And 'long their closing columns ran,
Commanding each to choose his man!
And ere the sound had died away,
Full many a ranting rebel lay
Gasping piteously for breath—
Struggling with the pangs of death,
From bayonet thrust or shining blade,
Plunged to the hilt by the Black Brigade.
    And thus they fought, and won a name—
None brighter on the scroll of Fame;
For out of one full corps of men,
But one remained unwounded, when

The dreadful fray had fully past—
All killed or wounded but the last!

And though they fell, as has been seen,
Each slept his lifeless foes between,
And marked the course and paved the way
To ushering in a better day.
Let Balaklava's cannons roar,
And Tennyson his hosts parade,
But ne'er was seen and never more
The equals of the Black Brigade!

Then nerve thy heart, gird on thy sword,
For dark Oppression's ruthless horde
And thy tried friends are in the field—
Say which shall triumph, which shall yield?
Shall they that heed not man nor God—
Vile monsters of the *gory rod*—
Dark forgers of the *rack* and *chain:*
Shall *they* prevail—and Thraldom's reign,
With all his dark unnumber'd ills,
Become eternal as the hills!
No! by the blood of freemen slain,
On hot-contested field and main,
And by the mingled sweat and tears,
Extorted through these many years
From Afric's patient sons of toil—
Weak victims of a braggart's spoil—
This bastard plant, the Upas tree,
Shall not supplant our liberty!

Sambo's Right To Be Kilt[2]

Charles Graham Halpine

Some tell us 'tis a burning shame
  To make the naygers fight;
An' that the thrade of bein' kilt
  Belongs but to the white:
But as for me, upon my sowl!
  So liberal are we here,
I'll let Sambo be murthered instead of myself,
  On every day in the year.
    On every day in the year, boys,
      And in every hour of the day;
    The right to be kilt I'll divide wid him,
      And divil a word I'll say.

In battle's wild commotion
  I shouldn't at all object
If Sambo's body should stop a ball
  That was comin' for me direct;
And the prod of a Southern bagnet,
  So ginerous are we here,
I'll resign, and let Sambo take it,
  On every day in the year!
    On every day in the year, boys,
      And wid none o' your nasty pride,
    All my right in a Southern bagnet prod,
      Wid Sambo I'll divide!

The men who object to Sambo
  Should take his place and fight;
And it's betther to have a nayger's hue
  Than a liver that's wake and white.

---

2. Published under the pseudonym Private Miles O'Reilly and collected in Halpine's *Life and Adventures, Songs, Services, and Speeches of Private Miles O'Reilly*, 1864, the source of our text. Some of the most virulent antiblack racism in the North came from the immigrant Irish. While the poem's first two stanzas are clearly racist, by the final stanza "Private O'Reilly" expresses a grudging admiration for the courage and skill of black soldiers. This mixture of prejudice and respect was representative of many white Union soldiers' attitudes toward black soldiers. See **Frances E. W. Harper**'s poem **"Lines to Miles O'Reiley."**

Though Sambo's black as the ace of spades,
His finger a thrigger can pull,
And his eye runs sthraight on the barrel-sights
From undher his thatch of wool.
So hear me all, boys darlin',
Don't think I'm tippin' you chaff,
The right to be kilt we'll divide wid him,
And give him the largest half!

Confederate Song of Freedom[3]

EMILY M. WASHINGTON

March on, ye children of the brave,
Descendants of the free!
On to the hero's bloody grave
Or glorious liberty!
On, on—with clashing sword and drum,
The foe!—they come! they come!—strike home,
For more than safety, or for life,
For more than mother, child, or wife,
Strike home for Liberty!

Charge, charge! nor shed the pitying tear,
Too long hath mercy plead!
Charge, charge! and share the hero's bier,
Or strike the foeman dead!
Charge, charge! for more than vital gains,
Strike home and rend the freeman's chains,
For more than safety, or for life,
For more than mother, child, or wife,
Strike home for Liberty!

Draw, draw—by every hope this hour
That animates the brave!
Draw!—strike!—and rend the foeman's power
Or fill the patriot's grave!
Strike—die—or conquer with the free,

3. Collected in the *Rebellion Record* Vol. 8, 1865.

Strike home, strike home, for Liberty—
For more than glory, safety, life,
For more than mother, child, or wife,
Strike home for Liberty!

At Fort Pillow*[4]

JAMES R. RANDALL

You shudder as you think upon
The carnage of the grim report,
The desolation when we won
The inner trenches of the fort.

But there are deeds you may not know,
That scourge the pulses into strife;
Dark memories of deathless woe
Pointing the bayonet and knife.

The house is ashes where I dwelt,
Beyond the mighty inland sea;
The tombstones shattered where I knelt,
By that old church at Pointe Coupee.

The Yankee fiends, that came with fire,
Camped on the consecrated sod,
And trampled in the dust and mire
The Holy Eucharist of God!

The spot where darling mother sleeps,
Beneath the glimpse of yon sad moon,
Is crushed, with splintered marble heaps,
To stall the horse of some dragoon.

God! when I ponder that black day
It makes my frantic spirit wince;

4. *Wilmington Journal* April 25, 1864; cited from *War Poetry*. In stanzas 1 and 16, the author responds to reports of the Confederacy's deliberate killing of black soldiers in this battle by claiming not to have participated in it. The entire poem constitutes a defense against the North's moral outrage at this battle, through the author's claim that he himself is responding to the moral outrages of the disturbance of his mother's grave and his sister's rape by a Union soldier.

I marched—with Longstreet*—far away,
But have beheld the ravage since.

The tears are hot upon my face,
When thinking what bleak fate befell
The only sister of our race—
A thing too horrible to tell.

They say that, ere her senses fled,
She rescue of her brothers cried;
Then feebly bowed her stricken head,
Too pure to live thus—so she died.

Two of those brothers heard no plea;
With their proud hearts forever still—
John shrouded by the Tennessee,
And Arthur there at Malvern Hill*.

But I have heard it everywhere,
Vibrating like a passing knell;
'Tis as perpetual as the air,
And solemn as a funeral bell.

By scorched lagoon and murky swamp
My wrath was never in the lurch;
I've killed the picket in his camp,
And many a pilot on his perch.

With steady rifle, sharpened brand,
A week ago, upon my steed,
With Forrest* and his warrior band,
I made the hell-hounds writhe and bleed.

You should have seen our leader go
Upon the battle's burning marge,
Swooping, like falcon, on the foe,
Heading the gray line's iron charge!

All outcasts from our ruined marts,
We heard th'undying serpent hiss,
And in the desert of our hearts
The fatal spell of Nemesis.

The Southern yell rang loud and high
  The moment that we thundered in,
Smiting the demons hip and thigh,
  Cleaving them to the very chin.

My right arm bared for fiercer play,
  The left one held the rein in slack;
In all the fury of the fray
  I sought the white man, not the black.

The dabbled clots of brain and gore
  Across the swirling sabers ran;
To me each brutal visage bore
  The front of one accursed man.

Throbbing along the frenzied vein,
  My blood seemed kindled into song—
The death-dirge of the sacred slain,
  The slogan of immortal wrong.

It glared athwart the dripping glaves,
  It blazed in each avenging eye—
The thought of desecrated graves,
  And some lone sister's desperate cry!

In the Wilderness[5]

George Henry Boker

Mangled, uncared for, suffering thro' the night
  With heavenly patience the poor boy had lain;
Under the dreary shadows, left and right,
  Groaned on the wounded, stiffened out the slain.
    What faith sustained his lone,
    Brave heart to make no moan,
To send no cry from that blood-sprinkled sod,
Is a close mystery with him and God.

5. Collected in *Poems of the War*; written in reference to the Battle of the Wilderness, May 7, 1864.

But when the light came, and the morning dew
   Glittered around him, like a golden lake,
And every dripping flower with deepened hue
   Looked through its tears for very pity's sake,
      He moved his aching head
      Upon his rugged bed,
And smiled as a blue violet, virgin-meek,
Laid her pure kiss upon his withered cheek.

At once there circled in his waking heart
   A thousand memories of distant home;
Of how those same blue violets would start
   Along his native fields, and some would roam
      Down his dear humming brooks,
      To hide in secret nooks,
And, shyly met, in nodding circles swing,
Like gossips murmuring at belated Spring.

And then he thought of the beloved hands
   That with his own had plucked the modest flower.
The blue-eyed maiden, crowned with golden bands,
   Who ruled as sovereign of that sunny hour.
      She at whose soft command
      He joined the mustering band,
She for whose sake he lay so firm and still,
Despite his pangs, nor questioned then her will.

So, lost in thought, scarce conscious of the deed,
   Culling the violets, here and there he crept
Slowly—ah! slowly,—for his wound would bleed;
   And the sweet flowers themselves half smiled, half wept,
      To be thus gathered in
      By hands so pale and thin,
By fingers trembling as they neatly laid
Stem upon stem, and bound them in a braid.

The strangest posy ever fashioned yet
   Was clasped against the bosom of the lad,
As we, the seekers for the wounded, set
   His form upon our shoulders bowed and sad;

Though he but seemed to think
How violets nod and wink;
And as we cheered him, for the path was wild,
He only looked upon his flowers and smiled.

Sonnet[6]

George Henry Boker

Brave comrade, answer! When you joined the war,
What left you? "Wife and children, wealth and friends,
A storied home whose ancient roof-tree bends
Above such thoughts as love tells o'er and o'er."
Had you no pang or struggle? "Yes; I bore
Such pain on parting as at hell's gate rends
The entering soul, when from its grasp ascends
The last faint virtue which on earth it wore."
You loved your home, your kindred, children, wife;
You loathed yet plunged into war's bloody whirl!—
What urged you? "Duty! Something more than life.
That which made Abraham bare the priestly knife,
And Isaac kneel, or that young Hebrew girl
Who sought her father coming from the strife."

The Patriot Ishmael Day[7]

William H. Hayward

Come forth, my muse, now don't refuse;
Assist me in this lay,
To sing of one—"My Maryland's" son—
The patriot Ishmael Day.

6. Collected in *Poems of the War*; Boker did not title this sonnet.

7. According to the *Baltimore Sun* and the memoir of Colonel Harry Gilmore, *Four Years In The Saddle* (1866), in July 1864, a sixty-five-year-old Maryland farmer named Ishmael Day shot Confederate army ordnance sergeant Eugene Fields, who tried to remove the Union flag that Day had refused to take down from his house after being ordered to do so. Day's house was then looted and burned by the Confederate forces. See **James Randall**'s **"My Maryland."** Collected in CWSS.

One Monday morn, at early dawn,
The hour when good men pray,
A rebel host, with threats and boast,
Came on to scare old Day.

He soon had word—the noise he heard
In the distance far away—
That Gilmore's men were coming then
To capture Ishmael Day.

"That's what's the matter—O, what a clatter!
I'll keep them awhile at bay,
Till I hoist my flag, of which I brag—"
Said the brave old Ishmael Day.

On rushed the crowd, with curses loud,
Begrimed with dust and gray;
"My flag I'll nail to the garden pale,
And die by it," said Day.

The thieving horde came down the road—
They had no time to stay.
"Our flag is here—touch it who dare!"
Shouted old Ishmael Day.

A trooper rushed, with whiskey flushed,
Swore he'd take that rag away.
"Let any man dare try that plan,
I'll shoot him," says old Day.

He feared the cock of his old flint-lock
Might miss, so this prayer did say:
That a load of duck-shot might pepper him hot
By the hands of Ishmael Day.

On the raider came—old Day was game;
Reb swore that flag shouldn't stay;
With a curse and a frown, cried, "Down with it, down!"
Bang! blazed away Ishmael Day.

Flint-lock he could trust, for down in the dust
The traitorous rebel lay,
Crying, "Spare my life, I'm tired of this strife."
"So am I," said Ishmael Day.

Now let each loyal heart in our cause take a part,
  Do his duty, watch, fight, and pray;
Shoulder his gun, stand by, never run,
  And imitate Ishmael Day.

Then we boldly say, a few men like Day,
  With guns, ammunition at hand,
We need not be afraid of Gilmore's next raid
  On the soil of "My Maryland."

I now close my song, for fear it's too long;
  On this subject I could much more say;
Let us all shout hosanna to the Star-spangled Banner,
  And hurrah for brave Ishmael Day.

The Pride of Battery B[8]

Frank H. Gassaway

South Mountain towering on our right,
  Far off the river lay,
And over on the wooded height
  We held their lines at bay.

At last the muttering guns were still,
  The day died slow and wan;
At last the gunner's pipes did fill,
  The sergeant's yarns began.

When, as the wind a moment blew
  Aside the fragrant flood
Our brierwoods raised, within our view
  A little maiden stood.

A tiny tot of six or seven,
  From fireside fresh she seemed
(Of such a little one in heaven
  One soldier often dreamed).

8. This poem refers to the countryside around Sharpsburg, Maryland, where the Battle of Antietam was fought; there was at least one Battery B in both Union and Confederate armies. Cited from *Blue and Gray*.

And as we stared, her little hand
  Went to her curly head
In grave salute. "And who are you?"
  At length the sergeant said.

"And where's your home?" He growled again,
  She lisped out, "Who is me?
Why, don't you know? I'm little Jane,
  The pride of Battery B.

"My home? Why, that was burned away,
  And Pa and Ma are dead,
And so I ride the guns all day,
  Along with Sergeant Ned.

"And I've a drum that's not a toy,
  A cap with feathers, too,
And I march beside the drummer boy
  On Sundays at review.

"But now, our 'bacca's all give out,
  The men can't have their smoke.
And so they're cross. Why, even Ned
  Won't play with me and joke!

"And the big colonel said today—
  I hate to hear him swear—
He'd give a leg for a good pipe
  Like the Yank had over there.

"And so I thought, when beat the drum,
  And the big guns were still,
I'd creep beneath the tent and come
  Down here across the hill,

"And beg, good Master Yankee men,
  You give me some Lone Jack,
Please do; when we get some again
  I'll surely bring it back.

"Indeed! I will, for Ned, says he,
  If I do what I say
I'll be a general yet, maybe,
  And ride a prancing bay."

We brimmed her tiny apron o'er;
You should have heard her laugh
And each man from his scanty store
Shook out a generous half!

To kiss the little mouth, stooped down
A score of grimy men,
Until the sergeant's husky voice
Said, "'Tention, squad!" and then

We gave her escort, till good-night
The pretty waif we bid,
And watched her toddle out of sight
Or else 'twas tears that hid

Her tiny form—nor turned about
A man, nor spoke a word,
Till after awhile a far, hoarse shout
Upon the wind we heard.

We sent it back, then cast sad eyes
Upon the scene around;
A baby's hand had touched the ties
That brothers once had bound.

That's all—save when the dawn awoke
Again the work of hell,
And through the sullen clouds of smoke
The screaming missiles fell.

Our general often rubbed his glass
And marveled much to see
Not a single shell that whole day fell
In the camp of Battery B.

Sheridan's Ride*[9]

THOMAS BUCHANAN READ

Up from the South, at break of day,
Bringing to Winchester fresh dismay,
The affrighted air with a shudder bore,
Like a herald in haste, to the chieftain's door,
The terrible grumble and rumble and roar,
Telling the battle was on once more,
And Sheridan twenty miles away.

And wider still those billows of war
Thundered along the horizon's bar,
And louder yet into Winchester rolled
The roar of that red sea, uncontrolled,
Making the blood of the listener cold
As he thought of the stake in that fiery fray,
With Sheridan twenty miles away.

But there is a road from Winchester town,
A good, broad highway leading down;
And there, through the flush of the morning light,
A steed as black as the steeds of night,
Was seen to pass, as with eagle flight:
As if he knew the terrible need,
He stretched away with his utmost speed.
Hills rose and fell; but his heart was gay,
With Sheridan fifteen miles away.

Still sprang from those swift hoofs, thundering south,
The dust, like smoke from the cannon's mouth,
Or the trail of a comet, sweeping faster and faster,
Foreboding to traitors the doom of disaster;
The heart of the steed, and the heart of the master
Were beating, like prisoners assaulting their walls,

9. This poem was evidently written soon after the event and has remained the most famous of several poems written about Sheridan's* ride. Republicans used the poem at political rallies to raise the level of patriotic fervor, in support of Lincoln's reelection. See **Melville**'s **"Sheridan at Cedar Creek."** Cited from CWSS.

Impatient to be where the battle-field calls;
Every nerve of the charger was strained to full play,
With Sheridan only ten miles away.

Under his spurning feet the road
Like an arrowy Alpine river flowed;
And the landscape sped away behind
Like an ocean flying before the wind;
And the steed, like a bark fed with furnace ire,
Swept on, with his wild eye full of fire.
But, lo! he is nearing his heart's desire;
He is snuffing the smoke of the roaring fray,
With Sheridan only five miles away.

The first that the General saw were the groups
Of stragglers, and then the retreating troops,
What was done—what to do—a glance told him both;
Then, striking his spurs, with a terrible oath,
He dashed down the line 'mid a storm of huzzas,
And the wave of retreat checked its course there because
The sight of the master compelled it to pause.
With foam and with dust, the black charger was gray.
By the flash of his eye, and his red nostril's play,
He seemed to the whole great army to say:
"I have brought you Sheridan, all the way
From Winchester down, to save the day."

Hurrah! hurrah for Sheridan!
Hurrah! hurrah for horse and man!
And when their statues are placed on high,
Under the dome of the Union sky—
The American soldiers' Temple of Fame,—
There with the glorious General's name,
Be it said, in letters both bold and bright:
   "Here is the steed that saved the day
By carrying Sheridan into the fight,
   From Winchester, twenty miles away!"

Brother, Tell Me of the Battle[10]

THOMAS MANAHAN

Brother, tell me of the battle,
    How the soldiers fought and fell;
Tell me of the weary marches,
    She who loves will listen well.

Brother, draw thee close beside me,
    Lay your head upon my breast,
While you're telling of the battle,
    Let your fevered forehead rest.

Brother, tell me of the battle,
    For they said your life was o'er;
They all told me you had fallen,
    That I'd never see you more.

Oh, I've been so sad and lonely,
    Filled my breast has been with pain,
Since they said my dearest brother
    I should never see again.

Brother, tell me of the battle,
    I can bear to hear it now;
Lay your head upon my bosom,
    Let me soothe your fevered brow.

Tell me, are you badly wounded?
    Did we win the deadly fight?
Did the vict'ry crown our banner?
    Did you put the foe to flight?

---

10. Collected in the Chappell Music Company's *Heartsongs. Melodies of Days Gone By*, 1909, and in *Blue and Gray*, our source for this text, where it was published as written by George F. Root, a popular composer who set the poem to music.

The Empty Sleeve[11]

J. R. Bagby

Tom, old fellow, I grieve to see
  The sleeve hanging loose at your side;
The arm you lost was worth to me
  Every Yankee that ever died.
But you don't mind it at all;
  You swear you've a beautiful stump,
And laugh at that damnable ball—
Tom, I knew you were always a trump.

A good right arm, a nervy hand,
  A wrist as strong as a sapling oak,
Buried deep in the Malvern* sand—
  To laugh at that, is a sorry joke.
Never again your iron grip
  Shall I feel in my shrinking palm—
Tom, Tom, I see your trembling lip;
  All within is not so calm.

Well! The arm is gone, it is true;
  But the one that is nearest the heart
Is left—and that's as good as two;
  Tom, old fellow, what makes you start?
Why, man, *she* thinks that empty sleeve
  A badge of honor; so do I,
And all of us:—I do believe
  The fellow is going to cry!

"She deserves a perfect man," you say;
  "You were not worth her in your prime."
Tom! The arm that has turned to clay,
  Your whole body has made sublime;
For you have placed in the Malvern earth
  The proof and pledge of a noble life—
And the rest, henceforward of higher worth,
  Will be dearer than all to your wife.

11. Collected in *War Poetry*.

I see the people in the street
  Look at your sleeve with kindling eyes;
And you know, Tom, there's naught so sweet
  As homage shown in mute surmise.
Bravely your arm in battle strove,
  Freely for Freedom's sake, you gave it;
It has perished—but a nation's love
  In proud remembrance will save it.

Go to your sweetheart, then, forthwith—
  You're a fool for staying so long—
Woman's love you'll find no myth,
  But a truth; living, tender, strong.
And when around her slender belt
  Your left is clasped in fond embrace,
Your right will thrill, as if it felt,
  In its grave, the usurper's place.

As I look through the coming years,
  I see a one-armed married man;
A little woman, with smiles and tears,
  Is helping as hard as she can.
To put on his coat, to pin his sleeve,
  Tie his cravat, and cut his food;
And I say, as these fancies I weave,
  "That is Tom, and the woman he wooed."

The years roll on, and then I see
  A wedding picture, bright and fair;
I look closer, and its plain to me
  That is Tom with the silver hair.
He gives away the lovely bride,
  And the guests linger, loth to leave
The house of him in whom they pride—
  "Brave old Tom with the empty sleeve."

Reading the List[12]

Anonymous

"Is there any news of the war?" she said.
"Only a list of the wounded and dead,"
Was the man's reply,
Without lifting his eye
To the face of the woman standing by.
" 'Tis the very thing I want," she said;
"Read me a list of the wounded and dead."
He read the list—'twas a sad array
Of the wounded and killed in the fatal fray.
In the very midst, was a pause to tell
Of a gallant youth who fought so well
That his comrades asked: "Who is he, pray?"
"The only son of the Widow Gray,"
Was the proud reply
Of his captain nigh. . . .
What ails the woman standing near?
Her face has the ashen hue of fear!
"Well, well, read on; is he wounded? Quick!
O God! But my heart is sorrow-sick!
Is he wounded?" "No; he fell, they say,
Killed outright on that fatal day!"
But see, the woman has swooned away!

Sadly she opened her eyes to the light;
Slowly recalled the events of the fight;
Faintly she murmured: "Killed outright!
It has cost me the life of my only son;
But the battle is fought, and the victory won,
The will of the Lord, let it be done!"

God pity the cheerless Widow Gray,
And send from the halls of eternal day
The light of His peace to illumine her way.

12. In *Bugle Echoes* Browne lists the poem as written by a Southerner.

Only One Killed[13]

Julia L. Keyes

Only one killed—in company B,
'Twas a trifling loss—one man!
A charge of the bold and dashing Lee*—
While merry enough it was, to see
The enemy, as he ran.

Only one killed upon our side—
Once more to the field they turn.
Quietly now the horsemen ride—
And pause by the form of the one who died,
So bravely, as now we learn.

Their grief for the comrade loved and true
For a time was unconcealed;
They saw the bullet had pierced him through;
That his pain was brief—ah! very few
Die thus, on the battle-field.

The news has gone to his home, afar—
Of the short and gallant fight,
Of the noble deeds of the young La Var
Whose life went out as a falling star
In the skirmish of that night.

"Only one killed! It was my son,"
The widowed mother cried.
She turned but to clasp the sinking one,
Who heard not the words of the victory won,
But of him who had bravely died.

Ah! death to her were a sweet relief,
The bride of a single year.
Oh! would she might, with her weight of grief,
Lie down in the dust, with the autumn leaf
Now trodden and brown and sere!

13. Written in response to a Montgomery, Alabama, newspaper account of a battle in 1864, using the phrase "only one killed"; collected in *War Poetry*, 1866.

But no, she must bear through coming life
Her burden of silent woe,
The aged mother and youthful wife
Must live through a nation's bloody strife,
Sighing, and waiting to go.

Where the loved are meeting beyond the stars,
Are meeting no more to part,
They can smile once more through the crystal bars—
Where never more will the woe of wars
O'ershadow the loving heart.

Fredericksburg[14]

Thomas Bailey Aldrich

The increasing moonlight drifts across my bed,
And on the churchyard by the road, I know
It falls as white and noiselessly as snow.
'Twas such a night two weary summers fled;
The stars, as now, were waning overhead.
Listen! Again the shrill-lipped bugles blow
Where the swift currents of the river flow
Past Fredericksburg: far off the heavens are red
With sudden conflagration: on yon height,
Linstock in hand, the gunners hold their breath:
A signal-rocket pierces the dense night,
Flings its spent stars upon the town beneath:
Hark!—the artillery massing on the right,
Hark!—the black squadrons wheeling down to Death!

14. Cited from *Bugle-Echoes*.

The Confederacy[15]

JANE T. H. CROSS

Born in a day, full-grown, our Nation stood,
The pearly light of heaven was on her face;
Life's early joy was coursing in her blood;
A thing she was of beauty and of grace.

She stood, a stranger on the great broad earth,
No voice of sympathy was heard to greet
The glory-beaming morning of her birth,
Or hail the coming of the unsoiled feet.

She stood, derided by her passing foes;
Her heart beat calmly 'neath their look of scorn;
Their rage in blackening billows round her rose—
Her brow, meanwhile, as radiant as the morn.

Their poisonous coils about her limbs are cast,
She shakes them off in pure and holy ire,
As quietly as Paul, in ages past,
Shook off the serpent in the crackling fire.

She bends not to her foes, nor to the world,
She bears a heart for glory, or for gloom;
But with her starry cross, her flag unfurled,
She kneels amid the sweet magnolia bloom.

She kneels to Thee, O God, she claims her birth,
She lifts to Thee her young and trusting eye,
She asks of Thee her place upon the earth—
For it is Thine to give or to deny.

Oh, let *Thine* eye but recognize her right!
Oh, let *Thy* voice but justify her claim!
Like grasshoppers are nations in Thy sight,
And all their power is but an empty name.

15. *Southern Christian Advocate* 1864; cited from *Blue and Gray*.

Then listen, Father, listen to her prayer!
  Her robes are dripping with her children's blood;
Her foes around "like bulls of Bashan stare,"
  They fain would sweep her off, "as with a flood."

The anguish wraps her close around, like death,
  Her children lie in heaps about her slain;
Before the world she bravely holds her breath,
  Nor gives one utterance to a note of pain.

But 'tis not like Thee to forget the oppressed,
  Thou feel'st within her heart the stifled moan—
Thou Christ! Thou Lamb of God! oh, give her rest!
  For Thou hast called her!—is she not Thine own?

1865

"The Halt"—A Scene in the Georgia Campaign. Painting by Thomas Nast, reproduced as an engraving in *Harper's Weekly*, June 30, 1866. General Research Division, The New York Public Library, Astor, Lenox and Tilden Foundations.

My Autumn Walk[1]

William Cullen Bryant

On woodlands ruddy with autumn
  The amber sunshine lies;
I look on the beauty round me,
  And tears come into my eyes.

For the wind that sweeps the meadows
  Blows out of the far South-west,
Where our gallant men are fighting,
  And the gallant dead are at rest.

The golden-rod is leaning,
  And the purple aster waves
In a breeze from the land of battles,
  A breath from the land of graves.

Full fast the leaves are dropping
  Before that wandering breath;
As fast, on the field of battle,
  Our brethren fall in death.

Beautiful over my pathway
  The forest spoils are shed;
They are spotting the grassy hillocks
  With purple and gold and red.

Beautiful is the death-sleep
  Of those who bravely fight
In their country's holy quarrel,
  And perish for the Right.
But who shall comfort the living,
  The light of whose homes is gone:

1. *Atlantic Monthly* January 1865; composed October 1864. Bryant adds a note to the poem saying that he has literally translated the botanical name of the Virginia creeper—*Ampelopsis*—as "mock-grape" in stanza 11 because "Virginia creeper" is "too cumbrous for verse."

The bride that, early widowed,
  Lives broken-hearted on;

The matron, whose sons are lying
  In graves on a distant shore;
The maiden, whose promised husband
  Comes back from the war no more?

I look on the peaceful dwellings
  Whose windows glimmer in sight,
With croft and garden and orchard
  That bask in the mellow light;

And I know, that, when our couriers
  With news of victory come,
They will bring a bitter message
  Of hopeless grief to some.

Again I turn to the woodlands,
  And shudder as I see
The mock-grape's blood-red banner
  Hung out on the cedar-tree;

And I think of days of slaughter,
  And the night-sky red with flames,
On the Chattahoochee's meadows,
  And the wasted banks of the James.

Oh, for the fresh spring-season,
  When the groves are in their prime,
And far away in the future
  Is the frosty autumn-time!

Oh, for that better season,
  When the pride of the foe shall yield,
And the hosts of God and Freedom
  March back from the well-won field;

And the matron shall clasp her first-born
  With tears of joy and pride;
And the scarred and war-worn lover
  Shall claim his promised bride!

The leaves are swept from the branches;
  But the living buds are there,
With folded flower and foliage,
  To sprout in a kinder air.

I'm Dying, Comrade[2]

MARY H. C. BOOTH

I think I'm dying, comrade,
    The day is growing dark;
And that is not the bob-o-link,
    Nor yet the meadow-lark:
It cannot be the distant drum;
    It cannot be the fife,
For why should drum, or bob-o-link,
    Be calling me from life?

I do not think I'm wounded;
    I cannot feel a pain;
And yet I've fallen, comrade,
    Never to rise again.
The last that I remember,
    We charged upon the foe;
I heard a sound of victory,
    And that is all I know.

I think we must have conquered,
    For all last night it seemed
That I was up in Paradise—
    Among the blest, it seemed.
And there, beside the Throne of God,
    I saw a banner wave,
The good old Stars and Stripes, my boy,
    O'er victory and the grave.

A hundred thousand soldiers
    Stood at the right of God;

2. *Wayside Blossoms* 1865.

And old John Brown, he stood before,
    Like Aaron with his rod:
A slave was there beside him,
    And Jesus Christ was there;
And over God, and Christ, and all,
    The banner waved in air.

And now I'm dying, comrade,
    And there is old John Brown
A standing at the Golden Gate,
    And holding me a crown.
I do not hear the bob-o-link,
    Nor yet the drum and fife;
I only know the voice of God
    Is calling me from life.

The Voices of the Guns[3]

Anonymous

Within a green and shadowy wood,
Circled with Spring, alone I stood:
The nook was peaceful, fair, and good.

The wild-plum blossoms lured the bees,
The birds sang madly in the trees,
Magnolia scents were on the breeze.

All else was silent; but the ear
Caught sounds of distant bugle clear,
And heard the bullets whistle near,—

When from the winding river's shore
The Rebel guns began to roar,
And ours to answer, thundering o'er;

And, echoed from the wooded hill,
Repeated and repeated still,
Through all my soul they seemed to thrill;

3. Collected in *Bugle-Echoes*.

For, as their rattling storm awoke,
And loud and fast the discord broke,
In rude and trenchant *words* they spoke:

"We *hate!*" boomed fiercely o'er the tide;
"We fear not!" from the other side;
"We *strike!*" the Rebel guns replied.

Quick roared our answer: "We defend!"
"*Our rights!*" the battle-sounds contend;
"The rights of all!" we answer send.

"We *conquer!*" rolled across the wave;
"We persevere!" our answer gave;
"*Our chivalry!*" they wildly rave.

"Ours are the brave!" "Be ours the free!"
"Be ours the slave, the masters we!"
"On us their blood no more shall be!"

As when some magic word is spoken
By which a wizard spell is broken,
There was a silence at that token.

The wild birds dared once more to sing,
I heard the pine bough's whispering,
And trickling of a silver spring.

Then, crashing forth with smoke and din,
Once more the rattling sounds begin;
Our iron lips roll forth: "We win!"

And dull and wavering in the gale
That rushed in gusts across the vale
Came back the faint reply : "*We fail!*"

And then a word, both stern and sad,
From throat of huge Columbiad:
"Blind fools and traitors! Ye are mad!"

Again the Rebel answer came,
Muffled and slow, as if in shame:
"*All, all is lost!*" in smoke and flame.

Now bold and strong and stern as Fate
The Union guns sound forth : "We wait!"
Faint comes the distant cry: "*Too late!*"

"Return, return!" our cannon said;
And, as the smoke rolled overhead,
"*We dare not!*" was the answer dread.

Then came a sound both loud and clear,
A Godlike word of hope and cheer:
"Forgiveness!" echoed far and near;

As when beside some death-bed still
We watch, and wait God's solemn will,
A bluebird warbles his soft trill.

I clenched my teeth at that blest word,
And, angry, muttered, "Not so, Lord!
The only answer is the sword!"

I thought of Shiloh's tainted air,
Of Richmond's prisons*, foul and bare,
And murdered heroes, young and fair,—

Of block and lash and overseer,
And dark, mild faces pale with fear,
Of baying hell-hounds panting near.

But then the gentle story told
My childhood in the days of old
Rang out its lessons manifold.

O prodigal and lost! arise,
And read the welcome blest that lies
In a kind Father's patient eyes!

Thy elder brother grudges not
The lost and found should share his lot,
And wrong in concord be forgot.

Thus mused I, as the hours went by,
Till the relieving guard drew nigh,
And threw as challenge and reply.

And as I hastened back to line,
It seemed an omen half divine
That "Concord" was the countersign.

Driving Home the Cows[4]

Kate Putnam Osgood

Out of the clover and blue-eyed grass,
He turned them into the river-lane;
One after another he let them pass,
Then fastened the meadow bars again.

Under the willows and over the hill,
He patiently followed their sober pace;
The merry whistle for once was still,
And something shadowed the sunny face.

Only a boy! and his father had said
He never could let his youngest go:
Two already were lying dead
Under the feet of the trampling foe.

But after the evening work was done,
And the frogs were loud in the meadow-swamp,
Over his shoulder he slung his gun,
And stealthily followed the foot-path damp,—

Across the clover and through the wheat,
With resolute heart and purpose grim,
Though cold was the dew on his hurrying feet,
And the blind bats flitting startled him.

Thrice since then had the lanes been white,
And the orchards sweet with apple-bloom;
And now, when the cows came back at night,
The feeble father drove them home.

For news had come to the lonely farm
That three were lying where two had lain;

4. Published anonymously in CWSS.

And the old man's tremulous, palsied arm
  Could never lean on a son's again.

The summer day grew cold and late;
  He went for the cows when the work was done;
But down the lane, as he opened the gate,
  He saw them coming, one by one,—

Brindle, Ebony, Speckle, and Bess,
  Shaking their horns in the evening wind,
Cropping the buttercups out of the grass—
  But who was it following close behind?

Loosely swang in the idle air
  The empty sleeve of army blue;
And worn and pale, from the crisping hair,
  Looked out a face that the father knew;—

For Southern prisons* will sometimes yawn,
  And yield their dead unto life again;
And the day that comes with a cloudy dawn
  In golden glory at last may wane.

The great tears sprang to their meeting eyes;
  For the heart must speak when the lips are dumb,
And under the silent evening skies
  Together they followed the cattle home.

"Stack Arms"[5]

Joseph Blythe Allston

"Stack Arms!" I've gladly heard the cry
  When, weary with the dusty tread
Of marching troops, as night drew nigh,
  I sank upon my soldier bed,

5. According to its informational epigraph, as published in *War Poetry,* this poem was written in the Prison of Fort Delaware, on hearing of the surrender of General Lee in April 1865. To "stack arms" is to put up your weapons. At the end of the war, the Confederate army formally surrendered its weapons to the Union army, under the command "stack arms."

And calmly slept; the starry dome
Of heaven's blue arch my canopy,
And mingled with my dreams of home,
The thoughts of Peace and Liberty.

"Stack Arms!" I've heard it, when the shout
Exulting, rang along our line,
Of foes hurled back in bloody rout,
Captured, dispersed; its tones divine
Then came to mine enraptured ear.
Guerdon of duty nobly done,
And glistened on my cheek the tear
Of grateful joy for victory won.

"Stack Arms!" In faltering accents, slow
And sad, it creeps from tongue to tongue,
A broken, murmuring wail of woe,
From manly hearts by anguish wrung.
Like victims of a midnight dream,
We move, we know not how nor why,
For life and hope but phantoms seem,
And it would be relief—to die!

Doffing the Gray[6]

ROBERT FALLIGANT

Off with your gray suits, boys—
Off with your rebel gear—
They smack too much of the cannons' peal,
The lightning flash of your deadly steel,
The terror of your spear.

Their color is like the smoke
That curled o'er your battle-line;
They call to mind the yell that woke
When the dastard columns before you broke,
And their dead were your fatal sign.

6. Collected in *War Poetry*, 1866.

Off with the starry wreath,
  Ye who have led our van;
To you 'twas the pledge of glorious death,
When we followed you over the gory heath,
  Where we whipped them man to man.

Down with the cross of stars—
  Too long hath it waved on high;
'Tis covered all over with battle scars,
But its gleam the Northern banner mars—
  'Tis time to lay it by.

Down with the vows we've made,
  Down with each memory—
Down with the thoughts of our noble dead—
Down, down to the dust, where their forms are laid
  And down with Liberty.

Ashes of Glory[7]

Augustus Julian Requier

Fold up the gorgeous silken sun,
  By bleeding martyrs blest,
And heap the laurels it has won
  Above its place of rest.

No trumpet's note need harshly blare—
  No drum funereal roll—
Nor trailing sables drape the bier
  That frees a dauntless soul!

It lived with Lee*, and decked his brow
  From Fate's empyreal Palm:
It sleeps the sleep of Jackson* now—
  As spotless and as calm.

7. One of several poems written in response to Abram Joseph Ryan's "The Conquered Banner," written after Lee's surrender and ending with the lines "Let it droop there, furled forever, / For its people's hopes are dead!" Simms prints "Ashes of Glory" as the final poem in *War Poetry*.

It was outnumbered—not outdone;
  And they shall shuddering tell,
Who struck the blow, its latest gun
  Flashed ruin as it fell.

Sleep, shrouded Ensign! not the breeze
  That smote the victor tar,
With death across the heaving seas
  Of fiery Trafalgar;

Not Arthur's knights, amid the gloom
  Their knightly deeds have starred;
Nor Gallic Henry's matchless plume,
  Nor peerless-born Bayard;

Not all that antique fables feign,
  And Orient dreams disgorge;
Nor yet, the Silver Cross of Spain,
  And Lion of St. George,

Can bid thee pale! Proud emblem, still
  Thy crimson glory shines
Beyond the lengthened shades that fill
  Their proudest kingly lines.

Sleep! In thine own historic night,—
  And be thy blazoned scroll,
A warrior's Banner takes its flight,
  To greet the warrior's soul!

The Death of Lincoln[8]

WILLIAM CULLEN BRYANT

Oh, slow to smite and swift to spare,
Gentle and merciful and just!
Who, in the fear of God, didst bear
The sword of power, a nation's trust!

8. Composed April 1865; cited from *Political Writings of William Cullen Bryant*, 1882.

In sorrow by thy bier we stand,
Amid the awe that hushes all,
And speak the anguish of a land
That shook with horror at thy fall.

Thy task is done; the bond are free:
We bear thee to an honored grave,
Whose proudest monument shall be
The broken fetters of the slave.

Pure was thy life; its bloody close
Hath placed thee with the sons of light,
Among the noble host of those
Who perished in the cause of Right.

The Death-Blow[9]

Christopher Pearse Cranch

But yesterday the exulting nation's shout
Swelled on the breeze of victory through our streets;
But yesterday our gay flags flaunted out
Like flowers the south-wind wooes from their retreats,—
Flowers of the Union, blue and white and red,
Blooming on balcony and spire and mast,
Telling us that war's wintry storm had fled,
And spring was more than spring to us at last.
To-day,—the nation's heart lies crushed and weak;
Drooping and draped in black our banners stand.
Too stunned to cry revenge, we scarce may speak
The grief that chokes all utterance through the land.
God is in all. With tears our eyes are dim,
Yet strive through darkness to look up to Him!

9. This and the following sonnet are part of a seven-sonnet sequence titled "Poems for the Times, April, 1865." They first appeared in book form in Cranch's *The Bird and the Bell with Other Poems*, 1875 (our source), but were almost certainly published previously, in 1865 or 1866.

The Martyr

CHRISTOPHER PEARSE CRANCH

No, not in vain he died, not all in vain,—
Our good, great President. This people's hands
Are linked together in one mighty chain,
Knit tighter now in triple woven bands,
To crush the fiends in human mask, whose might
We suffer, O, too long! No league or truce
Save *men* with *men*. The devils we must fight
With fire. God wills it in this deed. This use
We draw from the most impious murder done
Since Calvary. Rise, then, O countrymen!
Scatter these marsh-light hopes of union won
Through pardoning clemency. Strike, strike again!
Draw closer round the foe a girdling flame!
We are stabbed whene'er we spare. Strike, in God's name!

A Second Review of the Grand Army[10]

BRET HARTE

I read last night of the grand review
In Washington's chiefest avenue,—
Two hundred thousand men in blue,
    I think they said was the number,—
Till I seemed to hear their trampling feet,
The bugle blast and the drum's quick beat,
The clatter of hoofs in the stony street,
The cheers of people who came to greet,
And the thousand details that to repeat
    Would only my verse encumber,—
Till I fell in a reverie, sad and sweet,
    And then to a fitful slumber.

10. *The Californian* July 1, 1865, under the name "Bret"; cited from *Poems*. On May 24, 1865, Union troops marched in review through Washington, D.C. Harte here imagines Lincoln and other war dead joining this procession.

When, lo! in a vision I seemed to stand
In the lonely Capitol. On each hand
Far stretched the portico, dim and grand
Its columns ranged like a martial band
Of sheeted spectres, whom some command
    Had called to a last reviewing.
And the streets of the city were white and bare;
No footfall echoed across the square;
But out of the misty midnight air
I heard in the distance a trumpet blare,
And the wandering night-winds seemed to bear
    The sound of far tattooing.

Then I held my breath with fear and dread;
For into the square, with a brazen tread,
There rode a figure whose stately head
    O'erlooked the review that morning,
That never bowed from its firm-set seat
When the living column passed its feet,
Yet now rode steadily up the street
    To the phantom bugle's warning:

Till it reached the Capitol square, and wheeled,
And there in the moonlight stood revealed
A well-known form that in State and field
    Had led our patriot sires:
Whose face was turned to the sleeping camp,
Afar through the river's fog and damp,
That showed no flicker, nor waning lamp,
    Nor wasted bivouac* fires.

And I saw a phantom army come,
With never a sound of fife or drum,
But keeping time to a throbbing hum
    Of wailing and lamentation:
The martyred heroes of Malvern Hill*,
Of Gettysburg and Chancellorsville,
The men whose wasted figures fill
    The patriot graves of the nation.

And there came the nameless dead,—the men
Who perished in fever swamp and fen,

The slowly-starved of the prison pen*;
    And, marching beside the others,
Came the dusky martyrs of Pillow's* fight,
With limbs enfranchised and bearing bright;
I thought—perhaps 't was the pale moonlight—
    They looked as white as their brothers!

And so all night marched the nation's dead,
With never a banner above them spread,
Nor a badge, nor a motto brandishèd;
No mark—save the bare uncovered head
    Of the silent bronze Reviewer;
With never an arch save the vaulted sky;
With never a flower save those that lie
On the distant graves—for love could buy
    No gift that was purer or truer.

So all night long swept the strange array,
So all night long till the morning gray
I watched for one who had passed away;
    With a reverent awe and wonder,—
Till a blue cap waved in the length'ning line,
And I knew that one who was kin of mine
Had come; and I spake—and lo! that sign
    Awakened me from my slumber.

The Dying Words of Jackson*[11]

SIDNEY LANIER

"Order A. P. Hill to prepare for battle."
"Tell Major Hawks to advance the Commissary train."
"Let us cross the river and rest in the shade."

The stars of Night contain the glittering Day,
And rain his glory down with sweeter grace

11. Composed at Scotts Mill, near Macon, Georgia, September 24, 1865; published posthumously in 1884, with "Stonewall" add to the title. Our source is Lanier's *Works*, vol. 1, 1945. In the confusion following the battle of Chancellorsville (May 1–5, 1863), Jackson was fatally shot by his own troops; his last words are quoted in the epigraph. Lanier was stationed at nearby Franklin, Virginia.

Upon the dark World's grand, enchanted face
All loth to turn away.

And so the Day, about to yield his breath,
Utters the Stars unto the listening Night
To stand for burning fare-thee-wells of light
Said on the verge of death.

O hero-life that lit us like the Sun!
O hero-words that glittered like the Stars
And stood and shone above the gloomy wars
When the hero-life was done!

The Phantoms of a battle came to dwell
I' the fitful vision of his dying eyes—
Yet even in battle-dreams, he sends supplies
To those he loved so well.

His army stands in battle-line arrayed:
His couriers fly: all's done—now God decide!
And not till then saw he the Other Side
Or would accept the Shade.

Thou Land whose Sun is gone, thy Stars remain!
Still shine the words that miniature his deeds—
O Thrice-Beloved, where'er thy great heart bleeds,
Solace hast thou for pain!

Ethiopia's* Dead[12]

Sarah E. Shuften

A tribute to the memory of her sons who have fallen in the great struggle for liberty and independence.

Brave hearts! brave Ethiopia's dead
On hills, in valleys lie,
On every field of strife, made red
With gory victory.

12. *Colored American* 1865; cited from NAWP.

Each valley, where the battle poured
Its purple swelling tide,
Beheld brave Ethiopia's sword
With slaughter deeply dyed.

Their bones bleach on the Southr'n hill,
And on the Southern plain,
By [brook], and river, lake and rill,
And by the roaring main.

The land is holy where they fought,
And holy where they fell;
For by their blood, that land was bought
That land they loved so well—
Then glory to that valiant band,
The honored saviors of the land.

Oh! few and weak their numbers were,
A handful of brave men,
But up to God they sent their prayer,
And rushed to battle, then
The God of battle heard their cry,
And crowned their deeds with victory.

From east to west, from hill to vale,
Then be their names adored—
Europe, with all thy millions, hail!
The Peace bought by their sword.

Asia, and Africa shall ring
From shore to shore, their fame;
And fair Columbia shall sing,
Their glory, and their name.

Peace, with her olive branch, shall spread
Her wings, o'er sea and shore,
And hearts no more with terror dread
The battle's clashing roar.

Fair Afric's *free* and valiant sons,
Shall join with Europe's band,

To celebrate in varied tongues,
        Our *free* and happy land

Till freedom's golden fingers trace,
        A line that knows no end,
And man shall meet in every face,
        A brother and a friend.

The Aftermath of the War

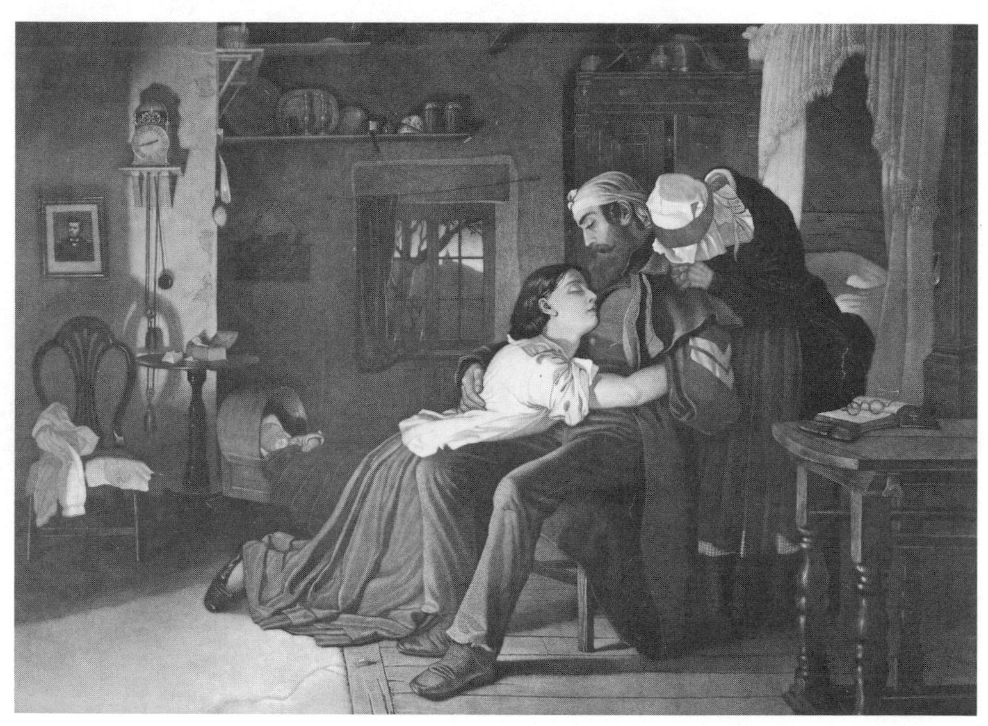

“Home from Andersonville.” Engraving by William Sartain, after a painting by Joseph Noel Paton. Courtesy of The Lincoln Museum, Fort Wayne, Indiana (#4148).

"Is There, Then, No Hope for the Nations?"[1]

Anonymous

Is there, then, no hope for the nations?
  Must the record of Time be the same?
And shall History, in all her narrations,
  Still close each last chapter in shame?
Shall the valor which grew to be glorious,
  Prove the shame, as the pride of a race:
And a people, for ages victorious,
  Through the arts of the chapman, grow base?

Greek, Hebrew, Assyrian, and Roman,
  Each strides o'er the scene and departs!
How valiant their deeds 'gainst the foeman,
  How wondrous their virtues and arts!
Rude valor, at first, when beginning,
  The nation through blood took its name;
Then the wisdom, which hourly winning
  New heights in its march, rose to Fame!

How noble the tale for long ages,
  Blending Beauty with courage and might!
What Heroes, what Poets, and Sages,
  Made eminent stars for each height!
While their people, with reverence ample,
  Brought tribute of praise to the Great,
Whose wisdom and virtuous example,
  Made virtue the pride of the State!

Ours, too, was as noble a dawning,
  With hopes of the Future as high:
Great men, each a star of the morning,
  Taught us bravely to live and to die!

1. Cited from *War Poetry*.

We fought the long fight with our foeman,
And through trial—well-borne—won a name,
Not less glorious than Grecian or Roman,
And worthy as lasting a fame!

* * * * *

Shut the Book! We must open another!
O Southron! if taught by the Past,
Beware, when thou choosest a brother,
With what ally thy fortunes are cast!
Beware of all foreign alliance,
Of their pleadings and pleasings beware,
Better meet the old snake with defiance,
Than find in his charming a snare!

Killed at the Ford[2]

Henry Wadsworth Longfellow

He is dead, the beautiful youth,
The heart of honor, the tongue of truth,—
He, the life and light of us all,
Whose voice was blithe as a bugle call,
Whom all eyes followed with one consent,
The cheer of whose laugh, and whose pleasant word,
Hushed all murmurs of discontent.

Only last night, as we rode along
Down the dark of the mountain gap,
To visit the picket-guard at the ford,
Little dreaming of any mishap,
He was humming the words of some old song:
"Two red roses he had on his cap,
And another he bore at the point of his sword."

2. *Atlantic Monthly* April 1866.

Sudden and swift, a whistling ball
Came out of a wood, and the voice was still;
Something I heard in the darkness fall,
And for a moment my blood grew chill;
I spake in a whisper, as he who speaks
In a room where some one is lying dead;
But he made no answer to what I said.

We lifted him up on his saddle again,
And through the mire and the mist and the rain
Carried him back to the silent camp,
And laid him as if asleep on his bed;
And I saw by the light of the surgeon's lamp
Two white roses upon his cheeks,
And one just over his heart, blood-red!

And I saw in a vision how far and fleet
That fatal bullet went speeding forth,
Till it reached a town in the distant North,
Till it reached a house in a sunny street,
Till it reached a heart that ceased to beat
Without a murmur, without a cry;
And a bell was tolled in that far-off town,
For one who had passed from cross to crown,—
And the neighbors wondered that she should die.

The Sword of Robert Lee*[3]

Abram Joseph Ryan

Forth from its scabbard, pure and bright,
  Flashed the sword of Lee!
Far in the front of the deadly fight,
High o'er the brave in the cause of Right
Its stainless sheen, like a beacon light,
  Led us to Victory!

3. Collected in W. L. Fagan's *Southern War Songs. Camp-Fire, Patrotic and Sentimental*, 1890; cited from *Blue and Gray*.

Out of its scabbard, where, full long,
It slumbered peacefully,
Roused from its rest by the battle's song,
Shielding the feeble, smiting the strong,
Guarding the right, avenging the wrong,
Gleamed the sword of Lee!

Forth from its scabbard, high in the air
Beneath Virginia's sky—
And they who saw it gleaming there,
And knew who bore it, knelt to swear
That where that sword led they would dare
To follow—and to die!

Out of its scabbard! Never hand
Waved sword from stain as free,
Nor purer sword led braver band,
Nor braver bled for a brighter land,
Nor brighter land had a cause so grand,
Nor cause a chief like Lee!

Forth from its scabbard! How we prayed
That sword might victor be;
And when our triumph was delayed,
And many a heart grew sore afraid,
We still hoped on while gleamed the blade
Of noble Robert Lee!

Forth from its scabbard all in vain
Bright flashed the sword of Lee;
'Tis shrouded now in its sheath again,
It sleeps the sleep of our noble slain,
Defeated, yet without a stain,
Proudly and peacefully!

Let the Banner Proudly Wave[4]

*Written after the surrender of Lee**

Joshua McCarter Simpson

Our glorious flag is floating,
 Triumphantly at last;
Our nation is exulting,
 The rebel's die is cast;
Rebellion now is conquered,
 No more to lift its head,
And best of all we now can sing,
 Old Slavery is dead.

Chorus: Let it wave, let it wave!
 Let the banner proudly wave;
 Let it wave, let it wave!
 But never o'er a slave.

We are a happy nation,
 Because our country's free
From war and desolation,
 And from bold tyranny.
The tyrant's arm is broken
 Nor more to hold a slave,
This is the year of jubilee,
 So let our banner wave.

We've stood and fought like demons,
 Upon the battle-field;
Both slaves and Northern freemen
 Have faced the glowing steel.
Our blood beneath this banner
 Has mingled with the whites,
And 'neath its folds we now demand
 Our just and equal rights.

4. Probably published in a newspaper or magazine shortly after the war, this poem was collected in Simpson's *The Emancipation Car*, 1874. It is written to the tune of "Nearer to Our Happy Home."

The world has seen our valor,
 And nations now confess
That man is not in color,
 In fashion nor in dress;
In Charleston* and old Richmond*,
 In spite of Lee* and Bragg*,
We drove the Rebs in wild dismay,
 And planted there our flag.

Port Hudson and Fort Pillow*,
 And Wagner's rugged crag,
Where many a colored soldier
 Was murdered for this flag.
And Petersburg, Oulusta,
 And Nashville, all can tell,
Who were the boys that stood in front,
 And for this banner fell.

We've fed the Union soldiers,
 When fleeing from the foe;
We've led them through the mountains,
 Where white men dare not go;
Our "hoe-cake" and our cabbage,
 And pork we freely gave,
That this old flag might be sustained.
 Now let it proudly wave.

We've fought like men and brethren,
 And we defy the world
To say we've ever faltered,
 Beneath this flag unfurled;
Our guns have broke our fetters,
 And justice now demands
That we shall never more be slaves,
 With muskets in our hands.

Christmas, South, 1866[5]

Mary Eliza Tucker

Laughing, merry, childish voices, woke us in their eager glee,
When the rosy blush of morning in the east we scarce could see:
Surely, ne'er a Christmas morning was so cold and drear as this;
Can it be our hearts are frozen with the sere frost's icy kiss?
Ah, stern want and desolation has a heavy, heavy hand,
And no mirth should ever issue from beneath the iron band.
Now the voices draw still nearer—bless the children, all are here!
"Mother, don't weep, they won't mind it; oh, God help thee, mother, dear!"

One by one they took their stockings, gazed upon the store, then turned:
"Sissie," said the bravest rebel, "did Santee have his cotton burned?"
"Hush, hush, Buddie; don't say nothing; just see how poor mamma cries."
Now the repentant Buddy to his mother's bedside hies—
"I'm so sorry, mother, darling: when I'm grown you shan't be poor;
I'll write for the Yankee papers, that will make us rich once more."
Off I turned to hide my feelings—feelings deep by care refined,—
Ah! my child, like sister Annie's, your poor piece may be declined.

Ah, there is some joy in sorrow! in the door two freed-men creep:
"Christmas gif, ole Miss, Miss Annie—why, what fur you white folks weep?
All dis time you give us Christmas; now, we going to give to you:
Here, old Missus, here, Miss Annie—children, here's your Christmas, too!"
In black bosoms true love lingers, deeply by our kindness riven,
And the tender tie that binds us, can be severed save by heaven.
O'er the day that dawned so sadly, that kind act a ray imparts,
And we grasp the sunbeam gladly, for it cheers our aching hearts.

5. *Poems*, 1867. In the final stanza, the line "And the tender tie that binds us, can be severed save by heaven" is grammatically confusing but clearly means that these ties can be severed only by heaven.

"Ay De Mi, Alhama!"[6]

William Gilmore Simms

i

Ah! woe is me, my Dixie Land!
I weep for thee, my Dixie Land!
I weep o'er all that glorious Band,
That bore thy Banner and thy Brand,
From mountain height to ocean strand,
And bled, and died, for thee, O! Dixie Land!
My Dixie Land! My Dixie Land.

ii

Thy wail of wo, my Dixie Land!
From homes laid low, my Dixie Land,
From plains once glorious in the glow,
Of summer fruits, and blooms of snow,
Speaks for the brave that sleep below,
Thy braves, thy graves, their virtues and thy woe,
My Dixie Land! My Dixie Land!

iii

Yet not in vain, O! Dixie Land!
Thy Heroes slain, O! Dixie Land!
Thy ruin'd realm, thy blacken'd fane,—
Thy agonies of heart and brain,
If still thy spirit mounts amain,
And sings for Freedom one, the grand refrain
Of Dixie Land! Of Dixie Land.

iv

Each lowly grave, my Dixie Land!
Where sleeps your brave, my Dixie Land!
Becomes a shrine that yet shall save,
If, keeping faith, your fathers gave,

6. Published anonymously in the *Charleston Mercury* January 11, 1867; cited from *Selected Poems*. The title is from the refrain of a sixteenth-century Spanish ballad and means "Woe is me, Alhama"—as Simms suggests in his first line. The ballad laments the conquest of the citadel of Alhama in Grenada, as part of the Spanish reconquest of Spain from the Moors; Simms composed the poem while walking through the ruins of his plantation.

Ye rend the shackles, which enslave,
And sharp for happier fields your battle glaive,
Oh! Dixie Land! O! Dixie Land!

v

Though often crost, O! Dixie Land!
No cause is lost, my Dixie Land!
While still remain a generous Host;
That hold the Faith, that keep the post,
And still invoke each glorious ghost,
That was your people's Beauty and their Boast,
Oh! Dixie Land! O! Dixie Land!

vi

Tender and True, my Dixie Land!
Though faint and few, my Dixie Land!
We keep the Faith our Fathers knew,
For which they bled, in which we grew,
And at their graves our vows renew,—
For nought is lost of truth, where Faith keeps true,
Oh! Dixie Land! O! Dixie Land!

To Our Hills[7]

Sidney Lanier

Dear Mother-Earth
Of giant-birth,
Yon hills are thy large breasts, and often I
Have climbed to their top nipples, fain to lie
And drink my mother's-milk so near the sky.

But, Mother Earth
Of giant-birth,
Thy mother milk comes curdled thick with woe.
Friends, blood is in the milk whereby we grow,
And life is heavy and death is marvelous slow.

7. Written July 14, 1867; revised in December 1867—the source of our text, cited from Lanier's *Works*, vol, 1, 1945. The poem first appeared in print in 1916.

Mark yon hill-stains,
Red, for all rains!
The blood that made them was all shed for us:
The hearts that paid them are all dead for us:
The trees that shade them groan with lead, for us.

O ye hill-sides,
Like giants' brides
Ye sleep in ravine-rumpled draperies,
And weep your springs in tearful memories
Of green bride-robes, now turned to bloody frieze.

Sad furrowed hills
By full-wept rills,
The stainers have decreed the stains shall stay.
What clement hands might wash the stains away
Are chained, to make us rue a mournful day.

O coward hand
Of the Northland,
That after honorable war couldst smite
Cheeks grimed in adverse battle, to wreak spite
For dainty Senators that lagged the fight.

O monstrous crime
Of a sick Time:
—Forever waging war that peace may be
And serving God by cheating on bent knee
And freeing slaves by chaining down the free.

Thou sorrow height
We climb by night,
Hast thou no hiding for a Southern face?
Forever will the Heavens brook disgrace?
Shall Hope sit always cooing to the base?

The Blue and the Gray[8]

Francis Miles Finch

The women of Columbus, Mississippi, animated by nobler sentiments than are many of their sisters, have shown themselves impartial in their offerings made to the memory of the dead. They strewed flowers alike on the graves of the Confederate and of the National soldiers.

New York Tribune

By the flow of the inland river,
Whence the fleets of iron have fled,
Where the blades of the grave-grass quiver,
Asleep are the ranks of the dead;—
Under the sod and the dew,
Waiting the judgment day;—
Under the one, the Blue;
Under the other, the Gray.

These in the robings of glory,
Those in the gloom of defeat,
All with the battle-blood gory,
In the dusk of eternity meet;—
Under the sod and the dew,
Waiting the judgment day;—
Under the laurel, the Blue;
Under the willow, the Gray.

From the silence of sorrowful hours
The desolate mourners go,
Lovingly laden with flowers
Alike for the friend and the foe;—
Under the sod and the dew
Waiting the judgment day;—
Under the roses, the Blue;
Under the lilies, the Gray.

So with an equal splendor
The morning sun-rays fall,

8. *Atlantic Monthly* September 1867.

With a touch, impartially tender,
On the blossoms blooming for all;
Under the sod and the dew,
Waiting the judgment day;—
Broidered with gold, the Blue;
Mellowed with gold, the Gray.

So, when the Summer calleth,
On forest and field of grain
With an equal murmur falleth
The cooling drip of the rain;—
Under the sod and the dew,
Waiting the judgment day;—
Wet with the rain, the Blue;
Wet with the rain, the Gray.

Sadly, but not with upbraiding,
The generous deed was done;
In the storm of the years that are fading,
No braver battle was won;—
Under the sod and the dew,
Waiting the judgment day;—
Under the blossoms, the Blue,
Under the garlands, the Gray.

No more shall the war-cry sever,
Or the winding rivers be red;
They banish our anger forever
When they laurel the graves of our dead!
Under the sod and the dew,
Waiting the judgment day;—
Love and tears for the Blue,
Tears and love for the Gray.

Little Giffen[9]

Francis Orray Ticknor

Out of the focal and foremost fire,
Out of the hospital walls as dire,
Smitten of grape-shot and gangrene
(Eighteenth battle and he sixteen!)
Spectre such as you seldom see,
Little Giffen of Tennessee.

"Take him—and welcome!" the surgeon said,
"Much your doctor can help the dead!"
And so we took him and brought him where
The balm was sweet on the summer air;
And we laid him down on a wholesome bed—
Utter Lazarus, heel to head!

Weary war with the bated breath,
Skeleton boy against skeleton Death.
Months of torture, how many such!
Weary weeks of the stick and crutch!
And still a glint in the steel-blue eye
Spoke of the spirit that would not die.

And didn't! nay, more! in death's despite
The crippled skeleton learned to write!
"Dear Mother" at first, of course: and then,
"Dear Captain" inquiring about "the men."
Captain's answer—"Of eighty and five,
Giffen and I are left alive!"

"Johnston's pressed at the front, they say!"
Little Giffen was up and away.
A tear, his first, as he bade good-by,
Dimmed the glint of his steel-blue eye.
"*I'll write, if spared.*" There was news of a fight,
But none of Giffen. He did not write!

9. *The Land We Love* November 1867; cited from *Bugle-Echoes*.

I sometimes fancy that were I king
Of the princely knights of the Golden Ring,
With the song of the minstrel in mine ear,
And the tender legend that trembles here,
I'd give the best, on his bended knee,
The whitest soul of my chivalry,
For Little Giffen of Tennessee.

Gettysburg Ode[10]

Bayard Taylor

Dedication of the National Monument, July 1, 1869.

After the eyes that looked, the lips that spake
Here, from the shadows of impending death,
    Those words of solemn breath,
    What voice may fitly break
The silence, doubly hallowed, left by him?
We can but bow the head, with eyes grown dim,
And, as a Nation's litany, repeat
The phrase his martyrdom hath made complete,
Noble as then, but now more sadly-sweet;
"Let us, the Living, rather dedicate
Ourselves to the unfinished work, which they
Thus far advanced so nobly on its way,
    And save the perilled State!
Let us, upon this field where they, the brave,
Their last full measure of devotion gave,
Highly resolve they have not died in vain!—
That, under God, the Nation's later birth
    Of Freedom, and the people's gain
Of their own Sovereignty, shall never wane
And perish from the circle of the earth!"
From such a perfect text, shall Song aspire
        To light her faded fire,

10. *Putnam's Magazine* 1869; reprinted as "Lincoln at Gettysburg" in *Blue and Gray*. Cited from *Poetical Works of Bayard Taylor*, 1894.

And into wandering music turn
Its virtue, simple, sorrowful, and stern?
His voice all elegies anticipated;
For, whatsoe'er the strain,
We hear that one refrain:
"We consecrate ourselves to them, the Consecrated!"

Lincoln[11]

Henrietta Cordelia Ray

To-day, O martyred chief, beneath the sun
We would unveil thy form; to thee who won
Th'applause of nations for thy soul sincere,
A loving tribute we would offer here.
'T was thine not worlds to conquer, but men's hearts;
To change to balm the sting of slavery's darts;
In lowly charity thy joy to find,
And open "gates of mercy on mankind."
And so they come, the freed, with grateful gift,
From whose sad path the shadows thou didst lift.

Eleven years have rolled their seasons round,
Since its most tragic close thy life-work found.
Yet through the vistas of the vanished days
We see thee still, responsive to our gaze,
As ever to thy country's solemn needs.
Not regal coronets, but princely deeds
Were thy chaste diadem; of truer worth
Thy modest virtues than the gems of earth.
Stanch, honest, fervent in the purest cause,
Truth was thy guide; her mandates were thy laws.

Rare heroism, spirit-purity,
The storied Spartan's stern simplicity,
Such moral strength as gleams like burnished gold
Amid the doubt of men of weaker mould,

11. Read at the unveiling of the Freedmen's Monument in 1876 and published as *Lincoln* in 1893, our source for this text.

Were thine. Called in thy country's sorest hour,
When brother knew not brother—mad for power—
To guide the helm through bloody deeps of war,
While distant nations gazed in anxious awe,
Unflinching in the task, thou didst fulfill
Thy mighty mission with a deathless will.

Born to a destiny the most sublime,
Thou wert, O Lincoln! in the march of time,
God bade thee pause and bid the oppressed go free—
Most glorious boon giv'n to humanity.
While slavery ruled the land, what deeds were done?
What tragedies enacted 'neath the sun!
Her page is blurred with records of defeat,
Of lives heroic lived in silence, meet
For the world's praise; of woe, despair and tears,
The speechless agony of weary years.

Thou utteredst the word, and Freedom fair
Rang her sweet bells on the clear winter air;
She waved her magic wand, and lo! from far
A long procession came. With many a scar
Their brows were wrinkled, in the bitter strife,
Full many had said their sad farewell to life
But on they hastened, free, their shackles gone;
The aged, young,—e'en infancy was borne
To offer unto thee loud paeans of praise,—
Their happy tribute after saddest days.

A race set free! The deed brought joy and light!
It bade calm Justice from her sacred height,
When faith and hope and courage slowly waned,
Unfurl the stars and stripes, at last unstained!
The nations rolled acclaim from sea to sea,
And Heaven's vault rang with Freedom's harmony.
The angels 'mid the amaranths must have hushed
Their chanted cadences, as upward rushed
The hymn sublime: and as the echoes pealed,
God's ceaseless benison the action sealed.

As now we dedicate this shaft to thee,
True champion! in all humility
And solemn earnestness, we would erect
A monument invisible, undecked,
Save by our allied purpose to be true
To Freedom's loftiest precepts, so that through
The fiercest contests we may walk secure,
Fixed on foundations that may still endure,
When granite shall have crumbled to decay,
And generations passed from earth away.

Exalted patriot! illustrious chief!
Thy life's immortal work compels belief.
To-day in radiance thy virtues shine,
And how can we a fitting garland twine?
Thy crown most glorious to a ransomed race!
High on our country's scroll we fondly trace,
In lines of fadeless light that softly blend,
Emancipator, hero, martyr, friend!
While Freedom may her holy sceptre claim,
The world shall echo with Our Lincoln's name.

Part II

COLLECTIONS AND VOLUMES OF CIVIL WAR POETRY

George Moses Horton (1797?–1883)

The remarkable career of George Moses Horton is a testament to one man's perseverance and resourcefulness. Born into slavery in North Carolina, Horton spent his childhood working on his masters' farms. As a young man, he began traveling to Chapel Hill where he worked as a jack-of-all-trades and also sold his poems to university students. By the time he turned twenty, Horton had become so successful at these enterprises that he made this trip almost weekly; he no doubt benefited from the fact that in the 1820s, North Carolina had some of the most liberal slavery laws of any Southern state. By the 1830s, Horton had persuaded his master to let him purchase his own time. Although he had taught himself to read as a child, he did not learn to write until around this time, well after he was widely known as a poet. Horton had quickly proved himself an expert at composing love poems and acrostics for students—composing in his head and then dictating to paying customers. He was able to make a remarkably good living by means of this work.

In the meantime, Horton was also composing his own poetry. With the help of white sponsors, he began to publish in Southern and Northern newspapers in the late 1820s; he also dictated and published his first collection, with the aim of purchasing his freedom. *The Hope of Liberty* (1829) did not lead to Horton's emancipation; it was, however, reprinted in the North, where abolitionists used it as evidence of the injustice of slavery. This volume was the first book published by an African American living in the South. In 1845, Horton published a second collection, enlisting the support of nearly a hundred subscribers. *The Poetical Works of George M. Horton, the Colored Bard of North Carolina* included forty-five poems, as well as an autobiographical essay. Much of the information we have about Horton's life is drawn from this source. Though Horton married and had two children, little is known about his life for the next two decades. In the 1830s, North Carolina began to tighten restrictions on slaves and free blacks in response to several slave uprisings. In view of these changes, it is not surprising that Horton's *Poetical Works* includes no antislavery poems, although *The Hope of Liberty* does.

When Union forces arrived in North Carolina in April 1865, the sixty-eight-year-old Horton traveled for three months with the 9th Michigan Cavalry Volunteers under the command of Captain William Banks. Once again Horton supported himself by writing love poems for young white men, this time for Union soldiers. With the sponsorship of Banks, a third collection of Horton's poems, *Naked Genius,* was printed that summer; Horton wrote most of the poems in this collection while he was on the march. It was probably about a year later that he moved from Chapel Hill to Philadelphia. While Horton's poetry is a remarkable accomplishment in and of itself, his body of work also shows a surprising range of themes and forms, including religious verse, arguments for abolition and temperance, sentimental stances, paeans to the natural world, and reflections on the Civil War in particular and war in general. Although modern critics initially dismissed Horton's work as derivative, more recently scholars have begun to consider the ways in which Horton uses imitative postures and irony to express through indirection what a Southern slave could never have expressed directly.

Slavery[1]

By a Carolinian Slave named George Horton

When first my bosom glowed with hope,
I gaz'd as from a mountain top
  On some delightful plain;
But oh! how transient was the scene—
It fled as though it had not been,
    And all my hopes were vain.

How oft this tantalizing blaze
Has led me through deception's maze;
  My friend became my foe—
Then like a plaintive dove I mourn'd,
To bitter all my sweets were turn'd,
    And tears began to flow.

Why was the dawning of my birth
Upon this vile accursed earth,
    Which is but pain to me?
Oh! that my soul had winged its flight,
When first I saw the morning light,
    To worlds of liberty!

1. *Freedom's Journal* July 18, 1828; cited from *The Black Bard of North Carolina: George Moses Horton and His Poetry*, ed. Joan R. Sherman (Chapel Hill: University of North Carolina Press, 1997).

Come melting Pity from afar
And break this vast, enormous bar
Between a wretch and thee;
Purchase a few short days of time,
And bid a vassal rise sublime
On wings of liberty.

Is it because my skin is black,
That thou should'st be so dull and slack,
And scorn to set me free?
Then let me hasten to the grave,
The only refuge for the slave,
Who mourns for liberty.

The wicked cease from trouble there;
No more I'd languish or despair—
The weary there can rest.
Oppression's voice is heard no more,
Drudg'ry and pain, and toil are o'er.
Yes! there I shall be blest.

Lines[2]

On hearing of the intention of a gentleman to purchase the poet's freedom

When on life's ocean first I spread my sail,
I then implored a mild auspicious gale;
And from the slippery strand I took my flight,
And sought the peaceful haven of delight.

Tyrannic storms arose upon my soul,
And dreadful did their mad'ning thunders roll;
The pensive muse was shaken from her sphere,
And hope, it vanished in the clouds of fear.

At length a golden sun broke through the gloom,
And from his smiles arose a sweet perfume—
A calm ensued, and birds began to sing,
And lo! the sacred muse resumed her wing.

2. *Register* October 7, 1828; cited from *The Black Bard*.

With frantic joy she chanted as she flew,
And kiss'd the clement hand that bore her through;
Her envious foes did from her sight retreat,
Or prostrate fall beneath her burning feet.

'Twas like a proselyte, allied to Heaven—
Or rising spirits' boast of sins forgiven,
Whose shout dissolves the adamant away,
Whose melting voice the stubborn rocks obey.

'Twas like the salutation of the dove,
Borne on the zephyr through some lonesome grove,
When Spring returns, and Winter's chill is past,
And vegetation smiles above the blast.

'Twas like the evening of a nuptial pair,
When love pervades the hour of sad despair—
'Twas like fair Helen's sweet return to Troy,
When every Grecian bosom swell'd with joy.

The silent harp which on the osiers hung,
Was then attuned, and manumission sung;
Away by hope the clouds of fear were driven,
And music breathed my gratitude to Heaven.

Hard was the race to reach the distant goal,
The needle oft was shaken from the pole;
In such distress who could forbear to weep?
Toss'd by the headlong billows of the deep!

The tantalizing beams which shone so plain,
Which turned my former pleasures into pain—
Which falsely promised all the joys of fame,
Gave way, and to a more substantial flame.

Some philanthropic souls as from afar,
With pity strove to break the slavish bar;
To whom my floods of gratitude shall roll,
And yield with pleasure to their soft control.

And sure of Providence this work begun—
He shod my feet this rugged race to run;
And in despite of all the swelling tide,
Along the dismal path will prove my guide.

Thus on the dusky verge of deep despair,
Eternal Providence was with me there;
When pleasure seemed to fade on life's gay dawn,
And the last beam of hope was almost gone.

The Poet's Feeble Petition[3]

Bewailing mid the ruthless wave,
  I lift my feeble hand to thee.
Let me no longer live a slave
  But drop these fetters and be free.

Why will regardless fortune sleep
  Deaf to my penitential prayer,
Or leave the struggling Bard to weep,
  Alas, and languish in despair?

He is an eagle void of wings
  Aspiring to the mountain's height;
Yet in the vale aloud he sings
  For Pity's aid to give him flight.

Then listen all who never felt
  For fettered genius heretofore—
Let hearts of petrifaction melt
  And bid the gifted Negro soar.

General Grant* —The Hero of the War[4]

Brave Grant, thou hero of the war,
Thou art the emblem of the morning star,
Transpiring from the East to banish fear,
Revolving o'er a servile Hemisphere,
At large thou hast sustained the chief command

3. This poem was included in an unmailed letter to Horace Greeley, September 11, 1852; cited from *The Black Bard.*

4. *Naked Genius*, 1865. All other poems reprinted here were first published in and are cited from Horton's *Naked Genius*, 1865; the poems are cited in the order in which they appear there.

And at whose order all must rise and stand,
To hold position in the field is thine,
To sink in darkness or to rise and shine.

Thou art the leader of the Fed'ral band,
To send them at thy pleasure through the land,
Whose martial soldiers never did recoil
Nor fail in any place to take the spoil,
Thus organized was all the army firm,
And led unwavering to their lawful term,
Never repulsed or made to shrink with fear,
Advancing in their cause so truly dear.

The love of Union burned in every heart,
Which led them true and faithful from the start,
Whether upon water or on land,
They all obeyed their marshal's strict command,
By him the regiments were all surveyed,
His trumpet voice was by the whole obeyed,
His order right was every line to form,
And all be well prepared to front the storm.

Ye Southern gentlemen must grant him praise,
Nor on the flag of Union fail to gaze;
Ye ladies of the South forego the prize,
Our chief commander here to recognize,
From him the stream of general orders flow,
And every chief on him some praise bestow,
The well-known victor of the mighty cause
Demands from every voice a loud applause.

What more has great Napoleon ever done,
Though many battles in his course he won?
What more has Alexander e'er achieved,
Who left depopulated cities grieved?
To him we dedicate the whole in song,
The verses from our pen to him belong,
To him the Union banners are unfurled,
The star of peace the standard of the world.

The Southern Refugee

What sudden ill the world await,
From my dear residence I roam;
I must deplore the bitter fate,
To straggle from my native home.

The verdant willow droops her head,
And seems to bid a fare thee well;
The flowers with tears their fragrance shed,
Alas! their parting tale to tell.

'Tis like the loss of Paradise,
Or Eden's garden left in gloom,
Where grief affords us no device;
Such is thy lot, my native home.

I never, never shall forget
My sad departure far away,
Until the sun of life is set,
And leaves behind no beam of day.

How can I from my seat remove
And leave my ever devoted home,
And the dear garden which I love,
The beauty of my native home?

Alas! sequestered, set aside,
It is a mournful tale to tell;
'Tis like a lone deserted bride
That bade her bridegroom fare thee well.

I trust I soon shall dry the tear
And leave forever hence to roam,
Far from a residence so dear,
The place of beauty—my native home.

Lincoln Is Dead

He is gone, the strong base of the nation,
  The dove to his covet has fled;
Ye heroes lament his privation,
  For Lincoln is dead.

He is gone down, the sun of the Union,
  Like Phoebus, that sets in the west;
The planet of peace and communion,
  Forever has gone to his rest.

He is gone down from a world of commotion,
  No equal succeeds in his stead;
His wonders extend with the ocean,
  Whose waves murmur, Lincoln is dead.

He is gone and can ne'er be forgotten,
  Whose great deeds eternal shall bloom;
When gold, pearls and diamonds are rotten,
  His deeds will break forth from the tomb.

He is gone out of glory to glory,
  A smile with the tear may be shed,
O, then let us tell the sweet story,
  Triumphantly, Lincoln is dead.

Like Brothers We Meet

Dedicated to the Federal and Late Confederate Soldiers

Like heart-loving brothers we meet,
  And still the loud thunders of strife,
The blaze of fraternity kindles most sweet,
  There's nothing more pleasing in life.

The black cloud of faction retreats,
  The poor is no longer depressed,
See those once discarded resuming their seats,
  The lost strangers soon will find rest.

The soldier no longer shall roam,
  But soon shall land safely ashore,
Each soon will arrive at his own native home,
  And struggle in warfare no more.

The union of brothers is sweet,
  Whose wives and children do come,
Their sons and fair daughters with pleasure they greet,
  When long absent fathers come home.

They never shall languish again,
  Nor discord their union shall break,
When brothers no longer lament and complain,
  Hence never each other forsake.

Hang closely together like friends,
  By peace killing foes never driven,
The storm of commotion eternally ends,
  And earth will soon turn into Heaven.

The Dying Soldier's Message

Weep, mother, weep, it must be so,
  A tear when parting must be shed,
  The falling tribute is due the dead,
Which leaves the world in gloom below.
  Go flitting bird that splits the sky,
Where sits my mother sighing,
  And should she rise and ask you why,
O, tell her I am dying.

Weep, Father, I shall soon be gone;
  I travel to return no more,
  But sorrow cannot life restore,
I leave the whole to God alone.
  Go, gentle zephyrs, bear the tale,
While sweet the dove is sighing,
  Tell mother never long bewail,
However, I am dying.

Weep, brother, for fraternal love,
Death is about to close the scene—
Short is the space that lies between
My soul and better worlds above.
Let thunder storms my fate betray,
Ye sable vapors flying,
Sound that my life has past away,
Tell mother I am dying.

Weep, sister, love was born to grieve
For one thus passing out of time;
From this to other worlds sublime,
I shut my eyes and take my leave.
The favorite bird will soon have fled;
The fate there's no denying,
I soon shall lodge among the dead,
For I am surely dying.

The Spectator of the Battle of Belmont[5]

November 6, 1863

O, brother spectators, I long shall remember,
The blood-crimson veil which spreads over the field,
When battle commenc'd on the sixth of November,
With war-beaming aspect, the sword and the shield.

The sound of destruction breaks loud from the mortars,
The watchman is tolling the death-tuning knell,
The heroes are clustering from quarter to quarter;
What mortal, the fate of this combat shall tell?

Blood breaks from its vein like a stream from its fountain;
Spectators the pain of the conflict explore;
The fugitives fly to the cave on the mountain,
Betray'd by the vestige of blood in their gore.

5. The Battle of Belmont* took place on November 7, 1861. Although Horton or his printer may have mistaken the date, it is more likely that Horton adjusted the date to fit the meter of the poem.

The conflict begins from the twang of the drummer,
   And ends with the peal of a tragical tale;
O yes, its subsides like a storm into summer,
   No less for the dead shall the living bewail.

I've heard of the battles of many foreign nations;
   I've heard of the wonderful conflict of Troy,
And battles, with bloodshed, thro' all generations,
   But nothing like this could my feelings annoy.

The dark dirge of destiny, sung by a spirit,
   Alone can the scene of the combat display,
For surely no dull earthly mortal can merit
   A wonder to equal this tragical lay.

The Terrors of War

He bids the comet play,
   And empires tremble at his burning tail;
Commanding troops without delay,
The distant land his calls obey,
Ye proud imperial powers give way,
   And at the cause bewail.

Along the common tide,
   Pallid he floated with a hideous yell;
Napoleon bellowed at his side,
And saw compassion all denied;
Beneath his stroke, ten thousand died,
   And wounded millions fell.

Ye breathe a doleful strain,
   Pursued at once by heavy rending peals;
He heaved his thunders from the main,
In purple gore he dyed the plain,
Then boasted his legions slain,
   Beneath the ruthless wheel.

Pregnant with every ill,
   He breathed his stenched diseases from afar;

A quiet world no more was still,
And terrors broke from hill to hill,
Whose bloody thirst was all to kill,
  Which stood before his car.

Jefferson in a Tight Place[6]

The Fox Is Caught

The blood hounds, long upon the trail,
Have rambled faithful, hill and dale;
But mind, such creatures never fail,
  To run the rebel down.
His fears forbid him long to stop,
Altho' he gains the mountain top,
He soon is made his tail to drop,
  And fleets to leave the hounds.

Alas! He speeds from place to place,
Such is the fox upon the chase;
To him the mud is no disgrace,
  No lair his cause defends.
He leaves a law and seeks a dell,
And where to fly 'tis hard to tell;
He fears before to meet with hell;
  Behind he has no friends.

But who can pity such a fox,
Though buried among the rocks?
He's a nuisance among the flocks.
  And sucks the blood of geese.
He takes advantage of the sheep,
His nature is at night to creep,
And rob the flocks while the herdsmen sleep,
  When dogs can have no peace.

6. The title refers to Jefferson Davis*, who was captured by Union forces in Georgia on May 10, 1865. Northern papers falsely reported that Davis was disguised in women's clothing at the time of his capture.

But he is now brought to a bay,
However fast he run away,
He knows he has not long to stay,
And assumes a raccoon's dress.
Found in a hole, he veils his face,
And fain would take a lady's place,
But fails, for he has run his race,
And falls into distress.

The fox is captured in his den,
The martial troops of Michigan
May hence be known the fleetest men,
For Davis is their prey.
Great Babylon has fallen down,
A King is left without a crown,
Stripped of honors and renown,
The evening ends the day.

The Soldier on His Way Home

Soon, soon we shall depart,
Like light ascending out of gloom;
We now are ready to depart,
To our dear native home.

Adieu, ye noisy drums,
No more we hear dread monsters roar;
Adieu, ye thunder teeming guns,
Ye shake our camp no more.

We surely must rejoice,
We have no longer hence to roam;
Left like a trump, each joy prevail,
We're on our journey home.

Home is the sweetest place,
Who will not be contented there;
Rather than rove thro' woods apace,
With sorrow, gloom and fear.

Sound a loud tap before,
  And let our kindred know we come,
Let voices like sweet thunder war,
  We soon shall land at home.

The fields in rich array,
  And streamlets bubbling as they flow,
Allure the pensive mind away,
  Whilst vallies smile below.

We now anticipate,
  Our gardens teeming fresh in bloom,
And kindred meet us at the gate,
  Glad that we are home.

Weep

Weep for the country in its present state,
And of the gloom which still the future waits;
The proud confederate eagle heard the sound,
And with her flight fell prostrate to the ground!

Weep for the loss the country has sustained,
By which her now dependent is in jail;

The grief of him who now the war survived,
The conscript husbands and the weeping wives!

Weep for the seas of blood the battle cost,
And souls that ever hope forever lost!
The ravage of the field with no recruit,
Trees by the vengeance blasted to the root!

Weep for the downfall o'er your heads and chief,
Who sunk without a medium of relief;
Who fell beneath the hatchet of their pride,
Then like the serpent bit themselves and died!

Weep for the downfall of your president,
Who far too late his folly must repent;
Who like the dragon did all heaven assail,
And dragged his friends to limbo with his tail!

Weep o'er peculiar swelling coffers void,
Our treasures left, and all their banks destroyed;
Their foundless notes replete with shame to all,
Expecting every day their final fall,
In quest of profit never to be won,
Then sadly fallen and forever down!

John Greenleaf Whittier (1807–1892)

John Greenleaf Whittier thought of himself first as an abolitionist and second as a poet, although he was revered as a poet by the time of his death and published several volumes of poems. Born on December 17, 1807, in rural Massachusetts to a Quaker family struggling to hold on to their failing farm, Whittier spent a childhood and youth in hard labor, with little time or energy for formal schooling but an interest in books. The regional dialect poetry of Robert Burns inspired Whittier to think he, too, could write about the homely experiences he knew firsthand. In 1826, at the age of nineteen, he published his first poem in a journal edited by William Lloyd Garrison, and the two men became friends. Garrison encouraged the social reforming conscience of Whittier's Quaker upbringing, and Whittier soon began writing as an outspoken abolitionist. In 1833 he published an important abolitionist manifesto, *Justice and Expediency*; in 1835 he was elected as Massachusetts representative to Congress for one term; and in 1839 he helped to found the antislavery Liberty Party. During the 1830s and 1840s, abolitionist politics were generally unpopular in the North as well as in the South, and Whittier suffered for his radical views. Not only did his outspoken politics probably incline many readers away from his poems, but his publication and public speaking also led to his being mobbed and stoned and to a raid on his office, which was burned. During these years, Whittier also edited various newspapers and published *Legends of New England* (1831), *Lays of My Home* (1843), *Supernaturalism of New England* (1847), and *Leaves from Margaret Smith's Journal* (1849).

By the 1850s, many Northerners had adopted antislavery views. As a consequence, during the war, Whittier's many antislavery and pro-Union poems were well received. "Barbara Frietchie" in particular was widely reprinted. The prestigious *Atlantic Monthly*, founded in 1857, also helped Whittier's literary fortunes by publishing much of his work. Following the war, Whittier continued to write. His work was primarily in the realist vein associated with "local color" writing by regionalists such as Sarah Orne Jewett, whom Whittier admired and assisted. With the publication of his poem "Snow-Bound" in 1866, his reputation was secure. This poem brought him national acclaim and financial security, for the first time in his life. In a poem called "The Tent on the Beach," Whittier portrays a dreamer who makes "his rustic reed of song / A weapon in the war with wrong" (*The Tent on the Beach and Other Poems*, 1867). This description fits well his own sense of priority in understanding his work for abolitionism as a higher calling than his literary production. Like others in his family, Whittier never married. He died a famous poet on September 7, 1892.

The Hunters of Men[1]

Have ye heard of our hunting, o'er mountain and glen,
Through cane-brake and forest,—the hunting of men?
The lords of our land to this hunting have gone,
As the fox-hunter follows the sound of the horn;
Hark! the cheer and the hallo! The crack of the whip,
And the yell of the hound as he fastens his grip!
All blithe are our hunters, and noble their match,
Though hundreds are caught, there are millions to catch.
So speed to their hunting, o'er mountain and glen,
Through cane-brake and forest,—the hunting of men!

Gay luck to our hunters! how nobly they ride
In the glow of their zeal, and the strength of their pride!
The priest with his cassock flung back on the wind,
Just screening the politic statesman behind;
The saint and the sinner, with cursing and prayer,
The drunk and the sober, ride merrily there.
And woman, kind woman, wife, widow, and maid,
For the good of the hunted, is lending her aid:
Her foot's in the stirrup, her hand on the rein,
How blithely she rides to the hunting of men!

Oh, goodly and grand is our hunting to see,
In this "land of the brave and this home of the free."
Priest, warrior, and statesman, from Georgia to Maine,
All mounting the saddle, all grasping the rein;
Right merrily hunting the black man, whose sin
Is the curl of his hair and the hue of his skin!
Woe, now, to the hunted who turns him at bay!
Will our hunters be turned from their purpose and prey?

1. *The Liberator* 1834; all Whittier poems reprinted here are cited from *Whittier: The Cambridge Poets*, ed. Horace E. Scudder (Boston: Houghton Mifflin, 1894).

Will their hearts fail within them? their nerves tremble, when
All roughly they ride to the hunting of men?

Ho! alms for our hunters! all weary and faint,
Wax the curse of the sinner and prayer of the saint.
The horn is wound faintly, the echoes are still,
Over cane-brake and river, and forest and hill.
Haste, alms for our hunters! the hunted once more
Have turned from their flight with their backs to the shore:
What right have they here in the home of the white,
Shadowed o'er by our banner of Freedom and Right?
Ho! alms for the hunters! or never again
Will they ride in their pomp to the hunting of men!

Alms, alms for our hunters! why will ye delay,
When their pride and their glory are melting away?
The parson has turned; for, on charge of his own,
Who goeth a warfare, or hunting, alone?
The politic statesman looks back with a sigh,
There is doubt in his heart, there is fear in his eye.
Oh, haste, lest that doubting and fear shall prevail,
And the head of his steed take the place of the tail.
Oh, haste, ere he leave us! for who will ride then,
For pleasure or gain, to the hunting of men?

A Word for the Hour[2]

The firmament breaks up. In black eclipse
Light after light goes out. One evil star,
Luridly glaring through the smoke of war,
As in the dream of the Apocalypse,
Drags others down. Let us not weakly weep
Nor rashly threaten. Give us grace to keep
Our faith and patience; wherefore should we leap
On one hand into fratricidal fight,

2. Written on January 16, 1861, responding to the secession of South Carolina, Mississippi, Florida, and Alabama from the United States; published in the *Boston Evening Transcript* January 1861.

Or, on the other, yield eternal right,
Frame lies of laws, and good and ill confound?
What fear we? Safe on freedom's vantage-ground
Our feet are planted: let us there remain
In unrevengeful calm, no means untried
Which truth can sanction, no just claim denied,
The sad spectators of a suicide!
They break the links of Union: shall we light
The fires of hell to weld anew the chain
On that red anvil where each blow is pain?
Draw we not even now a freer breath,
As from our shoulders falls a load of death
Loathsome as that the Tuscan's victim bore
When keen with life to a dead horror bound?
Why take we up the accursed thing again?
Pity, forgive, but urge them back no more
Who, drunk with passion, flaunt disunion's rag
With its vile reptile-blazon. Let us press
The golden cluster on our brave old flag
In closer union, and, if numbering less,
Brighter shall shine the stars which still remain.

Ein feste Burg ist unser Gott[3]

We wait beneath the furnace-blast
    The pangs of transformation;
Not painlessly doth God recast
    And mould anew the nation.
        Hot burns the fire
        Where wrongs expire;
        Nor spares the hand
    That from the land
Uproots the ancient evil.

The hand-breadth cloud the sages feared
    Its bloody rain is dropping;

3. The title of a hymn by Martin Luther, sung in U.S. Protestant churches as "A Mighty Fortress Is Our God"; Whittier's poem was written in 1861.

The poison plant the fathers spared
  All else is overtopping.
    East, West, South, North,
    It curses the earth;
    All justice dies,
  And fraud and lies
Live only in its shadow.

What gives the wheat-field blades of steel?
  What points the rebel cannon?
What sets the roaring rabble's heel
  On the old star-spangled pennon?
    What breaks the oath
    Of the men o' the South?
    What whets the knife
  For the Union's life?—
Hark to the answer: Slavery!

Then waste no blows on lesser foes
  In strife unworthy freemen.
God lifts today the veil, and shows
  The features of the demon!
    O North and South
    Its victims both,
    Can ye not cry,
  "Let slavery die!"
And union find in freedom?

What though the cast-out spirit tear
  The nation in his going?
We who have shared guilt must share
  The pang of his o'erthrowing!
    Whate'er the loss,
    Whate'er the cross,
    Shall they complain
  Of present pain
Who trust in God's hereafter?

For who that leans on His right arm
  Was ever yet forsaken?
What righteous cause can suffer harm

If He its part has taken?
Though wild and loud,
And dark the cloud,
Behind its folds
His hand upholds
The calm sky of tomorrow.

Above the maddening cry for blood,
Above the wild war-drumming,
Let Freedom's voice be heard, with good
The evil overcoming.
Give prayer and purse
To stay the Curse
Whose wrong we share,
Whose shame we bear,
Whose end shall gladden Heaven!

In vain the bells of war shall ring
Of triumphs and revenges,
While still is spared the evil thing
That severs and estranges.
But blest the ear
That yet shall hear
The jubilant bell
That rings the knell
Of Slavery forever!

Then let the selfish lip be dumb,
And hushed the breath of sighing;
Before the joy of peace must come
The pains of purifying.
God give us grace
Each in his place
To bear his lot,
And, murmuring not,
Endure and wait and labor!

At Port Royal*[4]

The tent-lights glimmer on the land,
The ship-lights on the sea;
The night-wind smooths with drifting sand
Our track on lone Tybee.

At last our grating keels outslide,
Our good boats forward swing;
And while we ride the land-locked tide,
Our negroes row and sing.

For dear the bondman holds his gifts
Of music and of song:
The gold that kindly Nature sifts
Among his sands of wrong;

The power to make his toiling days
And poor home-comforts please;
The quaint relief of mirth that plays
With sorrow's minor keys.

Another glow than sunset's fire
Has filled the west with light,
Where field and garner, barn and byre,
Are blazing through the night.

The land is wild with fear and hate,
The rout runs mad and fast;
From hand to hand, from gate to gate
The flaming brand is passed.

The lurid glow falls strong across
Dark faces broad with smiles:
Not theirs the terror, hate, and loss
That fire yon blazing piles.

With oar-strokes timing to their song,
They weave in simple lays

---

4. *Atlantic Monthly* February 1862. Whittier took particular interest in the Port Royal* experiment that followed the Union victory at Port Royal Sound in late 1861. The "Song of the Negro Boatmen" included in this poem is Whittier's imitation of a slave song.

The pathos of remembered wrong,
    The hope of better days,—

The triumph-note that Miriam sung,
    The joy of uncaged birds:
Softening with Afric's mellow tongue
    Their broken Saxon words.

SONG OF THE NEGRO BOATMEN

Oh, praise an' tanks! De Lord he come
    To set de people free;
An' massa tink it day ob doom,
    An' we ob jubilee.
De Lord dat heap de Red Sea waves
    He jus' as 'trong as den;
He say de word: we las' night slaves;
    To-day, de Lord's free men.
        De yam will grow, de cotton blow,
            We'll hab de rice an' corn;
        Oh nebber you fear, if nebber you hear
            De driver blow his horn!

Ole massa on he trabbels gone;
    He leaf de land behind:
De Lord's breff blow him furder on,
    Like corn-shuck in de wind.
We own de hoe, we own de plough,
    We own de hands dat hold;
We sell de pig, we sell de cow,
    But nebber chile be sold.
        De yam will grow, de cotton blow,
            We'll hab de rice an' corn;
        Oh nebber you fear, if nebber you hear
            De driver blow his horn!

We pray de Lord: he gib us signs
    Dat some day we be free;
De norf-wind tell it to de pines,
    De wild-duck to de sea;
We tink it when de church-bell ring,
    We dream it in de dream;

De rice-bird mean it when he sing,
De eagle when he scream.
De yam will grown, de cotton blow,
We'll hab de rice an' corn;
Oh nebber you fear, if nebber you hear
De driver blow his horn!

We know de promise nebber fail,
An' nebber lie de word;
So, like de 'postles in de jail,
We waited for de Lord:
An' now he open ebery door,
An' trow away de key;
He tink we lub him so before,
We lub him better free.
De yam will grow, de cotton blow,
He'll gib de rice an' corn;
Oh nebber you fear, if nebber you hear
De driver blow his horn!

So sing our dusky gondoliers;
And with a secret pain,
And smiles that seem akin to tears,
We hear the wild refrain.

We dare not share the negro's trust,
Nor yet his hope deny;
We only know that God is just,
And every wrong shall die.

Rude seems the song; each swarthy face,
Flame-lighted, ruder still:
We start to think that hapless race
Must shape our good or ill;

That laws of changeless justice bind
Oppressor with oppressed;
And, close as sin and suffering joined,
We march to Fate abreast.

Sing on, poor hearts! your chant shall be
Our sign of blight or bloom,

The Vala-song of Liberty,
    Or death-rune of our doom!

The Battle Autumn of 1862[5]

The flags of war like storm-birds fly,
    The charging trumpets blow,
Yet rolls no thunder in the sky,
    No earthquake strives below.

And, calm and patient, Nature keeps
    Her ancient promise well,
Though o'er her bloom and greenness sweeps
    The battle's breath of hell.

And still she walks in golden hours
    Through harvest-happy farms,
And still she wears her fruits and flowers
    Like jewels on her arms.

What mean the gladness of the plain,
    This joy of eve and morn,
The mirth that shakes the beard of grain
    And yellow locks of corn?

Ah! eyes may be full of tears,
    And hearts with hate are hot;
But even-paced come round the years,
    And Nature changes not.

She meets with smiles our bitter grief,
    With songs our groans of pain;
She mocks with tint of flower and leaf
    The war-field's crimson stain.

Still, in the cannon's pause, we hear
    Her sweet thanksgiving-psalm;
Too near to God for doubt or fear,
    She shares the eternal calm.

5. *Atlantic Monthly* October 1862.

She knows the seed lies safe below
The fires that blast and burn;
For all the tears of blood we sow
She waits the rich return.

She sees with clearer eye than ours
The good of suffering born—
The hearts that blossom like her flowers,
And ripen like her corn.

Oh, give to us, in times like these,
The vision of her eyes;
And make her fields and fruited trees
Our golden prophecies!

Oh, give to us her finer ear!
Above this stormy din.
We too would hear the bells of cheer
Ring peace and freedom in.

What the Birds Said[6]

The birds against the April wind
Flew northward, singing as they flew;
They sang, "The land we leave behind
Has swords for corn-blades, blood for dew."

"O wild-birds, flying from the South,
What saw and heard ye, gazing down?"
"We saw the mortar's upturned mouth,
The sickened camp, the blazing town!

"Beneath the bivouac's* starry lamps,
We saw your march-worn children die;
In shrouds of moss, in cypress swamps,
We saw your dead uncoffined lie.

"We heard the starving prisoner's* sighs
And saw, from line and trench, your sons

6. *Atlantic Monthly* May 1863.

Follow our flight with home-sick eyes
    Beyond the battery's smoking guns."

"And heard and saw ye only wrong
    And pain," I cried, "O wing-worn flocks?"
"We heard," they sang, "the freedman's song,
    The crash of Slavery's broken locks!

"We saw from new, uprising States
    The treason-nursing mischief spurned,
As, crowding Freedom's ample gates,
    The long-estranged and lost returned.

"O'er dusky faces, seamed and old,
    And hands horn-hard with unpaid toil,
With hope in every rustling fold,
    We saw your star-dropt flag uncoil.

"And struggling up through sounds accursed,
    A grateful murmur clomb the air;
A whisper scarcely heard at first,
    It filled the listening heavens with prayer.

"And sweet and far, as from a star,
    Replied a voice which shall not cease,
Till, drowning all the noise of war,
    It sings the blessed song of peace!"

So to me, in a doubtful day
    Of chill and slowly greening spring,
Low stooping from the cloudy gray,
    The wild-birds sang or seemed to sing.

They vanished in the misty air,
    The song went with them in their flight;
But lo! they left the sunset fair,
    And in the evening there was light.

Barbara Frietchie[7]

Up from the meadows rich with corn,
Clear in the cool September morn,

The clustered spires of Frederick stand
Green-walled by the hills of Maryland.

Round about them orchards sweep,
Apple and peach tree fruited deep,

Fair as the garden of the Lord
To the eyes of the famished rebel horde,

On that pleasant morn of the early fall
When Lee* marched over the mountain wall;

Over the mountains winding down,
Horse and foot, into Frederick town.

Forty flags with their silver stars,
Forty flags with their crimson bars,

Flapped in the morning wind: the sun
Of noon looked down, and saw not one.

Up rose old Barbara Frietchie then,
Bowed with her fourscore years and ten;

Bravest of all in Frederick town,
She took up the flag the men hauled down;

In her attic window the staff she set,
To show that one heart was loyal yet.

Up the street came the rebel tread,
Stonewall Jackson* riding ahead.

Under his slouched hat left and right
He glanced; the old flag met his sight.

"Halt!"—the dust-brown ranks stood fast.
"Fire!"—out blazed the rifle-blast.

7. *Atlantic Monthly* October 1863. Whittier repeatedly asserted the truth of this incident.

It shivered the window, pane and sash;
It rent the banner with seam and gash.

Quick, as it fell, from the broken staff
Dame Barbara snatched the silken scarf.

She leaned far out on the window-sill,
And shook it forth with a royal will.

"Shoot, if you must, this old gray head,
But spare your country's flag," she said.

A shade of sadness, a blush of shame,
Over the face of the leader came;

The nobler nature within him stirred
To life at that woman's deed and word;

"Who touches a hair of yon gray head
Dies like a dog! March on!" he said.

All day long through Frederick street
Sounded the tread of marching feet:

All day long that free flag tossed
Over the heads of the rebel host.

Ever its torn folds rose and fell
On the loyal winds that loved it well;

And through the hill-gaps sunset light
Shone over it with a warm good-night.

Barbara Frietchie's work is o'er,
And the Rebel rides on his raids no more.

Honor to her! and let a tear
Fall, for her sake, on Stonewall's bier.

Over Barbara Frietchie's grave,
Flag of Freedom and Union, wave!

Peace and order and beauty draw
Round thy symbol of light and law;

And ever the stars above look down
On thy stars below in Frederick town!

Walt Whitman (1819–1892)

Walt Whitman, one of the greatest American poets, is also a significant writer on the Civil War. Born on Long Island, Whitman moved to Brooklyn as an adolescent to begin a life involving most aspects of journalism and literature, working his way up from errand boy and typesetter to editor, poet, and novelist. Through the 1840s, he was modestly successful in his journalism and in publishing relatively conventional stories, poems, and a temperance novel. In 1855, he published the first of what are now regarded as his great works, a slim volume of radically unconventional poems titled *Leaves of Grass*. For the next thirty-seven years, Whitman republished *Leaves of Grass*, and it grew from twelve untitled poems to hundreds of pages of poetry divided into thematic groupings representing several aspects and stages of his philosophical, cultural, and personal reflections. In 1891–92, shortly before his death, Whitman supervised a revision of the sixth edition (1881–82) of his poems, resulting in one of the great volumes and bodies of world poetry. Heralded as both the first truly "American" poet and as the most significant forerunner of twentieth-century free verse movements, Whitman revolutionized poetic form through his stylistic innovations and breadth of content. He took on a number of topics previously considered taboo in verse (male and female sexuality, homosexuality, frank celebration of parts of the body considered below the dignity of the elevated genre of poetry, radical religious ecumenicalism), in the name of making a poem large and "natural" enough to encompass all aspects of the United States, considering the nation itself to be the world's greatest "poem."

From his early years as a journalist, Whitman engaged seriously in national politics as well as in philosophical and aesthetic issues. Long a Free-Soiler, with some personal ambivalence toward African Americans, at the outbreak of the war Whitman wrote fervently in support of the Union and soon began writing the poems that would appear as *Drum-Taps* in 1865. Early in the war he also visited sick and wounded soldiers at New York Hospital. In December 1862, on hearing that his brother George had been wounded, Whitman traveled to the front in Virginia and then settled in Washington, D.C., where he supported himself through part-time clerical work and spent the majority of his time and money tending the wounded as an unofficial nurse in military hospitals. He describes this experience in his poem "The Wound-Dresser" and reflects at greater length and more broadly on the war in a journal later published as *Specimen Days*. This journal/essay sequence provides a historically significant and illuminating account of the war years and of military camps and hospitals.

A great admirer of President Lincoln, Whitman was shocked and grieved by his assassination and wrote a number of poems immediately following the event, including his great elegy "When Lilacs Last in the Dooryard Bloom'd." Among his few entirely popular performances were his repeated lectures on Lincoln and on Lincoln's death. It was also while living in D.C. at the end of the war that Whitman met Peter Doyle and began the only known extended romantic-sexual relationship of his life. Although Whitman was not a popular poet in the United States during his lifetime, before his death he had received letters or visits of admiration from some of the most popular and important writers of his day, including **Ralph Waldo Emerson** (who had praised Whitman's poems as early as 1855), **Henry David Thoreau,** Alfred, Lord Tennyson, William M. Rosetti, and Oscar Wilde. Partially paralyzed in 1873, Whitman died an invalid, dependent on the friends and supporters who saw in his work a prophecy of literary and cultural changes they hoped would come.

Eighteen Sixty-One[1]

Arm'd year—year of the struggle,
No dainty rhymes or sentimental love verses for you terrible year,
Not you as some pale poetling seated at a desk lisping cadenzas piano,
But as a strong man erect, clothed in blue clothes, advancing, carrying a rifle on your shoulder,
With well-gristled body and sunburnt face and hands, with a knife in the belt at your side,
As I heard you shouting loud, your sonorous voice ringing across the continent,
Your masculine voice O year, as rising amid the great cities,
Amid the men of Manhattan I saw you as one of the workmen, the dwellers in Manhattan,
Or with large steps crossing the prairies out of Illinois and Indiana,

1. The following poems were first published in *Drum-Taps*, 1865, or *Sequel to Drum-Taps*, 1865–66, except for three poems added subsequently to the poems of this series: "Adieu to a Soldier" and "Ethiopia Saluting the Colors" (1871) and "Virginia—The West" (1872). The order of poems printed here is from the 1881–82 *Leaves of Grass*, as explained in the preface. All poems reprinted here are cited from *Walt Whitman: Leaves of Grass, A Textual Variorum of the Printed Poems*, ed. Sculley Bradley, Harold W. Blodgett, Arthur Golden, and William White (New York: New York University Press, 1980).

Rapidly crossing the West with springy gait, and descending the Alleghanies,
Or down from the great lakes or in Pennsylvania, or on deck along the Ohio river,
Or southward along the Tennessee or Cumberland rivers, or at Chattanooga on the mountain top,
Saw I your gait and saw I your sinewy limbs clothed in blue, bearing weapons, robust year,
Heard your determin'd voice launch'd forth again and again,
Year that suddenly sang by the mouths of the round-lipp'd cannon,
I repeat you, hurrying, crashing, sad, distracted year.

Beat! Beat! Drums!

Beat! beat! drums!—blow! bugles! blow!
Through the windows—through doors—burst like a ruthless force,
Into the solemn church, and scatter the congregation,
Into the school where the scholar is studying;
Leave not the bridegroom quiet—no happiness must he have now with his bride,
Nor the peaceful farmer any peace, ploughing his field or gathering his grain,
So fierce you whirr and pound you drums—so shrill you bugles blow.

Beat! beat! drums! —blow! bugles! blow!
Over the traffic of cities—over the rumble of wheels in the streets;
Are beds prepared for sleepers at night in the houses? no sleepers must sleep in those beds,
No bargainers' bargains by day—no brokers or speculators—would they continue?
Would the talkers be talking? would the singer attempt to sing?
Would the lawyer rise in the court to state his case before the judge?
Then rattle quicker, heavier drums—you bugles wilder blow.

Beat! beat! drums!—blow! bugles! blow!
Make no parley—stop for no expostulation,
Mind not the timid—mind not the weeper or prayer,
Mind not the old man beseeching the young man,
Let not the child's voice be heard, nor the mother's entreaties,
Make even the trestles to shake the dead where they lie awaiting the hearses,
So strong you thump O terrible drums—so loud you bugles blow.

Virginia—The West

The noble sire fallen on evil days,
I saw with hand uplifted, menacing, brandishing,
(Memories of old in abeyance, love and faith in abeyance,)
The insane knife toward the Mother of All.

The noble son on sinewy feet advancing,
I saw, out of the land of prairies, land of Ohio's waters and of Indiana,
To the rescue the stalwart giant hurry his plenteous offspring,
Drest in blue, bearing their trusty rifles on their shoulders.

Then the Mother of All with calm voice speaking,
As to you Rebellious, (I seemed to hear her say,) why strive against me, and why seek my life?
When you yourself forever provide to defend me?
For you provided me Washington—and now these also.

Cavalry Crossing a Ford

A line in long array where they wind betwixt green islands,
They take a serpentine course, their arms flash in the sun—hark to the musical clank,
Behold the silvery river, in it the splashing horses loitering stop to drink,
Behold the brown-faced men, each group, each person a picture, the negligent rest on the saddles,
Some emerge on the opposite bank, others are just entering the ford—while,
Scarlet and blue and snowy white,
The guidon flags flutter gayly in the wind.

Bivouac* on a Mountain Side

I see before me now a traveling army halting,
Below a fertile valley spread, with barns and the orchards of summer,
Behind, the terraced sides of a mountain, abrupt, in places rising high,
Broken, with rocks, with clinging cedars, with tall shapes dingily seen,
The numerous camp-fires scatter'd near and far, some away up on the mountain,

The shadowy forms of men and horses, looming, large-sized, flickering,
And over all the sky—the sky! far, far out of reach, studded, breaking out, the eternal stars.

An Army Corps on the March

With its cloud of skirmishers in advance,
With now the sound of a single shot snapping like a whip, and now an irregular volley,
The swarming ranks press on and on, the dense brigades press on,
Glittering dimly, toiling under the sun—the dust-cover'd men,
In columns rise and fall to the undulations of the ground,
With artillery interspers'd—the wheels rumble, the horses sweat,
As the army corps advances.

By the Bivouac's* Fitful Flame

By the bivouac's fitful flame,
A procession winding around me, solemn and sweet and slow—but first I note,
The tents of the sleeping army, the fields' and woods' dim outline,
The darkness lit by spots of kindled fire, the silence,
Like a phantom far or near an occasional figure moving,
The shrubs and trees, (as I lift my eyes they seem to be stealthily watching me,)
While wind in procession thoughts, O tender and wondrous thoughts,
Of life and death, of home and the past and loved, and of those that are far away;
A solemn and slow procession there as I sit on the ground,
By the bivouac's fitful flame.

Come Up from the Fields Father

Come up from the fields father, here's a letter from our Pete,
And come to the front door mother, here's a letter from thy dear son.

Lo, 'tis autumn,
Lo, where the trees, deeper green, yellower and redder,

Cool and sweeten Ohio's villages with leaves fluttering in the moderate wind,
Where apples ripe in the orchards hang and grapes on the trellis'd vines,
(Smell you the smell of the grapes on the vines?
Smell you the buckwheat where the bees were lately buzzing?)

Above all, lo, the sky so calm, so transparent after the rain, and with wondrous clouds,
Below too, all calm, all vital and beautiful, and the farm prospers well.

Down in the fields all prospers well,
But now from the fields come father, come at the daughter's call,
And come to the entry mother, to the front door come right away.

Fast as she can she hurries, something ominous, her steps trembling,
She does not tarry to smooth her hair nor adjust her cap.

Open the envelope quickly,
O this is not our son's writing, yet his name is sign'd,
O a strange hand writes for our dear son, O stricken mother's soul!
All swims before her eyes, flashes with black, she catches the main words only,
Sentences broken, *gunshot wound in the breast, cavalry skirmish, taken to hospital,*
At present low, but will soon be better.

Ah now the single figure to me,
Amid all teeming and wealthy Ohio with all its cities and farms,
Sickly white in the face and dull in the head, very faint,
By the jamb of a door leans.

Grieve not so, dear mother, (the just-grown daughter speaks through her sobs,
The little sisters huddle around speechless and dismay'd,)
See, dearest mother, the letter says Pete will soon be better.

Alas poor boy, he will never be better, (nor may-be needs to be better, that brave and simple soul,)
While they stand at home at the door he is dead already,
The only son is dead.

But the mother needs to be better,
She with thin form presently drest in black,
By day her meals untouch'd, then at night fitfully sleeping, often waking,
In the midnight waking, weeping, longing with one deep longing,
O that she might withdraw unnoticed, silent from life escape and withdraw,
To follow, to seek, to be with her dear dead son.

Vigil Strange I Kept on the Field One Night

Vigil strange I kept on the field one night;
When you my son and my comrade dropt at my side that day,
One look I but gave which your dear eyes return'd with a look I shall never forget,
One touch of your hand to mine O boy, reach'd up as you lay on the ground,
Then onward I sped in the battle, the even-contested battle,
Till late in the night reliev'd to the place at last again I made my way,
Found you in death so cold dear comrade, found your body son of responding kisses, (never again on earth responding,)
Bared your face in the starlight, curious the scene, cool blew the moderate night-wind,
Long there and then in vigil I stood, dimly around me the battle-field spreading,
Vigil wondrous and vigil sweet there in the fragrant silent night,
But not a tear fell, not even a long-drawn sigh, long, long I gazed,
Then on the earth partially reclining sat by your side leaning my chin in my hands,
Passing sweet hours, immortal and mystic hours with you dearest comrade—not a tear, not a word,
Vigil of silence, love and death, vigil for you my son and my soldier,
As onward silently stars aloft, eastward new ones upward stole,
Vigil final for you brave boy, (I could not save you, swift was your death,
I faithfully loved you and cared for you living, I think we shall surely meet again,)
Till at latest lingering of the night, indeed just as the dawn appear'd,
My comrade I wrapt in his blanket, envelop'd well his form,
Folded the blanket well, tucking it carefully over head and carefully under feet,
And there and then and bathed by the rising sun, my son in his grave, in his rude-dug grave I deposited,
Ending my vigil strange with that, vigil of night and battle-field dim,
Vigil for boy of responding kisses, (never again on earth responding,)
Vigil for comrade swiftly slain, vigil I never forget, how as day brighten'd,
I rose from the chill ground and folded my soldier well in his blanket,
And buried him where he fell.

A March in the Ranks Hard-Prest, and the Road Unknown

A march in the ranks hard-prest, and the road unknown,
A route through a heavy wood with muffled steps in the darkness,
Our army foil'd with loss severe, and the sullen remnant retreating,
Till after midnight glimmer upon us the lights of a dim-lighted building,
We come to an open space in the woods, and halt by the dim-lighted building,
'Tis a large old church at the crossing roads, now an impromptu hospital,
Entering but for a minute I see a sight beyond all the pictures and poems ever made,
Shadows of deepest, deepest black, just lit by moving candles and lamps,
And by one great pitchy torch stationary with wild red flame and clouds of smoke,
By these, crowds, groups of forms vaguely I see on the floor, some in the pews laid down,
At my feet more distinctly a soldier, a mere lad, in danger of bleeding to death, (he is shot in the abdomen,)
I stanch the blood temporarily, (the youngster's face is white as a lily,)
Then before I depart I sweep my eyes o'er the scene fain to absorb it all,
Faces, varieties, postures beyond description, most in obscurity, some of them dead,
Surgeons operating, attendants holding lights, the smell of ether, the odor of blood,
The crowd, O the crowd of the bloody forms, the yard outside also fill'd,
Some on the bare ground, some on planks or stretchers, some in the death-spasm sweating,
An occasional scream or cry, the doctor's shouted orders or calls,
The glisten of the little steel instruments catching the glint of the torches,
These I resume as I chant, I see again the forms, I smell the odor,
Then hear outside the orders given, *Fall in, my men, fall in;*
But first I bend to the dying lad, his eyes open, a half-smile gives he me,
Then the eyes close, calmly close, and I speed forth to the darkness,
Resuming, marching, ever in darkness marching, on in the ranks,
The unknown road still marching.

A Sight in Camp in the Daybreak Gray and Dim

A sight in camp in the daybreak gray and dim,
As from my tent I emerge so early sleepless,
As slow I walk in the cool fresh air the path near by the hospital tent,
Three forms I see on stretchers lying, brought out there untended lying,
Over each the blanket spread, ample brownish woolen blanket,
Gray and heavy blanket, folding, covering all.
Curious I halt and silent stand,
Then with light fingers I from the face of the nearest the first just lift the blanket;
Who are you elderly man so gaunt and grim, with well-gray'd hair, and flesh all sunken about the eyes?
Who are you my dear comrade?

Then to the second I step—and who are you my child and darling?
Who are you sweet boy with cheeks yet blooming?

Then to the third—a face nor child nor old, very calm, as of beautiful yellow-white ivory;
Young man I think I know you—I think this face is the face of the Christ himself,
Dead and divine and brother of all, and here again he lies.

Not the Pilot

Not the pilot has charged himself to bring his ship into port, though beaten back and many times baffled;
Not the pathfinder penetrating inland weary and long,
By deserts parch'd, snows chill'd, rivers wet, perseveres till he reaches his destination,
More than I have charged myself, heeded or unheeded, to compose a march for these States,
For a battle-call, rousing to arms if need be, years, centuries hence.

Year That Trembled and Reel'd Beneath Me

Year that trembled and reel'd beneath me!
Your summer wind was warm enough, yet the air I breathed froze me,
A thick gloom fell through the sunshine and darken'd me,
Must I change my triumphant songs? said I to myself
Must I indeed learn to chant the cold dirges of the baffled?
And sullen hymns of defeat?

The Wound-Dresser

1

An old man bending I come among new faces,
Years looking backward resuming in answer to children,
Come tell us old man, as from young men and maidens that love me,
(Arous'd and angry, I'd thought to beat the alarum, and urge relentless war,
But soon my fingers fail'd me, my face droop'd and I resign'd myself
To sit by the wounded and soothe them, or silently watch the dead;)
Years hence of these scenes, of these furious passions, these chances,
Of unsurpass'd heroes, (was one side so brave? the other was equally brave;)
Now be witness again, paint the mightiest armies of earth,
Of those armies so rapid so wondrous what saw you to tell us?
What stays with you latest and deepest? of curious panics,
Of hard-fought engagements or sieges tremendous what deepest remains?

2

O maidens and young men I love and that love me,
What you ask of my days those the strangest and sudden your talking recalls,
Soldier alert I arrive after a long march cover 'd with sweat and dust,
In the nick of time I come, plunge in the fight, loudly shout in the rush of
successful charge,
Enter the captur'd works—yet lo, like a swift-running river they fade,
Pass and are gone they fade—I dwell not on soldiers' perils or soldiers' joys,
(Both I remember well—many the hardships, few the joys, yet I was content.)

But in silence, in dreams' projections,
While the world of gain and appearance and mirth goes on,

So soon what is over forgotten, and waves wash the imprints off the sand,
With hinged knees returning I enter the doors, (while for you up there,
Whoever you are, follow without noise and be of strong heart.)

Bearing the bandages, water and sponge,
Straight and swift to my wounded I go,
Where they lie on the ground after the battle brought in,
Where their priceless blood reddens the grass the ground,
Or to the rows of the hospital tent or under the roof'd hospital,
To the long rows of cots up and down each side I return,
To each and all one after another I draw near, not one do I miss,
An attendant follows holding a tray, he carries a refuse pail,
Soon to be fill'd with clotted rags and blood, emptied, and fill'd again.

I onward go, I stop,
With hinged knees and steady hand to dress wounds,
I am firm with each, the pangs are sharp yet unavoidable,
One turns to me his appealing eyes—poor boy! I never knew you,
Yet I think I could not refuse this moment to die for you, if that would save you.

3

On, on I go, (open doors of time! open hospital doors!)
The crush'd head I dress, (poor crazed hand tear not the bandage away,)
The neck of the cavalry-man with the bullet through and through I examine,
Hard the breathing rattles, quite glazed already the eye, yet life struggles hard,
(Come sweet death! be persuaded O beautiful death!
In mercy come quickly.)

From the stump of the arm, the amputated hand,
I undo the clotted lint, remove the slough, wash off the matter and blood,
Back on his pillow the soldier bends with curv'd neck and side-falling head,
His eyes are closed, his face is pale, he dares not look on the bloody stump,
And has not yet look'd on it.

I dress a wound in the side, deep, deep,
But a day or two more, for see the frame all wasted and sinking,
And the yellow-blue countenance see.

I dress the perforated shoulder, the foot with the bullet-wound,
Cleanse the one with a gnawing and putrid gangrene, so sickening, so offensive,
While the attendant stands behind aside me holding the tray and pail.

I am faithful, I do not give out,
The fractur'd thigh, the knee, the wound in the abdomen,
These and more I dress with impassive hand, (yet deep in my breast a fire, a
  burning flame.)

4

Thus in silence in dreams' projections,
Returning, resuming, I thread my way through the hospitals,
The hurt and wounded I pacify with soothing hand,
I sit by the restless all the dark night, some are so young,
Some suffer so much, I recall the experience sweet and sad,
(Many a soldier's loving arms about this neck have cross'd and rested,
Many a soldier's kiss dwells on these bearded lips.)

Dirge for Two Veterans

The last sunbeam
Lightly falls from the finish'd Sabbath,
On the pavement here, and there beyond it is looking,
Down a new-made double grave.

Lo, the moon ascending,
Up from the east the silvery round moon,
Beautiful over the house-tops, ghastly, phantom moon,
Immense and silent moon.

I see a sad procession,
And I hear the sound of coming full-key'd bugles,
All the channels of the city streets they're flooding,
As with voices and with tears.

I hear the great drums pounding,
And the small drums steady whirring,
And every blow of the great convulsive drums,
Strikes me through and through.

For the son is brought with the father,
(In the foremost ranks of the fierce assault they fell,
Two veterans son and father dropt together,
And the double grave awaits them.)

Now nearer blow the bugles,
And the drums strike more convulsive,
And the daylight o'er the pavement quite has faded,
And the strong dead-march enwraps me.

In the eastern sky up-buoying,
The sorrowful vast phantom moves illumin'd,
('Tis some mother's large transparent face,
In heaven brighter growing.)

O strong dead-march you please me!
O moon immense with your silvery face you soothe me!
O my soldiers twain! O my veterans passing to burial!
What I have I also give you.

The moon gives you light,
And the bugles and the drums give you music,
And my heart, O my soldiers, my veterans,
My heart gives you love.

Over the Carnage Rose Prophetic a Voice

Over the carnage rose prophetic a voice,
Be not dishearten'd, affection shall solve the problems of freedom yet,
Those who love each other shall become invincible,
They shall yet make Columbia victorious.

Sons of the Mother of All, you shall yet be victorious,
You shall yet laugh to scorn the attacks of all the remainder of the earth.

No danger shall balk Columbia's lovers,
If need be a thousand shall sternly immolate themselves for one.

One from Massachusetts shall be a Missourian's comrade,
From Maine and from hot Carolina, and another an Oregonese, shall be friends triune,
More precious to each other than all the riches of the earth.

To Michigan, Florida perfumes shall tenderly come,
Not the perfumes of flowers, but sweeter, and wafted beyond death.

It shall be customary in the houses and streets to see manly affection,
The most dauntless and rude shall touch face to face lightly,
The dependence of Liberty shall be lovers,
The continuance of Equality shall be comrades.

These shall tie you and band you stronger than hoops of iron,
I, ecstatic, O partners! O lands! with the love of lovers tie you.

(Were you looking to be held together by lawyers?
Or by an agreement on a paper? or by arms?
Nay, nor the world, nor any living thing, will so cohere.)

The Artilleryman's Vision

While my wife at my side lies slumbering, and the wars are over long,
And my head on the pillow rests at home, and the vacant midnight passes,
And through the stillness, through the dark, I hear, just hear, the breath of my infant,
There in the room as I wake from sleep this vision presses upon me;
The engagement opens there and then in fantasy unreal,
The skirmishers begin, they crawl cautiously ahead, I hear the irregular snap! snap!
I hear the sounds of the different missiles, the short *t-h-t! t-h-t!* of the rifle-balls,
I see the shells exploding leaving small white clouds, I hear the great shells shrieking as they pass,
The grape like the hum and whirr of wind through the trees, (tumultuous now the contest rages,)
All the scenes at the batteries rise in detail before me again,
The crashing and smoking, the pride of the men in their pieces,
The chief-gunner ranges and sights his piece and selects a fuse of the right time,
After firing I see him lean aside and look eagerly off to note the effect;
Elsewhere I hear the cry of a regiment charging, (the young colonel leads himself this time with brandish'd sword,)
I see the gaps cut by the enemy's volleys, (quickly fill'd up, no delay,)
I breathe the suffocating smoke, then the flat clouds hover low concealing all;
Now a strange lull for a few seconds, not a shot fired on either side,
Then resumed the chaos louder than ever, with eager calls and orders of officers,
While from some distant part of the field the wind wafts to my ears a shout of applause, (some special success,)

And ever the sound of the cannon far or near, (rousing even in dreams a devilish exultation and all the old mad joy in the depths of my soul,)
And ever the hastening of infantry shifting positions, batteries, cavalry, moving hither and thither,
(The falling, dying, I heed not, the wounded dripping and red I heed not, some to the rear are hobbling,)
Grime, heat, rush, aide-de-camps galloping by or on a full run,
With the patter of small arms, the warning *s-s-t* of the rifles, (these in my vision I hear or see,)
And bombs bursting in air, and at night the vari-color'd rockets.

Ethiopia* Saluting the Colors

Who are you dusky woman, so ancient hardly human,
With your woolly-white and turban'd head, and bare bony feet?
Why rising by the roadside here, do you the colors greet?

('Tis while our army lines Carolina's sands and pines,
Forth from thy hovel door thou Ethiopia com'st to me,
As under doughty Sherman* I march toward the sea.)

Me master years a hundred since from my parents sunder'd,
A little child, they caught me as the savage beast is caught,
Then hither me across the sea the cruel slaver brought.

No further does she say, but lingering all the day,
Her high-borne turban'd head she wags, and rolls her darkling eye,
And courtesies to the regiments, the guidons moving by.

What is it fateful woman, so blear, hardly human?
Why wag your head with turban bound, yellow, red and green?
Are the things so strange and marvelous you see or have seen?

Not Youth Pertains to Me

Not youth pertains to me,
Nor delicatesse, I cannot beguile the time with talk,
Awkward in the parlor, neither a dancer nor elegant,
In the learn'd coterie sitting constrain'd and still, for learning inures not to me,

Beauty, knowledge, inure not to me—yet there are two or three things inure
to me,
I have nourish'd the wounded and sooth'd many a dying soldier,
And at intervals waiting or in the midst of camp,
Composed these songs.

Look Down Fair Moon

Look down fair moon and bathe this scene,
Pour softly down night's nimbus floods on faces ghastly, swollen, purple,
On the dead on their backs with arms toss'd wide,
Pour down your unstinted nimbus sacred moon.

Reconciliation

Word over all, beautiful as the sky,
Beautiful that war and all its deeds of carnage must in time be utterly lost,
That the hands of the sisters Death and Night incessantly softly wash again,
and ever again, this soil'd world;
For my enemy is dead, a man divine as myself is dead,
I look where he lies white-faced and still in the coffin—I draw near,
Bend down and touch lightly with my lips the white face in the coffin.

How Solemn as One by One

(Washington City, 1865)

How solemn as one by one,
As the ranks returning worn and sweaty, as the men file by where I stand,
As the faces the masks appear, as I glance at the faces studying the masks,
(As I glance upward out of this page studying you, dear friend, whoever
you are,)
How solemn the thought of my whispering soul to each in the ranks, and
to you,
I see behind each mask that wonder a kindred soul,
O the bullet could never kill what you really are, dear friend,
Nor the bayonet stab what you really are;

The soul! yourself I see, great as any, good as the best,
Waiting secure and content, which the bullet could never kill,
Nor the bayonet stab O friend.

As I Lay with My Head in Your Lap Camerado

As I lay with my head in your lap camerado,
The confession I made I resume, what I said to you and the open air I resume,
I know I am restless and make others so,
I know my words are weapons full of danger, full of death,
For I confront peace, security, and all the settled laws, to unsettle them,
I am more resolute because all have denied me than I could ever have been had all accepted me,
I heed not and have never heeded either experience, cautions, majorities, nor ridicule,
And the threat of what is call'd hell is little or nothing to me,
And the lure of what is call'd heaven is little or nothing to me;
Dear camerado! I confess I have urged you onward with me, and still urge you, without the least idea what is our destination,
Or whether we shall be victorious, or utterly quell'd and defeated.

To a Certain Civilian

Did you ask dulcet rhymes from me?
Did you seek the civilian's peaceful and languishing rhymes?
Did you find what I sang erewhile so hard to follow?
Why I was not singing erewhile for you to follow, to understand—nor am I now;
(I have been born of the same as the war was born,
The drum-corps' rattle is ever to me sweet music, I love well the martial dirge,
With slow wail and convulsive throb leading the officer's funeral;)
What to such as you anyhow such a poet as I? therefore leave my works,
And go lull yourself with what you can understand, and with piano-tunes,
For I lull nobody, and you will never understand me.

Adieu to a Soldier

Adieu O soldier,
You of the rude campaigning, (which we shared,)
The rapid march, the life of the camp,
The hot contention of opposing fronts, the long manoeuvre,
Red battles with their slaughter, the stimulus, the strong terrific game,
Spell of all brave and manly hearts, the trains of time through you and like of you all fill'd,
With war and war's expression.

Adieu dear comrade,
Your mission is fulfill'd—but I, more warlike,
Myself and this contentious soul of mine,
Still on our own campaigning bound,
Through untried roads with ambushes opponents lined,
Through many a sharp defeat and many a crisis, often baffled,
Here marching, ever marching on, a war fight out—aye here,
To fiercer, weightier battles give expression.

Turn O Libertad

Turn O Libertad, for the war is over,
From it and all henceforth expanding, doubting no more, resolute, sweeping the world,
Turn from lands retrospective recording proofs of the past,
From the singers that sing the trailing glories of the past,
From the chants of the feudal world, the triumphs of kings, slavery, caste,
Turn to the world, the triumphs reserv'd and to come—give up that backward world,
Leave to the singers of hitherto, give them the trailing past,
But what remains remains for singers for you—wars to come are for you,
(Lo, how the wars of the past have duly inured to you, and the wars of the present also inure;)
Then turn, and be not alarm'd O Libertad—turn your undying face,
To where the future, greater than all the past,
Is swiftly, surely preparing for you.

To the Leaven'd Soil They Trod

To the leaven'd soil they trod calling I sing for the last,
(Forth from my tent emerging for good, loosing, untying the tent-ropes,)
In the freshness the forenoon air, in the far-stretching circuits and vistas again to peace restored,
To the fiery fields emanative and the endless vistas beyond, to the South and the North,
To the leaven'd soil of the general Western world to attest my songs,
To the Alleghanian hills and the tireless Mississippi,
To the rocks I calling sing, and all the trees in the woods,
To the plains of the poems of heroes, to the prairies spreading wide,
To the far-off sea and the unseen winds, and the sane impalpable air;
And responding they answer all, (but not in words,)
The average earth, the witness of war and peace, acknowledges mutely,
The prairie draws me close, as the father to bosom broad the son,
The Northern ice and rain that began me nourish me to the end,
But the hot sun of the South is to fully ripen my songs.

Pensive on Her Dead Gazing[2]

Pensive on her dead gazing I heard the Mother of All,
Desperate on the torn bodies, on the forms covering the battle-fields gazing,
(As the last gun ceased, but the scent of the powder-smoke linger'd,)
As she call'd to her earth with mournful voice while she stalk'd,
Absorb them well O my earth, she cried, I charge you lose not my sons, lose not an atom,
And you streams absorb them well, taking their dear blood,
And you local spots, and you airs that swim above lightly impalpable,
And all you essences of soil and growth, and you my rivers' depths,
And you mountain sides, and the woods where my dear children's blood trickling redden'd,
And you trees down in your roots to bequeath to all future trees,
My dead absorb or South or North—my young men's bodies absorb, and their precious precious blood,

2. Whitman omitted this poem from *Drum-Taps* after 1871.

Which holding in trust for me faithfully back again give me many a year hence,
In unseen essence and odor of surface and grass, centuries hence,
In blowing airs from the fields back again give me my darlings, give my
 immortal heroes,
Exhale me them centuries hence, breathe me their breath, let not an atom
 be lost,
O years and graves! O air and soil! O my dead, an aroma sweet!
Exhale them perennial sweet death, years, centuries hence.

When Lilacs Last in the Dooryard Bloom'd

1

When lilacs last in the dooryard bloom'd,
And the great star early droop'd in the western sky in the night,
I mourn'd, and yet shall mourn with ever-returning spring.

Ever-returning spring, trinity sure to me you bring,
Lilac blooming perennial and drooping star in the west,
And thought of him I love.

2

O powerful western fallen star!
O shades of night—O moody, tearful night!
O great star disappear'd—O the black murk that hides the star!
O cruel hands that hold me powerless—O helpless soul of me!
O harsh surrounding cloud that will not free my soul.

3

In the dooryard fronting an old farm-house near the white-wash'd palings,
Stands the lilac-bush tall-growing with heart-shaped leaves of rich green,
With many a pointed blossom rising delicate, with the perfume strong I love,
With every leaf a miracle—and from this bush in the dooryard,
With delicate-color'd blossoms and heart-shaped leaves of rich green,
A sprig with its flower I break.

4

In the swamp in secluded recesses,
A shy and hidden bird is warbling a song.

Solitary the thrush,
The hermit withdrawn to himself, avoiding the settlements,
Sings by himself a song.

Song of the bleeding throat,
Death's outlet song of life, (for well dear brother I know,
If thou wast not granted to sing thou would'st surely die.)

5

Over the breast of the spring, the land, amid cities,
Amid lanes and through old woods, where lately the violets peep'd from the ground, spotting the gray debris,
Amid the grass in the fields each side of the lanes, passing the endless grass,
Passing the yellow-spear'd wheat, every grain from its shroud in the dark-brown fields uprisen,
Passing the apple-tree blows of white and pink in the orchards,
Carrying a corpse to where it shall rest in the grave,
Night and day journeys a coffin.

6

Coffin that passes through lanes and streets,
Through day and night with the great cloud darkening the land,
With the pomp of the inloop'd flags with the cities draped in black,
With the show of the States themselves as of crape-veil'd women standing,
With processions long and winding and the flambeaus of the night,
With the countless torches lit, with the silent sea of faces and the unbared heads,
With the waiting depot, the arriving coffin, and the sombre faces,
With dirges through the night, with the thousand voices rising strong and solemn,
With all the mournful voices of the dirges pour'd around the coffin,
The dim-lit churches and the shuddering organs—where amid these you journey,
With the tolling tolling bells' perpetual clang,
Here, coffin that slowly passes,
I give you my sprig of lilac.

7

(Nor for you, for one alone,
Blossoms and branches green to coffins all I bring,

For fresh as the morning, thus would I chant a song for you O sane and sacred death.

All over bouquets of roses,
O death, I cover you over with roses and early lilies,
But mostly and now the lilac that blooms the first,
Copious I break, I break the sprigs from the bushes,
With loaded arms I come, pouring for you,
For you and the coffins all of you O death.)

8

O western orb sailing the heaven,
Now I know what you must have meant as a month since I walk'd,
As I walk'd in silence the transparent shadowy night,
As I saw you had something to tell as you bent to me night after night,
As you droop'd from the sky low down as if to my side, (while the other stars all look'd on,)
As we wander'd together the solemn night, (for something I know not what kept me from sleep,)
As the night advanced, and I saw on the rim of the west how full you were of woe,
As I stood on the rising ground in the breeze in the cool transparent night,
As I watch'd where you pass'd and was lost in the netherward black of the night,
As my soul in its trouble dissatisfied sank, as where you sad orb,
Concluded, dropt in the night, and was gone.

9

Sing on there in the swamp,
O singer bashful and tender, I hear your notes, I hear your call,
I hear, I come presently, I understand you,
But a moment I linger, for the lustrous star has detain'd me,
The star my departing comrade holds and detains me.

10

O how shall I warble myself for the dead one there I loved?
And how shall I deck my song for the large sweet soul that has gone?
And what shall my perfume be for the grave of him I love?

Sea-winds blown from east and west,
Blown from the Eastern sea and blown from the Western sea, till there on the prairies meeting,

These and with these and the breath of my chant,
I'll perfume the grave of him I love.

11

O what shall I hang on the chamber walls?
And what shall the pictures be that I hang on the walls,
To adorn the burial-house of him I love?

Pictures of growing spring and farms and homes,
With the Fourth-month eve at sundown, and the gray smoke lucid and bright,
With floods of the yellow gold of the gorgeous, indolent, sinking sun, burning, expanding the air,
With the fresh sweet herbage under foot, and the pale green leaves of the trees prolific,
In the distance the flowing glaze, the breast of the river, with a wind-dapple here and there,
With ranging hills on the banks, with many a line against the sky, and shadows,
And the city at hand with dwellings so dense, and stacks of chimneys,
And all the scenes of life and the workshops, and the workmen homeward returning.

12

Lo, body and soul—this land,
My own Manhattan with spires, and the sparkling and hurrying tides, and the ships,
The varied and ample land, the South and the North in the light,
Ohio's shores and flashing Missouri,
And ever the far-spreading prairies cover'd with grass and corn.

Lo, the most excellent sun so calm and haughty,
The violet and purple morn with just-felt breezes,
The gentle soft-born measureless light,
The miracle spreading bathing all, the fulfill'd noon,
The coming eve delicious, the welcome night and the stars,
Over my cities shining all, enveloping man and land.

13

Sing on, sing on you gray-brown bird,
Sing from the swamps, the recesses, pour your chant from the bushes,
Limitless out of the dusk, out of the cedars and pines.

Sing on dearest brother, warble your reedy song,
Loud human song, with voice of uttermost woe.

O liquid and free and tender!
O wild and loose to my soul—O wondrous singer!
You only I hear—yet the star holds me, (but will soon depart,)
Yet the lilac with mastering odor holds me.

14

Now while I sat in the day and look'd forth,
In the close of the day with its light and the fields of spring, and the farmers preparing their crops,
In the large unconscious scenery of my land with its lakes and forests,
In the heavenly aerial beauty, (after the perturb'd winds and the storms,)
Under the arching heavens of the afternoon swift passing, and the voices of children and women,
The many-moving sea-tides, and I saw the ships how they sail'd,
And the summer approaching with richness, and the fields all busy with labor,
And the infinite separate houses, how they all went on, each with its meals and minutia of daily usages,
And the streets how their throbbings throbb'd, and the cities pent—lo, then and there,
Falling upon them all and among them all, enveloping me with the rest,
Appear'd the cloud, appear'd the long black trail,
And I knew death, its thought, and the sacred knowledge of death.

Then with the knowledge of death as walking one side of me,
And the thought of death close-walking the other side of me,
And I in the middle as with companions, and as holding the hands of companions,
I fled forth to the hiding receiving night that talks not,
Down to the shores of the water, the path by the swamp in the dimness,
To the solemn shadowy cedars and ghostly pines so still.

And the singer so shy to the rest receiv'd me,
The gray-brown bird I know receiv'd us comrades three,
And he sang the carol of death, and a verse for him I love.

From deep secluded recesses,
From the fragrant cedars and the ghostly pines so still,
Came the carol of the bird.

And the charm of the carol rapt me,
As I held as if by their hands my comrades in the night,
And the voice of my spirit tallied the song of the bird.

Come lovely and soothing death,
Undulate round the world, serenely arriving, arriving,
In the day, in the night, to all, to each,
Sooner or later delicate death.

Prais'd be the fathomless universe,
For life and joy, and for objects and knowledge curious,
And for love, sweet love—but praise! praise! praise!
For the sure-enwinding arms of cool-enfolding death.

Dark mother always gliding near with soft feet,
Have none chanted for thee a chant of fullest welcome?
Then I chant it for thee, I glorify thee above all,
I bring thee a song that when thou must indeed come, come unfalteringly.

Approach strong deliveress,
When it is so, when thou hast taken them I joyously sing the dead,
Lost in the loving floating ocean of thee,
Laved in the flood of thy bliss O death.

From me to thee glad serenades,
Dances for thee I propose saluting thee, adornments and feastings for thee,
And the sights of the open landscape and the high-spread sky are fitting,
And life and the fields, and the huge and thoughtful night.

The night in silence under many a star,
The ocean shore and the husky whispering wave whose voice I know,
And the soul turning to thee O vast and well-veil'd death,
And the body gratefully nestling close to thee.

Over the tree-tops I float thee a song,
Over the rising and sinking waves, over the myriad fields and the prairies wide,
Over the dense-pack'd cities all and the teeming wharves and ways,
I float this carol with joy, with joy to thee O death.

15

To the tally of my soul,
Loud and strong kept up the gray-brown bird,
With pure deliberate notes spreading filling the night.

Loud in the pines and cedars dim,
Clear in the freshness moist and the swamp-perfume,
And I with my comrades there in the night.

While my sight that was bound in my eyes unclosed,
As to long panoramas of visions.

And I saw askant the armies,
I saw as in noiseless dreams hundreds of battle-flags,
Borne through the smoke of the battles and pierc'd with missiles I saw them,
And carried hither and yon through the smoke, and torn and bloody,
And at last but a few shreds left on the staffs, (and all in silence,)
And the staffs all splinter'd and broken.

I saw battle-corpses, myriads of them,
And the white skeletons of young men, I saw them,
I saw the debris and debris of all the slain soldiers of the war,
But I saw they were not as was thought,
They themselves were fully at rest, they suffer'd not,
The living remain'd and suffer'd, the mother suffer'd,
And the wife and the child and the musing comrade suffer'd,
And the armies that remain'd suffer'd.

16

Passing the visions, passing the night,
Passing, unloosing the hold of my comrades' hands,
Passing the song of the hermit bird and the tallying song of my soul,
Victorious song, death's outlet song, yet varying ever-altering song,
As low and wailing, yet clear the notes, rising and falling, flooding the night,
Sadly sinking and fainting, as warning and warning, and yet again bursting with joy,
Covering the earth and filling the spread of the heaven,
As that powerful psalm in the night I heard from recesses,
Passing, I leave thee lilac with heart-shaped leaves,
I leave thee there in the door-yard, blooming, returning with spring.

I cease from my song for thee,
From my gaze on thee in the west, fronting the west, communing with thee,
O comrade lustrous with silver face in the night.

Yet each to keep and all, retrievements out of the night,
The song, the wondrous chant of the gray-brown bird,
And the tallying chant, the echo arous'd in my soul,
With the lustrous and drooping star with the countenance full of woe,
With the holders holding my hand nearing the call of the bird,

Comrades mine and I in the midst, and their memory ever to keep, for the dead
I loved so well,
For the sweetest, wisest soul of all my days and lands—and this for his dear
sake,
Lilac and star and bird twined with the chant of my soul,
There in the fragrant pines and the cedars dusk and dim.

Herman Melville (1819–1891)

Though Melville is now best known for his novels, including his masterpiece *Moby-Dick*, he also wrote a substantial body of poetry over the course of his career. Born into a prosperous family in New York City, Melville experienced an abrupt change of fortunes at the age of twelve. The death of his father left the family in poverty, and Melville's formal education ended just a few years later. Lacking any job skills, he worked as a clerk, farmhand, and teacher; despairing at this narrow range of options, in 1839 Melville signed on as a sailor with a merchant ship bound for Liverpool, and thereafter he served for three years on whaling ships. Working side by side with men of all races and from all walks of life, Melville gained a perspective on the human condition that his privileged early childhood in New York could never have given him.

When Melville returned to the United States, he began drafting a fictionalized account of his travels. His first two books, *Typee: A Peep at Polynesian Life* (1846) and *Omoo* (1847), were great successes in spite of their sharp critique of white imperialism. This success enabled Melville to marry Elizabeth Shaw, daughter of Lemuel Shaw, the chief justice of the Massachusetts Supreme Court and a supporter of the Fugitive Slave Law*. Though Melville's experiences after his father's death had given him a powerful sense of empathy with the poor and dispossessed, his close relationship with his father-in-law and his desire to write commercially successful books led him to present his radical ideas in an oblique fashion. In his novels, Melville alternated between conventional and experimental strategies, hoping to write a book that would both satisfy public taste and express his arguments about the injustices of capitalism, slavery, and imperialism. In *Moby-Dick*, Melville represents a whaling voyage as an epic about the human struggle to assert mastery over nature at the same time as he indicts theories of white racial superiority. Though Melville wrote several novels and many short stories, he was never able to support his family with his writing. In 1866, a deeply depressed Melville accepted a job as a customs inspector in New York City; he held this position for the next twenty years.

Though *Battle-Pieces and Aspects of the War* (1866) was Melville's first published volume of poetry, he had been writing poetry for several years before the volume appeared. For the rest of his career, with the exception of a few short prose works, he would write nothing but poetry. As a crisis of national identity, the Civil War clearly brought Melville a renewed sense of purpose as a writer. Though he did not serve in the military, his family connections to the war were direct and numerous. One cousin was a naval commander, and Melville visited another cousin at the front; after touring battlefields, he rode out with the cavalry on a three-day mission. Melville also followed the war's moment-by-moment developments in the newspapers. In addition to his response to the war, one senses in *Battle-Pieces* Melville's desire to invent a new kind of poetry, a poetry that could look unflinchingly at the horrors of war even as it also questioned the possibility of representing those horrors in writing. *Battle-Pieces* offers a critical intervention into the lyric tradition, suggesting that poetry might meld traditional formal commitments with a new kind of realism that could encompass both the complexity of the ideologies which fuel wars and the ethical dilemmas which representing war poses for writers.

The Portent[1]

(1859)

Hanging from the beam,
Slowly swaying (such the law),
Gaunt the shadow on your green,
Shenandoah!
The cut is on the crown
(Lo, John Brown),
And the stabs shall heal no more.

Hidden in the cap
Is the anguish none can draw;
So your future veils its face,
Shenandoah!
But the streaming beard is shown
(Weird John Brown),
The meteor of the war.

1. The following poems are cited from *Battle-Pieces and Aspects of the War* (New York: Harper and Brothers, 1866). In "The Portent," Melville responds to John Brown's abortive uprising (see Time Line, October 1959) and his hanging, both of which took place in the Shenandoah River valley. This valley was also the site of particularly violent and destructive military campaigns during the war.

Apathy and Enthusiasm

(1860–61)

I.

O the clammy cold November,
 And the winter white and dead,
And the terror dumb with stupor,
 And the sky a sheet of lead;
And events that came resounding
 With the cry that *All was lost,*
Like the thunder-cracks of massy ice
 In intensity of frost—
Bursting one upon another
 Through the horror of the calm.
 The paralysis of arm
In the anguish of the heart;
And the hollowness and dearth.
 The appealings of the mother
 To brother and to brother
Not in hatred so to part—
And the fissure in the hearth
 Growing momently more wide.
Then the glances 'tween the Fates,
 And the doubt on every side,
And the patience under gloom
In the stoniness that waits
The finality of doom.

II.

So the winter died despairing,
 And the weary weeks of Lent;
And the ice-bound rivers melted,
 And the tomb of Faith was rent.
O, the rising of the People
 Came with springing of the grass,
They rebounded from dejection
 After Easter came to pass.
And the young were all elation

Hearing Sumter's* cannon roar.
And they thought how tame the Nation
In the age that went before.
And Michael seemed gigantical,
The Arch-fiend but a dwarf;
And at the towers of Erebus
Our striplings flung the scoff.
But the elders with foreboding
Mourned the days forever o'er,
And recalled the forest proverb,
The Iroquois' old saw:
Grief to every graybeard
When young Indians lead the war.

The March into Virginia,
Ending in the First Manassas
(July, 1861)

Did all the lets and bars appear
To every just or larger end,
Whence should come the trust and cheer?
Youth must its ignorant impulse lend—
Age finds place in the rear.
All wars are boyish, and are fought by boys,
The champions and enthusiasts of the state:
Turbid ardors and vain joys
Not barrenly abate—
Stimulants to the power mature,
Preparatives of fate.

Who here forecasteth the event?
What heart but spurns at precedent
And warnings of the wise,
Contemned foreclosures of surprise?
The banners play, the bugles call,
The air is blue and prodigal.
No berrying party, pleasure-wooed,

No picnic party in the May,
Ever went less loth than they
Into that leafy neighborhood.
In Bacchic glee they file toward Fate,
Moloch's uninitiate;
Expectancy, and glad surmise
Of battle's unknown mysteries.
All they feel is this: 'tis glory,
A rapture sharp, though transitory,
Yet lasting in belaureled story.
So they gayly go to fight,
Chatting left and laughing right.

But some who this blithe mood present,
As on in lightsome files they fare,
Shall die experienced ere three days are spent—
Perish, enlightened by the vollied glare;
Or shame survive, and, like to adamant,
The throe of Second Manassas share.

Ball's Bluff[2]

A Reverie

(October, 1861)

One noonday, at my window in the town,
I saw a sight—saddest that eyes can see—
Young soldiers marching lustily
Unto the wars,
With fifes, and flags in mottoed pageantry;
While all the porches, walks, and doors
Were rich with ladies cheering royally.

They moved like Juny morning on the wave,
Their hearts were fresh as clover in its prime
(It was the breezy summer time),

2. Union forces suffered both defeat and heavy casualties at the battle of Ball's Bluff on October 21, 1861. The fighting took place on cliffs overlooking the Potomac.

Life throbbed so strong,
How should they dream that Death in a rosy clime
Would come to thin their shining throng?
Youth feels immortal, like the gods sublime.

Weeks passed; and at my window, leaving bed,
By night I mused, of easeful sleep bereft,
On those brave boys (Ah War! thy theft);
Some marching feet
Found pause at last by cliffs Potomac* cleft;
Wakeful I mused, while in the street
Far footfalls died away till none were left.

Dupont's Round Fight[3]

(November, 1861)

In time and measure perfect moves
All Art whose aim is sure;
Evolving rhyme and stars divine
Have rules, and they endure.

Nor less the Fleet that warred for Right,
And, warring so, prevailed,
In geometric beauty curved,
And in an orbit sailed.

The rebel at Port Royal* felt
The Unity overawe,
And rued the spell. A type was here,
And victory of LAW.

3. Naval commander Samuel Dupont led Union ships to victory in a battle at Port Royal, South Carolina, on November 7, 1861, giving Union forces a strategic base for future operations on the coast.

Donelson

(February, 1862)

The bitter cup
  Of that hard countermand
Which gave the Envoys up,
Still was wormwood in the mouth,
  And clouds involved the land,
When, pelted by sleet in the icy street,
  About the bulletin-board a band
Of eager, anxious people met,
And every wakeful heart was set
On latest news from West or South.
"No seeing here," cries one—"don't crowd"—
"You tall man, pray you, read aloud."

IMPORTANT.

*We learn that General Grant,**
  Marching from Henry overland,
And joined by a force up the Cumberland sent
  (Some thirty thousand the command),
On Wednesday a good position won—
Began the siege of Donelson.

This stronghold crowns a river-bluff,
  A good broad mile of leveled top;
Inland the ground rolls off
  Deep-gorged, and rocky, and broken up—
A wilderness of trees and brush.
  The spaded summit shows the roods
Of fixed intrenchments in their hush;
  Breast-works and rifle-pits in woods
Perplex the base.—
            The welcome weather
  Is clear and mild; 'tis much like May.
The ancient boughs that lace together
Along the stream, and hang far forth,
  Strange with green mistletoe, betray
A dreamy contrast to the North.

Our troops are full of spirits—say
The siege won't prove a creeping one.
They purpose not the lingering stay
Of old beleaguerers; not that way;
But, full of vim *from Western prairies won,*
They'll make, ere long, a dash at Donelson.

Washed by the storm till the paper grew
Every shade of a streaky blue,
That bulletin stood. The next day brought
A second.

LATER FROM THE FORT.

Grant's investment is complete—
A semicircular one.
Both wings the Cumberland's margin meet,
Then, backward curving, clasp the rebel seat.
On Wednesday this good work was done;
But of the doers some lie prone.
Each wood, each hill, each glen was fought for;
The bold inclosing line we wrought for
Flamed with sharpshooters. Each cliff cost
A limb or life. But back we forced
Reserves and all; made good our hold;
And so we rest.

Events unfold.
On Thursday added ground was won,
A long bold steep: we near the Den.
Later the foe came shouting down
In sortie, which was quelled; and then
We stormed them on their left.
A chilly change in the afternoon;
The sky, late clear, is now bereft
Of sun. Last night the ground froze hard—
Rings to the enemy as they run
Within their works. A ramrod bites
The lip it meets. The cold incites
To swinging of arms with brisk rebound.
Smart blows 'gainst lusty chests resound.

Along the outer line we ward
A crackle of skirmishing goes on.
Our lads creep round on hand and knee,
They fight from behind each trunk and stone;
And sometimes, flying for refuge, one
Finds 'tis an enemy shares the tree.
Some scores are maimed by boughs shot off
In the glades by the Fort's big gun.
We mourn the loss of Colonel Morrison,
Killed while cheering his regiment on.
Their far sharpshooters try our stuff;
And ours return them puff for puff:
'Tis diamond-cutting-diamond work.
Woe on the rebel cannoneer
Who shows his head. Our fellows lurk
Like Indians that waylay the deer
By the wild salt-spring.—The sky is dun,
Foredooming the fall of Donelson.
Stern weather is all unwonted here.
The people of the country own
We brought it. Yea, the earnest North
Has elementally issued forth
To storm this Donelson.

FURTHER.

A yelling rout
Of ragamuffins broke profuse
To-day from out the Fort.
Sole uniform they wore, a sort
Of patch, or white badge (as you choose)
Upon the arm. But leading these,
Or mingling, were men of face
And bearing of patrician race,
Splendid in courage and gold lace—
The officers. Before the breeze
Made by their charge, down went our line;
But, rallying, charged back in force,
And broke the sally; yet with loss.
This on the left; upon the right

Meanwhile there was an answering fight;
Assailants and assailed reversed.
The charge too upward, and not down—
Up a steep ridge-side, toward its crown,
A strong redoubt. But they who first
Gained the fort's base, and marked the trees
Felled, heaped in horned perplexities,
And shagged with brush; and swarming there
Fierce wasps whose sting was present death—
They faltered, drawing bated breath,
And felt it was in vain to dare;
Yet still, perforce, returned the ball,
Firing into the tangled wall
Till ordered to come down. They came;
But left some comrades in their fame,
Red on the ridge in icy wreath
And hanging gardens of cold Death.
But not quite unavenged these fell;
Our ranks once out of range, a blast
Of shrapnel and quick shell
Burst on the rebel horde, still massed,
Scattering them pell-mell.
(This fighting—judging what we read—
Both charge and countercharge,
Would seem but Thursday's told at large,
Before in brief reported.—Ed.)
Night closed in about the Den
Murky and lowering. Ere long, chill rains.
A night not soon to be forgot,
Reviving old rheumatic pains
And longings for a cot.
No blankets, overcoats, or tents.
Coats thrown aside on the warm march here—
We looked not then for changeful cheer;
Tents, coats, and blankets too much care.
No fires; a fire a mark presents;
Near by, the trees show bullet-dents.
Rations were eaten cold and raw.

The men well soaked, came snow; and more—
A midnight sally. Small sleeping done—
But such is war;
No matter, we'll have Fort Donelson.

"Ugh! ugh!
'Twill drag along—drag along,"
Growled a cross patriot in the throng,
His battered umbrella like an ambulance cover
Riddled with bullet-holes, spattered all over.
"Hurrah for Grant!" cried a stripling shrill;
Three urchins joined him with a will,
And some of taller stature cheered.
Meantime a Copperhead* passed; he sneered.
"Win or lose," he pausing said,
"Caps fly the same; all boys, mere boys;
Any thing to make a noise.
Like to see the list of the dead;
These '*craven Southerners*' hold out;
Ay, ay, they'll give you many a bout."
"We'll beat in the end, sir,"
Firmly said one in staid rebuke,
A solid merchant, square and stout.
"And do you think it? that way tend, sir?"
Asked the lean Copperhead, with a look
Of splenetic pity. "Yes, I do."
His yellow death's head the croaker shook:
"The country's ruined, that I know."
A shower of broken ice and snow,
In lieu of words, confuted him;
They saw him hustled round the corner go,
And each by-stander said—Well suited him.

Next day another crowd was seen
In the dark weather's sleety spleen.
Bald-headed to the storm came out
A man, who, 'mid a joyous shout,
Silently posted this brief sheet:

GLORIOUS VICTORY OF THE FLEET!

FRIDAY'S GREAT EVENT!

THE ENEMY'S WATER-BATTERIES BEAT!

WE SILENCED EVERY GUN!

THE OLD COMMODORE'S COMPLIMENTS SENT
PLUMP INTO DONELSON!

"Well, well, go on!" exclaimed the crowd
To him who thus much read aloud.
"That's all," he said. "What! nothing more?"
"Enough for a cheer, though—hip, hurrah!
"But here's old Baldy come again—
"More news!"—And now a different strain.

(Our own reporter a dispatch compiles,
As best he may, from varied sources.)

Large re-enforcements have arrived—
Munitions, men, and horses—
For Grant, and all debarked, with stores.

The enemy's field-works extend six miles—
The gate still hid; so well contrived.

Yesterday stung us; frozen shores
Snow-clad, and through the drear defiles
And over the desolate ridges blew
A Lapland wind.
The main affair
Was a good two hours' steady fight
Between our gun-boats and the Fort.
The Louisville's wheel was smashed outright.
A hundred-and-twenty-eight-pound ball
Came planet-like through a starboard port,
Killing three men, and wounding all
The rest of that gun's crew,
(The captain of the gun was cut in two);
Then splintering and ripping went—
Nothing could be its continent.

In the narrow stream the Louisville,
Unhelmed, grew lawless; swung around,
And would have thumped and drifted, till
All the fleet was driven aground,
But for the timely order to retire.

Some damage from our fire, 'tis thought,
Was done the water-batteries of the Fort.

Little else took place that day,
Except the field artillery in line
Would now and then—for love, they say—
Exchange a valentine.
The old sharpshooting going on.
Some plan afoot as yet unknown;
So Friday closed round Donelson.

LATER.

Great suffering through the night—
A stinging one. Our heedless boys
Were nipped like blossoms. Some dozen
Hapless wounded men were frozen.
During day being struck down out of sight,
And help-cries drowned in roaring noise,
They were left just where the skirmish shifted—
Left in dense underbrush snow-drifted.
Some, seeking to crawl in crippled plight,
So stiffened—perished.
Yet in spite
Of pangs for these, no heart is lost.
Hungry, and clothing stiff with frost,
Our men declare a nearing sun
Shall see the fall of Donelson.
And this they say, yet not disown
The dark redoubts round Donelson,
And ice-glazed corpses, each a stone—
A sacrifice to Donelson;
They swear it, and swerve not, gazing on
A flag, deemed black, flying from Donelson.
Some of the wounded in the wood
Were cared for by the foe last night,

Though he could do them little needed good,
Himself being all in shivering plight.
The rebel is wrong, but human yet;
He's got a heart, and thrusts a bayonet.
He gives us battle with wondrous will—
This bluff's a perverted Bunker Hill.

The stillness stealing through the throng
The silent thought and dismal fear revealed;
They turned and went,
Musing on right and wrong
And mysteries dimly sealed—
Breasting the storm in daring discontent;
The storm, whose black flag showed in heaven,
As if to say no quarter there was given
To wounded men in wood,
Or true hearts yearning for the good—
All fatherless seemed the human soul.
But next day brought a bitterer bowl—
On the bulletin-board this stood:

Saturday morning at 3 A.M.
A stir within the Fort betrayed
That the rebels were getting under arms;
Some plot these early birds had laid.
But a lancing sleet cut him who stared
Into the storm. After some vague alarms,
Which left our lads unscared,
Out sallied the enemy at dim of dawn,
With cavalry and artillery, and went
In fury at our environment.
Under cover of shot and shell
Three columns of infantry rolled on,
Vomited out of Donelson—
Rolled down the slopes like rivers of hell,
Surged at our line, and swelled and poured
Like breaking surf. But unsubmerged
Our men stood up, except where roared
The enemy through one gap. We urged
Our all of manhood to the stress,

But still showed shattered in our desperateness.
Back set the tide,
But soon afresh rolled in;
And so it swayed from side to side—
Far batteries joining in the din,
Though sharing in another fray—
Till all became an Indian fight,
Intricate, dusky, stretching far away,
Yet not without spontaneous plan
However tangled showed the plight;
Duels all over 'tween man and man,
Duels on cliff-side, and down in ravine,
Duels at long range, and bone to bone;
Duels every where flitting and half unseen.
Only by courage good as their own,
And strength outlasting theirs,
Did our boys at last drive the rebels off.
Yet they went not back to their distant lairs
In strong-hold, but loud in scoff
Maintained themselves on conquered ground—
Uplands; built works, or stalked around.
Our right wing bore this onset. Noon
Brought calm to Donelson.

The reader ceased; the storm beat hard;
'Twas day, but the office-gas was lit;
Nature retained her sulking-fit,
In her hand the shard.
Flitting faces took the hue
Of that washed bulletin-board in view,
And seemed to bear the public grief
As private, and uncertain of relief;
Yea, many an earnest heart was won,
As broodingly he plodded on,
To find in himself some bitter thing,
Some hardness in his lot as harrowing
As Donelson.
That night the board stood barren there,
Oft eyed by wistful people passing,
Who nothing saw but the rain-beads chasing

Each other down the wafered square,
As down some storm-beat grave-yard stone.
But next day showed—

MORE NEWS LAST NIGHT.

STORY OF SATURDAY AFTERNOON.

VICISSITUDES OF THE WAR.

The damaged gun-boats can't wage fight
For days; so says the Commodore.
Thus no diversion can be had.
Under a sunless sky of lead
Our grim-faced boys in blackened plight
Gaze toward the ground they held before,
And then on Grant. He marks their mood,
And hails it, and will turn the same to good.
Spite all that they have undergone,
Their desperate hearts are set upon
This winter fort, this stubborn fort,
This castle of the last resort,
This Donelson.

I P.M.

An order given
Requires withdrawal from the front
Of regiments that bore the brunt
Of morning's fray. Their ranks all riven
Are being replaced by fresh, strong men.
Great vigilance in the foeman's Den;
He snuffs the stormers. Need it is
That for that fell assault of his,
That rout inflicted, and self-scorn—
Immoderate in noble natures, torn
By sense of being through slackness overborne—
The rebel be given a quick return:
The kindest face looks now half stern.
Balked of their prey in airs that freeze,
Some fierce ones glare like savages.
And yet, and yet, strange moments are—
Well—blood, and tears, and anguished War!

The morning's battle-ground is seen
In lifted glades, like meadows rare;
The blood-drops on the snow-crust there
Like clover in the white-weed show—
Flushed fields of death, that call again—
Call to our men, and not in vain,
For that way must the stormers go.

3 P.M.
The work begins.
Light drifts of men thrown forward, fade
In skirmish-line along the slope,
Where some dislodgments must be made
Ere the stormer with the strong-hold cope.

Lew Wallace, moving to retake
The heights late lost—
(Herewith a break.
Storms at the West derange the wires.
Doubtless, ere morning, we shall hear
The end; we look for news to cheer—
Let Hope fan all her fires.)

Next day in large bold hand was seen
The closing bulletin:

VICTORY!
Our troops have retrieved the day
By one grand surge along the line;
The spirit that urged them was divine.
The first works flooded, naught could stay
The stormers: on! still on!
Bayonets for Donelson!
Over the ground that morning lost
Rolled the blue billows, tempest-tossed,
Following a hat on the point of a sword.
Spite shell and round-shot, grape and canister,
Up they climbed without rail or banister—
Up the steep hill-sides long and broad,
Driving the rebel deep within his works.

'Tis nightfall; not an enemy lurks
In sight. The chafing men
Fret for more fight:
"To-night, to-night let us take the Den!"
But night is treacherous, Grant is wary;
Of brave blood be a little chary.
Patience! the Fort is good as won;
To-morrow, and into Donelson.

LATER AND LAST.

THE FORT IS OURS.

A flag came out at early morn
Bringing surrender. From their towers
Floats out the banner late their scorn.
In Dover, hut and house are full
Of rebels dead or dying.
The National flag is flying
From the crammed court-house pinnacle.
Great boat-loads of our wounded go
To-day to Nashville. The sleet-winds blow;
But all is right: the fight is won,
The winter-fight for Donelson.
Hurrah!
The spell of old defeat is broke,
The habit of victory begun;
Grant strikes the war's first sounding stroke
At Donelson.

For lists of killed and wounded, see
The morrow's dispatch: to-day 'tis victory.

The man who read this to the crowd
Shouted as the end he gained;
And though the unflagging tempest rained,
They answered him aloud.
And hand grasped hand, and glances met
In happy triumph; eyes grew wet.
O, to the punches brewed that night
Went little water. Windows bright

Beamed rosy on the sleet without,
And from the deep street came the frequent shout;
While some in prayer, as these in glee,
Blessed heaven for the winter-victory.
But others were who wakeful laid
  In midnight beds, and early rose,
  And feverish in the foggy snows,
Snatched the damp paper—wife and maid.
  The death-list like a river flows
      Down the pale sheet,
And there the whelming waters meet.

Ah God! may Time with happy haste
Bring wail and triumph to a waste,
  And war be done;
The battle flag-staff fall athwart
The curs'd ravine, and wither; naught
  Be left of trench or gun;
The bastion, let it ebb away,
Washed with the river bed; and Day
  In vain seek Donelson.

A Utilitarian View of the *Monitor*'s Fight[4]

Plain be the phrase, yet apt the verse,
  More ponderous than nimble;
For since grimed War here laid aside
His Orient pomp, 'twould ill befit
    Overmuch to ply
  The rhyme's barbaric cymbal.

Hail to victory without the gaud
  Of glory; zeal that needs no fans
Of banners; plain mechanic power

4. The *Monitor*, a Union ironclad ship, met the Confederate ironclad the *Merrimack* in battle on May 9, 1862; though effectively a draw, the battle saved the Union fleet from destruction. This was the first encounter of two ironclads and one of the first naval battles fought mainly under steam power.

Plied cogently in War now placed—
Where War belongs—
Among the trades and artisans.

Yet this was battle, and intense—
Beyond the strife of fleets heroic;
Deadlier, closer, calm 'mid storm;
No passion; all went on by crank,
Pivot, and screw,
And calculations of caloric.

Needless to dwell; the story's known.
The ringing of those plates on plates
Still ringeth round the world—
The clangor of the blacksmiths' fray.
The anvil-din
Resounds this message from the Fates:

War shall yet be, and to the end;
But war-paint shows the streaks of weather;
War yet shall be, but warriors
Are now but operatives; War's made
Less grand than Peace,
And a singe runs through lace and feather.

Shiloh

A Requiem

(April, 1862)

Skimming lightly, wheeling still,
The swallows fly low
Over the fields in clouded days,
The forest-field of Shiloh—
Over the field where April rain
Solaced the parched ones stretched in pain
Through the pause of night
That followed the Sunday fight
Around the church of Shiloh—

The church so lone, the log-built one,
That echoed to many a parting groan
And natural prayer
Of dying foemen mingled there—
Foemen at morn, but friends at eve—
Fame or country least their care:
(What like a bullet can undeceive!)
But now they lie low,
While over them the swallows skim,
And all is hushed at Shiloh.

Malvern Hill*

(July, 1862)

Ye elms that wave on Malvern Hill
In prime of morn and May,
Recall ye how McClellan's* men
Here stood at bay?
While deep within yon forest dim
Our rigid comrades lay—
Some with the cartridge in their mouth,
Others with fixed arms lifted South—
Invoking so
The cypress glades? Ah wilds of woe!

The spires of Richmond*, late beheld
Through rifts in musket-haze,
Were closed from view in clouds of dust
On leaf-walled ways,
Where streamed our wagons in caravan;
And the Seven Nights and Days
Of march and fast, retreat and fight,
Pinched our grimed faces to ghastly plight—
Does the elm wood
Recall the haggard beards of blood?

The battle-smoked flag, with stars eclipsed,
We followed (it never fell!)—

In silence husbanded our strength—
Received their yell;
Till on this slope we patient turned
With cannon ordered well;
Reverse we proved was not defeat;
But ah, the sod what thousands meet!—
Does Malvern Wood
Bethink itself, and muse and brood?

We elms of Malvern Hill
Remember every thing;
But sap the twig will fill:
Wag the world how it will,
Leaves must be green in Spring.

The House-top[5]

A Night Piece
(July, 1863)

No sleep. The sultriness pervades the air
And binds the brain—a dense oppression, such
As tawny tigers feel in matted shades,
Vexing their blood and making apt for ravage.
Beneath the stars the roofy desert spreads
Vacant as Libya. All is hushed near by.
Yet fitfully from far breaks a mixed surf
Of muffled sound, the atheist roar of riot.
Yonder, where parching Sirius set in drought
Balefully glares red Arson—there—and there.
The town is taken by its rats—ship-rats
And rats of the wharves. All civil charms
And priestly spells which late held hearts in awe—

5. Melville here responds to the draft riots (see Time Line, July 13–17, 1863). References to "ship-rats" and "rats of the wharves" allude to the role played by Irish immigrant dockworkers in the riots. The phrase "priestly spells" alludes to John Hughes, the Roman Catholic bishop of New York (himself Irish), who was asked by city leaders to help quell the violence and who supported the draft. "Draco" was a Greek statesman (seventh century B.C.E.) who was the author of harsh (or "Draconian") laws.

Fear-bound, subjected to a better sway
Than sway of self; these like a dream dissolve,
And man rebounds whole aeons back in nature.
Hail to the low dull rumble, dull and dead,
And ponderous drag that shakes the wall.
Wise Draco comes, deep in the midnight roll
Of black artillery; he comes, though late;
In code corroborating Calvin's creed
And cynic tyrannies of honest kings;
He comes, nor parlies; and the Town, redeemed,
Gives thanks devout; nor, being thankful, heeds
The grimy slur on the Republic's faith implied,
Which holds that Man is naturally good,
And—more—is Nature's Roman, never to be scourged.

Sheridan* at Cedar Creek[6]

(October, 1864)

Shoe the steed with silver
    That bore him to the fray,
When he heard the guns at dawning—
            Miles away;
When he heard them calling, calling—
          Mount! nor stay:
            Quick, or all is lost;
            They've surprised and stormed the post,
            They push your routed host—
    Gallop! retrieve the day!

House the horse in ermine—
    For the foam-flake blew
White through the red October;
    He thundered into view;
They cheered him in the looming;
    Horseman and horse they knew.

6. In the third stanza, Melville refers to Jubal Early, the Confederate general whom Sheridan* defeated at Cedar Creek. See **Thomas Buchanan Read**'s **"Sheridan's Ride."**

The turn of the tide began,
The rally of bugles ran,
He swung his hat in the van;
The electric hoof-spark flew.

Wreathe the steed and lead him—
For the charge he led
Touched and turned the cypress
Into amaranths for the head
Of Philip, king of riders,
Who raised them from the dead.
The camp (at dawning lost)
By eve recovered—forced,
Rang with laughter of the host
At belated Early fled.

Shroud the horse in sable—
For the mounds they heap!
There is firing in the Valley,
And yet no strife they keep;
It is the parting volley,
It is the pathos deep.
There is glory for the brave
Who lead, and nobly save,
But no knowledge in the grave
Where the nameless followers sleep.

In the Prison* Pen[7]

(1864)

Listless he eyes the palisades
And sentries in the glare;
'Tis barren as a pelican-beach—
But his world is ended there.

7. In stanza 4, Melville alludes to the fact that at Andersonville Prison in Georgia, Union prisoners were prohibited from having any sort of shelter.

Nothing to do; and vacant hands
 Bring on the idiot-pain;
He tries to think—to recollect,
 But the blur is on his brain.

Around him swarm the plaining ghosts
 Like those on Virgil's shore—
A wilderness of faces dim,
 And pale ones gashed and hoar.

A smiting sun. No shed, no tree;
 He totters to his lair—
A den that sick hands dug in earth
 Ere famine wasted there,

Or, dropping in his place, he swoons,
 Walled in by throngs that press,
Till forth from the throngs they bear him dead—
 Dead in his meagreness.

The College Colonel

He rides at their head;
 A crutch by his saddle just slants in view,
One slung arm is in splints, you see,
 Yet he guides his strong steed—how coldly too.

He brings his regiment home—
 Not as they filed two years before,
But a remnant half-tattered, and battered, and worn,
Like castaway sailors, who—stunned
  By the surf's loud roar,
 Their mates dragged back and seen no more—
Again and again breast the surge,
 And at last crawl, spent, to shore.

A still rigidity and pale—
 An Indian aloofness lones his brow;
He has lived a thousand years
Compressed in battle's pains and prayers,

Marches and watches slow.
There are welcoming shouts, and flags;
Old men off hat to the Boy,
Wreaths from gay balconies fall at his feet,
But to *him*—there comes alloy.

It is not that a leg is lost,
It is not that an arm is maimed,
It is not that the fever has racked—
Self he has long disclaimed.

But all through the Seven Days' Fight,
And deep in the Wilderness grim,
And in the field-hospital tent,
And Petersburg crater, and dim
Lean brooding in Libby,* there came—
Ah heaven!—what *truth* to him.

The Martyr

Indicative of the passion of the people on the 15th of April, 1865

Good Friday was the day
Of the prodigy and crime,
When they killed him in his pity,
When they killed him in his prime
Of clemency and calm—
When with yearning he was filled
To redeem the evil-willed,
And, though conqueror, be kind;
But they killed him in his kindness,
In their madness and their blindness,
And they killed him from behind.

There is sobbing of the strong,
And a pall upon the land;
But the People in their weeping
Bare the iron hand:
Beware the People weeping
When they bare the iron hand.

He lieth in his blood—
  The father in his face;
They have killed him, the Forgiver—
  The Avenger takes his place,
The Avenger wisely stern,
    Who in righteousness shall do
    What the heavens call him to,
And the parricides remand;
  For they killed him in his kindness,
  In their madness and their blindness,
And his blood is on their hand.

There is sobbing of the strong,
  And a pall upon the land;
But the People in their weeping
    Bare the iron hand:
Beware the People weeping
  When they bare the iron hand.

Rebel Color-bearers at Shiloh:[8]

A plea against the vindictive cry raised by civilians shortly after the surrender at Appomattox

The color-bearers facing death
White in the whirling sulphurous wreath,
  Stand boldly out before the line;
Right and left their glances go,
Proud of each other, glorying in their show;
Their battle-flags about them blow,
  And fold them as in flame divine:
Such living robes are only seen
Round martyrs burning on the green—
And martyrs for the Wrong have been.

8. As he reveals in a note, Melville bases this poem on a newspaper account of the battle of Shiloh (see Time Line, April 6–7, 1862); the piece describes how a Union colonel ordered his sharpshooters not to shoot Confederate color-bearers who had boldly stepped out in front of their line just as the engagement began. The poem's closing stanza refers to Grant's* meeting with Lee* at Appomattox (see Time Line, April 9, 1865); Melville here reminds readers of the generous terms of surrender that the Union general offered his Confederate counterpart.

Perish their Cause! but mark the men—
Mark the planted statues, then
Draw trigger on them if you can.

The leader of a patriot-band
Even so could view rebels who so could stand;
And this when peril pressed him sore,
Left aidless in the shivered front of war—
Skulkers behind, defiant foes before,
And fighting with a broken brand.
The challenge in that courage rare—
Courage defenseless, proudly bare—
Never could tempt him; he could dare
Strike up the leveled rifle there.

Sunday at Shiloh, and the day
When Stonewall* charged—McClellan's* crimson May,
And Chickamauga's wave of death,
And of the Wilderness the cypress wreath—
All these have passed away.
The life in the veins of Treason lags,
Her daring color-bearers drop their flags,
And yield. *Now* shall we fire?
Can poor spite be?
Shall nobleness in victory less aspire
Than in reverse? Spare Spleen her ire,
And think how Grant met Lee.

"Formerly a Slave"[9]

An idealized Portrait, by E. Vedder, in the Spring Exhibition of the National Academy, 1865

The sufferance of her race is shown,
And retrospect of life,
Which now too late deliverance dawns upon;
Yet is she not at strife.

9. Elihu Vedder's painting *Jane Jackson, formerly a Slave* was exhibited at the National Academy of Design in 1865.

Her children's children they shall know
    The good withheld from her;
And so her reverie takes prophetic cheer—
    In spirit she sees the stir

Far down the depth of thousand years,
    And marks the revel shine;
Her dusky face is lit with sober light,
    Sibylline, yet benign.

Magnanimity Baffled

"Sharp words we had before the fight;
        But—now the fight is done—
Look, here's my hand," said the Victor bold,
        "Take it—an honest one!
What, holding back? I mean you well;
    Though worsted, you strove stoutly, man;
The odds were great; I honor you;
            Man honors man.

"Still silent, friend? can grudges be?
        Yet am I held a foe?—
Turned to the wall, on his cot he lies—
        Never I'll leave him so!
Brave one! I here implore your hand;
    Dumb still? all fellowship fled?
Nay, then, I'll have this stubborn hand!"
    He snatched it—it was dead.

On the Slain Collegians[10]

Youth is the time when hearts are large,
        And stirring wars

10. In his note for this poem, Melville writes: "The records of Northern colleges attest what numbers of our noblest youth went from them to the battle-field. Southern members of the same classes arrayed themselves on the side of Secession, while Southern seminaries contributed large quotas. Of all these, what numbers marched who never returned except on the shield."

Appeal to the spirit which appeals in turn
To the blade it draws.
If woman incite, and duty show
(Though made the mask of Cain),
Or whether it be Truth's sacred cause,
Who can aloof remain
That shares youth's ardor, uncooled by the snow
Of wisdom or sordid gain?

The liberal arts and nurture sweet
Which give his gentleness to man—
Train him to honor, lend him grace
Through bright examples meet—
That culture which makes never wan
With underminings deep, but holds
The surface still, its fitting place,
And so gives sunniness to the face
And bravery to the heart; what troops
Of generous boys in happiness thus bred—
Saturnians through life's Tempe led,
Went from the North and came from the South,
With golden mottoes in the mouth,
To lie down midway on a bloody bed.

Woe for the homes of the North,
And woe for the seats of the South:
All who felt life's spring in prime,
And were swept by the wind of their place and time—
All lavish hearts, on whichever side,
Of birth urbane or courage high,
Armed them for the stirring wars—
Armed them—some to die.
Apollo-like in pride,
Each would slay his Python—caught
The maxims in his temple taught—
Aflame with sympathies whose blaze
Perforce enwrapped him—social laws,
Friendship and kin, and by-gone days—
Vows, kisses—every heart unmoors,
And launches into the seas of wars.
What could they else—North or South?

Each went forth with blessings given
By priests and mothers in the name of Heaven;
  And honor in both was chief.
Warred one for Right, and one for Wrong?
So be it; but they both were young—
Each grape to his cluster clung,
All their elegies are sung.

The anguish of maternal hearts
  Must search for balm divine;
But well the striplings bore their fated parts
  (The heavens all parts assign)—
Never felt life's care or cloy.
Each bloomed and died an unabated Boy;
Nor dreamed what death was—thought it mere
Sliding into some vernal sphere.
They knew the joy, but leaped the grief,
Like plants that flower ere comes the leaf—
Which storms lay low in kindly doom,
And kill them in their flush of bloom.

On the Slain at Chickamauga

Happy are they and charmed in life
  Who through long wars arrive unscarred
At peace. To such the wreath be given,
If they unfalteringly have striven—
  In honor, as in limb, unmarred.
Let cheerful praise be rife,
  And let them live their years at ease,
Musing on brothers who victorious died—
  Loved mates whose memory shall ever please.

And yet mischance is honorable too—
  Seeming defeat in conflict justified
Whose end to closing eyes is hid from view.
The will, that never can relent—
The aim, survivor of the bafflement,
  Make this memorial due.

An uninscribed Monument

on one of the Battle-fields of the Wilderness

Silence and Solitude may hint
  (Whose home is in yon piny wood)
What I, though tableted, could never tell—
The din which here befell,
  And striving of the multitude.
The iron cones and spheres of death
  Set round me in their rust,
    These, too, if just,
Shall speak with more than animated breath.
  Thou who beholdest, if thy thought,
Not narrowed down to personal cheer,
Take in the import of the quiet here—
  The after-quiet—the calm full fraught;
Thou too wilt silent stand—
Silent as I, and lonesome as the land.

Frances Ellen Watkins Harper (1825–1911)

Frances Ellen Watkins Harper was the most popular and highly respected African American poet before Paul Laurence Dunbar; in fact, Harper's dialect poems characterizing the speech and attitudes of former slaves helped to pave the way for his later success. Probably born on September 24, 1825, in Baltimore to free parents, Frances Watkins was raised by an aunt. There is no record of the names of either parent or of the aunt who took her in when she was three. At the age of thirteen, she left school to take on paid domestic and child care work. At the age of fourteen, however, Harper published her first essay. At the age of twenty, in 1845, she reputedly published a volume of poems and essays called *Forest Leaves*. This is a remarkable achievement for a young black woman having to support herself through domestic work; no copies of this publication survive. In 1850, Harper moved to Ohio and taught sewing and embroidery briefly as the first female teacher at Union Seminary. This was the first of a number of relatively short-lived positions that kept her moving around the country. She taught in New York, returned to Philadelphia, then moved to New England, taking employment with the Maine Anti-Slavery Society as a traveling lecturer. A radical abolitionist, Harper both grounded her remarks broadly in Christian moral philosophy and urged her listeners to political action. She was extremely successful as a lecturer, owing to both her great oratorical skill and eloquent writing. During this same period, Harper published *Poems on Miscellaneous Subjects* (1854), which was reprinted several times before the war and had sold ten thousand copies by 1857. In that year she returned to Philadelphia, continuing her lecturing for the Philadelphia Society for Promoting the Abolition of Slavery.

In 1860, Frances Watkins married the widower Fenton Harper, and together they purchased a farm in Ohio, where they lived until his death in 1864. Deeply in debt, Harper moved her daughter and three stepchildren to New England to rejoin the lecture circuit for the remainder of the Civil War. After the war, Harper turned her attention to the project of reconstruction and aiding newly freed slaves, lecturing throughout the South to a wide variety of audiences, black and white.

By the time of her death, Harper was among the best-known and most widely respected African Americans for her work in several social and political movements—abolition, temperance, black and women's suffrage, women's rights,

African American education, and racial justice. An activist as well as a writer throughout her life, she never stopped publishing essays and poems and in the later decades of her life also wrote novels. *Iola Leroy* (1892) was the first novel by an African American to deal directly with the Civil War and Reconstruction and remains the work by which Harper is best known today. She is almost equally famous, however, for her "Aunt Chloe" series of poems, published in *Sketches of Southern Life* (1872). These poems similarly present a story of enslavement, Civil War, and emancipation, but here through the single distinctive voice of a clear-sighted and uneducated woman. In total, Harper published at least nine volumes of poetry. After having been at the forefront of most major reform movements of the nineteenth century, Frances E. W. Harper died of heart failure in Philadelphia in 1911. She was celebrated at her death for her poetry, stories, and fiction and for her life of service to reform.

The Slave Mother[1]

Heard you that shriek? It rose
  So wildly on the air,
It seemed as if a burden'd heart
  Was breaking in despair.

Saw you those hands so sadly clasped—
  The bowed and feeble head—
The shuddering of that fragile form—
  That look of grief and dread?

Saw you the sad, imploring eye?
  Its every glance was pain,
As if a storm of agony
  Were sweeping through the brain.

She is a mother, pale with fear,
  Her boy clings to her side,

1. *Poems on Miscellaneous Subjects*, 1854. Most of Harper's poems were published first in periodicals, but records of first publication are difficult to find; we have depended for this information and for historical context on Frances Smith Foster, *A Brighter Coming Day: A Frances Ellen Watkins Harper Reader* (New York: Feminist Press, 1990) and on Paula Bernat Bennett, *Nineteenth-Century American Women Poets*. All poems reprinted here are cited from *A Brighter Coming Day*.

And in her kirtle vainly tries
His trembling form to hide.

He is not hers, although she bore
For him a mother's pains;
He is not hers, although her blood
Is coursing through his veins!

He is not hers, for cruel hands
May rudely tear apart
The only wreath of household love
That binds her breaking heart.

His love has been a joyous light
That o'er her pathway smiled,
A fountain gushing ever new,
Amid life's desert wild.

His lightest word has been a tone
Of music round her heart,
Their lives a streamlet blent in one—
Oh, Father! must they part?

They tear him from her circling arms,
Her last and fond embrace.
Oh! never more may her sad eyes
Gaze on his mournful face.

No marvel, then, these bitter shrieks
Disturb the listening air:
She is a mother, and her heart
Is breaking in despair.

Bible Defence of Slavery[2]

Take sackcloth of the darkest dye,
And shroud the pulpits round!
Servants of Him that cannot lie,
Sit mourning on the ground.

2. *Poems on Miscellaneous Subjects*, 1854.

Let holy horror blanch each cheek,
  Pale every brow with fears:
And rocks and stones, if ye could speak,
  Ye well might melt to tears!

Let sorrow breathe in every tone,
  In every strain ye raise;
Insult not God's majestic throne
  With th' mockery of praise.

A "reverend" man, whose light should be
  The guide of age and youth,
Brings to the shrine of Slavery
  The sacrifice of truth!

For the direst wrong by man imposed,
  Since Sodom's fearful cry,
The word of life has been unclosed,
  To give your God the lie.

Oh! when ye pray for heathen lands,
  And plead for their dark shores,
Remember Slavery's cruel hands
  Make heathens at your doors!

Eliza Harris[3]

Like a fawn from the arrow, startled and wild,
A woman swept by us, bearing a child;
In her eye was the night of a settled despair,
And her brow was o'ershaded with anguish and care.

She was nearing the river—in reaching the brink,
She heeded no danger, she paused not to think!
For she is a mother—her child is a slave—
And she'll give him his freedom, or find him a grave!

3. *The Liberator* December 16, 1853. This poem was frequently reprinted, sometimes without stanzas 11 and 12. References exist to an earlier publication of the poem in *Aliened American*, but no copy of this publication has been found. Eliza is a character from Harriet Beecher Stowe's *Uncle Tom's Cabin* (1852).

It was a vision to haunt us, that innocent face—
So pale in its aspect, so fair in its grace;
As the tramp of the horse and the bay of the hound,
With the fetters that gall, were trailing the ground!

She was nerv'd by despair, and strengthened by woe,
As she leap'd o'er the chasms that yawn'd from below;
Death howl'd in the tempest, and rav'd in the blast,
But she heard not the sound till the danger was past.

Oh! how shall I speak of my proud country's shame?
Of the stains on her glory, how give them their name?
How say that her banner in mockery waves—
Her "star spangled banner"—o'er millions of slaves?

How say that the lawless may torture and chase
A woman whose crime is the hue of her face?
How the depths of the forest may echo around
With the shrieks of despair, and the bay of the hound?

With her step on the ice, and her arm on her child,
The danger was fearful, the pathway was wild;
But, aided by Heaven, she gained a free shore,
Where the friends of humanity open'd their door.

So fragile and lovely, so fearfully pale,
Like a lily that bends to the breath of the gale,
Save the heave of her breast, and the sway of her hair,
You'd have thought her a statue of fear and despair.

In agony close to her bosom she press'd
The life of her heart, the child of her breast:—
Oh! love from its tenderness gathering might,
Had strengthen'd her soul for the dangers of flight.

But she's free—yes, free from the land where the slave
From the hand of oppression must rest in the grave;
Where bondage and torture, where scourges and chains,
Have plac'd on our banner indelible stains.

Did a fever e'er burning through bosom and brain,
Send a lava-like flood through every vein,
Till it suddenly cooled 'neath a healing spell,
And you knew, oh! the joy! you knew you were well?

So felt this young mother, as a sense of the rest
Stole gently and sweetly o'er *her* weary breast,
As her boy looked up, and, wondering, smiled
On the mother whose love had freed her child.

The bloodhounds have miss'd the scent of her way;
The hunter is rifled and foil'd of his prey;
Fierce jargon and cursing, with clanking of chains,
Make sounds of strange discord on Liberty's plains.

With the rapture of love and fulness of bliss,
She plac'd on his brow a mother's fond kiss:—
Oh! poverty, danger and death she can brave,
For the child of her love is no longer a slave!

The Slave Auction[4]

The sale began—young girls were there,
  Defenceless in their wretchedness,
Whose stifled sobs of deep despair
  Revealed their anguish and distress.

And mothers stood with streaming eyes,
  And saw their dearest children sold;
Unheeded rose their bitter cries,
  While tyrants bartered them for gold.

And woman, with her love and truth—
  For these in sable forms may dwell—
Gaz'd on the husband of her youth,
  With anguish none may paint or tell.

And men, whose sole crime was their hue,
  The impress of their Maker's hand,
And frail and shrinking children, too,
  Were gathered in that mournful band.

Ye who have laid your love to rest,
  And wept above their lifeless clay,

4. *Frederick Douglass' Paper* September 22, 1854.

Know not the anguish of that breast,
Whose lov'd are rudely torn away.

Ye may not know how desolate
Are bosoms rudely forced to part,
And how a dull and heavy weight
Will press the life-drops from the heart.

Bury Me in a Free Land[5]

Make me a grave where'er you will,
In a lowly plain or a lofty hill;
Make it among earth's humblest graves,
But not in a land where men are slaves.

I could not rest, if around my grave
I heard the steps of a trembling slave;
His shadow above my silent tomb
Would make it a place of fearful gloom.

I could not sleep, if I heard the tread
Of a coffle-gang to the shambles led,
And the mother's shriek of wild despair
Rise, like a curse, on the trembling air.

I could not rest, if I saw the lash
Drinking her blood at each fearful gash;
And I saw her babes torn from her breast,
Like trembling doves from their parent nest.

I'd shudder and start, if I heard the bay
Of a bloodhound seizing his human prey;
And I heard the captive plead in vain,
As they bound, afresh, his galling chain.

If I saw young girls from their mother's arms
Bartered and sold from their youthful charms,

5. *Anti-Slavery Bugle* November 20, 1858, reprinted in *Liberator* January 14, 1864. Harper sent a copy of this poem to one of John Brown's men awaiting execution after the raid on Harpers Ferry in 1859.

My eye would flash with a mournful flame,
My death-pale cheek grow red with shame.

I would sleep, dear friends, where bloated Might
Can rob no man of his dearest right;
My rest shall be calm in any grave
Where none can call his brother a slave.

I ask no monument, proud and high,
To arrest the gaze of the passers by;
All that my yearning spirit craves
Is—*Bury me not in a land of slaves!*

To the Cleveland Union-Savers:[6]

An Appeal from One of the Fugitive's Own Race

Men of Cleveland, had a vulture
  Clutched a timid dove for prey,
Would ye not, with human pity,
  Drive the gory bird away?

Had you seen a feeble lambkin
  Shrinking from a wolf so bold,
Would ye not, to shield the trembler,
  In your arms have made its fold?

But when she, a hunted sister,
  Stretched her hands that ye might save,
Colder far then Zembla's regions
  Was the answer that ye gave.

On your Union's bloody altar
  Was your helpless victim laid;

6. *Anti-Slavery Bugle* February 23, 1861, and *Liberator* March 8, 1861, the source of this text. The poem criticizes members of the Cleveland, Ohio, Republican Party (called the Union Party) for their support of the Fugitive Slave Law.* In 1861 an escaped slave named Sarah Lucy Bagby was seized by U.S. authorities in Cleveland. Although white abolitionists attempted to purchase her freedom, the court ruled in favor of returning her to her owner in Virginia. Bagby was the last slave compelled to return to a Southern state under the Fugitive Slave Law.

Mercy, truth, and justice shuddered,
  But your hands would give no aid.

And ye sent her back to torture,
  Stripped of freedom, robbed of right,—
Thrust the wretched, captive stranger
  Back to Slavery's gloomy night!

Sent her back where men may trample
  On her honor and her fame,
And upon her lips so dusky
  Press the cup of woe and shame.

There is blood upon your city,—
  Dark and dismal is the stain;
And your hands would fail to cleanse it,
  Though you should Lake Erie drain.

There's a curse upon your Union!
  Fearful sounds are in the air;
As if thunderbolts were forging
  Answers to the bondman's prayer.

Ye may bind your trembling victims,
  Like the heathen priests of old;
And may barter manly honor
  For the Union and for gold;—

But ye cannot stay the whirlwind,
  When the storm begins to break;
And our God doth rise in judgment
  For the poor and needy's sake.

And your guilty, sin-cursed Union
  Shall be shaken to its base,
Till ye learn that simple justice
  Is the right of every race.

Lines to Miles O'Reiley[7]

You've heard no doubt of Irish bulls,
And how they blunder, thick and fast;
But of all the queer and foolish things,
O'Reiley, you have said the last.

You say we brought the rebs supplies,
And gave them aid amid the fight,
And if you must be ruled by rebs,
Instead of black you want them white.

You blame us that we did not rise,
And pluck from a fiery brand,
When Little Mac* said if we did,
He'd put us down with iron hand.

And when we sought to join your ranks,
And battle with you, side by side,
Did men not curl their lips with scorn,
And thrust us back with hateful pride?

And when at last we gained the field,
Did we not firmly, bravely stand,
And help to turn the tide of death,
That spread its ruin o'er the land?

We hardly think we're worse than those
Who kindled up this fearful strife,
Because we did not seize the chance
To murder helpless babes and wife.

And had we struck, with vengeful hand,
The rebel where he most could feel,
Were you not ready to impale
Our hearts upon your Northern steel?

---

7. Published as "The Other Side" in the *Philadelphia Press* October 16, 1867, but most likely written during the war. Harper here addresses **Charles Graham Halpine,** who wrote poems and articles under the pen name "Private Miles O'Reilly," with particular reference to his poem **"Sambo's Right to be Kilt."** An "Irish bull" was a statement that was erroneous, patently absurd, or illogical.

O'Reiley, men like you should wear
The gift of song like some bright crown,
Nor worse than ruffians at the ring,
Strike at a man because he's down.

Words for the Hour[8]

Men of the North! it is no time
To quit the battle-field;
When danger fronts your rear and van
It is no time to yield.

No time to bend the battle's crest
Before the wily foe,
And, ostrich-like, to hide your heads
From the impending blow.

The minions of a baffled wrong
Are marshalling their clan,
Rise up! rise up, enchanted North!
And strike for God and man.

This is no time for careless ease;
No time for idle sleep;
Go light the fires in every camp,
And solemn sentries keep.

The foe ye foiled upon the field
Has only changed his base;
New dangers crowd around you
And stare you in the face.

O Northern men! within your hands
Is held no common trust;
Secure the victories won by blood
When treason bit the dust.

'Tis yours to banish from the land
Oppression's iron rule;

8. *Poems*, 1871.

And o'er the ruin'd auction-block
  Erect the common school.

To wipe from labor's branded brow
  The curse that shamed the land;
And teach the Freedman how to wield
  The ballot in his hand.

This is the nation's golden hour,
  Nerve every heart and hand,
To build on Justice, as a rock,
  The future of the land.

True to your trust, oh, never yield
  One citadel of right!
With Truth and Justice clasping hands
  Ye yet shall win the fight!

An Appeal to My Countrywomen[9]

You can sigh o'er the sad-eyed Armenian
  Who weeps in her desolate home.
You can mourn o'er the exile of Russia
  From kindred and friends doomed to roam.

You can pity the men who have woven
  From passion and appetite chains
To coil with a terrible tension
  Around their heartstrings and brains.

You can sorrow o'er little children
  Disinherited from their birth,
The wee waifs and toddlers neglected,
  Robbed of sunshine, music and mirth.

For beasts you have gentle compassion;
  Your mercy and pity they share.
For the wretched, outcast and fallen
  You have tenderness, love and care.

9. *Poems*, 1871.

But hark! from our Southland are floating
Sobs of anguish, murmurs of pain,
And women heart-stricken are weeping
Over their tortured and their slain.

On their brows the sun has left traces;
Shrink not from their sorrow in scorn.
When they entered the threshold of being
The children of a King were born.

Each comes as a guest to the table
The hand of our God has outspread,
To fountains that ever leap upward,
To share in the soil we all tread.

When ye plead for the wrecked and fallen,
The exile from far-distant shores,
Remember that men are still wasting
Life's crimson around your own doors.

Have ye not, oh, my favored sisters,
Just a plea, a prayer or a tear,
For mothers who dwell 'neath the shadows
Of agony, hatred and fear?

Men may tread down the poor and lowly,
May crush them in anger and hate,
But surely the mills of God's justice
Will grind out the grist of their fate.

Oh, people sin-laden and guilty,
So lusty and proud in your prime,
The sharp sickles of God's retribution
Will gather your harvest of crime.

Weep not, oh my well-sheltered sisters,
Weep not for the Negro alone,
But weep for your sons who must gather
The crops which their fathers have sown.

Go read on the tombstones of nations
Of chieftains who masterful trod,
The sentence which time has engraven,
That they had forgotten their God.

'Tis the judgment of God that men reap
    The tares which in madness they sow,
Sorrow follows the footsteps of crime,
    And Sin is the consort of Woe.

The Deliverance[10]

Master only left old Mistus
    One bright and handsome boy;
But she fairly doted on him,
    He was her pride and joy.

We all liked Mister Thomas,
    He was so kind at heart;
And when the young folks got in scrapes,
    He always took their part.

He kept right on that very way
    Till he got big and tall,
And old Mistus used to chide him,
    And say he'd spile us all.

But somehow the farm did prosper
    When he took things in hand;
And though all the servants liked him,
    He made them understand.

One evening Mister Thomas said,
    "Just bring my easy shoes:
I am going to sit by mother,
    And read her up the news."

Soon I heard him tell old Mistus
    "We're bound to have a fight;
But we'll whip the Yankees, mother,
    We'll whip them sure as night!"

10. *Sketches of Southern Life*, 1872. Late in this poem, Harper's speaker (Aunt Chloe) refers to "another president" who black people thought would "be the Moses / Of all the colored race"—namely, Andrew Johnson, who betrayed black expectation for his support; the president who broke up the Ku Klux Klan is Ulysses S. Grant.*

Then I saw old Mistus tremble;
She gasped and held her breath;
And she looked on Mister Thomas
With a face as pale as death.

"They are firing on Fort Sumpter*;
Oh! I wish that I was there!—
Why, dear mother! what's the matter?
You're the picture of despair."

"I was thinking, dearest Thomas,
'Twould break my very heart
If a fierce and dreadful battle
Should tear our lives apart."

"None but cowards, dearest mother,
Would skulk unto the rear,
When the tyrant's hand is shaking
All the heart is holding dear."

I felt sorry for old Mistus;
She got too full to speak;
But I saw the great big tear-drops
A running down her cheek.

Mister Thomas too was troubled
With choosing on that night,
Betwixt staying with his mother
And joining in the fight.

Soon down into the village came
A call for volunteers;
Mistus gave up Mister Thomas,
With many sighs and tears.

His uniform was real handsome;
He looked so brave and strong;
But somehow I couldn't help thinking
His fighting must be wrong.

Though the house was very lonesome,
I thought 'twould all come right,
For I felt somehow or other
We was mixed up in that fight.

And I said to Uncle Jacob,
  "Now old Mistus feels the sting,
For this parting with your children
  Is a mighty dreadful thing."

"Never mind," said Uncle Jacob,
  "Just wait and watch and pray,
For I feel right sure and certain,
  Slavery's bound to pass away;

"Because I asked the Spirit,
  If God is good and just,
How it happened that the masters
  Did grind us to the dust.

"And something reasoned right inside,
  Such should not always be;
And you could not beat it out my head,
  The Spirit spoke to me."

And his dear old eyes would brighten,
  And his lips put on a smile,
Saying, "Pick up faith and courage,
  And just wait a little while."

Mistus prayed up in the parlor
  That the Secesh* all might win;
We were praying in the cabins,
  Wanting freedom to begin.

Mister Thomas wrote to Mistus,
  Telling 'bout the Bull's Run fight,
That his troops had whipped the Yankees,
  And put them all to flight.

Mistus' eyes did fairly glisten;
  She laughed and praised the South,
But I thought some day she'd laugh
  On tother side her mouth.

I used to watch old Mistus' face,
  And when it looked quite long
I would say to Cousin Milly,
  The battle's going wrong;

Not for us, but for the Rebels.—
My heart 'would fairly skip,
When Uncle Jacob used to say,
"The North is bound to whip."

And let the fight go as it would—
Let North or South prevail—
He always kept his courage up,
And never let it fail.

And he often used to tell us,
"Children, don't forget to pray;
For the darkest time of morning
Is just 'fore the break of day."

Well, one morning bright and early
We heard the fife and drum,
And the booming of the cannon—
The Yankee troops had come.

When the word ran through the village,
The colored folks are free—
In the kitchens and the cabins
We held a jubilee.

When they told us Mister Lincoln*
Said that slavery was dead,
We just poured our prayers and blessings
Upon his precious head.

We just laughed, and danced, and shouted,
And prayed, and sang, and cried,
And we thought dear Uncle Jacob
Would fairly crack his side.

But when old Mistus heard it,
She groaned and hardly spoke;
When she had to lose her servants,
Her heart was almost broke.

'Twas a sight to see our people
Going out, the troops to meet,
Almost dancing to the music,
And marching down the street.

After years of pain and parting,
Our chains was broke in two,
And we was so mighty happy,
We did'nt know what to do.

But we soon got used to freedom,
Though the way at first was rough;
But we weathered through the tempest,
For slavery made us tough.

But we had one awful sorrow,
It almost turned my head,
When a mean and wicked cretur
Shot Mister Lincoln dead.

'Twas a dreadful solemn morning,
I just staggered on my feet;
And the women they were crying
And screaming in the street.

But if many prayers and blessings
Could bear him to the throne,
I should think when Mister Lincoln died,
That heaven just got its own.

Then we had another President,—
What do you call his name?
Well, if the colored folks forget him
They would'nt be much to blame.

We thought he'd be the Moses
Of all the colored race;
But when the Rebels pressed us hard
He never showed his face.

But something must have happened him,
Right curi's I'll be bound,
'Cause I heard'em talking 'bout a circle
That he was swinging round.

But everything will pass away—
He went like time and tide—
And when the next election came
They let poor Andy slide.

But now we have a President,
  And if I was a man
I'd vote for him for breaking up
  The wicked Ku-Klux Klan.

And if any man should ask me
  If I would sell my vote,
I'd tell him I was not the one
  To change and turn my coat;

If freedom seem'd a little rough
  I'd weather through the gale;
And as to buying up my vote,
  I hadn't it for sale.

I do not think I'd ever be
  As slack as Jonas Handy;
Because I heard he sold his vote
  For just three sticks of candy.

But when John Thomas Reeder brought
  His wife some flour and meat,
And told her he had sold his vote
  For something good to eat,

You ought to seen Aunt Kitty raise,
  And heard her blaze away;
She gave the meat and flour a toss,
  And said they should not stay.

And I should think he felt quite cheap
  For voting the wrong side;
And when Aunt Kitty scolded him,
  He just stood up and cried.

But the worst fooled man I ever saw
  Was when poor David Rand
Sold out for flour and sugar;
  The sugar was mixed with sand.

I'll tell you how the thing got out;
  His wife had company,
And she thought the sand was sugar,
  And served it up for tea.

When David sipped and sipped the tea,
Somehow it did'nt taste right;
I guess when he found he was sipping sand,
He was mad enough to fight.

The sugar looked so nice and white—
It was spread some inches deep—
But underneath was a lot of sand;
Such sugar is mighty cheap.

You'd laughed to seen Lucinda Grange
Upon her husband's track;
When he sold his vote for rations
She made him take 'em back.

Day after day did Milly Green
Just follow after Joe,
And told him if he voted wrong
To take his rags and go.

I think that Curnel Johnson said
His side had won that day,
Had not we women radicals
Just got right in the way.

And yet I would not have you think
That all our men are shabby;
But 'tis said in every flock of sheep
There will be one that's scabby.

I've heard, before election came
They tried to buy John Slade;
But he gave them all to understand
That he wasn't in that trade.

And we've got lots of other men
Who rally round the cause,
And go for holding up the hands
That gave us equal laws.

Who know their freedom cost too much
Of blood and pain and treasure,
For them to fool away their votes
For profit or for pleasure.

Learning to Read[11]

Very soon the Yankee teachers
   Came down and set up school;
But, oh! how the Rebs did hate it,—
   It was agin' their rule.

Our masters always tried to hide
   Book learning from our eyes;
Knowledge did'nt agree with slavery—
   'Twould make us all too wise.

But some of us would try to steal
   A little from the book,
And put the words together,
   And learn by hook or crook.

I remember Uncle Caldwell,
   Who took pot-liquor fat
And greased the pages of his book,
   And hid it in his hat.

And had his master ever seen
   The leaves upon his head,
He'd have thought them greasy papers,
   But nothing to read.

And there was Mr. Turner's Ben,
   Who heard the children spell,
And picked the words right up by heart,
   And learned to read 'em well.

Well, the Northern folks kept sending
   The Yankee teachers down;
And they stood right up and helped us,
   Though Rebs did sneer and frown.

And, I longed to read my Bible,
   For precious words it said;

11. *Sketches*; the speaker, Aunt Chloe, refers here to the laws in several Southern states making it a criminal activity to teach an African American to read.

But when I begun to learn it,
   Folks just shook their heads,

And said there is no use trying,
   Oh! Chloe, you're too late;
But as I was rising sixty,
   I had no time to wait.

So I got a pair of glasses,
   And straight to work I went,
And never stopped till I could read
   The hymns and Testament.

Then I got a little cabin—
   A place to call my own—
And I felt as independent
   As the queen upon her throne.

Henry Timrod (1828–1867)

Often called the "Poet Laureate of the Confederacy," Henry Timrod is considered by many scholars to be the most gifted of the Southern poets writing in this era. Born in Charleston, South Carolina, Timrod was descended on both sides of his family from military men. His father, who was also a poet, fought in Florida in the war against the Seminoles; he died while Timrod was still young as a result of an illness contracted during this campaign. After attending private school in Charleston, Timrod enrolled at the University of Georgia, but ill health and lack of funds forced him to withdraw before completing his degree. Thereafter, Timrod studied law briefly before deciding to embark on a career in teaching. When he was unable to find a position at a college, Timrod chose to work as a private tutor. During this time, he began to publish poetry; his pieces appeared first in Charleston newspapers and then in the prestigious *Southern Literary Messenger*. With his lifelong friend Paul Hamilton Hayne, Timrod was at the center of a vibrant community of writers in Charleston, despite his personal shyness. **William Gilmore Simms,** an early supporter of Timrod's work, sought to build relationships between local scholars and this younger generation of writers. It was this Charleston community that launched *Russell's Magazine*, where many of Timrod's poems and critical essays on poetry appeared. The success of Timrod's work in *Russell's* led to the publication of a volume of his poems in 1859 by Ticknor and Fields, one of the leading literary publishing houses in the North. The volume received favorable reviews in both the North and the South; it was to be the only volume published during Timrod's lifetime.

Timrod was a Southerner by birth and by vocation. Though he produced some of his finest poems during the war years, the fall of the Confederacy accelerated his decline into tuberculosis and poverty. He wrote some of his most powerful poems in the white heat of Southern patriotism that the first two years of the war prompted in him: "Ethnogenesis," "A Cry to Arms," "Charleston," and "The Cotton Boll" all date from this period. While the poems he wrote before the war often focus on the beauty of nature in the South, the political crisis of the war gives his representations of Southern landscapes a new vitality and force. Though Timrod attempted to serve in the military, poor health forced him to take a position as a war correspondent for the *Charleston Mercury* instead. In early January 1864, Timrod moved to Columbia, South Carolina, where he became an associate editor of the *South Carolinian*. Shortly thereafter he married Kate Goodwin; the couple's only child, a son, was born a year later. When Sherman's* forces arrived in Columbia in February 1865, Timrod went into hiding. When he reemerged, he found a devastated city; his infant son died in the autumn of that year. In the aftermath of the war, Timrod struggled to make ends meet and had little time for writing poetry; he worked for a time as an editor for the *Carolinian* and then as a clerk in the governor's office. Though "1866" ends on a moment of hope, one senses in the poem an undercurrent of sadness that reflects the losses Timrod endured in the final years of his life. Paul Hamilton Hayne edited a collection of Timrod's poems after his death, thereby preserving many poems that might otherwise have been lost.

Ethnogenesis[1]

I

Hath not the morning dawned with added light?
And shall not evening call another star
Out of the infinite regions of the night,
To mark this day in Heaven? At last, we are
A nation among nations; and the world
Shall soon behold in many a distant port
        Another flag unfurled!
Now, come what may, whose favor need we court?
And, under God, whose thunder need we fear?
        Thank Him who placed us here
Beneath so kind a sky—the very sun
Takes part with us; and on our errands run
All breezes of the ocean; dew and rain
Do noiseless battle for us; and the Year,
And all the gentle daughters in her train,
March in our ranks, and in our service wield
        Long spears of golden grain!

1. Published in the *Charleston Daily Courier* on February 23, 1861, as "Ode on Occasion of the Meeting of the Southern Congress"; the first Southern Congress met at Montgomery, Alabama. With the exception of "We May Not Falter," all poems reprinted here are cited from *The Collected Poems of Henry Timrod: A Variorum Edition*, ed. Edd Winfield Parks and Aileen Wells Parks (Athens: University of Georgia Press, 1965).

A yellow blossom as her fairy shield,
June flings her azure banner to the wind,
  While in the order of their birth
Her sisters pass, and many an ample field
Grows white beneath their steps, till now, behold
    Its endless sheets unfold
THE SNOW OF SOUTHERN SUMMERS! Let the earth
Rejoice! beneath those fleeces soft and warm
    Our happy land shall sleep
    In a repose as deep
  As if we lay intrenched behind
Whole leagues of Russian ice and Arctic storm!

II

And what if, mad with wrongs themselves have wrought,
    In their own treachery caught,
    By their own fears made bold,
    And leagued with him of old,
Who long since in the limits of the North
Set up his evil throne, and warred with God –
What if, both mad and blinded in their rage,
Our foes should fling us down their mortal gage,
And with a hostile step profane our sod!
We shall not shrink, my brothers, but go forth
To meet them, marshaled by the Lord of Hosts,
And overshadowed by the mighty ghosts
Of Moultrie and of Eutaw—who shall foil
Auxiliars such as these? Nor these alone,
    But every stock and stone
    Shall help us; but the very soil,
And all the generous wealth it gives to toil,
And all for which we love our noble land,
Shall fight beside, and through us, sea and strand,
    The heart of woman, and her hand,
Tree, fruit, and flower, and every influence,
    Gentle, or grave, or grand;
    The winds in our defence
Shall seem to blow; to us the hills shall lend
    Their firmness and their calm;

And in our stiffened sinews we shall blend
The strength of pine and palm!

III

Nor would we shun the battle-ground,
    Though weak as we are strong;
Call up the clashing elements around,
    And test the right and wrong!
On one side, creeds that dare to teach
What Christ and Paul refrained to preach;
Codes built upon a broken pledge,
And Charity that whets a poniard's edge;
Fair schemes that leave the neighboring poor
To starve and shiver at the schemer's door,
While in the world's most liberal ranks enrolled,
He turns some vast philanthropy to gold;
Religion, taking every mortal form
But that a pure and Christian faith makes warm,
Where not to vile fanatic passion urged,
Or not in vague philosophies submerged,
Repulsive with all Pharisaic leaven,
And making laws to stay the laws of Heaven!
And on the other, scorn of sordid gain,
Unblemished honor, truth without a stain,
Faith, justice, reverence, charitable wealth,
And, for the poor and humble, laws which give,
Not the mean right to buy the right to live,
    But life, and home, and health!
To doubt the end were want of trust in God,
    Who, if he has decreed
  That we must pass a redder sea
Than that which rang to Miriam's holy glee,
    Will surely raise at need
    A Moses with his rod!

IV

But let our fears—if fears we have—be still,
And turn us to the future! Could we climb
Some mighty Alp, and view the coming time,
    The rapturous sight would fill

Our eyes with happy tears!
Not for the glories which a hundred years
Shall bring us; not for lands from sea to sea,
And wealth, and power, and peace, though these shall be;
But for the distant peoples we shall bless,
And the hushed murmurs of a world's distress:
For, to give labor to the poor,
The whole sad planet o'er,
And save from want and crime the humblest door,
Is one among the many ends for which
God makes us great and rich!
The hour perchance is not yet wholly ripe
When all shall own it, but the type
Whereby we shall be known in every land
Is that vast gulf which laves our Southern strand,
And through the cold, untempered ocean pours
Its genial streams, that far off Arctic shores
May sometimes catch upon the softened breeze
Strange tropic warmth and hints of summer seas!

The Cotton Boll[2]

While I recline
At ease beneath
This immemorial pine,
Small sphere!
(By dusky fingers brought this morning here
And shown with boastful smiles),
I turn thy cloven sheath,
Through which the soft white fibres peer,
That, with their gossamer bands,
Unite, like love, the sea-divided lands,
And slowly, thread by thread,
Draw forth the folded strands,
Than which the trembling line,
By whose frail help yon startled spider fled

2. *Charleston Mercury* September 3, 1861.

Down the tall spear-grass from his swinging bed,
Is scarce more fine;
And as the tangled skein
Unravels in my hands,
Betwixt me and the noonday light,
A veil seems lifted, and for miles and miles
The landscape broadens on my sight,
As, in the little boll, there lurked a spell
Like that which, in the ocean shell,
With mystic sound,
Breaks down the narrow walls that hem us round,
And turns some city lane
Into the restless main,
With all his capes and isles!

Yonder bird,
Which floats, as if at rest,
In those blue tracts above the thunder, where
No vapors cloud the stainless air,
And never sound is heard,
Unless at such rare time
When, from the City of the Blest,
Rings down some golden chime,
Sees not from his high place
So vast a cirque of summer space
As widens round me in one mighty field,
Which, rimmed by seas and sands,
Doth hail its earliest daylight in the beams
Of gray Atlantic dawns;
And, broad as realms made up of many lands,
Is lost afar
Behind the crimson hills and purple lawns
Of sunset, among plains which roll their streams
Against the Evening Star!
And lo!
To the remotest point of sight,
Although I gaze upon no waste of snow,
The endless field is white;
And the whole landscape glows,
For many a shining league away,

With such accumulated light
As Polar lands would flash beneath a tropic day!
Nor lack there (for the vision grows,
And the small charm within my hands—
More potent even than the fabled one,
Which oped whatever golden mystery
Lay hid in fairy wood or magic vale,
The curious ointment of the Arabian tale—
Beyond all mortal sense
Doth stretch my sight's horizon, and I see,
Beneath its simple influence,
As if, with Uriel's crown,
I stood in some great temple of the Sun,
And looked, as Uriel, down!)
Nor lack there pastures rich and fields all green
With all the common gifts of God,
For temperate airs and torrid sheen
Weave Edens of the sod;
Through lands which look one sea of billowy gold
Broad rivers wind their devious ways;
A hundred isles in their embraces fold
A hundred luminous bays;
And through yon purple haze
Vast mountains lift their plumed peaks cloud-crowned;
And, save where up their sides the ploughman creeps,
An unhewn forest girds them grandly round,
In whose dark shades a future navy sleeps!
Ye Stars, which, though unseen, yet with me gaze
Upon this loveliest fragment of the earth!
Thou Sun, that kindlest all thy gentlest rays
Above it, as to light a favorite hearth!
Ye Clouds, that in your temples in the West
See nothing brighter than its humblest flowers!
And you, ye Winds, that on the ocean's breast
Are kissed to coolness ere ye reach its bowers!
Bear witness with me in my song of praise,
And tell the world that, since the world began,
No fairer land hath fired a poet's lays,
Or given a home to man!

But these are charms already widely blown!
His be the meed whose pencil's trace
Hath touched our very swamps with grace,
And round whose tuneful way
All Southern laurels bloom;
The Poet of "The Woodlands," unto whom
Alike are known
The flute's low breathing and the trumpet's tone,
And the soft west wind's sighs;
But who shall utter all the debt,
O Land wherein all powers are met
That bind a people's heart,
The world doth owe thee at this day,
And which it never can repay,
Yet scarcely deigns to own!
Where sleeps the poet who shall fitly sing
The source wherefrom doth spring
That mighty commerce which, confined
To the mean channels of no selfish mart,
Goes out to every shore
Of this broad earth, and throngs the sea with ships
That bear no thunders; hushes hungry lips
In alien lands;
Joins with a delicate web remotest strands;
And gladdening rich and poor,
Doth gild Parisian domes,
Or feed the cottage-smoke of English homes,
And only bounds its blessings by mankind!
In offices like these, thy mission lies,
My Country! and it shall not end
As long as rain shall fall and Heaven bend
In blue above thee; though thy foes be hard
And cruel as their weapons, it shall guard
Thy hearth-stones as a bulwark; make thee great
In white and bloodless state;
And haply, as the years increase—
Still working through its humbler reach
With that large wisdom which the ages teach—
Revive the half-dead dream of universal peace!

As men who labor in that mine
Of Cornwall, hollowed out beneath the bed
Of ocean, when a storm rolls overhead,
Hear the dull booming of the world of brine
Above them, and a mighty muffled roar
Of winds and waters, yet toil calmly on,
And split the rock, and pile the massive ore,
Or carve a niche, or shape the arched roof;
So I, as calmly, weave my woof
Of song, chanting the days to come,
Unsilenced, though the quiet summer air
Stirs with the bruit of battles, and each dawn
Wakes from its starry silence to the hum
Of many gathering armies. Still,
In that we sometimes hear,
Upon the Northern winds, the voice of woe
Not wholly drowned in triumph, though I know
The end must crown us, and a few brief years
Dry all our tears,
I may not sing too gladly. To Thy will
Resigned, O Lord! we cannot all forget
That there is much even Victory must regret.
And, therefore, not too long
From the great burthen of our country's wrong
Delay our just release!
And, if it may be, save
These sacred fields of peace
From stain of patriot or of hostile blood!
Oh, help us, Lord! to roll the crimson flood
Back on its course, and, while our banners wing
Northward, strike with us! till the Goth shall cling
To his own blasted altar-stones, and crave
Mercy; and we shall grant it, and dictate
The lenient future of his fate
There, where some rotting ships and crumbling quays
Shall one day mark the Port which ruled the Western seas.

I Know Not Why[3]

I know not why, but all this weary day,
Suggested by no definite grief or pain,
Sad fancies have been flitting through my brain:
Now it has been a vessel losing way
Rounding a stormy headland; now a gray
Dull waste of clouds above a wintry main;
And then a banner drooping in the rain,
And meadows beaten into bloody clay.
Strolling at random with this shadowy woe
At heart, I chanced to wander hither! Lo!
A league of desolate marsh-land, with its lush,
Hot grasses in a noisome, tide-left bed,
And faint, warm airs, that rustle in the hush
Like whispers round the body of the dead!

A Cry to Arms[4]

Ho! woodsmen of the mountain side!
    Ho! dwellers in the vales!
Ho! ye who by the chafing tide
    Have roughened in the gales!
Leave barn and byre, leave kin and cot,
    Lay by the bloodless spade;
Let desk, and case, and counter rot,
    And burn your books of trade.

The despot roves your fairest lands;
    And till he flies or fears,
Your fields must grow but armèd bands,
    Your sheaves be sheaves of spears!
Give up to mildew and to rust
    The useless tools of gain;

3. *Charleston Mercury* October 7, 1861.
4. *Charleston Mercury* and *Daily Courier* March 4, 1862.

And feed your country's sacred dust
  With floods of crimson rain!

Come, with the weapons at your call—
  With musket, pike, or knife;
He wields the deadliest blade of all
  Who lightest holds his life.
The arm that drives its unbought blows
  With all a patriot's scorn,
Might brain a tyrant with a rose,
  Or stab him with a thorn.

Does any falter? let him turn
  To some brave maiden's eyes,
And catch the holy fires that burn
  In those sublunar skies.
Oh! could you like your women feel,
  And in their spirit march,
A day might see your lines of steel
  Beneath the victor's arch.

What hope, O God! would not grow warm
  When thoughts like these give cheer?
The Lily calmly braves the storm,
  And shall the Palm-tree fear?
No! rather let its branches court
  The rack that sweeps the plain;
And from the Lily's regal port
  Learn how to breast the strain!

Ho! woodsmen of the mountain side!
  Ho! dwellers in the vales!
Ho! ye who by the roaring tide
  Have roughened in the gales!
Come! flocking gaily to the fight,
  From forest, hill, and lake;
We battle for our Country's right,
  And for the Lily's sake!

Charleston*[5]

Calm as that second summer which precedes
The first fall of the snow,
In the broad sunlight of heroic deeds,
The City bides the foe.

As yet, behind their ramparts stern and proud,
Her bolted thunders sleep—
Dark Sumter*, like a battlemented cloud,
Looms o'er the solemn deep.

No Calpe frowns from lofty cliff or scar
To guard the holy strand;
But Moultrie holds in leash her dogs of war
Above the level sand.

And down the dunes a thousand guns lie couched,
Unseen, beside the flood—
Like tigers in some Orient jungle crouched
That wait and watch for blood.

Meanwhile, through streets still echoing with trade,
Walk grave and thoughtful men,
Whose hands may one day wield the patriot's blade
As lightly as the pen.

And maidens, with such eyes as would grow dim
Over a bleeding hound,
Seem each one to have caught the strength of him
Whose sword she sadly bound.

Thus girt without and garrisoned at home,
Day patient following day,
Old Charleston looks from roof, and spire, and dome,
Across her tranquil bay.

Ships, through a hundred foes, from Saxon lands
And spicy Indian ports,

---

5. *Charleston Mercury* December 3, 1862. This poem is about the Union blockade of the port of Charleston.

Bring Saxon steel and iron to her hands,
    And summer to her courts.

But still, along yon dim Atlantic line,
    The only hostile smoke
Creeps like a harmless mist above the brine,
    From some frail, floating oak.

Shall the spring dawn, and she still clad in smiles,
    And with an unscathed brow,
Rest in the strong arms of her palm-crowned isles,
    As fair and free as now?

We know not; in the temple of the Fates
    God has inscribed her doom;
And, all untroubled in her faith, she waits
    The triumph or the tomb.

The Two Armies[6]

Two armies stand enrolled beneath
The banner with the starry wreath;
One, facing battle, blight and blast,
Through twice a hundred fields has passed;
Its deeds against a ruffian foe,
Stream, valley, hill, and mountain know,
Till every wind that sweeps the land
Goes, glory laden, from the strand.

The other, with a narrower scope,
Yet led by not less grand a hope,
Hath won, perhaps, as proud a place,
And wears its fame with meeker grace.
Wives march beneath its glittering sign,
Fond mothers swell the lovely line,
And many a sweetheart hides her blush
In the young patriot's generous flush.

6. *Southern Illustrated News* May 30, 1863.

No breeze of battle ever fanned
The colors of that tender band;
Its office is beside the bed,
Where throbs some sick or wounded head.
It does not court the soldier's tomb,
But plies the needle and the loom;
And, by a thousand peaceful deeds,
Supplies a struggling nation's needs.

Nor is that army's gentle might
Unfelt amid the deadly fight;
It nerves the son's, the husband's hand,
It points the lover's fearless brand;
It thrills the languid, warms the cold,
Gives even new courage to the bold;
And sometimes lifts the veriest clod
To its own lofty trust in God.

When Heaven shall blow the trump of peace,
And bid this weary warfare cease,
Their several missions nobly done,
The triumph grasped, and freedom won,
Both armies, from their toils at rest,
Alike may claim the victor's crest,
But each shall see its dearest prize
Gleam softly from the other's eyes.

Carmen Triumphale[7]

Go forth and bid the land rejoice,
    Yet not too gladly, O my song!
    Breathe softly, as if mirth would wrong
The solemn rapture of thy voice.

Be nothing lightly done or said
    This happy day! Our joy should flow

7. *Southern Illustrated News* June 7, 1863. Here Timrod celebrates Confederate victory over the April 7, 1863, attack of nine Union ironclad ships on Charleston; this was the first major naval assault against Charleston.

Accordant with the lofty woe
That wails above the noble dead.

Let him whose brow and breast were calm
While yet the battle lay with God,
Look down upon the crimson sod
And gravely wear his mournful palm;

And him, whose heart still weak from fear
Beats all too gaily for the time,
Know that intemperate glee is crime
While one dead hero claims a tear.

Yet go thou forth, my song! and thrill,
With sober joy, the troubled days;
A nation's hymn of grateful praise
May not be hushed for private ill.

Our foes are fallen! Flash, ye wires!
The mighty tidings far and nigh!
Ye cities! write them on the sky
In purple and in emerald fires!

They came with many a haughty boast;
Their threats were heard on every breeze;
They darkened half the neighboring seas,
And swooped like vultures on the coast.

False recreants in all knightly strife,
Their way was wet with woman's tears;
Behind them flamed the toil of years,
And bloodshed stained the sheaves of life.

They fought as tyrants fight, or slaves;
God gave the dastards to our hands;
Their bones are bleaching on the sands,
Or mouldering slow in shallow graves.

What though we hear about our path
The heavens with howls of vengeance rent?
The venom of their hate is spent;
We need not heed their fangless wrath.

Meantime the stream they strove to chain
Now drinks a thousand springs, and sweeps
With broadening breast, and mightier deeps,
And rushes onward to the main;

While down the swelling current glides
Our Ship of State before the blast,
With streamers poured from every mast,
Her thunders roaring from her sides.

Lord! bid the frenzied tempest cease,
Hang out thy rainbow on the sea!
Laugh round her, waves! in silver glee,
And speed her to the ports of peace!

The Unknown Dead[8]

The rain is plashing on my sill,
But all the winds of Heaven are still;
And so it falls with that dull sound
Which thrills us in the church-yard ground,
When the first spadeful drops like lead
Upon the coffin of the dead.
Beyond my streaming window-pane,
I cannot see the neighboring vane,
Yet from its old familiar tower
The bell comes, muffled, through the shower.
What strange and ususpected link
Of feeling touched, has made me think—
While with a vacant soul and eye
I watch that gray and stony sky—
Of nameless graves on battle-plains
Washed by a single winter's rains,
Where, some beneath Virginian hills,
And some by green Atlantic rills,
Some by the waters of the West,
A myriad unknown heroes rest.

8. *Southern Illustrated News* July 4, 1863.

Ah! not the chiefs who, dying, see
Their flags in front of victory,
Or, at their life-blood's noble cost
Pay for a battle nobly lost,
Claim from their monumental beds
The bitterest tears a nation sheds.
Beneath yon lonely mound—the spot
By all save some fond few forgot—
Lie the true martyrs of the fight,
Which strikes for freedom and for right.
Of them, their patriot zeal and pride,
The lofty faith that with them died,
No grateful page shall farther tell
Than that so many bravely fell;
And we can only dimly guess
What worlds of all this world's distress,
What utter woe, despair, and dearth,
Their fate has brought to many a hearth.
Just such a sky as this should weep
Above them, always, where they sleep;
Yet, haply, at this very hour,
Their graves are like a lover's bower;
And Nature's self, with eyes unwet,
Oblivious of the crimson debt
To which she owes her April grace,
Laughs gaily o'er their burial place.

We May Not Falter[9]

We may not falter, while there is an ell
    Of ground on which to strike a foeman dead;
    But count our means, and see how weak the dread
Which hears, in every skirmish lost, the knell
    Of freedom's fortunes. Plains as vast as realms,
Swamps, forests, valleys, which no hostile tread

9. *Daily South Carolinian* January 15, 1864. Cited from *The Uncollected Poems of Henry Timrod*, ed. Guy Cardwell (Athens: University of Georgia Press, 1942).

Hath yet profaned—mountains like mighty helms
All plumed with pines—men that would freely shed
Their heart's best blood and hopes, to win no more
Of the dear soil for which they lift their steel,
Than would suffice to drink one freeman's gore—
And women, with their tender souls so poured
In patriot strength, we feel as one might feel,
If God should turn his rainbow to a sword!

Ode[10]

Sung on the Occasion of Decorating the Graves of the Confederate Dead, at Magnolia Cemetery, Charleston, S.C., 1866.

Sleep sweetly in your humble graves,
Sleep, martyrs of a fallen cause!—
Though yet no marble column craves
The pilgrim here to pause.

In seeds of laurels in the earth,
The garlands of your fame are sown;
And, somewhere, waiting for its birth,
The shaft is in the stone.

Meanwhile, your sisters for the years
Which hold in trust your storied tombs,
Bring all they now can give you—tears,
And these memorial blooms.

Small tributes, but your shades will smile
As proudly on these wreaths to-day,
As when some cannon-moulded pile
Shall overlook this Bay.

Stoop, angels, hither from the skies!
There is no holier spot of ground,
Than where defeated valor lies
By mourning beauty crowned.

10. *Charleston Daily Courier* June 18, 1866; revised and reprinted in the *Charleston Daily Courier* July 23, 1866.

1866[11]

Addressed to the Old Year

Art thou not glad to close
    Thy wearied eyes, O saddest child of Time,
    Eyes which have looked on every mortal crime,
And swept the piteous round of mortal woes?

In dark Plutonian caves,
    Beneath the lowest deep, go, hide thy head;
    Or earth thee where the blood that thou hast shed
May trickle on thee from thy countless graves!

Take with thee all thy gloom
    And guilt, and all our griefs, save what the breast,
    Without a wrong to some dear shadowy guest,
May not surrender even to the tomb.

No tear shall weep thy fall,
    When, as the midnight bell doth toll thy fate,
    Another lifts the scepter of thy state,
And sits a monarch in thine ancient hall.

Him all the hours attend,
    With a new hope like morning in their eyes;
    Him the fair earth and him these radiant skies
Hail as their sovereign, welcome as their friend.

Him, too, the nations wait;
    "O lead us from the shadow of the Past,"
    In a long wail like this December blast,
They cry, and, crying, grow less desolate.

How he will shape his sway
    They ask not—for old doubts and fears will cling—
    And yet they trust that, somehow, he will bring
A sweeter sunshine than thy mildest day.

11. Probably published in the *Daily South Carolinian* December 31, 1866.

Beneath his gentle hand
    They hope to see no meadow, vale, or hill
    Stained with a deeper red than roses spill,
When some too boisterous zephyr sweeps the land.

A time of peaceful prayer,
    Of law, love, labor, honest loss and gain—
    These are the visions of the coming reign
Now floating to them on this wintry air.

Sarah Morgan Bryan Piatt (1836–1919)

In her extraordinarily long and productive career as a writer, Sarah Piatt published eighteen volumes of poetry, two of which she coauthored with her husband. She was also widely published in the leading magazines in the United States, England, and Ireland, placing an impressive thirty poems in the *Atlantic Monthly* and many others in *Harper's* and *Scribner's*. Born into a notable Kentucky family, Piatt lost her mother when she was still a child and thereafter lived with various Kentucky relatives; moving from plantation to plantation with the young Piatt was an elderly black slave who had been her mother's nurse. Piatt's memories of this relationship are tinged with love for her nurse, nostalgia for a lost world of Southern luxury, and a sense of guilt about the slavery that made that world possible; she represents this contradictory mix of emotions in a number of poems, including "The Black Princess." Piatt received her formal education from Henry Female College in New Castle, Kentucky; just as she was finishing her studies, she began publishing poems in the *Louisville Journal*. This early success encouraged her to send her work to the *New York Ledger*, which printed her pieces frequently in the late 1850s. Through the editor of the *Louisville Journal*, Piatt met her future husband, **John James Piatt.** A native of Ohio, he was also an aspiring poet, publishing his first volume of verse in 1860. In June 1861, just two months after the start of the war, the couple were married and went to live in Washington, D.C., where Piatt's husband worked in the Treasury Department.

Never as successful a writer as his wife and never quite able to support the family, John James's various political appointments and newspaper jobs would lead the Piatts and their several children to move many times between Washington and Ohio; the most successful stage of his political career came after the war when he served for eleven years as the U.S. consul to Ireland. In spite of the family's mobility and precarious finances, Sarah Piatt continued writing, and the Piatts moved in circles that included the leading literary figures of their day—**Henry Wadsworth Longfellow, Walt Whitman, Bret Harte, James Russell Lowell,** and **Edmund Clarence Stedman.**

Piatt's husband continued in his position at the Treasury Department until 1867, so Piatt observed the war from the vantage point of Washington. Born and raised in the South, yet living in the capital of the Union, Piatt clearly felt torn by her divided loyalties. Whereas poets like Whitman and **Herman Melville** often focus on representing battles, Piatt seeks in her poems to examine the domestic contexts which produce the passions that fuel wars. Through the lens of a genteel Victorian domesticity, she argues that both men and women are responsible for the violence wrought on battlefields; "Another War" is just one of many poems in which Piatt suggests that women help to indoctrinate children in a chivalric code of military honor. In "Mock Diamonds," Piatt represents a Confederate officer after the war through the eyes of a woman he had courted years before; it is an ironic portrait, emphasizing the hierarchies and hypocrisy of the Southern aristocracy. In "Shoulder-Rank," Piatt argues that the hierarchies of the military celebrate the achievements of a few great West Point graduates, while neglecting the bravery and accomplishments of the common soldier. Looking at these three poems alone, it is easy to imagine why Piatt's work—in spite of its wide circulation—met with mixed reviews. Her reliance on irony, her use of dialogic structures, and her mingling of genteel Victorian imagery with biting political critique all contribute to the complexity of her work.

Hearing the Battle.—July 21, 1861[1]

One day in the dreamy summer,
    On the Sabbath hills, from afar
We heard the solemn echoes
    Of the first fierce words of war.

Ah, tell me, thou veilèd Watcher
    Of the storm and the calm to come,
How long by the sun or shadow
    Till these noises again are dumb.

And soon in a hush and glimmer
    We thought of the dark, strange fight,
Whose close in a ghastly quiet
    Lay dim in the beautiful night.

Then we talk'd of coldness and pallor,
    And of things with blinded eyes

1. *Nests at Washington*, 1864. All poems reprinted here are cited from *Palace-Burner: Selected Poetry of Sarah Piatt*, ed. Paula Bernat Bennett (Urbana: University of Illinois Press, 2001). Brackets in poems are Bennett's. We have silently corrected apparent spelling errors.

That stared at the golden stillness
  Of the moon in those lighted skies;

And of souls, at morning wrestling
  In the dust with passion and moan,
So far away at evening
  In the silence of worlds unknown.

But a delicate wind beside us
  Was rustling the dusky hours,
As it gather'd the dewy odors
  Of the snowy jessamine-flowers.

And I gave you a spray of the blossoms,
  And said: "I shall never know
How the hearts in the land are breaking,
  My dearest, unless you go."

Army of Occupation[2]

At Arlington, 1866

The summer blew its little drifts of sound—
  Tangled with wet leaf-shadows and the light
Small breath of scattered morning buds—around
The yellow path through which our footsteps wound.
  Below, the Capitol rose glittering white.

There stretched a sleeping army. One by one,
  They took their places until thousands met;
No leader's stars flashed on before, and none
Leaned on his sword or stagger'd with his gun—
  I wonder if their feet have rested yet!

They saw the dust, they joined the moving mass,
  They answer'd the fierce music's cry for blood,
Then straggled here and lay down in the grass:—
Wear flowers for such, shores whence their feet did pass;
  Sing tenderly; O river's haunted flood!

2. *Harper's Weekly* 1866, reprinted in *Mac-A-Cheek Press*, 1867, Bennett's source text.

They had been sick, and worn, and weary, when
They stopp'd on this calm hill beneath the trees:
Yet if, in some red-clouded dawn, again
The country should be calling to her men,
Shall the r[e]veill[e] not remember these?

Around them underneath the mid-day skies
The dreadful phantoms of the living walk,
And by low moons and darkness with their cries—
The mothers, sisters, wives with faded eyes,
Who call still names amid their broken talk.

And there is one who comes alone and stands
At his dim fireless hearth—chill'd and oppress'd
By Something he has summon'd to his lands,
While the weird pallor of its many hands
Points to his rusted sword in his own breast!

Giving Back the Flower[3]

So, because you chose to follow me into the subtle sadness of night,
And to stand in the half-set moon with the weird fall-light on your glimmering hair,
Till your presence hid all of the earth and all of the sky from my sight,
And to give me a little scarlet bud, that was dying of frost, to wear,

Say, must you taunt me forever, forever? You looked at my hand and you knew
That I was the slave of the Ring, while you were as free as the wind is free.
When I saw your corpse in your coffin, I flung back your flower to you;
It was all of yours that I ever had; you may keep it, and—keep from me.

Ah? so God is your witness. Has God, then, no world to look after but ours?
May He not have been searching for that wild star, with the trailing plumage, that flew
Far over a part of our darkness while we were there by the freezing flowers,
Or else brightening some planet's luminous rings, instead of thinking of you?

3. *Galaxy* 1867. "Hear me, Norma" (mentioned in stanza 4) was a popular song based on Vincenzo Bellini's opera *Norma* (1832), in which a Druidic woman takes a Roman proconsul—that is, a political enemy—as her lover.

Or, if He was near us at all, do you think that He would sit listening there
Because you sang "Hear me, Norma," to a woman in jewels and lace,
While, so close to us, down in another street, in the wet, unlighted air,
There were children crying for bread and fire, and mothers who questioned His grace?

Or perhaps He had gone to the ghastly field where the fight had been that day,
To number the bloody stabs that were there, to look at and judge the dead;
Or else to the place full of fever and moans where the wretched wounded lay;
At least I do not believe that He cares to remember a word that you said.

So take back your flower, I tell you—of its sweetness I now have no need;
Yes; take back your flower down into the stillness and mystery to keep;
When you wake I will take it, and God, then, perhaps will witness indeed,
But go, now, and tell Death he must watch you, and not let you walk in your sleep.

Shoulder-Rank[4]

"West Point?" Yes, that was the one grand argument ever so long
At the capital, I remember now, in our far-back battledays:
If the hour's great Leader blundered and war, therefore, went wrong,
West Point would give a subtle faith in the great Leader's ways.

West Point—Ah, well, no doubt they can graduate generals there,
Why, I wonder they do not send them out, plumed, sworded, and ready-scarr'd,
And just because one when a boy has happened somehow to wear
The uniform of their cadets, let his shoulders be splendidly starr'd!

And if he in such starlight should grope on a little ahead
Of the failures of two or three others and fall in some shining high place,
Does that go to prove that not one in the dusty dim legions he led
Could give him his orders in secret and point him the way to your grace?

Oh, you fancy you honor where honor is due? But I feel
You may shake the hand that finished your work, nor guess at the head that planned;

4. *Capital* 1871. A majority of the military commanders in the Civil War, both Confederate and Union, were graduates of West Point. The poem's final two lines refer to Ulysses S. Grant.*

What if I tell you that one, who studied the science of steel,
In the nameless name of a Private commanded his chief to command!

If I say that he passed, through a wound in his breast, up the hill,
And lies buried where grave-marks by thousands at Arlington whiten the air—
Why—you will go on and believe that our very first warrior still
Sits smoking his pipe of Peace in the Presidential easy chair!

Another War[5]

Yes, they are coming from the fort—
Not weary they, nor dimm'd with dust;
Their march seems but a shining sport,
Their swords too new for rust.

You think the captains look so fine,
You like, I know, the long sharp flash,
The fair silk flags above the line,
The pretty scarlet sash?

You like the horses when they neigh,
You like the music most of all,
And, if they had to fight to-day,
You'd like to see them fall.

I wisely think the uniform
Was made for skeletons to wear,
But your young blood is quick and warm,
And so—you do not care.

You lift your eager eyes and ask:
"Could we not have another war?"
As I might give this fearful task
To armies near and far.

Another war? Perhaps we could,
Yet, child of mine with sunniest head,

5. *The Capital* 1872.

I sometimes wonder if I would
Bear then to see the dead!

But am I in a dream? For see,
My pretty boy follows the men—
Surely he did not speak to me,
Who could have spoken, then?

It was another child, less fair,
Less young, less innocent, I know,
Who lost the light gold from its hair
Most bitter years ago!

It was that restless, wavering child
I call Myself. No other, dear.
Perhaps you knew it when you smiled
Because none else was near.

Then not my boy, it seems, but I
Would wage another war?—to see
The shining sights, to hear the cry
Of ghastly victory?

No—for another war could bring
No second bloom to wither'd flowers,
No second song to birds that sing,
Lost tunes in other hours!

But, friend, since time is full of pain,
Whether men fall by field or hearth,
I want the old war back again
And nothing new on earth!

Mock Diamonds[6]

(At the Seaside.)

The handsome man there with the scar?—
(Who bow'd to me? Yes, slightly)—

6. *The Capital* 1872. The phrase "midnight-vengeance meetings" in stanza 3 refers to the Ku Klux Klan, founded in 1865 by Confederate soldiers.

A ghastly favor of the War,
Nor does he wear it lightly.

Such brigand-looking men as these
Might hide behind a dagger
In—ah, "the fellow, if I please,
With the low Southern swagger?

"One of the doubtful chivalry,
The midnight-vengeance meetings,
Who sends, from ghostly company,
Such fearful queer-spell'd greetings!"

No—but a soldier late to throw
(I see not where the harm is)
Lost Cause and Conquer'd Flag below
The dust of Northern armies.

What more? Before the South laid down
Her insolent false glory,
He was, at this fair seaside town,
The hero of—a story.

And painted Beauty scheming through
The glare of gilded station,
Long'd for the orange flowers—that grew
Upon his rich plantation.

I knew him then? Well, he was young
And I was—what he thought me;
And there were kisses hidden among
The thin bud-scents he brought me.

One night I saw a stranger here,—
"An heiress, you must know her,"
His mother whisper'd, sliding near.
Perhaps my heart beat lower.

The band play'd on, the hours declined,
His eyes looked tired and dreamy;
I knew her diamonds flash'd him blind—
He could no longer see me.

Leave your sweet jealousy unsaid:
Your bright child's fading mother
And that guerrilla from—the dead?
Are nothing to each other.

He rose before me on the sand
Through that damp sky's vague glimmer,
With shadows in his shadow, and
All the dim sea grew dimmer.

He spoke? He laughed? Men hear of men
Such words, such laughter never.
He said? "*She wore Mock-Diamonds*"—then,
Pass'd to the Past forever.

Over in Kentucky[7]

"This is the smokiest city in the world,"
A slight voice, wise and weary, said, "I know.
My sash is tied, and if my hair was curled,
I'd like to have my prettiest hat and go
There where some violets had to stay, you said,
Before your torn-up butterflies were dead—
Over in Kentucky."

Then one, whose half sad face still wore the hue
The North Star loved to light and linger on,
Before the war, looked slowly at me too,
And darkly whispered: "What is gone is gone.
Yet, though it may be better to be free,
I'd rather have things as they used to be
Over in Kentucky."

Perhaps I thought how fierce the master's hold,
Spite of all armies, kept the slave within;

7. *The Independent* 1872, reprinted in *Voyage to the Fortunate Isles*, 1874. The speakers are a white daughter (stanza 1), an African American woman (stanza 2), and a white mother (the remaining stanzas). Born in Kentucky, the mother now lives across the Ohio River in Cincinnati. Before the war, the river marked the boundary between a slave state and a free one.

How iron chains, when broken, turned to gold,
  In empty cabins, where glad songs had been,
Before the Southern sword knew blood and rust,
Before wild cavalry sprang from the dust,
    Over in Kentucky.

Perhaps—but, since two eyes, half-full of tears,
  Half-full of sleep, would love to keep awake
With fairy pictures from my fairy years,
  I have a phantom pencil that can make
Shadows of moons, far back and faint, to rise
On dewier grass and in diviner skies,
    Over in Kentucky.

For yonder river, wider than the sea,
  Seems sometimes in the dusk a visible moan
Between two worlds—one fair, one dear to me.
  The fair has forms of ever-glimmering stone,
Weird-whispering ruin, graves where legends hide,
And lies in mist upon the charmèd side,
    Over in Kentucky.

The dear has restless, dimpled, pretty hands,
  Yearning toward unshaped steel, unfancied wars,
Unbuilded cities, and unbroken lands,
  With something sweeter than the faded stars
And dim, dead dews of my lost romance, found
In beauty that has vanished from the ground,
    Over in Kentucky.

The Black Princess[8]

(A True Fable of My Old Kentucky Nurse.)

I knew a Princess: she was old,
  Crisp-haired, flat-featured, with a look
Such as no dainty pen of gold
  Would write of in a fairy book.

8. *The Independent* 1872.

So bent she almost crouched, her face
Was like the Sphinx's face, to me,
Touched with vast patience, desert grace,
And lonesome, brooding mystery.

What wonder that a faith so strong
As hers, so sorrowful, so still,
Should watch in bitter sands so long,
Obedient to a burdening will!

This Princess was a slave—like one
I read of in a painted tale;
Yet free enough to see the sun,
And all the flowers, without a vail.

Not of the lamp, not of the ring,
The helpless, powerful slave was she;
But of a subtler, fiercer thing—
She was the slave of Slavery.

Court lace nor jewels had she seen:
She wore a precious smile, so rare
That at her side the whitest queen
Were dark—her darkness was so fair.

Nothing of loveliest loveliness
This strange, sad Princess seemed to lack;
Majestic with her calm distress
She was, and beautiful, though black.

Black, but enchanted black, and shut
In some vague giant's tower of air,
Built higher than her hope was. But
The true knight came and found her there.

The Knight of the Pale Horse, he laid
His shadowy lance against the spell
That hid her self: as if afraid,
The cruel blackness shrank and fell.

Then, lifting slow her pleasant sleep,
He took her with him through the night,

And swam a river cold and deep,
    And vanished up an awful hight.

And in her Father's house beyond,
    They gave her beauty, robe, and crown:
On me, I think, far, faint, and fond,
    Her eyes to-day look, yearning, down.

The Old Slave-Music[9]

Blow back the breath of the bird,
    Scatter the song through the air;
There was music you never heard,
    And cannot hear anywhere.

It was not the sob of the vain
    In the old, old dark so sweet,
(I shall never hear it again,)
    Nor the coming of fairy feet.

It was music and music alone,
    Not a sigh from a lover's mouth;
Now it comes in a phantom moan
    From the dead and buried South.

It was savage and fierce and glad,
    It played with the heart at will;
Oh, what a wizard touch it had—
    Oh, if I could hear it still!

Were they slaves? They were not then;
    The music had made them free.
They were happy women and men—
    What more do we care to be?

There is blood and blackness and dust,
    There are terrible things to see,
There are stories of swords that rust,
    Between that music and me.

9. *The Capital* 1873.

Dark ghosts with your ghostly tunes
Come back till I laugh through tears;
Dance under the sunken moons,
Dance over the grassy years!

Hush, hush—I know it, I say;
Your armies were bright and brave,
But the music they took away
Was worth—whatever they gave.

Counsel—In the South[10]

My boy, not of your will nor mine
You keep the mountain pass and wait,
Restless, for evil gold to shine
And hold you to your fate.

A stronger Hand than yours gave you
The lawless sword—you know not why.
That you must live is all too true,
And other men must die.

My boy, be brigand if you must,
But face the traveller in your track:
Stand one to one, and never thrust
The dagger in his back.

Nay, make no ambush of the dark.
Look straight into your victim's eyes;
Then—let his free soul, like a lark,
Fly, singing, toward the skies.

My boy, if Christ must be betrayed,
And you must the betrayer be,
Oh, marked before the worlds were made!
What help is there for me?

Ah, if the prophets from their graves
Demand such blood of you as this,

10. *Galaxy* 1874.

Take Him, I say, with swords and staves,
But—never with a kiss!

A Child's Party[11]

Before my cheeks were fairly dry,
I heard my dusky playmate say:
"Well, now your mother's in the sky,
And you can always have your way.

"Old Mistress has to stay, you know,
And read the Bible in her room.
Let's have a party! Will you, though?"
Ah, well, the whole world was in bloom.

"A party would be fine, and yet—
There's no one here I can invite."
"Me and the children." "You forget—"
"Oh, please pretend that I am white."

I said, and think of it with shame,
"Well, when it's over, you'll go back
There to the cabin all the same,
And just remember you are black.

"I'll be the lady, for, you see,
I'm pretty," I serenely said.
"The black folk say that you would be
If—if your hair just wasn't red."

"I'm pretty anyhow, you know.
I saw this morning that I was."
"Old Mistress says it's wicked, though,
To keep on looking in the glass."

Our quarrel ended. At our feet
A faint green blossoming carpet lay,
By some strange chance, divinely sweet,
Just shaken on that gracious day.

11. *Wide-Awake* 1883. The ellipses in the penultimate stanza are Piatt's.

Into the lonesome parlor we
Glided, and from the shuddering wall
Bore, in its antique majesty,
The gilded mirror dim and tall.

And then a woman, painted by—
By Raphael, for all I care!
From her unhappy place on high,
Went with us to the outside air.

Next the quaint candlesticks we took.
Their waxen tapers every one
We lighted, to see how they'd look;—
A strange sight, surely, in the sun.

Then, with misgiving, we undid
The secret closet by the stair;—
There, with patrician dust half-hid,
My ancestors, in china, were.

(Hush, child, this splendid tale is true!)
Were one of these on earth to-day,
You'd know right well my blood was *blue;*
You'd own I was not common clay.

There too, long hid from eyes of men,
A shining sight we two did see.
Oh, there was solid silver then
In this poor hollow world—ah me!

We spread the carpet. By a great
Gray tree, we leant the mirror's glare,
And graven spoon and pictured plate
Were wildly scattered here and there.

And then our table:—Thereon gleamed,
Adorned with many an apple-bud,
Foam-frosted, dainty things that seemed
Made of the most delicious mud.

Next came our dressing. As to that,
I had the fairest shoes! (on each
Were four gold buttons) and a hat,
And the plume the blushes of the peach.

But there was my dark, elfish guest
    Still standing shabby in her place.
How could I use her to show best
    My own transcendent bloom and grace?

"You'll be my grandmamma," I sighed
    After much thought, somewhat in fear.
She, joyous, to her sisters cried:
    "Call me Old Mistress! Do you hear?"

About that little slave's weird face
    And rude, round form, I fastened all
My grandmamma's most awful lace
    And grandmamma's most sacred shawl.

Then one last sorrow came to me:
    "I didn't think of it before,
But at a party there should be
    One gentleman, I guess, or more."

"There's uncle Sam, you might ask him."
    I looked, and in an ancient chair,
Sat a bronze gray-beard, still and grim,
    On Sundays called Old Brother Blair.

Above a book his brows were bent.
    It was his pride as I had heard,
To study the New Testament
    (In which he could not spell one word).

"Oh, *he* is not a gentleman,"
    I said with my Caucasian scorn.
"He is," replied the African;
    "He is. He's quit a-plowing corn.

"He was so old they set him free.
    He preaches now, you ought to know.
I tell you, we are proud when he
    Eats dinner at our cabin, though."

"Well—ask him!" Lo, he raised his head.
    His voice was shaken and severe:
"Here, sisters in the church," he said.
    "Here—for old Satan's sake, come here!

"That white child's done put on her best
  Silk bonnet. (It looks like a rose.)
And this black little imp is drest
  In all Old Mistress' finest clothes.

"Come, look! They've got the parlor glass,
  And all the silver too. Come, look!
(Such plates as these, here on the grass!)"
  And Uncle Sam shut up his book.

The priestess of the eternal flame
  That warmed our Southern kitchen hearth
Rushed out. The housemaid with her came
  Who swept the cobwebs from the earth.

Then there was one bent to the ground,
  Her hair than lilies not less white,
With a bright handkerchief was crowned:
  Her lovely face was weird as night.

I felt the flush of sudden pride,
  The others soon grew still with awe,
For, standing bravely at my side,
  My mother's nurse and mine, they saw.

"Who blamed my child?" she said. "It makes
  My heart ache when they trouble you.
Here's a whole basket full of cakes,
  And I'll come to the party too." . . .

Tears made of dew were in my eyes.
  These after-tears are made of brine.
No sweeter soul is in the skies
  Than hers, my mother's nurse and mine.

Part III

UNPUBLISHED OR POSTHUMOUSLY PUBLISHED POEMS

Emily Dickinson (1830–1886)

Emily Dickinson is now widely acknowledged to be one of America's greatest poets, but during her lifetime, her work was unknown. Born in Amherst, Massachusetts, as the second of three children, Dickinson lived a life without obvious drama. Her father was a noted lawyer and one-term representative to Congress for the state of Massachusetts, and the family promoted good education for women as well as men. Dickinson graduated from Amherst Academy and attended Mount Holyoke Female Seminary (later Mount Holyoke College) for a year. Neither she nor her sister, Lavinia, married, and their brother, Austin, built a house directly next door to the family "Homestead" for his wife, Susan Huntington Gilbert Dickinson, and their children. Known as a precocious and witty child, Emily Dickinson had become relatively reclusive by the beginning of the Civil War and became increasingly so thereafter. As a rule, she did not submit her poems for publication, although she did include poems in letters to many acquaintances, and a handful of her poems were sent to newspapers or anthologies by these recipients. In 1864, Dickinson also permitted three poems to be published in *Drum-Beat*, a fund-raising newspaper for the Union army. Moreover, she copied nearly two-thirds of her poems into small booklets—some with hand-sewn binding—and she preserved both these booklets and many poems on loose sheets or scraps of paper until her death. After her death, Mabel Loomis Todd and Thomas Wentworth Higginson edited a few volumes of her poems, the first appearing in 1890. Since then her poems have been continuously in print, in various (and disputed) editions.

Because Dickinson rarely left the town of Amherst and wrote no poems containing explicit topical reference to the Civil War as such, critical commentary for decades assumed that the war was not a matter of pressing interest to her. Since the mid-1980s, however, critics have increasingly recognized the currency of Dickinson's information about the progress of the war, the number of poems she wrote in direct response or reference to the war, and the far greater number of poems that seem to have been influenced in their metaphors and concerns by the national conflict. There is no question that the war years constituted her period of greatest productivity; during 1862 and 1865, she wrote an average of two poems every three days, and during 1863, almost a poem a day. Even during 1864, when she spent several months undergoing eye treatment and was not allowed to write, she composed ninety-eight poems, according to Ralph W. Franklin's dating of manuscripts (and assuming that the extant copies of poems were produced not long after their initial composition). In no other period of her life did she have a comparable surge of creativity.

While Dickinson wrote some poems in response to battles, she responded more profoundly to the war by turning in her poetry to questions about the meaning of the terms touted daily in newspapers and preached from local pulpits. What do "victory" and "defeat" mean, in relation to each other and in relation to moral questions or to religious speculations about an afterlife? How does the individual deal with acute pain? How can one believe in a benevolent and protective God when men are dying by the thousands in the most violent circumstances? How does news of such cataclysmic dying affect the living, especially those living far from the war's battlefields—such as in Amherst? Such philosophical, religious, and moral questioning makes Dickinson among the most profound of the writers on the American Civil War.

To fight aloud, is very brave - [1]
But *gallanter*, I know
Who charge within the bosom
The Cavalry of Wo -

Who win, and nations do not see -
Who fall - and none observe -
Whose dying eyes, no Country
Regards with patriot love -

We trust, in plumed procession
For such, the Angels go -
Rank after Rank, with even feet -
And Uniforms of snow. (F 138) Early 1860

1. All poems in this section are taken from Ralph W. Franklin, *The Poems of Emily Dickinson* (Cambridge: Harvard University Press, 1998). Numbers assigned by Franklin in accord with their chronological progression appear after each poem in parenthesis; following that number is Franklin's estimated date of composition. We have followed Franklin in maintaining Dickinson's misspellings: "it's" for "its," "opon" for "upon," and so on.

Unto like Story - Trouble has enticed me -
How Kinsmen fell -
Brothers and Sisters - who preferred the Glory -
And their young will
Bent to the Scaffold, or in Dungeons - chanted -
Till God's full time -
When they let go the ignominy - smiling -
And Shame went still -

Unto guessed Crests, my moaning fancy, leads me,
Worn fair
By Heads rejected - in the lower country -
Of honors there -
Such spirit makes her perpetual mention,
That I - grown bold -
Step martial - at my Crucifixion -
As Trumpets - rolled -

Feet, small as mine - have marched in Revolution
Firm to the Drum -
Hands - not so stout - hoisted them - in witness -
When Speech went numb -
Let me not shame their sublime deportments -
Drilled bright -
Beckoning - Etruscan invitation -
Toward Light - (F 300) Early 1862

I like a look of Agony,
Because I know it's true -
Men do not sham Convulsion,
Nor simulate, a Throe -

The Eyes glaze once - and that is Death -
Impossible to feign
The Beads opon the Forehead
By homely Anguish strung. (F 339) Summer 1862

After great pain, a formal feeling comes -
The Nerves sit ceremonious, like Tombs -
The stiff Heart questions 'was it He, that bore,'
And 'Yesterday, or Centuries before'?

The Feet, mechanical, go round –
A Wooden way
Of Ground, or Air, or Ought -
Regardless grown,
A Quartz contentment, like a stone -

This is the Hour of Lead -
Remembered, if outlived,
As Freezing persons, recollect the Snow -
First - Chill - then Stupor - then the letting go -

(F 372) Autumn 1862

The name - of it - is "Autumn" -
The hue - of it - is Blood -
An Artery - opon the Hill -
A Vein - along the Road -

Great Globules - in the Alleys -
And Oh, the Shower of Stain -
When Winds - upset the Basin -
And spill the Scarlet Rain -

It sprinkles Bonnets - far below -
It gathers ruddy Pools -
Then - eddies like a Rose - away -
Opon Vermillion Wheels -

(F 465) Late 1862

He fought like those Who've nought to lose -
Bestowed Himself to Balls
As One who for a further Life
Had not a further Use -

Invited Death - with bold attempt -
But Death was Coy of Him
As Other Men, were Coy of Death.
To Him - to live - was Doom -

His Comrades, shifted like the Flakes
When Gusts reverse the Snow -
But He - was left alive Because
Of Greediness to die - (F 480) Late 1862

When I was small, a Woman died -
Today - her Only Boy
Went up from the Potomac -
His face all Victory

To look at her - How slowly
The Seasons must have turned
Till Bullets clipt an Angle
And He passed quickly round -

If pride shall be in Paradise -
Ourself cannot decide -
Of their imperial Conduct -
No person testified -

But, proud in Apparition -
That Woman and her Boy
Pass back and forth, before my Brain
As even in the sky -

I'm confident that Bravoes -
Perpetual break abroad
For Braveries, remote as this
In Yonder Maryland - (F 518) Spring 1863

It feels a shame to be Alive -
When Men so brave - are dead -
One envies the Distinguished Dust -
Permitted - such a Head -

The Stone - that tells defending Whom
This Spartan put away
What little of Him we - possessed
In Pawn for Liberty -

The price is great - Sublimely paid -
Do we deserve - a Thing -
That lives - like Dollars - must be piled
Before we may obtain?

Are we that wait - sufficient worth -
That such Enormous Pearl
As life - dissolved be - for Us -
In Battle's - horrid Bowl?

It may be - a Renown to live -
I think the Men who die -
Those unsustained – Saviors -
Present Divinity - (F 524) Spring 1863

One Anguish - in a Crowd -
A Minor thing - it sounds -
And yet, unto the single Doe
Attempted - of the Hounds

'Tis Terror as consummate
As Legions of Alarm
Did leap, full flanked, opon the Host -
'Tis Units - make the Swarm -

A Small Leech - on the Vitals -
The sliver, in the Lung -
The Bung out - of an Artery -
Are scarce accounted - Harms -

Yet mighty - by relation
To that Repealless thing -
A Being - impotent to end -
When once it has begun - (527) Spring 1863

They dropped like Flakes -
They dropped like Stars -
Like Petals from a Rose -
When suddenly across the June
A Wind with fingers - goes -

They perished in the seamless Grass -
No eye could find the place -
But God can summon every face
On his Repealless - List. - (F 545) Spring 1863

If any sink, assure that this, now standing -
Failed like Themselves - and conscious that it rose -
Grew by the Fact, and not the Understanding
How Weakness passed - or Force - arose -

Tell that the Worst, is easy in a Moment -
Dread, but the Whizzing, before the Ball -
When the Ball enters, enters Silence -
Dying - annuls the power to kill - (F 616) Second half of 1863

The Battle fought between the Soul
And No Man - is the One
Of all the Battles prevalent -
By far the Greater One -

No News of it is had abroad -
It's Bodiless Campaign
Establishes, and terminates -
Invisible - Unknown -

Nor History - record it -
As Legions of a Night
The Sunrise scatters - These endure -
Enact - and terminate - (F 629) Second half of 1863

No Rack can torture me -
My Soul - at Liberty -
Behind this mortal Bone
There knits a bolder One -

You cannot prick with Saw -
Nor pierce with Cimitar -
Two Bodies - therefore be -
Bind One - The Other fly -

The Eagle of his Nest
No easier divest -
And gain the Sky
Than mayest Thou -

Except Thyself may be
Thine Enemy -
Captivity is Consciousness -
So's Liberty - (F 649) Second half of 1863

My Portion is Defeat - today -
A paler luck than Victory -
Less Paeans - fewer Bells -
The Drums dont follow Me - with tunes -
Defeat - a somewhat slower - means -
More Arduous than Balls -

'Tis populous with Bone and stain -
And Men too straight to stoop again -
And Piles of solid Moan -
And Chips of Blank - in Boyish Eyes -
And scraps of Prayer -

And Death's surprise,
Stamped visible - in stone -

There's somewhat prouder, Over there -
The Trumpets tell it to the Air -
How different Victory
To Him who has it - and the One
Who to have had it, would have been
Contenteder - to die - (F 704) Second half of 1863

My Life had stood - a Loaded Gun -
In Corners - till a Day
The Owner passed - identified -
And carried Me away -

And now We roam in Sovreign Woods -
And now We hunt the Doe -
And every time I speak for Him -
The Mountains straight reply -

And do I smile, such cordial light
Opon the Valley glow -
It is as a Vesuvian face
Had let it's pleasure through -

And when at Night - Our good Day done -
I guard My Master's Head -
'Tis better than the Eider Duck's
Deep Pillow - to have shared -

To foe of His - I'm deadly foe -
None stir the second time -
On whom I lay a Yellow Eye -
Or an emphatic Thumb -

Though I than He - may longer live
He longer must - than I -
For I have but the power to kill,
Without - the power to die - (F 764) Late 1863

Color - Caste - Denomination -
These - are Time's Affair -
Death's diviner Classifying
Does not know they are -

As in sleep - all Hue forgotten -
Tenets - put behind -
Death's large - Democratic fingers
Rub away the Brand -

If Circassian - He is careless -
If He put away
Chrysalis of Blonde - or Umber -
Equal Butterfly -

They emerge from His Obscuring -
What Death - knows so well -
Our minuter intuitions -
Deem unplausible - (F 836) Early 1864

Dying! To be afraid of thee
One must to thine Artillery
Have left exposed a Friend -
Than thine old Arrow is a Shot
Delivered straighter to the Heart
The leaving Love behind -

Not for itself, the Dust is shy,
But, enemy, Beloved be
Thy Batteries divorce.
Fight sternly in a Dying eye
Two Armies, Love and Certainty
And Love and the Reverse - (F 946) 1865

My Triumph lasted till the Drums
Had left the Dead alone
And then I dropped my Victory

And chastened stole along
To where the finished Faces
Conclusion turned on me
And then I hated Glory
And wished myself were They.

What is to be is best descried
When it has also been -
Could Prospect taste of Retrospect
The tyrannies of Men
Were Tenderer, diviner
The Transitive toward -
A Bayonet's contrition
Is nothing to the Dead - (F 1212) 1871

I never hear that one is dead
Without the chance of Life
Afresh annihilating me
That mightiest Belief,

Too mighty for the Daily mind
That tilling it's abyss,
Had Madness, had it once or, twice
The yawning Consciousness,

Beliefs are Bandaged, like the Tongue
When Terror were it told
In any Tone commensurate
Would strike us instant Dead -

I do not know the man so bold
He dare in lonely Place
That awful stranger - Consciousness
Deliberately face - (F 1325) 1874

Obadiah Ethelbert Baker (1838–1923)

Born in Eden, New York, Obadiah Ethelbert Baker moved to Iowa with his family in 1856. There he taught school at Strawberry Point from 1859 until 1861; in 1860, he married Melissa Dalton, who had been one of his students. Baker enlisted in the 2nd Iowa Cavalry Volunteers in September 1861 and fought with this unit in several states, including Mississippi, Missouri, Louisiana, and Tennessee. The battles of Corinth and Booneville receive particularly detailed description in his writings. The journal entry about Corinth expresses shock at the carnage he witnessed during the fight and at the injured soldiers he saw in the following days. He describes to his wife how quickly his horror at the sight of wounded Confederate soldiers turned to sympathy for the men he had so recently fought against. The poem "After the Battle: The Dirge" was probably written shortly after this battle and reflects the conciliatory spirit of the prose in this entry.

Like many Civil War soldiers, Baker spent long periods of illness at military hospitals; these hospital stays may in part account for the volume of writing that he produced during the war. In the spring of 1863, he spent some months at Overton Hospital in Memphis before being transferred to a hospital in Saint Louis. In late May 1864, Baker returned home for a brief period of leave, rejoining the army in mid-July. He received his honorable discharge in April 1865.

During the years that he served in the war, Baker and his wife both wrote journals to each other, addressing the other at the start of each entry and exchanging these volumes regularly by mail. Both Baker and his wife included poems and fragments of verse in their journals. In some cases, Baker copies his own long poems into the journals, and he frequently closes out entries with a few lines of verse by way of farewell. It is clear that Baker had written some poetry before the war since both he and his wife discuss whether or not he will be able to continue writing. Baker wrote at least thirteen volumes of Civil War diaries; between his enlistment in 1861 and the 1890s, he wrote and revised about two hundred poems, not counting the brief verse fragments included in journal entries. While some of these poems can be dated based on their inclusion in the journals, the date of composition for many others is difficult to determine. In addition to his many poems describing battle scenes, Baker also wrote numerous love poems for and about his wife during the war years.

After the war, Baker worked as a teacher in Mississippi and Iowa. In 1874, financial troubles prompted the family to move to California; Baker remained there for the rest of his life. He and his wife had four children, including a son who died in infancy before the war. That the war was a defining moment for Baker becomes clear when one looks at the collection of poems, journals, and newspaper clippings he left behind, including carefully recopied versions of the journals and poems that he prepared two decades after the war had ended. Though Baker describes the terrors of combat in his wartime writings, both during and after the war he also expresses great pride in his ability to serve his country in the military. That Baker was not a professional writer is immediately evident from his poems; they are nonetheless powerful insofar as they make their writer come alive for a reader, through their very ungainliness and their awkward imitations of the stirring military ballads Baker clearly admired. They are also powerful insofar as they represent an epistolary and poetic style that was within the reach of many Civil War soldiers. Obadiah Ethelbert Baker was just one of many common soldiers, both Northern and Southern, who responded to the war by writing poems.

After the Battle: The Dirge[1]

O shine alike, sun, moon, and stars,
  O'er graves of Blue and Gray;
And may you all sweet vigils keep
  Till Resurrection day.
No more the well-known drum will beat,
  For these, the Blue and Gray;
No more the fife and bugle sound
  Will call them where they lay.

No more these many fallen braves,
  Shall in the battle meet;
No more will speed to battle line
  With willing, hurrying feet;

1. Baker copied this poem into his journal just after the entry for October 5, 1862, which he wrote in Corinth, Mississippi. In the Battle of Corinth (October 3–4, 1862), Confederate forces under Sterling Price and Earl Van Dorn attempted unsuccessfully to capture a crucial railroad center from Grant's troops. All poems of Obadiah Ethelbert Baker are reproduced by permission of the Huntington Library, San Marino, California.

No more at roll-call or parade,
    With comrades will they fly;
No more in dreams their lov'd ones meet
    And waking, heave a sigh.

The fife, the drum, the bugle blast,
    They never more will hear;
But in our hearts will ever live
    And claim the the falling tear.
The father he will praise his boy,
    For daring deeds here done;
And proud the loving mother be,
    As she weeps o'er her son.

The boy will praise his father gone
    Who fighting fell this day;
While grand-sires, they will sit and tell,
    Of deeds of Blue and Gray:
The brother will extol the deeds
    Of brother who here fell,
And as the battle he reads o'er,
    With pride his heart will swell.

The sister, though she weepeth sore,
    For him her brother dear
Will tell of deeds of valor done
    Though telling brings the tear.
Our countrymen never will forget,
    Deeds done here by the Blue;
And in our catalogue of Fame,
    Their deeds will e'er be new.

I praise the bravery of the Gray.
    It deserved a better cause;
But may the Lord each one forgive
    As also does our laws:
Then farewell, no ill I bear you.
    Ye who did wear the Gray;
But to the wearer of the Blue
    Hallow'd ground where you lay.

Nov. 30th To an absent Wife[2]

Wish I was sitting by thy side,
My dear beloved wife;
Far from the cannon's awful roar,
Far from this awful strife.

My thoughts are of thee through the day,
I dream of thee at night;
I long to kiss thy lips once more,
And see thy face so bright

O God! When will this strife be o'er?
When will we learn to war no more?

Do you[3]

Do you often think of me dear wife?
Am I dearer than all else in life?
Do you dream of me in the stilly night?
Do you see me mingle in the fight?
Do you hear the cannon's mighty roar?
Do you see men fall to rise no more?

My Army Birth[4]

I left my home in the distant north,
My much loved prairie home,
To help to fight my country's foes,
Not for a love to roam.

But because a rebel horde had scorned,
The banner of the free,

2. Baker includes this poem between journal entries for November 1862, while encamped in Mississippi.
3. This poem appears after the entry from Camp Corinth, Mississippi, dated January 25, 1863.
4. A note on the poem states that it was written on August 24, 1863, in Saint Louis, Missouri.

That bright and shining starry flag,
  Emblem of liberty.

I tried to be content at home,
  But no, I could not stay,
While rebel feet were tramping o'er,
  The flag that sheltered me.

The flag that waved o'er grandsire's head,
  That bore him through the strife,
I could not see dishonored now,
  Though I left a widowed wife.

And so I left one April day,
  And soon was in the strife,
Soon heard the booming cannon roar,
  Soon heard the drum and fife.

The Charge at Monterey[5]

I'm carried back again today
  To fields of sixty-two,
I'm carried down to Tennessee,
  Those fields look bright and new.
I see my regiment of horse,
  As in the days gone by,
I see them charge upon the foe,
  See dead and wounded lie.
We charged the foe at Monterey,
  For miles and miles they ran.
We took some prisoners that day
  'Way down in Dixie's Land.
We charged upon a battery,
  We had no coats of mail,
The very air where we did ride
  Was full of iron hail.

5. This and the following poem were probably written sometime between 1865 and the 1880s; the fighting described in the poems took place in Tennessee in late April and early May 1862, respectively.

My horse was shot, my noble steed,
  The best I ever strode.
The king of all our mounts was he,
  A daisy on the road.
In drill he knew all the commands,
  And did not need a goad.

The Charge at Farmington

At Farmington, the ninth of May,
  We charged upon the foe,
Adown a slope, and o'er that field
  Like fury we did go.
Great ditches yawned before our line,
  Worn by the waters wild,
Many a horse and rider bold
  Into their depths were piled.
We charged upon some batteries,
  Were in a half moon shape,
That field of Farmington that day
  Was like a fiery lake.
General Payne ordered this charge
  To get his troops away,
And well we charged through fire and smoke
  His orders to obey.
We drove them from their batteries,
  We held the foe at bay.
We gained the point for which we charged,
  Were victors of the day.
Promised support we did not have,
  And so we could not stay.
A mile across an open field,
  We charged upon the foe.
Across and enfilading fire
  Into our ranks did go.
Shrapnel and grape and canister,
  In fury it did pour.
But well we knew before the start

What they'd for us in store.
Besides the rain of iron hail,
Came the screaking, bursting shell;
That field of Farmington that day
Was like a fiery Hell.
Though Payne had blundered, we well knew
His army we must save.
Many a gallant boy in blue
Life for this blunder gave.
We did charge on fifteen thousand
Through a gauntlet of fire.
Sometimes a boy of tender years
Beside a gray-haired sire.
And many a one who charged that day
Did charge unto his pyre.

August 3rd, 1886[6]

"Tramp, Tramp, Tramp," the Grand Army are marching,
Marching, while the fife and drum
Stir sweet music which was sung,
In the days of sixty-one;
Days when blood like water run,
With the battles lost and won.

"Tramp, Tramp, Tramp," with shattered banners waving,
Living o'er the scenes passed through,
While sad memories bring to view
The blood-stained fields of sixty-two.
John Brown's form rises anew
'Mongst the noble boys in blue.

"Tramp, Tramp, Tramp," with your ranks fastly thinning,
Many a hero now is free,
Who risked his all to gain the key,
To victory in sixty-three.

6. The title is most likely the poem's date of composition.

While Lincoln's form in fancy I see,
Paving the way to Liberty.

"Tramp, Tramp, Tramp," trail arms as you march away,
Grant,* your leader is no more,
Who led you on in sixty-four,
Mac* and Hancock* have gone before,
To meet the brave on the other shore.

"Tramp, Tramp, Tramp," the boys in blue are marching,
May they for right forever strive,
For defeat and carnage strode aside,
And crowned them kings in sixty-five.
All are glad that's now alive,
For victory gained in sixty-five.

The Unknown Grave[7]

He's sleeping in an unknown grave,
A boy who wore the Blue;
He was an idol of my heart,
A soldier good and true.
'Twas after the siege of Vicksburg;
We held that great stronghold.
The starry flag of the Union
Waved o'er its heroes bold.

Yes, 'twas after months of fighting;
He'd wrote one letter more.
Peace dwelt on the mighty river;
Cannons had ceased to roar.
July of sixty three had gone,
And August passed away.
Next month brought tidings of his death,
No word where the hero lay.

He lieth in a distant state,
Far, far from home and friend;

7. A note on the poem says that it was written in Forestdale, California, on February 2, 1891.

Parents, nor brothers, nor sisters
    Can o'er his ashes bend.
Perchance near the mighty river
    Holly blossoms and waves,
Its branches of green above him
    O'er ashes of the brave.

Somewhere in the sunny Southland
    His ashes they must lie;
But his spirit is in Beulah,
    We'll meet him bye and bye.
His Testament came with his clothes
    And told of usage strong,
And many landmarks on the way
    Of route he went along.

His watch came also in the box,
    And in the back of case,
They wrote—died third of September
    But did not name the place.
Somewhere in the sunny South-land,
    Far, far from friends most dear,
His grave will never once receive
    A loving mother's tear.

CIVIL WAR POETRY GLOSSARY

Belmont (Missouri), the battle of: November 7, 1861, battle in which Grant led a largely unsuccessful raid against Confederate general Benjamin Cheatham.

bivouac: Temporary encampment made by soldiers in the field.

"Blue-Light Elder," "Old Blue Light," or "Old Blue Eyes": Nicknames for Confederate commander Thomas "Stonewall" Jackson, who had blue eyes.

Bragg, Braxton (1817–76): Commander of Confederate forces at the battle of Chickamauga.

Charleston, South Carolina: The location of Fort Sumter and capital of the first state to secede, thus considered the birthplace of the Confederacy.

contraband: Name given to escaped slaves, stemming from abolitionist general Benjamin Butler's declaration that escaped slaves were "contraband of war": the South regarded slaves as property, so the Union could claim them as "contraband." Butler and some other Union officers sheltered escaped slaves and put them to work in army camps even before they were allowed to fight, in 1863. The term did, however, reaffirm the idea that African Americans were property.

copperhead: Derogatory term for a Northerner who sympathizes with the South in supporting slavery or opposing the war against Southern secession.

Cumberland: The USS *Cumberland* and the USS *Congress* were defeated in a naval battle by the CSS *Virginia* on March 8, 1862. Several paintings and lithographs were made of the sinking of the *Cumberland,* and the name of the ship became a byword for gallant fighting.

Davis, Jefferson (1808–89): A graduate of West Point, Davis served in the U.S. Congress, in the Senate, and as secretary of war before being elected president of the Confederate States of America (1861–65).

Ethiopian: A commonly used reference in the nineteenth century to African Americans.

Forrest, Nathan Bedford (1821–77): Confederate general who was noted for his brilliant cavalry raiding and who led the attack on Fort Pillow. See Time Line, April 12, 1864.

Fugitive Slave Law: Legislation in 1850 stating that any federal marshal who did not arrest an alleged runaway slave would be fined and that a suspected runaway slave could be placed in custody of her or his alleged owner without warrant or proof of ownership other than the claimant's sworn testimony. Any person aiding a runaway slave was liable to six months' imprisonment or a fine of one thousand dollars.

Grant, Ulysses S. (1822–85): First brigadier general on the western front, then general in chief of U.S. forces (March 1864–March 1869); eighteenth president of the United States (1869–77).

Hancock, Winfield Scott (1824–86): Union general who served at Antietam, Fredericksburg, Chancellorsville, and Gettysburg, among other battles.

Jackson, Thomas Jonathan "Stonewall" (1824–63): Commander of Confederate troops at Bull Run, the Shenandoah Valley, and Antietam; a brilliant tactician.

Kansas—"Bleeding Kansas" or "Bloody Kansas": See Time Line, 1854.

Lee, Robert E. (1807–70): Commander of the Army of Northern Virginia (1862–65), then general in chief of Confederate armies (January–April 1865).

Libby Prison: Confederate army prison in Richmond, Virginia—after Andersonville (see Time Line, April 12, 1864), the most notorious of the Confederate army prisons for poor conditions for prisoners. See also Prisons/Prison-pen.

Lincoln, Abraham (1809–65): Sixteenth president of the United States, assassinated during his second term in 1865.

Longstreet, James (1821–1904): Senior general in the Confederate army; often fought directly under Lee's command.

"Mac" or "Little Mac": Nicknames for George McClellan.

Malvern Hill: The battle of Malvern Hill (July 1, 1862) was the final action in the Seven Days' battles (see Time Line, April–July 1862), McClellan's unsuccessful attempt to capture Richmond. Though Union artillery created heavy casualties among the Confederates, McClellan nonetheless ordered his forces to withdraw.

McClellan, George Brinton (1826–85): General in chief of the Union Army (November 1861–March 1862); removed by Lincoln owing to his reluctance to go on the attack; presidential candidate in 1864. Also called "Mac" or "Little Mac."

Meade, George Gordon (1815–72): General of the Union Army of the Potomac (July 1863–April 1865).

Morris, George Upham (1830–75): Commanding officer of the USS *Cumberland* in the heroically fought naval battle; although the *Cumberland* was defeated, Morris was promoted to lieutenant commander after the battle.

Pillow/Battle of Fort Pillow: After this April 12, 1864, Confederate victory, Northern troops claimed that the Confederates targeted black soldiers in particular and that many blacks were killed even after surrendering; the death rate for Northern black soldiers was more than twice that for Northern whites. See also Prisons/Prison-pen.*

Port Royal, South Carolina: In November 1861, the Federal fleet surrounded Port Royal Sound and conquered Port Royal, where the Ordinance of Secession was first drafted, and other towns in the area. Occupation of Beaufort and Hilton Head Island opened the way for Federal blockades of the South. On January 1, 1862, Sherman defeated Lee at Port Royal Ferry, giving the Union control of all the South Carolina Sea Islands. African American men from Hilton Head were briefly enlisted in the Union army (some by force) but then dismissed until 1863, when blacks were officially authorized to fight for the Union. Slaves were in effect freed by the Union occupation of this area, and the government established schools for former slaves and paid black men to work in the fields and for the Union army. This early exercise in emancipation was referred to as the "Port Royal experiment."

Potomac River: This river stretches across the states of Maryland, Pennsylvania, Virginia, and West Virginia and runs through Washington, D.C. For this reason it was considered an important marker of the progress of the Union and Confederate armies in their campaigns toward the South and North.

Prisons/Prison-pen: Following the Confederate victory at Fort Pillow* on April 12, 1864, Grant suspended all further prisoner exchanges until the South agreed to treat black and white prisoners on the same terms. When the South refused, prisons in both the North and South quickly became overcrowded. Crowding and deprivation were particularly acute at Andersonville Prison in Georgia, where nearly 30 percent of prisoners died of starvation and disease.

Richmond, Virginia: Capital city of the Confederate States of America.

Secesh: Northern slang for Southerner(s) (from "secession").

Sheridan, Philip (1831–88): On October 19, 1864, Confederate troops attacked Union forces at Cedar Creek, Virginia. Major General Philip Henry Sheridan received news of the battle while returning from a strategy conference in Washington, D.C., and rode directly to the front, initiating a successful counterattack.

Sherman, William Tecumseh (1820–91): Senior general in the Union army, who served in many battles, including Shiloh, Vicksburg, Chattanooga, and Atlanta and was responsible for widespread destruction of Southern cities and countryside.

Stonewall: See Jackson.

Stuart, James Ewell Brown (Jeb) (1833–64): A Confederate cavalry commander who provided Lee and other generals with important intelligence from reconnaissance missions. He served in many battles, including those at Antietam, Gettysburg, Chancellorsville, and the Wilderness, dying of a combat wound in 1864.

Sumter: Fort Sumter; see Time Line, April 1861.

BIOGRAPHIES OF POETS

Aldrich, Thomas Bailey (1836–1907)

A poet, novelist, and editor, Thomas Bailey Aldrich was born in Portsmouth, New Hampshire; as a child, he lived in New York, New Orleans, and Portsmouth. In New York, Aldrich met with success as a poet before the age of twenty. Thereafter, he worked as an editor for several journals and papers, including the *Evening Mirror* and the *Home Journal.* With the outbreak of war, Aldrich hoped to receive an appointment with either the army or the navy; when he received neither, he decided to serve instead as a war correspondent, working in that capacity until his return to New York in 1862. In 1865, he moved to Boston, became editor of *Every Saturday,* and married Lilian Woodman. Aldrich served as editor of the *Atlantic Monthly,* one of the most prestigious literary magazines in the country, from 1881 to 1890. In addition to writing short stories and several successful novels, including *The Story of a Bad Boy* (1870), he published seven volumes of poetry.

Allen, Elizabeth Anne Chase Akers (1832–1911)

An accomplished journalist and poet, Elizabeth Anne Chase grew up in Farmington, Maine, and attended Farmington Academy (later Maine State Teachers College). In 1855, she began to write for the *Portland Transcript* and in 1856, under the pseudonym Florence Percy, published her first book of verse, *Forest Buds from the Woods of Maine.* Sales from this volume funded her travel to Rome, where she served as a correspondent for American newspapers and met the sculptor Benjamin Paul Akers, whom she married in 1860. Although Benjamin Akers had died in 1861, in 1866 she still published *Poems* under the name Elizabeth Akers, even though in 1865 she had already married Elijah M. Allen, whom she met while working as a government clerk in Washington, D.C. (1863–65). After the war, she and her new husband moved to Richmond, Virginia, and then in 1874 to Portland, Maine, where she was literary editor of the *Daily Advertiser,* until they moved to Tuckahoe, New York, in 1881. In the remaining thirty years of her life, Allen published *Queen Catherine's Rose* (1885), *The High-Top Sweeting* (1891), and *The Ballad of the Bronx* (1901).

Allston, Joseph Blythe (1833–1904)

Born on a plantation in Georgetown, South Carolina, Joseph Allston was the son of General Joseph Allston. After graduating from South Carolina College in 1851, he began practicing law in Charleston. When the Civil War broke out, he volunteered and was made a captain. "Stack Arms" was written while Allston was a prisoner of war. He later published two chapbooks of poetry, *Sumter* (1874) and *The Battle of Lake Erie* (1897).

ANDERSON, R. M.

In his *Civil War in Song and Story,* Frank Moore adds a note to **"The Song of the South,"** stating that "Captain R. M. Anderson, of Louisville, Kentucky, offered his whole command, consisting of ninety rifles, to the Governor of South Carolina, stipulating that they would bear their own expenses in going to Charleston and returning to Kentucky." **William Gilmore Simms** collected a poem called "The New Star" by B. M. Anderson in his *War Poetry of the South* (1866). These two authors may be the same man.

BAGBY, J. R.

A physician from Virginia, J. R. Bagby wrote poems in support of the Confederacy. **"The Empty Sleeve"** was included in **William Gilmore Simms**'s collection *War Poetry of the South* (1866), suggesting that it enjoyed some popularity during the war.

BALL, CAROLINE AUGUSTA RUTLEDGE (1823–?)

From Charleston, South Carolina, Caroline Rutledge was educated in New Haven, Connecticut, and then returned to Charleston, where she married Isaac Ball. Although she began writing poetry as a young girl, until the Civil War she had never published under her own name. During the war, she published several poems supporting the Confederacy. Critics of her verse most often comment that it is written "from the heart," not studied or "transcendental" in style. Ball published *The Jacket of Gray and Other Fugitive Poems* in 1866.

BARTLESON, FREDERICK A. (1833–64)

Frederick A. Bartleson was a colonel of the One Hundredth Illinois Regiment in the Union army. His military service proved him to be a remarkably dedicated soldier. Bartleson enlisted in 1861, lost one arm in the battle at Shiloh, and was captured while leading a charge during the battle at Chickamauga. As a prisoner, he was taken to Libby Prison* for Union officers in Richmond, Virginia. After a year, Bartleson was exchanged and returned to the command of his regiment, where he died a few days later in the battle at Kennesaw Mountain in 1864. In 1956, Margaret W. Peele edited and published Bartleson's *Letters from Libby Prison, Being the Authentic Letters Written While in Confederate Captivity in the Notorious Libby Prison.* A lawyer, Bartleson was the son of a proprietor of the *Wheeling Times.*

BEERS, ETHELINDA ELIOT (1827–1879)

Born Ethelinda Eliot in Goshen, New York, Beers began publishing under the name "Ethel Lynn" while still an adolescent. After her marriage to William Beers in 1846, she continued to write, publishing as "Ethel Lynn Beers." Her poems and stories frequently appeared in the *New York Ledger.* The success of Beers's most famous poem (most often printed as "All Quiet Along the Potomac") resulted in a controversy over the identity of its author. Beers's poem appeared in *Harper's Magazine* in 1861 under the title **"The Picket-Guard."** It was subsequently reprinted anonymously in a Southern paper, along with a note claiming it had been found on the body of a slain Confederate soldier, and later two Southern writers claimed responsibility for it. Beers wrote the poem after reading a newspaper article titled "All Quiet along the Potomac" (a familiar phrase in 1861) followed by the smaller title "A Picket Shot." Beers had a lifelong superstition that she would die if her collected poems were ever published. Her collection *All Quiet Along the Potomac, and Other Poems* was published in 1879; she died suddenly the following day.

BELL, JAMES MADISON (1826–1902)

Born to a free black family in Gallipolis, Ohio, James Madison Bell moved to Cincinnati at the age of sixteen, where he worked as a plasterer and married Louisiana Sanderlin, with whom he had several children. In 1854, Bell moved to Canada West, Ontario, then in 1860 to San Francisco. He became an ally and fund-raiser for John Brown and in the mid-1850s began publishing and giving public readings of his poetry as well as lecturing nationwide for abolition and racial justice. After the war, he was briefly politically active in the Republican Party. Bell wrote a number of long poems recalling the history of slavery, the war, and Reconstruction. His publications include *Poems* (1862), *An Anniversary Entitled the Progress of Liberty* (1866), *A Poem, Entitled the Triumph of Liberty* (1870), and the collection *Poetical Works* (1901). Madison's liveliest poem is "Modern Moses, or 'My Policy' Man," a witty satire of President Andrew Johnson, ridiculing Johnson's personal flaws and his broken pledges, especially to African Americans, such as his pardoning of Southern rebels, his restoring to rebels confiscated land that had been promised to freedmen, and his veto of the Freedman's Bureau Bill and Civil Rights Bill, both nonetheless passed by Congress in 1866.

BLUNT, ELLEN LLOYD KEY (1821–1884)

The granddaughter of Francis Scott Key (author of "The Star-Spangled Banner"), Ellen Blunt published both fiction and poetry. In 1859, she published "Poetical Readings," one of her several broadsides. Her works of fiction include *The Christmas Star for the Poor* (1856) and *Bread to My Children* (1856), a work combining fiction, poems, and songs.

BOKER, GEORGE HENRY (1823–1890)

A playwright, poet, and diplomat, George Boker was born in Philadelphia and educated at what is now Princeton University. In 1848 he published his first volume of poetry and saw the first of his several plays produced. His most famous literary production was *Francesca da Rimini,* a verse drama based on the fifth canto of Dante's *Inferno,* which opened in 1855 but was popular only in later, revised productions. Both a series of lackluster reviews of his plays and the urgency of the war prompted Boker to return to poetry, and in 1864 he published *Poems of the War.* Although a Democrat, after the attack on Fort Sumter,* Boker became a fervent supporter of the Union, helping to found the Union League of Philadelphia and directing its fund-raising and enlistment efforts. Among his many poems, Boker wrote over three hundred sonnets, several dealing with public affairs. In 1871 he became the U.S. foreign minister to Turkey, then assumed a diplomatic post in Russia, returning to Philadelphia and his career in writing in 1878.

BOOTH, MARY H. C. (1831–1865)

Born in Connecticut, Mary Booth married a journalist and in the early 1850s moved with him to Milwaukee, Wisconsin. Because of her poor health, Booth lived for several years in Zurich, Switzerland, writing for American magazines. Before returning to the United States, she published a volume of poems, including both original pieces and translations; the collection was titled *Wayside Blossoms among Flowers from German Gardens* (1864). In the terminal stages of tuberculosis, Booth returned to the United States; arriving in New York, she was able to complete a revised edition of these poems just before her death.

BRYANT, WILLIAM CULLEN (1794–1878)

One of the leading poets and editors of his day, William Cullen Bryant began his writing career at the age of thirteen, when his first published poem appeared in the *Hampshire Gazette.* Lacking the money for tuition at Yale, Bryant studied law instead and practiced as a lawyer for ten years. The success he met with as a poet during this decade prompted him to move to New York, where he became editor in chief of the *Evening Post.* Bryant's position at the *Post* led him to take a leading role in political debates of the day; for example, he advocated prison reform and the abolition of slavery. A staunch supporter of Lincoln's candidacy for president, Bryant introduced Lincoln* before his 1860 speech at Cooper Union in New York City and corresponded with Lincoln throughout the war years. He also used the columns of the *Post* to urge Lincoln's administration toward more decisive military action. After the president's assassination, in April 1865, Bryant read **"The Death of Lincoln"** to a crowd of grieving New Yorkers in Union Square. In spite of the demands of his career as an editor, Bryant also published several volumes of poems during his lifetime.

CAMPBELL, ALFRED GIBBS (1826?–?)

African American writer and journalist Alfred Gibbs Campbell founded and edited the *Alarm Bell,* a monthly newspaper published in Paterson, New Jersey, and devoted to a number of reform issues, including abolition. Campbell also published poems and essays supporting temperance, women's rights, and individualism and wrote frequently about religion. His writing ranged from the whimsically playful to the urgently political. He married Anne Hutchinson in 1852 and became vice president of the American Anti-Slavery Society in 1857. His activities during the Civil War are unknown. In 1883, he published his only book, titled *Poems.*

Cary, Phoebe (1824–1871)

Born into a farming family in Ohio, Phoebe Cary met with astonishing success in inventing a literary life for herself. After a childhood shaped by hard work and the death of her mother, Cary began publishing her poetry at the age of fourteen. Like her older sister Alice, Cary gained a national readership when Rufus Griswold included her work in his *Female Poets of America* (1849). Together the two sisters published *The Poems of Alice and Phoebe Cary* the following year. In 1851, Phoebe joined Alice in New York, and the sisters became leading figures in New York's literary circles. A less productive writer than Alice, Phoebe nonetheless published two collections of her own: *Poems and Parodies* (1854) and *Poems of Faith, Hope, and Love* (1868). Though reluctant to speak in public, Phoebe was known for her brilliant wit. Similarly, although she privately argued for women's rights and temperance, she preferred not to work for those causes in a public way. Neither sister married; they shared a home in New York until Alice's death in July 1871. Dependent on Alice in many ways, Phoebe Cary died five months later.

Cranch, Christopher Pearse (1813–1892)

A Unitarian minister, poet, and painter, Cranch completed his divinity studies at Harvard in 1835. Although he preached at several churches, he never settled permanently with one congregation. A member of the Transcendental Club, Cranch was a frequent contributor to the *Dial* in its earliest issues. From 1837 to 1839 he lived in the Ohio Valley, where he helped edit the *Western Messenger,* a Transcendentalist magazine. In 1842, Cranch took up painting as a profession and moved to New York. After two years of studying art in Italy, he lived and painted in Paris for ten years. By the time Cranch returned to New York in 1863, he was a recognized landscape painter, in the style of the Hudson River school. Throughout his painting career, Cranch was also a productive writer, publishing poems, essays, reviews, translations, a libretto, and stories for children. Considered a leading Transcendentalist poet, Cranch published three volumes of poetry: *Poems* (1844), *The Bird and the Bell, with Other Poems* (1874), and *Ariel and Caliban, with other Poems* (1887).

Cross, Jane Tandy Chinn Hardy (1817–1870)

A popular South Carolina poet, Jane T. H. Cross published several poems in support of the Confederacy under this abbreviation of her name. A newspaper clipping containing one of her poems dedicated to friends in Spartanburg, South Carolina, suggests that she may have lived in that town. In Nashville, Tennessee, in 1868, A. H. Redford published a novel written by Cross titled *Azile.*

Dickson, Samuel Henry (1798–1872)

Samuel Henry Dickson enrolled in Yale College at the age of thirteen. After graduation, he proceeded to the University of Pennsylvania, where he was awarded his M.D. in 1819. At that point, he returned to Charleston, South Carolina, his birthplace. After serving as director of the Marine and Yellow Fever Hospitals there, Dickson founded the Medical College of South Carolina, where he taught as a professor until 1855. He then returned to Philadelphia, where he taught in the Jefferson Medical College. Dickson wrote frequently for professional journals and published as well on literary and current topics—including an 1845 pamphlet on slavery asserting the inferiority of the "Negro" race. **"I Sigh for the Land of the Cypress and Pine"** is the only poem for which Dickson is now known. His sole volume of poems appeared in 1844.

DOUGLASS, SARAH MAPPS (1806–1882)

Daughter of prominent African American abolitionists Robert and Grace Bustill Douglass, Sarah Mapps Douglass was active in political causes from an early age. Extremely well educated for a young woman of her age—black or white—Douglass became a teacher, writer, and lecturer. She founded a school for black children in 1827, which was later run by the Philadelphia Female Anti-Slavery Society, an organization her mother had helped to found. In 1831, Douglass became secretary of the newly founded Female Literary Association for free black women, and in 1837, she attended the Anti-Slavery Convention of American Women. Douglass was appointed supervisor of the Institute for Colored Youth, a teacher-training institute, holding that position from the time it opened in 1853 until 1877; during the war she also devoted herself to antislavery activities. She married the Episcopal minister William Douglass in 1855. After the Civil War, Douglass became vice-chair of the Woman's Pennsylvania Branch of the American Freedmen's Aid Commission. During her lifetime she published several poems under the pseudonyms "Ella" and "Sophronisba"; some of her letters and speeches were published later in collections of African American abolitionist papers.

EMERSON, RALPH WALDO (1803–1882)

One of four children of an impoverished widow, Ralph Waldo Emerson studied at Harvard College and Divinity School. He was ordained in 1829, a time of national religious turmoil, and developed a theology independent of historical Christianity. In 1832 he resigned his post as minister because he felt he could not preach what he did not believe. After a period of travel in Europe, Emerson returned to the United States to begin a career as a public lecturer and writer. Initially roundly condemned by conservative and moderate thinkers, Emerson became one of the most influential thinkers of his day and is now acknowledged worldwide as one of the most significant American philosophers. His first book, *Nature,* articulated his idealist, Transcendentalist philosophy; with the publication of *Essays* (1841 and 1844) he became internationally renowned. Like his good friend **Henry David Thoreau,** Emerson spoke out in support of the abolition of slavery more than a decade before the war began, giving antislavery lectures around the country and publishing poems promoting the Union and condemning slavery. His journals are also dominated by his concerns for the political and moral issues facing the nation. There, for example, he refers to Lincoln's* election in 1860 as a "sublime" event and calls himself an abolitionist "of the most absolute abolition." Later he wrote, "You can no more keep out of politics than you can keep out of the frost." While known today primarily for his essays, during the mid-nineteenth century Emerson was also celebrated as a poet. His *Poems* was published in 1846 and *May-Day and Other Pieces* in 1867. Emerson's first wife died shortly after their marriage; with his second wife he had three children, two of whom survived.

Emmett, Daniel Decatur (1815–1904)

A white minstrel performer and composer, Dan Emmett was a self-taught musician with little education. Born in Ohio, Emmett enlisted in the army in 1834 and became a skilled drummer and fifer. After being discharged from the army, he began to perform in blackface as a banjo player, fiddler, and singer, first with circuses in the Midwest, then with minstrel troupes in New York. In 1843, Emmett and three other performers formed the Virginia Minstrels; they were one of the first groups of black impersonators to offer a show made up entirely of imitations of black art forms, including singing, playing, dancing, and stories. Like all blackface troupes, the Virginia Minstrels represented blacks as comic, stereotyped buffoons for the amusement of white audiences; the tremendous success of the Virginia Minstrels effectively launched a national minstrel craze among whites. In 1858, Emmett signed on with Dan Bryant's Minstrels in New York. While with this company, he wrote the lyrics and the music for the finale of many shows, a section known as the "walk-around," when all the performers came back onstage to sing, play, and dance. Now better known as "Dixie," "I Wish I Was in Dixie's Land" is the most famous of the walk-arounds Emmett wrote. It was played at Jefferson Davis's* inauguration in February 1861, and was thereafter identified as a Southern anthem. Though Emmett continued to perform through the 1880s, later in life he lost his voice, and his music waned in popularity. His later years were marked by poverty. Emmett published some thirty songs and left another twenty-five in manuscript at his death.

Falligant, Robert (1839–1902)

A judge and a soldier, Robert Falligant was descended from a long line of military men. Born in Savannah, Georgia, he was educated at Cherokee Baptist College (Cassville, Georgia) and at the University of Virginia. The war began while Falligant was a student at Virginia; joining up with a party of other college students, he was one of the group that seized Harpers Ferry during the Virginia secession convention. Falligant served in the Army of Northern Virginia until the war's end, eventually fighting in the artillery; after Antietam, he was promoted to lieutenant by special order from General Robert E. Lee.* Returning to Georgia after the war, Falligant became a lawyer and was elected first state representative and then state senator. Starting in the 1870s, he served for seventeen years as a commander in the state militia, and in 1889, he was appointed judge of the superior court of the eastern judicial circuit of Georgia.

FINCH, FRANCIS MILES (1827–1903)

Francis Miles Finch, a celebrated judge, dean of Cornell Law School, and Cornell professor of law, was remembered by his Yale undergraduate classmates as a songwriter, speechmaker, and wit. During class reunions, Finch frequently read recent compositions, the most memorable of which was **"The Blue and the Gray,"** written and published in 1867. Finch was a strong advocate of higher education. He served as one of the first trustees of Cornell University and as its legal counsel even before his appointment to the law school. He married Elizabeth Brooke in 1853 and had three children. His poems have not been collected for publication.

FLAGG, ELLEN (?–?)

Probably the pseudonym for a Northern poet.

FORTEN, SARAH LOUISA (1814–1883)

Born in Philadelphi and descended from African American slaves on her father's side and from African American, Native American, and Caucasian ancestors on her mother's, Sarah Louisa Forten grew up in a wealthy free family. Her family was well educated and active politically. Her father, James Forten, a shipbuilder, was the principal patron of William Lloyd Garrison's abolitionist newspaper the *Liberator,* and as an adult Sarah Forten was a charter member of the Philadelphia Female Anti-Slavery Society. Under the pseudonym "Ada," Forten published fifteen poems in the 1830s before her marriage to Joseph Purvis and their move from the city to a farm, where she bore and raised eight children. Although Forten returned to Philadelphia and her parents' house after her husband's death, she did not resume writing poetry. Her niece, **Charlotte Forten Grimké,** was also a poet.

GASSAWAY, FRANK HARRISON (?–1923)

Frank Gassaway was born in Maryland. Little is known about his life until he moved to California after the Civil War. There Gassaway published humorous travel letters under the name of "Derrick Dodd" in the *San Francisco Evening Post.* In 1882, some of these letters were collected in a volume called *Summer Saunterings, by "Derrick Dodd." A Series of Semi-Humorous, Semi-Descriptive letters about Santa Barbara, Santa Cruz, Monterey, San Jose, Napa Soda Springs, Sausalito, San Rafael, Santa Rosa, Cloverdale, Calistoga, Cliff House, etc. etc. etc. and the Yosemite.* Gassaway resided in Oakland from 1880 until his death.

GIBBONS, JAMES SLOAN (1810–1892)

American financier and philanthropist James Sloan Gibbons was born in Wilmington, Delaware, and moved to Philadelphia to become a dry-goods merchant. In 1835 he moved to New York and worked in finance and banking. Gibbons, like his wife Abigail Hopper Gibbons and her family, was a Quaker and fervent abolitionist. In fact, he expressed his abolitionist convictions so strongly and so much earlier than those of many in the North that he and his father-in-law were dropped from the membership of the New York Quaker Society in 1841. According to one story, Gibbons took his support for the *National Anti-Slavery Standard* so far as to mortgage his furniture to keep it in publication. During the draft riots of 1863, the Gibbons's house was one of the first to be attacked because his and his wife's antislavery sentiments were well known. Gibbons's financial success enabled his wife's reform activities and their mutual abolitionist work; together they had six children. Although Gibbons published in various financial and literary journals, his poem **"Three Hundred Thousand More"** was by far his most popular publication. Almost immediately after its first printing it was reprinted widely and set to music by several composers.

Grimké, Charlotte L. Forten (1837–1914)

The daughter of one of the most prominent African American families in the North and niece of **Sarah Louisa Forten,** Charlotte Forten grew up among active abolitionists. She was educated by tutors at home in Philadelphia and then attended the Higginson School and Salem Normal School in Massachusetts, where she began to keep journals (now published in two volumes) and was active in antislavery activities. After leaving school, Forten turned to teaching, and from late 1862 to 1864 taught freed slaves on St. Helena Island in South Carolina with Laura Towne and **Ellen Murray,** as part of the Port Royal* experiment. After the war she moved to Washington, D.C., and in 1878 married Francis James Grimké, a minister who, like her, was devoted to working for racial equality. Grimké published relatively little. Her fifteen poems and approximately fifteen essays appeared in leading black periodicals between 1855 and the 1890s.

Halpine, Charles Graham (1829–1868)

Born in Ireland, Charles Graham Halpine was educated at Trinity College, Dublin, and grew up in the world of journalism; his father, Reverend Nicholas Halpine, edited the chief Protestant Dublin paper, the *Evening Mail.* After his father's death, Halpine moved to England, where he made his own reputation as a journalist. In 1852, he immigrated to the United States, settling in New York, where he eventually became associate editor of the *New York Times* and editor of the *Leader.* At the beginning of the Civil War, he enlisted and rose through the ranks to the level of colonel. While serving in the army, he also published several burlesque poems in the *New York Herald* in the character of an unlearned Irish private, "Miles O'Reilly." In 1864, he published the *Life and Adventures, Songs, Services, and Speeches of Private Miles O'Reilly, 47th Regiment, New York Volunteers,* and in 1866, *Baked Meats of the Funeral: A Collection of Essays, Poems, Speeches, and Banquets, by Private Miles O'Reilly . . . Collected, Revised, and Edited, with the Requisite Corrections of Punctuation, Spelling, and Grammar, by an Ex-Colonel of the Adjutant-General's Department, with whom the Private formerly served as Lance Corporal of Orderlies.* He left the army in 1864, returning to New York. After his death, his poems were collected as *The Poetical Works of Charles G. Halpine (Miles O'Reilly)* (1869).

HARTE, BRET (1836–1902)

Francis ("Frank") Bret Harte was born in Albany, New York, into a family of Dutch, English, Huguenot, and Jewish descent, with Catholic and Episcopalian parents. In 1853, his widowed mother moved with her children to Oakland, California, where, after pursuing a variety of jobs, Harte began writing for newspapers. During the Civil War, he was interested primarily in developing his journalistic skills, although a Unitarian preacher enlisted his aid in writing for abolitionist causes. Harte enjoyed a brief period of great national acclaim immediately following the war (1868–71), when he published several stories and poems about rough-and-ready local life in California and served as founding editor of the *Overland Monthly.* During these same years he was the acknowledged leader of a diverse literary community in San Francisco, including among others the young Mark Twain, Ambrose Bierce, and Ina Coolbrith. By this time, he had also chosen the shortened Bret Harte as pen and personal name. In 1871, he moved with his wife and children to New York and thereafter to England, continuing to write but never again with the vitality or financial success of his early publishing in California.

HAYWARD, WILLIAM H. (1813–1876)

In 1864, General William H. Hayward published a volume titled *Camp Songs for the Soldier, and Poems of Leisure Moments* in Baltimore, Maryland. His poem "The Flag with Thirty-Four Stars" was published as sheet music in Boston in 1862.

HOLMES, OLIVER WENDELL (1809–1894)

A leading scientist and one of the most famous writers of his day, Oliver Wendell Holmes received both his bachelor and medical degrees from Harvard. After practicing medicine, he moved into medical research, teaching at both Dartmouth and Harvard, where he served as the dean of the medical school. In addition to publishing in the field of medicine, Holmes began to publish poetry while a student at Harvard. His first collection, a group of witty occasional verses, appeared in 1836. Holmes proposed the name of the *Atlantic Monthly* and became a frequent contributor after the magazine was launched in 1857. His famous series of breakfast-table sketches, later collected under the title *The Autocrat of the Breakfast-Table,* first appeared in the *Atlantic Monthly.* These fictionalized essays, set in a Boston boardinghouse, reveal Holmes's charm and wit and include two of his best-known poems, "The Deacon's Masterpiece" and "The Chambered Nautilus." Holmes's poems range from the witty to the philosophical to the patriotic, and his work often includes satirical attacks on Calvinism. Between 1862 and 1891, Holmes published five collections of poems, three novels, and two biographies, including a study of **Emerson.** His oldest son, Oliver Wendell Holmes Jr., served as a first lieutenant in the 20th Massachusetts Regiment of Volunteers in the Civil War and later became a justice of the U.S. Supreme Court.

Howe, Julia Ward (1819–1910)

Poet, playwright, and reformer, Julia Ward was born in New York City into an illustrious and well-to-do family. She received an excellent private education and had already published several essays on modern European writers before her marriage to Samuel Gridley Howe, director of the Perkins Institute for the Blind and well known for his active reform work. Her husband, however, did not approve of the participation of a married woman in public life, and it was over his initial strong opposition that Howe continued to pursue her literary career—eventually publishing five volumes of poems, two of travel sketches, a play, a memoir, and numerous essays, while raising five children. Both Howes, however, were ardent abolitionists and together helped to organize antislavery activity in their Boston home and edited an antislavery paper. The publication of the **"Battle Hymn of the Republic"** catapulted Howe to national attention, bringing her a kind of celebrity enjoyed by few nineteenth-century women. For the rest of her life she participated actively in several reform movements, giving frequent public lectures and publishing on a variety of topics.

Jonas, S. A. (?–?)

S. A. Jonas was an editor and poet in Aberdeen, Mississippi, who served as a major in the Confederate army. He published poetry in support of the Confederate cause, and his "Lines on the Back of a Confederate Note" was widely reprinted and very popular. Jonas also published several books during and following the war, including *The Lost Cause* (1872) and *Two Years After the Ratification of a Treaty of Peace Between Confederate States and the United States* (1900). After the war, Jonas was a member of the first Constitutional Convention held in Mississippi and edited the *Examiner,* one of the state's most important newspapers.

Keyes, Julia L. (1829–1877)

After the fall of the Confederacy, Julia Keyes emigrated from Montgomery, Alabama, to Brazil with her husband, who was a physician. A collection of her poems was published in Brazil after her death (*Poems,* 1918).

Lanier, Sidney (1842–1881)

Born in Macon, Georgia, Sidney Lanier studied at Oglethorpe College in Atlanta in 1860. When war broke out, Lanier joined the Second Georgia Battalion of the Macon Volunteers. He participated in several battles, including the Seven Days' fight. After his transfer to the signal service, Lanier was captured by Union forces in the fall of 1864 while running the blockades off the coast of North Carolina. During his imprisonment at Point Lookout, Maryland, he contracted tuberculosis, which would eventually kill him. In the decade after the war, Lanier began publishing poems in magazines; he also published the novel *Tiger-Lilies* (1867), based on his wartime experiences. After a number of years of practicing law, he traveled to Texas for his health, writing several essays based on his travels. A gifted musician, Lanier accepted a position as first flutist with the Peabody Orchestra in Baltimore in 1873. Deeply interested in the relationship between poetry and music, he also published articles in which he developed his theories on the physics of sound. He had already gained national recognition as poet through his magazine publications when his first volume of poems, *The Song of the Chattahoochee,* appeared in 1877. Following his appointment to Johns Hopkins University in 1879, Lanier published studies of verse technique, Shakespeare, and the novel; an expanded collection of his poems was published three years after his death.

LARCOM, LUCY (1824–1893)

The ninth of ten children, Lucy Larcom began working in the Lowell, Massachusetts, mills when she was eleven years old—after the death of her father and her mother's move to Lowell from Beverly, the seaport town where Lucy had been born. Ambitious to educate herself, Larcom took full advantage of the mill owners' encouragement for their employees to read and write, eventually publishing in the *Lowell Offering.* Larcom completed her education in Illinois, where she also taught briefly; later she taught at the Wheaton Seminary in Norton, Massachusetts. In 1862 she gave up teaching to focus exclusively on writing and editing (for example, the children's magazine *Our Young Folks* from 1865 to 1873), and in 1884 she was honored to be selected as one of only three nineteenth-century American women to have a complete poems published during her lifetime: a "household edition" of her poems by Houghton and Mifflin. While best known as a religious poet and for her prose and poetic descriptions of her New England childhood and life in the Lowell mills, Larcom also wrote some poems in support of the Union. In addition, she published *An Idyl of Work* and *A New England Girlhood, Outlined from Memory.*

LONGFELLOW, HENRY WADSWORTH (1807–1882)

A professor of literature first at Bowdoin College (where he received his undergraduate degree, along with classmate and lifelong friend Nathaniel Hawthorne) and then at Harvard University, Henry Wadsworth Longfellow was the first U.S. poet to achieve international renown. By the 1880s he had become the most popular poet writing in the English-speaking world. When he gave up teaching in 1855 to write full-time, he had already published thirteen books, including the 1842 *Poems on Slavery,* a manifestation of his early and deep conviction that slavery should be abolished. Although quiet in his political expression, Longfellow articulated strong antislavery views before many more radical and more famous abolitionists in the North did, and one of his closest friends was Charles Sumner, the radical abolitionist senator. During the war years, Longfellow also published several poems supporting the Union, while working on longer narrative-verse poems. The success of his professional life was not matched in his personal life: both Longfellow's wives died unexpectedly, leaving him bereaved after each loss. At the death of his second wife in 1861, Longfellow was also left with six children to raise.

Lowell, James Russell (1819–1891)

James Russell Lowell was educated at Harvard and briefly practiced as a lawyer before devoting himself to literary pursuits. Between 1841 and 1848, he published four collections of poetry, thereby establishing his reputation as one of the country's leading young poets. After his marriage to the poet Maria White, Lowell became increasingly active in the abolition movement and in other progressive causes. Starting in the 1840s, he published many antislavery articles and poems; he also served as an editorial writer for both the *Pennsylvania Freeman* and the *National Anti-Slavery Standard.* In *The Bigelow Papers* (1848), Lowell used satirical verse and a cast of comic Yankee characters to indict the imperialism of the Mexican War. Lowell's personal life, however, was marked by terrible losses: between 1845 and 1853, he lost three of his four children and his first wife. In 1856, he began teaching literature at Harvard, and in 1857, he married Frances Dunlap. In that same year, he launched the *Atlantic Monthly,* a publication that quickly became one of the foremost magazines in the United States. The *Atlantic Monthly* was among the first major periodicals to support abolition and, as a result, exercised a shaping influence in political debates. Though Lowell resigned the editorship in 1861, he continued to be a frequent contributor, publishing several political articles during the Civil War. Considered the leading man of letters of his generation, Lowell published numerous volumes of poetry, essays, and criticism.

Manahan, Thomas (1827?–?)

On April 20, 1861, Thomas Manahan enlisted as a musician in the 69th Infantry New York. He wrote many war songs during the Civil War.

Mason, Caroline Atherton Briggs (1823–1890)

Born into a family of ten children in Marblehead, Massachusetts, Caroline Atherton Briggs attended the Bradford Academy. One of her sisters also wrote poetry, and the sister to whom Caroline was closest became a missionary in Persia. As a young woman, Briggs published in local papers under the name "Caro." An early poem, "Do They Miss Me at Home," was set to music and became extremely popular in the United States and England—catapulting the author to minor fame. Her first volume, *Utterances, or Private Voices to the Public Heart,* appeared in 1852. In 1853, she married lawyer Charles Mason. Later, she published stories, essays, hymns, and letters as well as poetry, often under the initials C. A. M. With her husband, Mason actively promoted women's local and national suffrage and strongly supported the Union during the war. Many of her hymns continue to be sung in the Unitarian Church.

Meek, Alexander Beaufort (1814–1865)

Born in Columbia, South Carolina, Alexander Meek grew up in Alabama, where his family moved when he was five. After graduating from the University of Alabama in 1833, he studied law. At the age of twenty-three, he was appointed attorney general of

Alabama—a clear measure of his early success in his profession. In 1845, President Polk appointed Meek assistant secretary of the treasury. While continuing his legal practice and public service, Meek edited the *Tuscaloosa Flag of the Union* for one year and the *Mobile Register* for five years. He wrote poetry intermittently throughout his life. His most famous poem, "The Red Eagle," was a lyrical epic about a Creek Indian chief. During his lifetime, he published a Phi Beta Kappa oration called *Americanism in Literature* and *Romantic Passages in Southwestern History, Including Orations, Sketches, and Essays* and two books of poetry, *The Red Eagle, A Poem of the South* and *Songs and Poems of the South.*

MURRAY, ELLEN (1834–1908)

Ellen Murray taught on St. Helena Island, South Carolina, from June 1862 until 1904. There, with her lifelong friend Laura M. Towne and, later, with **Charlotte Grimké,** Murray helped to found the Penn Normal School, named for the Pennsylvania abolitionists and Freedmen Society that sponsored this project. Part of the Port Royal* Experiment, this was the first school opened in the South to educate freed slaves; it took in boarders and eventually taught trades and self-sufficiency skills as well as basic literacy and math. Towne and Murray also eventually adopted and raised several African American children. Murray published pamphlets in addition to her poems.

NEALL, MRS. JAMES (?–?)

Mrs. Neall was probably the wife of James Neall (1820–1903), a western writer, according to Paula Bennett in NAWP. Hannah and James Neall had a granddaughter, Marie de Nervaud Dun, who published western adventure novels and stories. It is unknown whether Hannah is the "Mrs. James Neall" who wrote "The Harvest-Field of 1861."

OSGOOD, KATE PUTNAM (?–?)

Born into a prestigious family that included an uncle who was governor of Maine, Kate Putnam married Henry B. Osgood (a brother of her uncle's wife) and, later, Judge Goodenough of Alfred, Maine. Her poem "Driving Home the Cows" was immensely popular and was frequently reprinted in the decades after the war.

PABOR, WILLIAM E. (1834?–1911)

Editor of the *Harlem Times* at the age of nineteen, William E. Pabor apparently spent at least part of the war years in Harlem. He moved to Colorado in 1870, where he helped found the Colorado Editorial Association and served as an officer in companies that established the towns of Greeley, Fort Collins, and Colorado Springs; he himself founded the town of Fruita. A pioneering horticulturist and tireless promoter of the new state, Pabor brought the first carload of apple trees into the Grand Valley and wrote *Colorado as an Agricultural State* to extol the fruit-growing potential of this region. Pabor was known as both a poet and a journalist; among other papers, he wrote for the *Rocky*

Mountain News, the *Colorado Farmer*, and the *Fruita Star*. Around 1891, after being told he had to leave the high altitude of Colorado to preserve his health, Pabor moved to Florida and began again the work of founding towns and agricultural pioneering—this time in the growing of pineapples.

Palmer, John Williamson (1825–1906)

John Williamson Palmer was born in Baltimore and studied medicine at the University of Maryland. In the midst of the gold rush of 1849, he traveled to San Francisco and worked as a physician. Thereafter, he sailed for Hawaii and then further east, serving as a surgeon in the East India Company's navy in the Second Burmese War. After traveling in India and China, he settled in New York, where he contributed to *Harper's*, *Putnam's*, and the *Atlantic Monthly*, writing travel sketches that he collected in two volumes (1856 and 1859). Palmer was writing for the *New York Times* when the war broke out. A Southern sympathizer, he offered to write a series describing life in the South. Though the *Times* would not print the first article he wrote from Richmond, the *New York Tribune* later agreed to publish his reporting as a Southern correspondent. Late in the war, Palmer joined the Confederate army and served on John C. Breckinridge's staff. In the years following the war, he published a study of cholera and edited a volume of the poetry of courtship. He returned to New York and to editorial work in 1870. Palmer's only novel, *After His Kind*, was published in 1886.

Piatt, John James (1835–1917)

Born in Indiana and raised there and in Ohio, John James Piatt was an editor, journalist, and poet who held a number of political appointments during and following the Civil War—including clerk to the U.S. Treasury Department (1861–67), clerk and librarian to the U.S. House of Representatives (1870–82), and consul to Cork and Dublin (1882–93). Known as a poet of midwestern experience and landscape, Piatt published several volumes of poetry, including two with his more famous wife, **Sarah Morgan Bryan Piatt.** Together they had eight children. After political changes brought about the end of his public career, he returned to journalism, editing journals, book reviews, and collections of poems in addition to continuing to write his own poetry.

Randall, James Ryder (1839–1908)

Known throughout the South as the author of **"My Maryland,"** called "the Marseillaise of the Confederate cause," James R. Randall was born and educated in that state. After his health necessitated that he spend some time in South America and further south in the United States, he began teaching English and Latin at Poydras College in Louisiana. Randall's health prevented him from enlisting in the Confederate army. After the war, he became associate editor of a Georgia paper, continuing in newspaper work for the rest of his life. Randall married Katherine Hammond in 1866; they had eight children. His poems were collected in a posthumous volume in 1910.

RAY, HENRIETTA CORDELIA (1850/52?–1916)

Henrietta Ray was born into a prominent black family in New York City that could trace its heritage back through Indian, Euro-American, and black ancestors for four or five generations; her father, Charles Bennett Ray, was a Congregationalist minister and edited the *Colored American.* After earning a master's degree at the University of the City of New York in 1891, Ray taught music, math, and languages (she knew French, Greek, and Latin) in the public schools and gave education classes for teachers in English literature. She wrote and published poetry throughout her adulthood and published two collections of her verse, *Sonnets* in 1893 and *Poems* in 1910. Her poem **"Lincoln,"** read to great acclaim at the unveiling of the Freedmen's Monument in Washington, D.C., in 1876, also appeared as a chapbook in 1893. She and her elder sister Florence, her lifelong companion, also published a biography of their father.

READ, THOMAS BUCHANAN (1822–1872)

Poet, painter, and sculptor Thomas Read was born in Chester County, Pennsylvania, and served in the Civil War as a major under General Lew Wallace. After the death of his father, Read had a variety of odd jobs and moved frequently until landing with an elder sister in Cincinnati, where he was hired to work for a sculptor. During the late 1830s and 1840s, Read published some verse in newspapers and worked as an itinerant portrait painter, enjoying considerable success in New York and Boston. In 1843, he married Mary J. Pratt of Gambier, Ohio, with whom he had three children. In 1846, they moved to Philadelphia, where he published several volumes of poetry and continued to paint. From 1850 on, Read and his family divided their time between several European cities, where he was well received, and Philadelphia. **"Sheridan's Ride"** remains Read's best-known poem. Read also depicted Sheridan's* ride in several paintings and sculpted at least two busts of the general.

REQUIER, AUGUSTUS JULIAN (1825–1887)

Like many of his fellow poets from the South, A. J. Requier was a lawyer. Descended from French parents from Haiti and Marseille, Requier was born and raised in Charleston, South Carolina, and passed the bar there in 1844. His first published work, *The Spanish Exile* (1842), was a drama in blank verse. Set in pre-Revolutionary South Carolina, his second book, *The Old Sanctuary* (1846), was a romance. Though Requier published in several genres, poetry was his first interest; the collection *Poems* appeared in 1860. In later verse, Requier offered praise of Shakespeare and meditated on Emanuel Swedenborg's philosophy. In addition to the romantic poem *The Legend of Tremaine* (1864), Requier also wrote poems in response to the war. Before the war, Requier had been appointed U.S. district attorney for Alabama; during the war, he served as district attorney for the Confederacy. Requier moved to New York in 1866, where he worked as a lawyer and as assistant district attorney.

Rockett, F. T. (?–?)

F. T. (perhaps F. V.) Rockett's **"Melt the Bells"** was published in *War Poetry of the South* (1866), edited by **William Gilmore Simms.**

R. R.

No information can be found about the user of this pseudonym.

Ryan, Abram Joseph (1838–1886)

The son of Irish immigrants, Abram Ryan grew up in St. Louis, Missouri, and took his orders as a Catholic priest in 1856. In 1862 Ryan joined the Confederate army as a chaplain. While his primary duties were tending the sick, hearing confession, and performing mass, he also fought on occasion. Fiercely loyal to the seceded South, Ryan saw it as his postwar duty to keep the memory of the Confederacy alive. Several of his poems were enormously popular, and many were set to music and taught in Southern schools. He called his 1866 "The Conquered Banner" the "requiem of the Lost Cause." Ryan served as a curate in various parts of Mississippi, Tennessee, Georgia, and Alabama. He edited journals, was a popular lecturer, and toured frequently to raise funds for the relief of Southern widows and orphans. Although he had little regard for his own verse, Ryan allowed volumes to be published in 1879 and 1880. In 1882 he published a volume of devotional verse. Ryan was so beloved in the South that at his death schoolchildren gave dimes to erect a monument in his memory.

Shepherd, Nathaniel Graham (1835–1869)

Born in New York City, Nathaniel Shepherd studied art in New York and then taught drawing in Georgia for several years. After returning to New York, he worked in the insurance business, studying and writing poetry in his spare time. At the start of the war, Shepherd became a journalist, working as a war correspondent for the *New York Tribune.* He was a frequent contributor to magazines and journals and won popular acclaim for his poems and war songs, which circulated widely. "The Dead Drummer Boy," "A Summer Reminiscence," and **"Roll Call"** were three of his best-known poems. Shepherd continued to work as a journalist after the war.

Shuften, Sarah E. (?–?)

Sarah Shuften published the poem **"Ethiopia's Dead."** According to Paula Bennett in NAWP, she is the wife of John T. Shuften, who was a graduate of Howard University and a lawyer. John Shuften was also editor and proprietor of the *Colored American,* the first African American newspaper published in Georgia, in 1865–66. Later, John Shuften moved to Jacksonville, Florida, where he was also among Florida's first African American journalists.

SIGNAIGO, J. AUGUSTINE (1835–1876)

Born in Italy in 1835, J. Augustine Signaigo immigrated to the United States, where he launched the *Grenada Sentinel* in Grenada, Mississippi, in 1854. Signaigo wrote the libretto for a popular Civil War–era operetta called *The Vivandiere*; his Civil War poetry was also popular. After the war, Signaigo served as president of the Mississippi Press Association. He is buried next to his wife and child in Grenada.

SIMMS, WILLIAM GILMORE (1806–1870)

One of the South's most influential and acclaimed writers, William Gilmore Simms was prolific, publishing numerous romances, essays, historical studies of the South, biographies, and works of criticism, as well as eighteen volumes of poetry. Born in Charleston, South Carolina, Simms was admitted to the bar but chose to pursue writing as a career. Active in both political and literary circles, he served as a state legislator in South Carolina from 1844 to 1846, and over the course of his career edited several newspapers and magazines, including the *Magnolia,* the *Southern and Western,* and, from 1849 to 1856, the influential proslavery *Southern Quarterly Review.* An ardent supporter of Southern nationalism, Simms advocated both the annexation of Texas and the founding of a Southern empire in the Caribbean. During the war years, Simms advised several Southern politicians; his beloved plantation Woodlands was destroyed in the final months of the war. In the war's aftermath, Simms's large family was impoverished; late in his life, Simms worked tirelessly—and to the detriment of his health—at various writing and editorial tasks, in a dogged attempt to support his family. Among other projects, he edited an influential anthology titled *War Poetry of the South* (1866).

SIMPSON, JOSHUA MCCARTER (1820?–1876)

Born a free black in Morgan County, Ohio, Joshua McCarter Simpson grew up in poverty and enjoyed only three months of schooling before he taught himself to write and gained entrance to Oberlin College, where he studied from 1844 until 1848. In 1852 he published a pamphlet called *Original Anti-slavery Songs,* and in 1874 he collected fifty-three of his song-poems in a volume called *The Emancipation Car,* described as "an original composition of anti-slavery ballads, composed exclusively for the Underground Railroad." McCarter married in 1847, in Zanesville, Ohio, the town where he lived for the rest of his life. There he worked as an herb doctor and wrote and performed his song-poems, as well as writing a few satirical essays. McCarter used song tunes with irony and wit, often as a barbed comment on white American society. His songs were highly popular, especially among escaping and escaped slaves.

STEDMAN, EDMUND CLARENCE (1833–1908)

Born in Hartford, Connecticut, and educated at Yale, Edmund Clarence Stedman had been employed by the *New York World* for less than a year when the Civil War began and he was sent to the front. Stedman covered the war in Virginia until 1862, when he left journalism to work for Attorney General Edward Bates. In 1863, he became a Wall Street broker and eventually founded his own very successful firm. Known as the Bard of Wall Street, Stedman was an esteemed member of New York's lively intellectual and literary circle and helped initiate a reevaluation of American poetry through his critical writing and by editing two anthologies, one on Victorian and another on American poetry. He also wrote poetry throughout his life. His most popular war poems were "John Brown's Invasion" and a campaign song called "Honest Abe of the West."

Stoddard, Elizabeth Barstow (1823–1902)

Elizabeth Drew Barstow was born into a prosperous family in Mattapoisett, Massachusetts. She attended Wheaton Female Seminary, read widely in the library of a local Congregationalist minister, and published her first sketch in 1851. In 1852 she married **Richard Stoddard,** an impoverished writer. Their circle of poet friends included **Bayard Taylor** and **George Henry Boker.** Stoddard contributed to family income through writing bimonthly columns for the *San Francisco Daily Alta California* from 1854 to 1858 and by publishing three novels and several short stories, sketches, and poems. A realist and protofeminist, Stoddard's fiction was not much heralded during her day. Now, however, *The Morgesons* (1862) is regarded as an important early experiment with social and psychological realism that mocks the values of sentimental fiction and questions the pieties of the midcentury. Under increasing pressure to earn money, Stoddard sold nearly forty stories and sketches, including a collection of children's tales, and a dozen poems between 1867 and 1874; her only volume of poetry, *Poems,* appeared in 1895.

Stoddard, Richard Henry (1825–1903)

Richard Henry Stoddard offers a remarkable example of one man's rise from poverty to a literary life. Born in Hingham, Massachusetts, he came from a seafaring family; his father, a ship's captain, died in 1828. When Stoddard's mother remarried in 1835, the family moved to New York. After a brief stint of schooling, Stoddard went to work in an iron foundry, studying literature in the evenings. By 1845 he had begun publishing poems in the *Rover,* the *Southern Literary Messenger,* and *Godey's Lady's Book,* among other magazines. In 1849, he self-published a collection titled *Foot-Prints.* Quickly realizing its weaknesses, he destroyed all copies but the one that had already been sold. A second volume of more polished poems appeared in 1851 and was well received. Soon thereafter, Stoddard married another writer, **Elizabeth (Barstow) Stoddard.** Thanks to Nathaniel Hawthorne, a distant cousin of his wife's, Stoddard was offered a position at the New York customhouse, where he worked for the next seventeen years. Starting in 1860, he wrote literary reviews for the *World,* and in 1865 he completed *Abraham Lincoln: An Horation Ode.* In addition to publishing many volumes of verse, Stoddard published critical studies, anthologies, and children's books.

TAYLOR, BAYARD (1825–1878)

Best known as a travel writer for his accounts of journeys in the Middle East, India, China, and Japan, Taylor was also a poet and illustrator. Born in Kennett Square, Pennsylvania, Taylor began his career as a printer's apprentice and then newspaper correspondent. After an assignment in Europe, resulting in the publication of *Views Afoot, or Europe Seen with Knapsack and Staff,* Taylor was sent to California via the Panama Canal to report on the gold rush. These newspaper stories became the basis of *El Dorado, or Adventures in the Path of Empire* (1850), a volume which was immediately popular in the United States and Europe and which heralded his continued success as a travel writer. Taylor's first publication, however, was a volume of poems, published in 1844, and he continued to write poetry throughout his life, producing lyric and narrative poems, lyrical drama, and a verse translation of *Faust.* Later in his life, Taylor taught German at Cornell University and was then appointed ambassador to Germany, where he died a few months after his arrival in Berlin.

THOMPSON, MERIWETHER JEFF (1826–1876)

Meriwether Jeff Thompson was serving as the mayor of St. Joseph, Missouri, when the war began. Born in Virginia, Thompson was loyal to the South and voluntarily organized a pro-Southern Missouri battalion when fighting broke out at Fort Sumter.* Known as the "Swamp Fox" (no doubt in allusion to Francis Marion, a daring South Carolina Revolutionary War soldier), Thompson led a battalion known as the Swamp Rats. Claiborne Jackson, the governor of Missouri, had refused Lincoln's* call to organize Union troops from that state, but he also refused the services of Thompson's Swamp Rats. Thereafter, Thompson took matters into his own hands and marched with five thousand men to Girardeau, Missouri. When John C. Frémont issued his emancipation proclamation in August 1861, Thompson issued a counterproclamation of his own and carried out a series of raids along the border. By the close of 1861, Thompson had become a legendary Confederate fighter, operating independently in southeast Missouri. In 1862 he joined Earl Van Dorn's command and saw action in many western battles. Captured in August 1863, he was imprisoned until his exchange in 1864. Thompson was one of the last Confederate commanders to surrender, in May 1865, and lived in New Orleans after the war.

THOREAU, HENRY DAVID (1817–1862)

Best known for his prose works *Walden* and "Resistance to Civil Government" (often called "Civil Disobedience"), Thoreau also wrote some two hundred poems. Born in Concord, Massachusetts, where he lived for most of his life, he was educated at Concord Academy and at Harvard. Like his friend and mentor **Ralph Waldo Emerson,** Thoreau was a lifelong writer of journals and used these writings as sourcebooks for his published works. In 1840, Thoreau published both an essay and a poem in the *Dial,* the literary magazine of the Transcendentalist circle, and thereafter he contributed regularly to the magazine. Though known as a serious writer among his friends, Thoreau published only two books during his lifetime: *A Week on the Concord and Merrimack Rivers* (1849) and *Walden* (1854). An outspoken opponent of slavery, Thoreau argued against both the institution and the government that condoned it; in particular, he condemned the Fugitive Slave Law* and defended the actions of John Brown. Thoreau died of tuberculosis in 1862.

Ticknor, Francis Orray (1822–1874)

Born in Fortville, Georgia, Francis ("Frank") Ticknor studied at the Philadelphia College of Medicine and then returned to rural Georgia, where he spent the rest of his life as a country doctor, with his wife and eight children. A poet and horticulturalist, Ticknor published frequently in southern periodicals. Although he wrote many Civil War poems, his primary fame as a poet is based on his account of treating and befriending a young Tennessee soldier named Isaac Newton Giffen, who returned to the ranks of the Confederate army as soon as he was able. Ticknor's ballad **"Little Giffen"** was widely reprinted following the war. A collection of Ticknor's poems was published posthumously, in 1879, and then republished in an expanded version in 1911.

Tucker, Mary Eliza (1838–?)

Mary Eliza Tucker was born in Cahawba, Alabama, and educated in a boarding school in New York. She later married John M. Tucker and moved to Georgia. During the Civil War, when her husband and her father lost all their property, she returned to New York to work as a journalist. In 1871 she married Colonel James H. Lambert and moved to Philadelphia, where she edited a journal. Tucker published two books in 1867, *Poems* (dedicated to the notoriously anti-Reconstructionist governor of Georgia, Charles J. Jenkins, and his wife) and a long poem titled *Loew's Bridge: A Broadway Idyl.* In 1868 she published the biography of a New York newspaper publisher, *Life of Mark M. Pomeroy.*

Wallis, Severn Teackle (1816–1894)

For half a century, Severn Wallis was regarded as Maryland's foremost lawyer, arguing thousands of cases before state courts and many before the United States Supreme Court. Always a reformer, he contributed frequent polemical articles to the daily press, notable for their pungency and wit. Born in Maryland, Wallis devoted his life to professional, reform, and political service to the state, never marrying. Before the war, he called for a constitutional amendment to protect slavery and defended the rights of Southern states to secede, although he contended that because of its military vulnerability Maryland should not secede. Once the war began, he vehemently opposed President Lincoln's* decision to defend the Union by force. When arrested for plotting secession, he refused to sign a loyalty oath and was imprisoned for fourteen months. An author of verse, two books on Spain, and several essays, Wallis was so widely admired for his thoughtful, terse intelligence and eloquence that friends collected his writings in a four-volume memorial edition two years after his death.

WARFIELD, CATHERINE ANN WARE (1816–1877)

A poet and novelist, Catherine Ware was born in Natchez, Mississippi, into a distinguished family. After the mental decline of her mother in 1820, the family moved to Philadelphia, where Ware's mother could receive better medical treatment and the children could receive superior cultural advantages and education. In 1833 she married Robert Elisha Warfield, with whom she moved to Lexington, Kentucky, and had six children; later they moved to a rural estate near Louisville. During the 1840s, Warfield coauthored two volumes of verse with her sister. After the deaths of both her sister and father, she published eight novels. During the Civil War, she returned to verse to express her strong Confederate sympathies. None of Warfield's fiction dealt explicitly with political issues, although some of her novels reveal the complications of slavery and of Southern conventions of femininity amid their often celebratory descriptions of Southern domestic life.

WASHINGTON, EMILY M. (?–?)

Emily M. Washington's **"Confederate Song of Freedom"** was published in volume 8 of the *Rebellion Record* in 1865.

WEEKS, DELLA JERMAN (?–?)

Della Jerman Weeks (who may also have published under the name Delia R. German) published a group of her poems in a volume titled *Legends of the War* in Boston in 1863. The volume was printed for private circulation.

INDEX OF AUTHORS AND TITLES

"A Battle Hymn," 77
"A Child's Party," 344
"A Cry to Arms," 320
"A March in the Ranks Hard-Prest, and the Road Unknown," 237
"A Prayer for Peace," 128
"A Second Review of the Grand Army," 173
"A Sight in Camp in the Daybreak Gray and Dim," 238
"A Southern Scene," 97
"A Thought," 66
"A Utilitarian View of the *Monitor*'s Fight," 275
"A Word for the Hour," 218
"Adieu to a Soldier," 247
"After great pain, a formal feeling comes -," 354
"After the Battle: The Dirge," 363
Aldrich, Thomas Bailey, 156
Allen, Elizabeth Akers, 110
Allston, Joseph Blythe, 168
"An Appeal to My Countrywomen," 300
"An Army Corps on the March," 234
"An uninscribed Monument," 288
Anderson, R. M., 82
"Anomalies," 76
Anonymous ("A Southern Scene"), 97
Anonymous ("Chickamauga, 'The Stream of Death!'"), 117
Anonymous ("Conservative Chorus"), 109
Anonymous ("Cotton-Doodle"), 62
Anonymous ("'Is There, Then, No Hope for the Nations?'"), 181
Anonymous ("Let My People Go: A Song of the 'Contrabands'"), 69
Anonymous ("My Army Cross Over"), 122
Anonymous ("Negro Song of Mission Ridge"), 121
Anonymous ("Reading the List"), 154
Anonymous ("Ride In, Kind Saviour"), 123
Anonymous ("Soldiers' Aid Societies"), 67
Anonymous ("The Voices of the Guns"), 164
"Another War," 336
"Apathy and Enthusiasm," 259
"Army of Occupation," 333
"As I Lay with My Head in Your Lap Camerado," 246
"Ashes of Glory," 170
"At Fort Pillow," 140
"At Port Royal," 222
"August 3rd, 1886," 368
"'Ay De Mi, Alhama!,'" 188

Bagby, J. R., 152
Baker, Obadiah Ethelbert, 362–370
Ball, Caroline A., 124
"Ball's Bluff," 261
"Barbara Frietchie," 228
Bartleson, Frederick A., 130
"Battle Hymn of the Republic," 75
"Beat! Beat! Drums!," 232
Beers, Ethelinda, 65
Bell, James Madison, 135
"Bible Defence of Slavery," 291
"Bivouac on a Mountain Side," 233
Blunt, Ellen Key, 56
Boker, George Henry, 77, 78, 112, 142, 144
Booth, Mary H. C., 96, 163

"Boston Hymn," 105
"Brother Jonathan's Lament for Sister Caroline," 54
"Brother, Tell Me of the Battle," 151
"Bury Me in a Free Land," 295
Bryant, William Cullen, 61, 161, 171
"By the Bivouac's Fitful Flame," 234

Campbell, Alfred Gibbs, 38
"Carmen Triumphale," 324
Cary, Phoebe, 123
"Cavalry Crossing a Ford," 233
"Charleston," 322
"Chickamauga, 'The Stream of Death!,'" 117
"Christmas, South, 1866," 187
"Clouds in the West," 91
"Color - Caste - Denomination -," 360
"Come Up from the Fields Father," 234
"Confederate Song of Freedom," 139
"Conservative Chorus," 109
"Cotton-Doodle," 62
"Counsel—In the South," 343
Cranch, Christopher Pearse, 172, 173
Cross, Jane T. H., 51, 157

"Death the Peacemaker," 125
Dickinson, Emily, 351–361
Dickson, Samuel Henry, 32
"Dirge for Two Veterans," 241
"Do You," 365
"Doffing the Gray," 169
"Donelson," 263
Douglass, Sarah Mapps, 28
"Driving Home the Cows," 167
"Dupont's Round Fight," 262
"Dying! To be afraid of thee," 360

"Eighteen Sixty-One," 231
"1866," 329
"Ein feste Burg ist unser Gott," 219
"Eliza Harris," 292
Ella, 28
"Emancipation," 93
Emerson, Ralph Waldo, 105
Emmett, Dan, 40
"Ethiopia Saluting the Colors," 244
"Ethiopia's Dead," 176
"Ethnogenesis," 312

Falligant, Robert, 169
Finch, Francis Miles, 191
Flagg, Ellen, 125
"'Formerly a Slave,'" 284
Forten, Sarah Louisa, 27
"Fredericksburg," 156

Gassaway, Frank H., 146
"General Grant—The Hero of the War," 205
"Gettysburg Ode," 194
Gibbons, James Sloan, 92
"Giving Back the Flower," 334
Grimké, Charlotte Forten, 41

"Half Way," 94
Halpine, Charles Graham, 138
Harper, Frances Ellen Watkins, 289–310
Harte, Bret, 108, 127, 173
Hayward, William H., 144
"He fought like those Who've nought to lose -," 354
"Hearing the Battle.— July 21, 1861," 332
Holmes, Oliver Wendell, 54
Horton, George Moses, 201–215
"How Solemn as One by One," 245
Howe, Julia Ward, 75

"I Know Not Why," 320
"I like a look of Agony," 353
"I never hear that one is dead," 361
"I Sigh for the Land of the Cypress and Pine," 32

"I Wish I Was in Dixie's Land," 40
"I'm Dying, Comrade," 163
"If any sink, assure that this, now standing -," 357
"In Libby Prison—New Year's Eve 1863–4," 130
"In the Prison Pen," 280
"In the Wilderness," 142
"'Is There, Then, No Hope for the Nations?,'" 181
"It feels a shame to be Alive -," 356

"Jefferson in a Tight Place," 212
Jonas, S. A., 109

Keyes, Julia L., 155
"Killed at the Ford," 182

Lanier, Sidney, 175, 189
Larcom, Lucy, 48, 86
"Learning to Read," 309
"Let My People Go: A Song of the 'Contrabands,'" 69
"Let the Banner Proudly Wave," 185
"Like Brothers We Meet," 208
"Lincoln," 195
"Lincoln Is Dead," 208
"Lines" (Alfred Gibbs Campbell), 38
"Lines" (George Moses Horton), 203
"Lines to Miles O'Reiley, 298
"Little Giffen," 193
Longfellow, Henry Wadsworth, 80, 182
"Look Down Fair Moon," 245
Lowell, James Russell, 29

"Magnanimity Baffled," 285
"Malvern Hill," 277
Manahan, Thomas, 151
"Manassas," 60
Mason, Caroline, 76
Meek, Alexander Beaufort, 114
"Melt the Bells," 99
Melville, Herman, 257–288
"Mock Diamonds," 337
Murray, Ellen, 94
"My Army Birth," 365
"My Army Cross Over," 122
"My Autumn Walk," 161
"My Country," 27
"My Life had stood - a Loaded Gun -," 359
"My Maryland," 49
"My Portion is Defeat - today -," 358
"My Triumph lasted till the Drums," 360

Neall, Mrs. James, 55
"Negro Song of Mission Ridge," 121
"No Rack can torture me -," 358
"Not the Pilot," 238
"Not Yet," 61
"Not Youth Pertains to Me," 244
"Nov. 30th To an Absent Wife," 365

"Ode," 328
"On the Heights of Mission Ridge," 120
"On the Slain at Chickamauga," 287
"On the Slain Collegians," 285
"One Anguish - in a Crowd -," 356
"Only a Soldier's Grave," 109
"Only One Killed," 155
Osgood, Kate Putnam, 167
"Our Faith in '61," 58
"Over in Kentucky," 339
"Over the Carnage Rose Prophetic a Voice," 242
"Over the River," 51

Pabor, William E., 93
Palmer, John Williamson, 85
"Pensive on Her Dead Gazing," 248
Platt, John James, 89

Piatt, Sarah Morgan Bryan, 331–347
"Price's Appeal to Missouri," 64

R. R., 83
Randall, James R., 49, 140
Ray, Henrietta Cordelia, 195
Read, Thomas Buchanan, 149
"Reading the List," 154
"Ready," 123
"Rebel Color-bearers at Shiloh," 283
"Reconciliation," 245
Requier, Augustus Julian, 58, 91, 170
"Ride In, Kind Saviour," 123
Rockett, F. T., 99
"Roll Call," 100
Ryan, Abram Joseph, 183

"Sambo's Right To Be Kilt," 138
Shepherd, Nathaniel Graham, 100
"Sheridan at Cedar Creek," 279
"Sheridan's Ride," 149
"Shiloh," 276
"Shoulder-Rank," 335
Shuften, Sarah E., 176
Signaigo, J. Augustine, 120
Simms, William Gilmore, 33, 35, 188
Simpson, Joshua McCarter, 37, 185
"Slavery," 202
"Soldiers' Aid Societies," 67
"Song of the 'Aliened American,'" 37
"Song of the South," 35
"Sonnet," 144
"Southern Ode," 33
"Spring at the Capital," 110
"'Stack Arms,'" 168
Stedman, Edmund Clarence, 89
Stoddard, Elizabeth, 66
Stoddard, Richard Henry, 47
"Stonewall Jackson's Way," 85

Taylor, Bayard, 194
"The Artilleryman's Vision," 243
"The Battle Autumn of 1862," 225
"The Battle fought between the Soul," 357
"The Black Princess," 340
"The Black Regiment," 112
"The Blue and the Gray," 191
"The Charge at Farmington," 367
"The Charge at Monterey," 366
"The College Colonel," 281
"The Confederacy," 157
"The Copperhead," 127
"The Cotton Boll," 315
"The Cumberland," 80
"The Day and the War" (excerpt), 135
"The Death of Lincoln," 171
"The Death-Blow," 172
"The Deliverance," 302
"The Dying Soldier's Message," 209
"The Dying Words of Jackson," 175
"The Empty Sleeve," 152
"The Harvest-Field of 1861," 55
"The House-top," 278
"The Hunters of Men," 217
"The Jacket of Gray," 124
"The March into Virginia," 260
"The Martyr" (Christopher Pearse Cranch), 173
"The Martyr" (Herman Melville), 282
"The Mother and Her Captive Boy," 28
"The name - of it - is 'Autumn' -," 354
"The Nineteenth of April," 48
"The Old Rifleman," 52
"The Old Slave-Music," 342
"The Patriot Ishmael Day," 144
"The Picket-Guard," 65
"The Poet's Feeble Petition," 205
"The Portent," 258
"The Present Crisis," 29
"The Pride of Battery B," 146
"The Reveille," 108
"The Slave Auction," 294
"The Slave Mother," 290

"The Soldier on His Way Home," 213
"The Song of the South," 82
"The Southern Cross," 56
"The Southern Refugee," 207
"The Spectator of the Battle of Belmont," 210
"The Stars and Bars," 83
"The Sword of Robert Lee," 183
"The Sword-Bearer," 78
"The Terrors of War," 211
"The Two Armies," 323
"The Two Voices," 41
"The Unknown Dead," 326
"The Unknown Grave," 369
"The Vessel of Love, the Vessel of State," 38
"The Voices of the Guns," 164
"The Wood of Gettysburg," 115
"The Wound-Dresser," 239
"They dropped like Flakes -," 357
Thompson, M. Jeff, 64
Thoreau, Henry David, 38
"Three Hundred Thousand More," 92
Ticknor, Francis Orray, 52, 193
Timrod, Henry, 311–330
"To a Certain Civilian," 246
"To Abraham Lincoln," 89
"To fight aloud, is very brave -,"352
"To Our Hills," 189
"To the Cleveland Union-Savers," 296
"To the Leaven'd Soil They Trod," 248
"To the Men of the North and West," 47
Tucker, Mary Eliza, 187
"Turn O Libertad," 247

"Unto like Story - Trouble has enticed me -," 353

"Vigil Strange I Kept on the Field One Night," 236
"Virginia—The West," 233

Wallis, Severn Teackle, 128
"Wanted—A Man," 89
Warfield, Catherine A. W., 60
Washington, Emily M., 139
"We May Not Falter," 327
"Weaving," 86
Weeks, Della Jerman, 115
"Weep," 214
"What the Birds Said," 226
"When I was small, a Woman died -," 355
"When Lilacs Last in the Dooryard Bloom'd," 249
"'While God He Leaves Me Reason, God He Will Leave Me Jim,'" 96
Whitman, Walt, 230–256
Whittier, John Greenleaf, 216–229
"Words for the Hour," 299
"Wouldst Thou Have Me Love Thee," 114

"Year That Trembled and Reel'd Beneath Me," 239

Faith Barrett is an assistant professor of English at Lawrence University in Wisconsin. She is currently working on two book projects: one focuses on the rhetoric of lyric voice in Emily Dickinson's poetry; the other examines stances of address in American poetry written in response to the Civil War, including the work of canonical and popular writers as well as unpublished poems by soldiers.

Cristanne Miller is W. M. Keck Distinguished Professor in the English Department at Pomona College. Her book publications include *Emily Dickinson: A Poet's Grammar; Marianne Moore: Questions of Authority; Cultures of Modernism: Marianne Moore, Mina Loy, Else Lasker-Schüler: Gender and Literary Community in New York and Berlin;* and *The Emily Dickinson Handbook* (coedited with Gudrun Grabher and Roland Hagenbüchle). Her next project will trace the conception of the poet in the United States from the antebellum writings of Emerson and Whitman through the beginnings of Modernism.